Berkley Prime Crime titles by Betty Hechtman

HOOKED ON MURDER

DEAD MEN DON'T CROCHET

BY HOOK OR BY CROOK

A STITCH IN CRIME

YOU BETTER KNOT DIE

BEHIND THE SEAMS

IF HOOKS COULD KILL

Behind the Seams

BETTY HECHTMAN

BERKLEY PRIME CRIME, NEW YORK

THE BERKLEY PUBLISHING GROUP
Published by the Penguin Group
Penguin Group (USA) Inc.
375 Hudson Street, New York, New York 10014, USA
Penguin Group (Canada), 90 Eglinton Avenue East, Suite 700, Toronto, Ontario M4P 2Y3, Canada
(a division of Pearson Penguin Canada Inc.) • Penguin Books Ltd., 80 Strand, London WC2R 0RL,
England • Penguin Group Ireland, 25 St. Stephen's Green, Dublin 2, Ireland (a division of Penguin
Books Ltd.) • Penguin Group (Australia), 250 Camberwell Road, Camberwell, Victoria 3124, Australia
(a division of Pearson Australia Group Pty. Ltd.) • Penguin Books India Pvt. Ltd., 11 Community
Centre, Panchsheel Park, New Delhi—110 017, India • Penguin Group (NZ), 67 Apollo Drive,
Rosedale, Auckland 0632, New Zealand (a division of Pearson New Zealand Ltd.) • Penguin Books
(South Africa) (Pty.) Ltd., 24 Sturdee Avenue, Rosebank, Johannesburg 2196, South Africa

Penguin Books Ltd., Registered Offices: 80 Strand, London WC2R 0RL, England

This is a work of fiction. Names, characters, places, and incidents either are the product of the author's
imagination or are used fictitiously, and any resemblance to actual persons, living or dead, business
establishments, events, or locales is entirely coincidental. The publisher does not have any control over
and does not assume any responsibility for author or third-party websites or their content.

PUBLISHER'S NOTE: The recipes contained in this book are to be followed exactly as written. The
publisher is not responsible for your specific health or allergy needs that may require medical supervision.
The publisher is not responsible for any adverse reactions to the recipes contained in this book.

BEHIND THE SEAMS

A Berkley Prime Crime Book / published by arrangement with the author

PUBLISHING HISTORY
Berkley Prime Crime hardcover edition / November 2011
Berkley Prime Crime mass-market edition / November 2012

Copyright © 2011 by Betty Hechtman.
Excerpt from *If Hooks Could Kill* by Betty Hechtman copyright © 2012 by Betty Hechtman.
Cover illustration by Cathy Gendron.
Cover design by Rita Frangie.
Interior text design by Kristin del Rosario.

ISBN: 978-0-425-25527-8

BERKLEY® PRIME CRIME
Berkley Prime Crime Books are published by The Berkley Publishing Group,
a division of Penguin Group (USA) Inc.,
375 Hudson Street, New York, New York 10014.
BERKLEY® PRIME CRIME and the PRIME CRIME logo are trademarks of
Penguin Group (USA) Inc.

PRINTED IN THE UNITED STATES OF AMERICA

10 9 8 7 6 5 4 3 2 1

ALWAYS LEARNING   PEARSON

Acknowledgments

Once again, Sandy Harding has done a great job of editing. I am so glad to be working with her. My agent, Jessica Faust, amazes me how she manages to do it all so well. Natalee Rosenstein continues to make Berkley Prime Crime a great place to be. The art department has come up with another fantastic cover.

I want to thank my team—Roberta Martia for crochet and yarn, Judy Libby for legal, LAPD officer Kathy Bennett for cop questions and Dr. Howard Marx for everything medical. Thank you, Michael Duffy, for sharing your rescue story. Burl, thanks for letting me tag along on all the backstage adventures. Max and Samantha, I wouldn't have made it to the Palm Springs Aerial Tramway without you.

Linda Hopkins offered invaluable help with the crochet patterns. Thank you for your generosity and eye for detail.

Rene Biederman, Connie Cabon, Najme Chawdhry, Alice Chiredjian, Terry Cohen, Tricia Culkin, Clara Feeney, Pamela Feuer, Lily Gillis, Winnie Hineson, Linda Hopkins, Debbie Kratofil, Reva Mallon, Elayne Moschin, Margaret Prentice, Tillie Sanchez and Blanche Tutt are my knit and crochet group. I keep learning so much from them. Paula Tesler has turned the group into something special.

Burl, Max and Samantha, you guys are still the best!

CHAPTER 1

"Okay, action," I said. "Sorry, I don't have one of those little black chalkboards to click."

"Dear, those are only when you're actually filming. This is just a run-through," CeeCee Collins said. Whatever it was called, CeeCee instantly went into character and gestured toward the setup for a cooking demonstration spread out in front of her. A series of glass bowls with ingredients, a mixing bowl and a nine-by-thirteen pan, along with an assortment of cooking tools, sat on the dark wood trestle table in her dining room.

She looked the picture of domesticity with her apron, and it was obvious she'd gone into character, because the real CeeCee didn't know which end of a wooden spoon was up.

"I'm so glad to be here," CeeCee said, all smiles as she glanced over at us as if we were the audience. "And to be able to share one of the Collins' family recipes is a real treat. I know this recipe so well, I could make it with my eyes closed." She picked up one of the small bowls, checking the label I'd attached to it. "Let's start with the cinnamon." Before anyone could stop her, she'd poured it into the large bowl. Continuing to chat on about how she'd learned to cook by watching her mother, she added the contents of each of the small bowls to the larger one, then grabbed a spoon and began to stir everything together. We all cried out no in unison as she upturned the bowl and the clump of ingredients thudded into the baking pan amid a puffy brown cloud of cinnamon.

My name is Molly Pink and the *we* are the Tarzana Hookers. That's hookers as in crochet. And the Tarzana refers to the Southern California San Fernando Valley community where we meet. We've been together for a while now and our lives have become intertwined. That's not to say we're all sugary and sweet about each other, exactly. It's more like a family—you have your differences but accept each other anyway. In lieu of our regular meeting at the bookstore, we had gathered at CeeCee's, and instead of crocheting, we were playing audience for CeeCee. Only our one male member, Eduardo, hadn't been able to come.

Along with being the leader of our group of yarn fans, CeeCee was our resident celebrity. Up until recently, she'd always been referred to as a veteran actress, which really meant career over. She'd had her own sitcom years ago, and then had been in some movies and television shows before her career slid into the occasional cameo appearance. Everything had changed when she became host of *Making Amends*. But the reality show turned out to be small change compared to the boost her career had just received from her new film. Though the role she'd gotten was as a secondary character, *Caught By a Kiss* was a hit movie from the moment it premiered a couple of weeks ago.

CeeCee ignored our nos and, smiling all the while, headed toward the part of the table we'd designated as the oven—without any concern that all the ingredients were in a big mound in the middle of the baking pan.

"Anybody got any yellow tape?" Rhoda Klein said. "Because this looks like a crime scene to me." Rhoda was one of our newer members. She'd lived in Southern California for over twenty years but had never lost her New York no-nonsense attitude, or her accent.

"I don't understand. What did I do wrong?" CeeCee said, glancing around at us as I grabbed the pan and set it aside.

The recipe for Apple Bumble Crumble was really my recipe, and even though I'd already shown her how to assemble the ingredients, apparently it hadn't sunk in that everything didn't get thrown in the bowl together. So far, the only part she'd excelled at was tasting the recipe at the end of my demonstration.

While I prepared a new setup of ingredients, I tried once again to explain that she needed to spread the apple slices and raisins in the baking pan, then measure the cinnamon and sugar, then in a separate bowl cut the butter into the flour, and finally add the brown sugar, oatmeal and nuts. She reacted to the word *cut* like it was a foreign language. It wasn't much better when I demonstrated with the pastry blender.

"This is ridiculous. You should be doing a crochet demonstration," Adele Abrams said. She'd popped out of her chair and glared at CeeCee. "You're going to be on a national talk show with millions of viewers. Imagine showing off the wonders of crochet."

CeeCee sank into a chair. "Tell me about it. Do you think I would choose to do something I'm clueless about? Believe me, a cooking demonstration was not my idea. But getting on the *Barbara Olive Overton* show is a real coup. They're devoting the whole show to me. Do you know what that means? So when they were insistent about having me do something on the show and they wanted cooking, I wasn't about to make waves. I was told they wanted to have something to serve the audience at the end."

"I'm with Adele," Elise Belmont said. Her voice was a little on the wispy side and we barely heard her. It didn't help that she wasn't facing the group, but instead was admiring the movie poster propped on a chair. It featured a photo of Hugh Jackman with just the hint of fangs, holding a crochet hook. The title, *Caught By a Kiss*, was in red letters across the top. They'd done something to the lettering to make it look like dripping blood. Under the information about the female lead, it said, "Featuring CeeCee Collins as Ophelia."

"I just think they ought to have you and Hugh on together. Maybe you could both crochet something." Even before the movie, Elise had been enamored with the series of books featuring Anthony, the urbane, handsome vampire who'd learned to control his lust for blood by crocheting and was now trying to use his immortality to help mankind and also snag his love interest. She wasn't the only one to love the series. It was still a huge seller at Shedd & Royal Books and More where I worked. Elise had just been a little more over the top than the rest of us.

"I see your point," CeeCee said, taking one of the apple slices out of the pan and dipping it in some sugar before eating it. "You'd think since I had such a great comeback-kid story and there was already Oscar buzz for me and the movie is barely out, that I'd have carte blanche to do what I want."

My late husband, Charlie, had worked in public relations and I'd helped out with his business, so I knew a bit about how things went. Barbara Olive Overton was the top talk show host. In the scheme of things, she trumped CeeCee in importance, so if she wanted CeeCee to cook, it was that or nothing.

Adele saw her opening and went for it. She leaned her beanie-covered head toward CeeCee. As usual, she'd gotten a little carried away with crochet. The hat was so covered with flowers, it made her head look like it had lumps on top.

"We have to do something. The knitters"—Adele interrupted herself with a harrumph sound as she threw up her hands in frustration—"have all kinds of people. I read that

Sandra Bullock keeps calm by knitting, and Julia Roberts knits. Even Russell Crowe. And the list goes on and on. Just think if you could teach Barbara how to crochet on the show. I'm telling you, we need more celebrity crocheters. All we have is Vanna White," Adele said.

"Excuse me," CeeCee interjected.

"Right, we have you, too," Adele said. "But we need more. We need someone big and splashy."

Nell Collins, CeeCee's niece, came in at the end of the interchange and stopped in the doorway. Adele saw her and her face lit up.

"Can't you do something about getting your aunt to do a crochet demonstration on the talk show? You work on it, don't you?"

Nell looked like a much younger version of her aunt. Only the brown of her long hair was all natural. She had come out from Ohio a few months ago with the idea of getting into the entertainment industry and was staying with CeeCee. But unlike her aunt, Nell was really interested in working on the production end rather than in front of the camera. She laughed at Adele's comment. "I'm a production assistant, which basically means I'm a gofer. I already get a lot of grief because some people think Aunt CeeCee got me the job, so I try not to bring up any connection." Nell sighed. "But I think I know why they didn't want you to teach Barbara how to crochet. I heard one of the segment producers has a show coming up in a few weeks with some celebrity knitters, and they're going to teach Barbara how to work her needles on the show. Everybody knows about Barbara's battle with her weight, nail biting and general anxiety. The knitters claim to have a cure-all for that."

Adele jumped up at the word knitters. We all understood Adele had her reasons for seeing it as being the crocheters versus the knitters. It went back to a Cinderella-type stepmother and stepsisters who were all aggressive knitters who shamed Adele about her yarn hobby. We all loved crochet but weren't as reactionary as Adele. Still, this time I could see her point. It irked me that the knitters were getting a platform on the show but the crocheters weren't.

"I'm telling you that host needs a crochet intervention. She's always going on about her weight problems and her nail biting. Knitting isn't going to help that. All those clacking needles will just make her more nervous," Adele said.

Sheila Altman said, "Hear, hear" from the corner. If anyone knew about the therapeutic aspect of crochet, it was her. Sheila had sensitive nerves and she'd learned to handle her anxiety attacks with crochet. In fact, this whole discussion seemed to have stirred things up for her, and I noticed she'd taken out a hook and string she always carried. She didn't even have to look as she made a bunch of chains and went back over them with single crochet stitches.

"Ladies, we're getting off track here," Dinah Lyons said. Along with being a fellow hooker, she was my best friend. She taught English at a community college to reluctant students and knew how to keep things on subject. "The show is tomorrow and CeeCee needs to get this recipe down cold." Dinah bristled with energy as she looked over the setup. She added numbers to the labels on the small bowls, showing the order they should be used. I wrote out a list of steps and put it next to the large bowl. It still took a few more tries before CeeCee ended up with a pan of apple slices correctly covered with the bumble-crumble topping. This time, she put it in the real oven—with us looking on to make sure she did it right. It came out smelling delicious. We all congratulated CeeCee on her success at cooking, and she triumphantly put some on plates for all of us.

"It seems a little plain," CeeCee said, looking at the serving she'd taken for herself. "Can't we jazz it up a little. How about whipped cream?"

CeeCee was astonished to hear there was a way to make it

besides squirting it out of a can. I made a fast grocery store run and came back with some heavy cream. Luckily I got several containers, knowing CeeCee was likely to have a problem. She went wild with the hand mixer and ended up turning the first attempt into butter.

"Dear, this is fascinating," she said, taking a taste of her creation and deciding it would be tasty on scones. She went slower with the next batch and stopped when it was still whipped cream. CeeCee added a dollop to each of our plates, and we all dug in. "This is wonderful. I can't believe I actually made it," she said, punctuating her comment with her musical laugh.

As we ate, she took the list of steps I'd written out and said she'd make a cheat sheet on her hand for the show. She'd call her agent to make sure they wrote the ingredients on the bowls and to make sure they had whipping cream and a mixer.

The baking smells must have wafted through the house because I heard CeeCee's two Yorkies barking and scratching from the service porch where she'd put them to keep them out of the way.

"I appreciate that you all want to come to the taping and give me moral support, but its really not necessary," CeeCee said. I knew what CeeCee was really saying was that she didn't want the group to come. Not that they got it. Everyone insisted it was no problem and was thrilled when Nell started to hand out the tickets.

"Getting these is the only real thing I've done," Nell said as she gave the last one out. Right after that, everyone took off. Even Dinah, which surprised me. My friend usually hung around until I left. I couldn't help but wonder what was up with that.

I hadn't been sure what kitchen equipment CeeCee had, so I'd brought the ingredients, bowls and pan. I took everything in the kitchen and started to wash the dishes. CeeCee said I could have left them for her housekeeper to deal with in the morning, but I felt funny about giving her extra work.

When everything was clean and packed up, I passed through the dining room and heard voices coming from the living room, and the tone sounded like somebody was unhappy. I peeked in the living room with the idea of saying good-bye. Nell and her aunt were sitting on the sofa, and the younger woman's face was twisted in frustration. It didn't seem right to interrupt, so before they saw me, I backed out of sight.

"I don't know what I'm going to do. Robyn is on my case all the time. She keeps bringing up that I got the job because of my connection to you, or as she puts it, I took the easy way, while she got in all on her own." Nell slumped farther. "She screwed something up and then made me take the blame. It's just so unfair. My life would be so much simpler if she was out of the way."

CeeCee seemed at a loss for suggestions and uncertain about how to comfort her niece. She started to put her arm around Nell, then took it back. Finally, she sighed. "I didn't get the job for you. I made some calls and my agent got you the interview. You got the job on your own merit."

Poor Nell. She was just out of college, where there was some effort to keep things fair, and she was getting her first taste of the unfairness of the world. Apparently, CeeCee was thinking the same thing. She told the girl she'd just have to deal with the woman who was causing all the problems. There was no magic cure.

If anybody knew about things not being fair, it was CeeCee. When her dentist-husband died, she found out he'd lost all their money and she had to start over. CeeCee might be a little self-absorbed at times, but she wasn't all fluff. Hidden behind the sparkling eyes and tinkling laugh was a will of steel. Though at one time she'd been the star of the *CeeCee Collins Show*, when that ended, she set aside her pride and had taken any small part or cameo role she could get. She had even hosted an infomercial. She made it a point to be easy to work with, knowing it would help her get more and hopefully better parts. Her determination had paid off.

I waited a moment longer and made sure Nell was done before I walked in to say good-bye.

"Thank you, Molly. What would I have done without you?" CeeCee got up and walked me to the door. Nell had let the dogs out and they were actively searching my shoes for crumbs. "You're coming to the show, aren't you?" CeeCee said, stopping in the foyer.

"Actually, I wasn't planning to. Adele has her heart set on going, and it's hard for both of us to be gone from the bookstore at the same time."

CeeCee's smile faded, and she grabbed my hands in a frantic manner. "You have to come. You really do. Molly, we can't have the Hookers in the audience on their own. Who knows what they'll do." I knew she was really talking about Adele, and since I'd seen what Adele could do when left on her own, I agreed to work it out so I could go.

I came home with the magic combination of food and animal scents, and my two dogs stuck to me like glue after I walked into my kitchen. Blondie, the strawberry blond terrier mix, and Cosmo, the small black mutt, were joined by Holstein and Cat Woman, the two cats my son had brought with him when he moved back home.

I'd had my share of cats over the years and was always amazed at how distinct each of their personalities were. Holstein was more like a cat-dog. He joined the dogs in following me around the house and couldn't get enough attention. Cat Woman was more like the generic idea of a cat. She tended to be more aloof except around food. She always sat at my feet and patted my leg with her paw until she got a taste.

I did a double take when I heard hammering coming from the other room. Supposedly I had been living alone since my husband Charlie died, but then my son Samuel lost the place where he was staying and moved back in with the cats. And then there was Barry Greenberg. . . .

I followed the sound to the dining room. The lights were on and the skeleton of a shelving unit was on the floor. Barry set down his hammer and looked up as I walked in. He wiped some sawdust off on his faded jeans and rolled up the sleeve that had come undone on his blue and black plaid flannel shirt. "What do you think?" He gestured toward his work. Last time I'd seen it, it was a pile of wood in the back of his Tahoe. The change was definitely impressive.

"Great," I said, trying to sound one hundred percent enthusiastic. Really, I was still getting used to the changes around here.

I used to be upset at referring to Barry as my boyfriend. I mean, he's in his fifties and a homicide detective. To me, the title *boyfriend* was somewhere along the lines of wearing clothes that were too young for you. Even if you still had the legs to wear a short little skirt, it looked off. I really didn't have to worry about the boyfriend title anymore anyway. When Barry presented me with the blue velvet box with a diamond ring inside at Christmas, everything changed, including the title he was after.

He's been talking about us getting married long before the ring, and I know most women would have been thrilled. But it was just that I was still getting over Charlie's death. And to be honest, there was something more. I'd married young and had never been on my own to try my wings. I was in my late forties and finally getting that chance. I liked it; I really did. I'd started a whole new life with my job at the bookstore and the crochet group.

There were other issues, too. Barry's job, for one. Forget about making any plans. If he picked up a murder, he could practically disappear for days with barely a call. And then out of nowhere, show up at my door with just a call from his cell phone to let me know he was there. I wasn't sure how I could deal with a husband who did that.

And there was the communication thing. Charlie had worked in public relations and talked about it extensively. I'd helped out with his business, too, so it was always in the open. But Barry wanted to shut the door on his day when he came over. I understood, but it still felt uncomfortable, as though I was shut out of a large portion of his life. Again, it was one thing if that was going on with someone you were going out with, another if you were married to them.

But I pretty much forgot about those problems when he was around. Even if he wouldn't talk about it, I found it exciting that his work world was dark and dangerous. I felt safe with him. Maybe it had to do with how he was able to fix anything that broke in my house. It felt like he could take care of things. And, of course, there was this chemical thing when he was around. Barry was hot. What could I say?

I glanced down at my bare left hand. The ring was still in the box in my dresser drawer. I'd thought his getting the ring was a romantic gesture and all, but I still wasn't ready to be a fiancée.

Barry wasn't happy with my fence-sitting and dealt with it by ignoring it. He'd begun leaving more of his things at my house and had gone ahead and started making changes, like building this shelving unit to add to what I already had for my yarn. Those shelves were already overflowing and there were grocery bags filled with my stash on the floor again.

Barry rocked back on his heels before standing and slinging his arm around my shoulder. "I've been thinking, babe. We should get our own place." He caught my look of surprise and quickly added. "That is if you decide to say yes." He said *if*, but I knew he meant *when*. Once he'd thrown out that qualifier, he continued on. "It would be better to start fresh, no memories." He didn't say it, but I knew he was thinking, *And no baggage, either.* My son Samuel had just walked in the room and was looking over Barry's work-in-progress.

He gave Barry a cursory nod and turned all his attention toward me. "I'm leaving," he said. "I'm filling in at that new restaurant that opened up in the Village Walk." Samuel was a musician waiting for his big break. In the meantime, he was a barista at a local coffee place and took whatever gigs he could get. He picked up his guitar case and headed toward the door.

Barry made a noise as Samuel left. Something along the lines of a displeased grunt. You didn't have to be an expert to pick up on the undercurrent of hostility between Barry and Samuel. Barry didn't think I should have let Samuel move back in when he lost the place he was sharing with a bunch of guys. And Samuel was still getting over his father's death and wasn't comfortable with someone taking Charlie's place in my life.

It put me smack in the middle. I would always be Samuel's mother and this was still his home when needed. But I could understand Barry's point of view, too. I was Barry's whatever—if I didn't like the term *boyfriend*, being referred to as a *girlfriend* really didn't work for me—and he was part of my life now and had a right not to be treated like an invader.

"There's Thai takeout in the refrigerator," Barry said. I'd been too busy helping CeeCee with her demo to do anything more than taste the Apple Bumble Crumble and was definitely hungry. I checked the fridge and saw the line of white cartons. He'd even gotten my favorite pad thai vegetables.

I went back to the dining room to thank him, but he was on his cell phone. I could tell by the serious set of his mouth and his measured tone that it was work. I watched him go from building Barry to detective Barry right before my eyes. He hugged me with one arm as he headed toward the living room. I nuzzled closer, drinking in the scent that was just his.

"I've got to get Jeffrey," Barry said before sticking his head in the doorway of the den. He didn't have to say anything. As soon as his son saw him, he sighed and started to gather up his homework.

"Yeah, we gotta go. So what else is new?" Jeffrey said in a fourteen-year-old's version of a world-weary voice.

"He can stay," I said and gestured for Jeffrey to stop packing up. "He can sleep here and I'll get him to school." Barry's work face disappeared and his eyes softened as he hugged me closer.

"You're the best. It's good to have somebody watching my back." Barry pulled free and headed for the door, almost at a sprint. No matter the long hours, the interrupting calls, Barry loved his job.

This wasn't the first time Jeffrey had stayed over. I'd taken the bedroom I'd used as an office and moved the computer and desk into the overcrowded crochet room and made a room for Jeffrey.

There was something old school about him. Jeffrey was polite and nice to talk to. He wasn't hostile or sullen the way some boys his age were. He was still soft around the edges and tried to look more manly by gelling his brown hair into a spiky style. His clothing choice wasn't typical, either. He wore a lot of suit jackets with jeans. Did I mention that Jeffrey wanted to be an actor, was an actor already, if you counted school plays and that he'd gone on some auditions for commercials. Barry didn't like the idea, and disliked it even more when Jeffrey started calling himself Columbia.

Barry was still struggling with being a full-time parent, even though Jeffrey had been living with his father for the past couple of years after things hadn't worked out with him living with his mother.

"Are you hungry? I was going to have some of the take-out," I said. Jeffrey nodded and closed up his homework. I made up plates for both of us and we took them in the den. I flipped on the TV.

A repeat of the *Barbara Olive Overton* show was on. "I'm going to that show tomorrow," I said. I explained about CeeCee being on the show, and when he heard what movie she was in, he was impressed. Who knew Jeffrey was a fan of Anthony, the vampire who crocheted?

Talking about Anthony reminded me of the bookstore. "Oh no," I said suddenly, as I was gathering up the plates. I'd promised CeeCee that I'd go to the show, but I'd forgotten to discuss getting time off with my boss.

CHAPTER 2

"I'M SORRY FOR ASKING YOU AT THE LAST MINUTE," I said to Mrs. Shedd. It was the last hour before closing and the bookstore had only a few customers. I glanced toward the bookstore café and saw that Bob, our barista and cookie baker, was already in the process of cleaning up the café. "I thought I could do some of the things I was planning to do in the morning now." I'd come in to ask my boss for the morning off to go to the talk show and to take care of a few things.

I had invited Jeffrey to come along to the store and was surprised when he agreed. He had immediately gone off to look at the big section we had on theater arts.

"As long as you're here by noon, it shouldn't be a problem. Funny you should bring up the *Barbara Olive Overton* program. I just had a call from someone there today," Mrs. Shedd said, putting back a copy of *Caught By the Hook*, which was the first of the Anthony books and the basis for the movie *Caught By a Kiss*. "They want to film something here for one of their background pieces. She said they would pay us a small fee and give us a promotional consideration in the credits. The mention in the credits would be nice, but I was thinking maybe we could slip something with the bookstore's name in the shot." Mrs. Shedd sighed. "Anything we can do to help business is a plus." Mrs. Shedd had made some bad investments with the bookstore's money and was doing whatever she could to make up for the losses. "The woman I spoke to said she comes in the café all the time and that's why she thought of Shedd and Royal. I'm not that familiar with the café customers and I'm so bad with names. Hers was something Freed—maybe Rachel. Do you know her?"

I didn't know much about the café customers, either, and shook my head. "Did she explain what they wanted to film?"

"More or less. They're doing an upcoming show to coincide with the release of a book called *Back from Hell*. Timing wise, there won't have been any actual book signings, so they want us to set up a fake one. Are you familiar with the author, D. J. Florian?"

Mrs. Shedd and her formerly silent partner, Mr. Royal, had been spending more time at the bookstore lately, but apparently she hadn't paid attention to all the upcoming releases. "His book is one of those blogoirs." Mrs. Shedd looked puzzled and I explained it was a mixture of a blog and a memoir. "He's the one who was struggling with a drug problem and started writing a blog more to help himself, but you know how it is these days. Somehow it got caught up in the blogosphere and he got a lot of followers. What was different about him was his blog was funny and literate and not totally self-centered." I recalled reading some interview with him where he'd talked about his life going in a downward spiral. He'd lost his place to live, his job, his friends, everything and ended up living on the street. "His turnaround was very dramatic. Something about hitting bottom and being on the street at five minutes to midnight on the last day of the year. A lot of people were inspired by his journey. He's actually local."

Mrs. Shedd appeared unimpressed and turned toward the display of Anthony books. "I'd rather have another hot vampire book."

"You know, CeeCee's niece works on the *Barbara Olive Overton* show," I said.

Mrs. Shedd didn't seem particularly surprised. The entertainment industry was woven into the everyday life of the San Fernando Valley. It was home to a number of production studios and television stations, who employed a lot of Valley residents. The area was often used for filming. It was a common sight to see a line of trucks and generators and mobile dressing rooms parked on residential streets. Actors, writers, directors and producers lived in the area, particularly in the communities nestled against the Santa Monica Mountains like Studio City, Sherman Oaks, Encino, Tarzana and Woodland Hills. It wasn't that unusual to find yourself standing behind some soap opera actor or news anchor in the grocery store checkout line, and every dog groomer and cleaners had framed eight-by-tens of their celebrity customers. But the bookstore had never gone that route. CeeCee would have had a place of honor if we had.

"Have I met CeeCee's niece?" Mrs. Shedd asked. She caught her reflection in the large windows that faced Ventura Boulevard and smoothed a stray blond hair back in place. Her hair was so perfect, it almost looked like a wig. Mrs. Shedd was in her late sixties without a hint of gray. The silky texture, however, suggested the blond was natural.

"I don't know," I said. "Her aunt is trying to get her to take up the hook and keeps dragging her to our group's meetings."

We were trying to make the events at the bookstore really large events. So instead of having a single author signing their latest books, we were teaming up with local business owners to put on something bigger that would attract more people and help us all. Shedd & Royal already had a reputation for their events. Let's just say they seemed to court disaster, but in a good way. No matter what happened, they always turned out to have good book sales, so Mrs. Shedd had learned not to mind if there was a miniriot.

I noticed that Jeffrey had gone into the café. Bob had given him some of the end-of-the-day leftover cookies and the last of the lemonade. Bob had his laptop set up on the table and the two of them were talking. No doubt they were discussing the science-fiction screenplay Bob had been writing for as long as I'd worked at the bookstore. Maybe Jeffrey was trying to get a part in it. I'd never asked too many questions about it, but Bob was always banging away at the laptop when business was slow. He looked like somebody who would write a science-fiction screenplay, with his pale skin, light brown hair and some glob of hair growing between his chin and his mouth. It wasn't a beard, more like a puff ball.

I was relieved Mrs. Shedd was okay about me going to the show. CeeCee had been almost panicky, and I figured I could sit in front and coach her if necessary. I took the signs for the Salute to Chocolate event I was holding and slipped them into frames. I put the biggest one near the front door and then placed the others around the bookstore. It was going to be an all-chocolate evening, with a highlight of having Alain Des Plaines, a chef on the food channel, sign his ultimate chocolate cookbook: *Melts at Body Heat*.

When I'd finished with the signs and put out a stack of schedules for the month, I went back to the yarn department. It was the newest addition and my favorite part of the store. We'd arranged the yarn by colors. There was a permanent wood table for the Hookers or anyone who wanted to stop by and work with yarn, along with some easy chairs. I picked up a few stray skeins and put them back where they belonged. All our yarn was high end, and Mrs. Shedd had wanted a crocheted and knitted swatch for each of the yarns we sold. Getting the crocheted ones was no problem, as Adele and the

Hookers all pitched in. I'd been left to do the knitted ones and still had a lot to finish.

Mrs. Shedd and I had decided that to make our yarn department stand out, we'd let people try it before they bought it. Each bin had a skein available to cut a sample from. We'd recently gotten in some variegated wool, worsted-weight yarn from Japan. The colors went from pumpkin to deep purple, with a lot of colors in between. I was curious how the colors would look when crocheted and cut a length from the sample skein. We kept a bunch of hooks and needles for the samples, and I pulled out a K-size hook and sat down at the table.

"There you are," a male voice said. I turned just as Mason Fields reached the table. "I called your house and your Black-Berry and got no answer. I just happened to be picking something up at Le Grande Fromage and saw your car in the store's parking lot."

"You called my cell phone?" I said. My purse was sitting on the table next to me. It took a while to find the black phone in the dark cavity of my purse. But when I checked it, sure enough, it showed that Mason had called while I was in the store. I realized I'd heard some ringing but never associated it with my phone. When I told Mason the problem, he grinned and asked for my BlackBerry.

"I can fix that." He walked away for a few moments and I resumed crocheting. When he returned, he handed back the phone and told me to bury it in my purse. Then he punched in the number.

Suddenly a high-pitched voice started squawking from my purse. "Hey, get me out of here. Help me, please! Somebody, pick me up. Hurry before it's too late." We both laughed and Mason explained he'd used the feature to record your own ring along with his best impression of a cartoon character in distress.

"Well, I certainly won't mix that up with other people's phones," I said, taking the phone out and making the "ring" stop. "Thanks, I guess," I said with a grin and a roll of my eyes.

"Why are you sitting here alone?" He slid into the chair next to me. I recapped the chain of events that had gotten me there, and Mason asked to see what I was making. As I held up the swatch of yarn, he caught my hand and looked at it.

"Still empty, Sunshine? The detective must be upset that the ring is still in the box hidden away somewhere."

I pulled my hand back. Mason was a high-powered criminal attorney and my good friend. Though *good friend* sounded kind of weak. He was so much more than a friend. Unlike Barry, who always told me to stay out of things, Mason helped me get information and even helped in my sleuthing activities. When Barry and I had broken up, Mason and I had almost gotten together, but our definition of relationship had been different. He kept telling me that his definition wasn't written in stone, but by then it was too late. Like Barry, Mason was divorced, but unlike Barry, he wasn't looking to get married again. He had a solid build, earthy brown eyes and brown hair sprinkled with a little silver, a lock of which usually fell across his forehead, giving him an earnest look.

I was glad when he dropped the subject. I knew I was going to have to do something about the ring in the drawer eventually, but in the meantime, I didn't want to think about it. "Why were you looking for me?" I asked.

"Oh, just to see what was up with you. If any dead bodies had fallen in your lap. If you wanted to get a cup of coffee."

"So you just wanted to see me," I said, and he nodded.

"And hopefully without an entourage," he added with a grin.

"Molly, they're turning off the lights," Jeffrey said as he joined us at the table. He noticed Mason and they traded nods of acknowledgment. They knew each other from numerous get-togethers at my house. Both of them looked disappointed at seeing the other.

CHAPTER 3

"PINK, I THOUGHT YOU WEREN'T GOING?" ADELE said with a mixture of surprise and disappointment, leaning over the seat of her Matrix as I followed Dinah and got in the backseat. Sheila was already sitting on the passenger side in the front. The Hookers who were going to the show had decided to carpool and arranged to meet in front of the bookstore. Rhoda and Elise opted to take Rhoda's car rather than have four of us squashed in the backseat. Adele sensed there was something up and grilled me until I admitted that CeeCee had asked me to come. I mentioned that she wanted me to be there to coach her, just in case. I did not mention that CeeCee had really been more concerned about me keeping the Hookers, well, Adele in line.

Doing this show was a big moment for CeeCee. It signified that she was back in the main spotlight.

I hadn't been to a TV show taping in years, and I'd always gone with Charlie when he was there in a business capacity. That meant special parking, going in the backstage entrance, and hanging out in the green room, with its array of drinks and snacks, while Charlie schmoozed with his client. It was a little different when you were just going to be part of the audience.

We had to park a million miles away and didn't even go inside the studio grounds. We had to line up on the street in front of the audience entrance. I must admit the *Barbara Olive Overton* show had everything well organized once we got inside. First up was signing a release that said we agreed to be seen on TV with no remuneration.

As we moved along the narrow hallway, we were relieved of our coats and purses and given a claim number. There were signs all over saying, "No phones, cameras or recording devices allowed in the show." Still, when we went through the metal detectors, a number of them showed up. Excuses were mumbled as the staff member took them and promised to return them after the show. Personally, I was glad not to have mine and have to worry about answering it. Adele was in line ahead of me. It was hard to miss her. She didn't wear clothes so much as costumes. Often I was inspired to give them names. Today's was clearly ode to crochet. Adele never seemed to get that less was more. If the jacket had been black with granny-square pockets, it would have been striking, but instead, the whole thing was made of the squares, which had multicolored centers surrounded by black. She looked like she was wrapped in an afghan. Adele liked hats, they just didn't like her. She'd worn a wide-brimmed black hat she'd made by mixing a strand of suede yarn with one of worsted-weight acrylic, so it had body. She'd trimmed it with a circle of loose-hanging hot pink pom-poms that bounced whenever she moved.

"Uh-oh," Dinah said, and we watched as Adele went through the metal detector. We both held our breath, expecting some kind of alarm to go off because I was sure she had some metal crochet hooks stashed in her pocket. But she was all smiles and there were no pings or beeps.

After our trip through the metal detector, Dinah followed me into a narrow room with chairs around the sides, or what appeared to be the green room for the audience. Dinah glanced around. "Hmm, I guess we don't get any perks." I'd told her about my backstage experiences.

"What do you mean?" I joked, pointing toward the drinking fountain and restrooms. During our brief stay in the room, I noticed Adele showed off her outfit to several people. I nudged Dinah.

"Adele seems to be more *out there* than usual and I have a bad feeling. I don't want anything to wreck this for CeeCee. She's got enough worries keeping her bowls straight. If I sit next to Adele, maybe she'll behave." Dinah saw my point, and when we finally stood to file into the studio where the taping was done, she stayed behind with the other Hookers as I pushed ahead and more or less cut in line to get next to Adele.

I had promised CeeCee I'd try to sit in the front. It was no problem now that I was shadowing Adele. She charged through the crowd with me in close pursuit and nabbed seats in the very first row.

When everyone was seated, a guy in jeans, high-top sneakers and a suit jacket came out to warm up the audience. He told a few jokes, then launched into the rules. He tried to be funny as he listed them, but basically there was no talking during the taping. During the question-and-answer segment, anyone with a question was to raise their hand, then wait until someone came with a microphone.

There was a moment of silence afterward as everyone waited for Barbara to come out. It was as if everyone sucked in their breath at once. No sooner had she walked out onto the stage when everyone started booing her. What was going on? The warm-up comedian seemed unconcerned as he left the stage. And the dark-haired woman with soft curves smiled at the crowd. Was she smiling to hide her embarrassment? I almost choked when Adele started pumping her fist and yelling along with the rest of the crowd.

I grabbed Adele's arm to make her stop and she shot me a dark look. "What's your problem, Pink?"

"My problem? You're the one who's booing the host of the show."

Adele rolled her eyes. "Pink, you need to get out more." She pointed toward the name of the show being projected on the blue wall at the back of the stage. "*Barbara Olive Overton* or *BOO* for short," Adele said, shaking her head at my obvious stupidity.

Okay, I got it, but I didn't join in the *BOO*-calling and was glad when it stopped. Adele had certainly snagged us good seats. We were so close I could see the white's of Barbara's eyes and figure out that all that poufy hair probably wasn't hers.

Adele was twitching in her seat, and it was making me nervous. She had something up her sleeve, but what? Maybe she was jiggling to keep the bright pink pom-poms on her hat bopping around to get people's attention.

The audience cheered when CeeCee came out and cheered again when the host talked about how CeeCee's career had been on the sidelines but now had come back full force.

"You know, there's already an Oscar buzz about my performance in *Caught By a Kiss*," CeeCee said. The audience applauded and CeeCee basked in all the attention. The only time her bright smile dimmed was when Barbara said something about how well CeeCee was doing for a woman of her age.

While they broke for a commercial break, they brought in the kitchen setup, and CeeCee and Barbara got ready for the cooking demonstration.

"You can tell us about your movie while you show off your recipe," Barbara said after they were back on the air. I watched nervously as CeeCee put on her apron and stepped up to the counter and the array of ingredients.

"This is an old Collins' family recipe," she said. She glanced over the ingredients and I held my breath, afraid she was going to dump the cinnamon again. If I ever doubted CeeCee's acting ability, I didn't anymore. I believed it was an old family recipe. She showed off the pan that was already lined with sliced apples and raisins. She measured the sugar and cinnamon and then sprinkled the mixture over the apples. Then, as if she'd been doing it all her life, she dropped the hunks of butter in the flour and used a pastry blender to mix it in. She did just enough to show how to do it. They had another bowl with the butter already cut into the flour, and she just had to add the brown sugar, oatmeal and walnuts. She poured the contents over the pan of apples, telling the audience to be sure to spread it evenly. Forget the movie, she deserved an Academy Award for this. I felt my breath release when she put it in the fake oven. They already had a finished version off to the side, which they now brought in. Apparently, they'd cut corners, and instead of having her make the whipped cream, they just had a can.

"Well, tell us about your movie. And what it feels like to be thinking about an Academy Award," Barbara said. "Vampires are everywhere. And now there's one who knits."

Adele was out of her seat before I could stop her. "He crochets," Adele said in an indignant tone. CeeCee's eyes flew up at the comment and she looked directly at me. I pulled Adele back in her seat as the talk show host chuckled and tried to cover the awkward moment. "Knit, crochet? What's the difference? They both use yarn."

The pink pom-poms on Adele's hats were jiggling big time now. Her face was red and she seemed to be trying to restrain herself. Her hand shot up in the air. No one came with a microphone and I tried to pull her arm down and told her between gritted teeth that they weren't taking questions now.

Suddenly, she couldn't hold back anymore and jumped out of her seat again and started waving a plastic size P crochet hook. The fact that it looked like a minibaseball bat and was bright turquoise made it hard to miss. Adele glanced around her and tugged at me to stand with her.

"Crocheters unite," she cried. "We will not be the stepsisters of knitting anymore." She turned squarely toward the talk show host. "And crochet and knitting are not the same."

CeeCee looked away from us and began to talk quickly about her movie and how wonderful it had been to work with Hugh Jackman.

A serious-looking woman with a Martha Stewart hairstyle and a headset appeared out of nowhere and grabbed Adele's arm and started to pull her toward the exit. Adele wasn't going to go easily. She clamped onto my arm, and the next thing I knew, she was dragging me along.

Adele might try to annoy me by calling me by my last name and slinging barbs at me all the time, but the minute there was trouble, I became her best friend. Before I could blink, we were going through the studio doors. I thought the woman was going to take us right to the street exit, but instead she led us to the audience waiting room and ordered us to sit. I had a sinking feeling. What if she was detaining us until the cops could get there?

It turned out to be much more mundane than that. They'd collected our stuff when we came in and there was no way to give it back during the show, so we had to wait around until the show finished.

"I don't understand what the fuss was about. I was merely trying to correct Barbara," Adele said. I rolled my eyes. Typical Adele. She never seemed to grasp the results of her behavior.

There was basically nothing to do but look at the photos of Barbara with assorted famous people that adorned the walls while we waited for the show to end. Adele took out the giant hook and a ball of purple yarn she'd kept in her pocket and began to crochet a loopy flower.

The woman who'd brought us in had sat down in one of the chairs and eyed us with a sour look. There was an air of authority about her, and I heard her talking into her headset, saying something about having better things to do than baby-sit a couple of troublemakers.

A door marked "Staff Only" opened and CeeCee's niece Nell walked in carrying one of those cardboard drink holders with one lidded coffee cup in it. She seemed disconcerted and her gaze went right to our babysitter. "There you are."

"I suppose it's cold by now," the woman said, reaching for the cup. "Such a simple job of getting me a hot latte and you can't seem to manage it. Did you think because your aunt was doing the show, you could slough off?"

Nell's face clouded and she seemed to be trying to restrain herself but lost the battle.

"Today at work is just like any other day to me, Robyn. The only reason I went into Ms. Collins' dressing room was to tell her it was time to go on," she sputtered. "And how was I supposed to know you'd be in here. You're never in the audience pretaping room during the show," Nell said, defiantly. I began to figure that Robyn was the woman Nell had been talking about to her aunt.

Robyn eyed her darkly. "Not that I have to explain anything to you, but our audience usually behaves. But these two," she said, gesturing toward us. I belatedly realized that by coming with Adele, I was considered as naughty as she was.

For the first time, Nell looked at Adele and me long enough to register our identities. I suppose Nell thought she was already in enough trouble with Robyn and didn't need the added burden of admitting that she knew us because she regarded us as if we were complete strangers. I had to nudge Adele and give her my best impression of CeeCee's cease-and-desist look to keep her from saying anything.

No wonder Nell had been crying on her aunt's shoulder about this woman. I was sure if she made this much of an issue about a possibly lukewarm latte, she was just looking to hassle Nell.

Finally Robyn took the coffee cup from the holder and looked at the empty spots around it. "Did you forget my sweetener?"

Nell appeared flustered and embarrassed as she rushed out through the door.

Robyn's mouth seemed stuck in an angry expression, and I thought of telling her that being so upset wasn't good for her health, but reconsidered, realizing she would probably just get angrier at the comment. She leaned back in the hard chair, pulled out her iPhone and began flipping through things. Adele had taken to staring at her and I was going to nudge her to try to get her to stop, but Adele spoke first.

"I knew you looked familiar. I've seen you in the café of Shedd and Royal."

The woman barely nodded and Adele continued. "You know I could probably get you some coupons for free lattes. Bob would make sure they were hot." Adele leaned closer and held up the rows of double crochets hanging off her hook. "I scratch your back. You scratch mine." She punctuated it with a wink. "You'd be doing your boss a favor by putting on a show dedicated to crochet. She bites her nails, she's always trying some new diet, and I heard her say she wanted to learn how to meditate." Adele held the hook higher, and the stitched yarn swung back and forth. "All the answers are right before your eyes."

Robyn responded with a dismissive shrug and a roll of her eyes. Adele got that crazed look again and I had to restrain her. Luckily Nell's return distracted Adele. Nell took something out of her denim shirt pocket. I hadn't noticed before, but there was a tiny darker blue motif made out of crochet thread sewn onto the pocket. CeeCee must have made it for her.

Robyn snatched the packet with an impatient groan and

added the contents to her cup. She gave the drink a quick stir and picked it up.

I didn't realize it at first, but I was already cringing, expecting some kind of outburst since the coffee drink couldn't possibly still be hot.

Robyn put the drink to her lips and finally drank some. She appeared hostile as she turned to Nell. "It's cold," Robyn barked as she pushed the cup toward Nell. "Go and get me . . ." Her voice trailed off as the cup fell from her hand. It hit the floor and splattered, making a large beige puddle on the charcoal gray carpet. When I looked up, I was shocked to see foam coming out of Robyn's mouth, and then she began to convulse.

Nell seemed frozen in her spot as the producer fell forward out of the chair and onto the floor.

I grabbed Robyn's iPhone and dialed 911.

CHAPTER 4

I'D NEVER BEFORE SEEN ANYBODY DIE RIGHT IN front of my eyes. The three of us stood around helplessly trying to figure out what to do as Robyn lay writhing on the floor. Adele got disgruntled with our inactivity, and with her pink pom-poms flying, leaned over the woman and tried to at least raise her shoulders. I bent down to help. It was a horrific sight as Robyn thrashed around and kept slipping from our grasp. The convulsing went on for a few minutes, and then abruptly Robyn was stone still. It all happened so fast I didn't think the paramedics would have been able to do anything even if they'd found us right away.

The logistics of the whole episode were a mess. Nell had never handled anything like this before and didn't realize she needed to contact security so the paramedics could get in and find us. She pretty much had a meltdown, and by the time the paramedics finally showed up, she had fainted and was on the floor, too. The man and woman in the dark blue uniforms had much more success treating her.

They just had to roll Nell on her back and put her feet up.

But Robyn showed no signs of life and there was nothing they could do to help her.

I was in shock to put it mildly. One minute the young woman with the Martha Stewart haircut was complaining about her latte, and a few minutes later, she was gone.

Adele was hanging on to me for dear life. "I tried to give her first aid," she said to the paramedic pair, "but nothing seemed to help." Adele let go and tried calming herself with her crochet hook and yarn. I was surprised to see something I'd never seen before. Her stitches were a mess.

I lost track of the time, and security people came in and took the three of us out into the hall. They asked a lot of questions and then a bunch of uniforms showed up and asked more questions about what had happened. The most I could find out was that despite what was going on, it hadn't interrupted the show. Then just when I thought they were going to let us go, the cops separated us. I don't know where they took Adele and Nell, but I was taken to a small lounge and told to wait to speak to a detective. When I tried to find out why, it became abundantly clear that they only asked questions and didn't answer them. After what seemed like eternity, the door opened and Barry walked in. He was completely in his detective mode, flipping open his notebook. Only when he looked up did his expression break.

"Molly?" Barry said. There was a squeak of surprise in his voice, and then he began shaking his head, obviously realizing that once again he was going to have to step down from a case because I was involved. "What are you doing here?"

I told him the whole story and he shook his head again. "Why didn't you tell me you were going to the show last night?"

I actually thought he might be more upset that I hadn't told him about my plans than the fact that I had just witnessed someone dying. I reminded him that he'd left rather abruptly and explained the plans had been last minute.

I glanced vaguely in the direction of the audience waiting room where everything had taken place. "She must have had some kind of attack?" I said before describing what had happened. Barry had on his cop face again and he just looked at me when I'd finished. "That's right, isn't it, you're just here investigating because she died suddenly and not in a hospital, right?"

Barry's face showed no emotion. It was maddening how he could do that. But then he'd been at his job long enough, it must have been second nature to hold it all in.

"You're all right, then?" he said. There was a flicker of emotion in his eyes, which was a relief from robot Barry. He knew that I knew that his not confirming what I'd said meant they suspected foul play. He looked toward the doorway, which was empty, and crossed the space between us and hugged me. "Just answer the questions and let it go, okay?"

Before he could realize that I wasn't agreeing with his order, he was out the door.

Murder? It couldn't be murder. They had to be wrong.

I had a pretty good idea who was going to replace him investigating. Detective Heather showed up a few minutes later in a cloud of Vera Wang perfume. Okay, her real name was Heather Gilmore, but in my head and when speaking among my friends, I referred to her as Detective Heather. I always said if they ever made a homicide detective Barbie, she'd look like Heather. I'm sure her extreme prettiness worked well when questioning men. They'd probably confess just to be able to spend more time with her.

This was not to say that she was just a pretty face. She had it all, brains and beauty and youth. She was more than ten years younger than I was. But despite all her attributes, I had managed to solve some cases she hadn't been able to crack. There was an additional undercurrent of hostility between us because I had something she wanted badly. Barry Greenberg. I don't think she could understand how he possibly could have chosen me over her. I could kind of see her point. They would have been the homicide division's golden couple. Though I had to wonder what it would be like for two people whose daily work really was a life-and-death matter to deal with something mundane like whose turn it was to take out the trash.

She had questioned me a number of times before, and I began to wonder if she just kept a sheet in her little notebook with all my vitals. The first few times we'd gone through this, I'd been the docile answerer of questions, but by now I asked as many as I answered.

"Why do you think it's murder?" I asked. Detective Heather rocked her head with frustration. I might ask questions, but it didn't mean she wanted to answer them.

"What's this?" she asked, ignoring my question and pointing to the giant turquoise crochet hook with the tangle of purple yarn sticking out of my pocket. Adele had been frustrated with her messy stitches and tossed it aside and I had picked it up. Did I mention that on top of all her other talents, Heather was a first-class knitter? Lucky for her, she'd gotten me to question. Adele knew about her knitting talents and would have either thrown a fit or taken the opportunity to try to convert her to crochet.

I explained the whole audience incident and how it was that Adele and I had ended up in the waiting room. "And you were going to tell me why you think there was foul play," I said with an expectant air.

"Nothing is certain until the coroner determines the cause of death. We're just investigating. What makes you think we think it's murder? We could just be following up on a sudden death," she said. How could I tell her it was all based on Barry's reactions?

"Because if you didn't think it was, you would just say it wasn't." I rolled my eyes at the tongue twister. I wished what she was saying was true. If it was murder, the three of us who were with Robyn were the most likely suspects. And I had a bad feeling that when I finished answering all of Detective Heather's questions, the suspects would be whittled down to just one.

She knew I had caught her and dealt with it by ignoring my comment. "So then, why don't you tell me what happened," she said with her pen poised.

I was shocked at how long Detective Heather kept questioning me. Once she realized who Nell was and that I knew her, she was relentless, going over and over what happened. I was pretty relentless, too, asking her over and over again why they thought it was murder.

"I give up, Molly," she said finally. "If I tell you what we found, will you let it go and just answer my questions?" I sucked in my breath in anticipation while I nodded. I wanted to know and not know at the same time.

"One of the paramedics noticed a smell on the victim and . . ."

"I know what you're going to say," I interrupted. I had noticed it, too, but hadn't put it together until now. When we were hovering over Robyn and the spilled drink, I'd noticed a faint almond smell. It didn't register then. Though I'd had a fleeting thought that the drink had one of those flavored syrups added. But of course it didn't; Robyn wouldn't have needed sweetener if it had.

"Cyanide?" I said.

"You promised no more questions," Detective Heather said.

Even though she didn't confirm it, I was pretty sure I was right. I knew from a past experience that one of the signatures of cyanide was the scent of almonds and that it didn't take much to do the job, and it acted very fast. For a moment, I felt a little less guilty. If it was cyanide, we couldn't have done anything to save her. But the relief didn't last as the question of how her drink became laced with cyanide filled my thoughts.

Detective Heather asked again about the sequence of events. And again I gave her the facts. I explained Nell had come in with a coffee drink for Robyn. There had been some issue about it being cold and then about the absence of sweetener.

"Did the victim drink any of the latte before she added the sweetener?" Heather asked.

"So, you think whatever killed her was in the sweetener?" I said. Detective Heather gave me a blank look and asked me if I knew what brand it was. I said I hadn't realized it was going to be important and hadn't paid any attention to it.

"It's called Nature's Sweetie," Detective Heather said. She waited to see if that would generate a comment from me. Then she said she was surprised I hadn't heard of it. It was the newest sugar replacement. "For people watching their weight," Heather added. Was it my imagination or did her gaze immediately go to my middle? A not-so-subtle reminder that I was a little soft in that area.

I knew eventually Heather was going to ask me what I knew about Nell and Robyn's relationship. Even if I hadn't overheard Nell's conversation with CeeCee, seeing their exchange over the coffee drink made it pretty clear they didn't get along. I tried to think of something that wasn't a lie and also wouldn't make Nell look bad. Who would have thought that without meaning to, Detective Heather made that easy for me with her next question?

"Do you have any idea who might have wanted to harm Ms. Freed?" Detective Heather asked.

"Freed, her last name is Freed?" I said quickly. The subject never got to Nell and Robyn's relationship and went directly to me explaining Mrs. Shedd's phone call from the victim. I think by then Heather was as tired of questioning me as I was being questioned. Besides, it wasn't like she didn't know where to find me. She was actually a customer of our new yarn department.

* * *

By the time I was finally reunited with my purse and jacket and escorted to the door, I had a tension and hunger headache. I hadn't even had my cell phone to call Mrs. Shedd and tell her why Adele and I were going to be delayed getting to the bookstore. When you're questioned by the cops, it's all on their terms. As soon as I was out on the street, I regretted being an audience member again. When I'd gone to shows with Charlie, we left by the backstage entrance and went right into the parking lot. It was all gated and secure and no one was going to stick a microphone in your face.

But now, the exit I went out put me right on the sidewalk. A bevy of reporters were clumped nearby, and I realized they were all set up to do remotes for the evening news from there. As soon as Kimberly Wang Diaz from channel three saw me, she practically knocked her colleagues out of the way to get to me.

She smiled. "Molly Pink? You must know what's going on." I edged away but she stuck close to me. I'd met the persistent reporter a number of times in the past. She was close enough to me that I could see the stage makeup on her face and smell the ton of hair spray that kept her black hair in an unmoving helmet. I wanted to get away before she trotted out her nickname for me. The last thing I wanted was to have that title broadcast to the greater L.A. area again. "C'mon, give us the details," she said as I picked up speed. She was hampered by having to let her cameraman keep up with us. I ran across the street just as she yelled, "I know you know what happened. Crime scene groupie."

She let go of the chase and I stopped running when I got across the street. It was then I realized a disconcerting fact. Adele had driven and was nowhere to be seen. I tried calling her and all the other Hookers, and all I got were voice mail answers. Were they still inside? There was no way of telling. I had to face it, I didn't have a ride home. I considered my options. Ventura Boulevard was a few blocks ahead and it ran west all the way across the Valley to Tarzana.

I was pretty sure there was a bus that would get me to Shedd & Royal or close enough to walk. It was embarrassing to admit that I didn't even know how much the bus cost. Over the years, the public transportation options had improved, but the truth was most people who had cars treated taking public transportation like a special event.

I found the bus stop and leaned against the glass enclosure around the bench. It was rush hour and the traffic clogged in the intersection when the light changed. Even when the light went to green, the cars moved so slowly in front of me, I had time to look at the occupants. It was the end of April and the weather was all over the place temperature wise. The mornings were usually cloudy and cool, the afternoons sunny and hot and then the evenings went back to chilly. Since I'd expected to just be getting in and out of a car, I'd worn only a thin rust-colored suede jacket with my khaki slacks. Even the black vest I'd put on over the white collared shirt didn't add much warmth. And the events of the day didn't help, either.

My head pounded and I shivered as I waited. The people in the cars had nice little cocoons of temperature control, and silly as it seems, I felt like a lost child a million miles from home as I saw them go by. I watched a woman take a paper cup of coffee out of her drink holder. I could almost taste it as she held the cup to her lips. Her car moved on and I glanced down the street, hoping to catch sight of a bus. Another car inched in front of me, then slowed to a stop. Suddenly the tinted window lowered.

"Molly?" a male voice said. I thought I was hearing things, but then the black Mercedes came into focus and I saw Mason was the driver. "Get in," he said with a quick wave of his hand.

Before anyone could even honk at the hold up, I was in the car pulling the door shut. As the car began to inch along, we both said, "What are you doing here?"

I let Mason go first. The eastern part of the Valley was

home to a number of movie and TV studios, and he'd had a meeting at one of them. Mason was the high-level attorney naughty celebrities turned to when they got in trouble. He had a reputation for keeping them out of jail or at least keeping their stay short. He didn't give me exact details, but he'd been at Warner Brothers talking to a client who was accused of hit-and-run involving a knocked-over "No Parking" sign.

"And you?" he said, giving me a concerned glance.

I spilled the whole story while he made a detour through a Starbucks drive-thru and got me a coffee and a roll. My stomach was growling loud enough that he could hear it across the car.

He listened without comment, but I knew what he was thinking—Nell Collins was in big trouble. She had motive. I had overheard her complaining about Robyn and wishing she was out of the way. No doubt she had expressed similar feelings to her coworkers, who were likely to be questioned by the cops. She had opportunity, since she'd been the one to bring the packet of sweetener, which she could have doctored. To cap it off, she had means. As a production assistant, she had to know how to do all kinds of things and get hold of whatever somebody told her to get. It wasn't a stretch that she could figure out how to get some cyanide.

"Poor CeeCee. Nell's the closest thing she has to a daughter," I said. The coffee and roll had taken a little of the edge off my hunger and headache, but thinking about the situation made me feel bad all over again.

"Do you want me to talk to her?" Mason said and I nodded.

"I'm sure she didn't do it. She couldn't have," I said. Mason caught my eye as we got to a stoplight, and again I knew what he was thinking. But what if she did?

The freeway wasn't a good option as it looked like even more of a parking lot than the street, so Mason headed toward Burbank Boulevard. It ran across the Valley and through the Sepulveda Dam area, which was the flood area for the L.A. river and was empty of development except for a golf course and various parks.

By then it all began to catch up with me. Someone had died in front of me and I had been helpless to save them. It started with my eyes getting watery and ended with me sobbing. Mason pulled off the wide street into the golf course parking lot. There was a walking track around it and the after-work exercise crowd were getting out of their cars and stretching before they began their trek.

Mason offered just what I needed. A shoulder to cry on. He put his arm around me and handed me a wad of tissue. It all came out now. An appropriate place because I felt like the dam had broken and my tears just flooded out. When I was done crying, I felt a sense of relief. His assurance that I couldn't have done anything to change the outcome helped.

He took his arm away and moved back into driving position. "Is there anything else on your mind?" I slumped and wondered if on top of all his other talents, Mason had become psychic. There had been an undercurrent of thought that had been percolating for a while. It had surfaced when Barry had shown up at the studio. Maybe I was being foolish. Maybe I should take the ring out of the box and just say yes.

"I have been thinking maybe I should just go ahead and become Molly Greenberg."

I heard Mason choke. I guess his supposed psychic powers weren't strong enough to have figured what else I was upset about. Mason took a moment to compose himself before he spoke.

"Speaking as your friend," he began, "I can just say one thing. Don't do it." Mason had been divorced for a while and had managed to keep a decent relationship with his ex-wife. His kids were grown and had lives of their own, but he was always there for family celebrations. When I'd first gotten to know him, it was very clear he didn't plan to get married again and was only interested in casual relationships. So, I could understand his reaction, though the emotion in his voice was a little stronger than I'd expected.

"Why change anything? If you were Mrs. Greenberg, would we even be sitting here now?"

I felt a slump coming again. I hadn't wanted to consider it, but I knew he was right about that. Barry didn't like that I was friends with Mason and would certainly *ixnay* it if we were married. And what about all the time I spent with the Hookers? He didn't seem altogether happy with it now. If we were married and he felt he had a say in my activities—I didn't even want to finish the thought. It brought forward all the reasons I didn't want to get married again. I liked being in charge of my own life.

I saw Mason surreptitiously check his watch and I apologized for barging into his day. "You have someplace to be, don't you?" I said.

"Sorry, Sunshine. But I have a dinner meeting." He started the car and rejoined the traffic. He dropped me back at the bookstore where I'd left my car. "If anything comes up, call me. Anything—like you start thinking of wedding-dress shopping," he said with a chuckle.

CHAPTER 5

MRS. SHEDD CAUGHT ME AS I WAS COMING IN THE door of Shedd & Royal. "Molly, where have you been? You said you'd be here by noon." She stopped and took a good look at me. I hadn't seen my reflection, but judging by Mrs. Shedd's expression, the long day, a tension headache, someone dying before my eyes and the sob fest with Mason must have left their mark. "Did something happen?" Now she sounded concerned.

I apologized for being late and not calling. By the time I'd gotten my phone back, calling to say I'd been delayed seemed kind of beside the point. I thought it would be better to just explain when I got to the bookstore. I began with Adele's crochet moment, and Mrs. Shedd rolled her eyes.

"She didn't mention Shedd and Royal, did she?" Mrs. Shedd asked with worry in her voice. A little laugh at the absurdity of her concern under the circumstances escaped my lips before I continued to describe the chain of events. I got as far as Robyn's dying practically at my feet when Mrs. Shedd put her hand on my shoulder. "Not another dead body," she said, shaking her head. "I'd be afraid to go anywhere with you."

I suppose I should have been grateful she didn't call me a crime scene groupie. She gasped when I mentioned that the victim was the woman she'd spoken to on the phone, and then gasped again when I mentioned that it seemed to be murder.

"The police don't think you or Adele had anything to do with it, do they—or me since I did speak with her on the phone?"

I tried to reassure Mrs. Shedd. "Speaking to someone on the phone once hardly made you a suspect. I don't think Adele or I are likely to be considered suspects, either." My voice sort of trailed off at the end. I hated to, but I finally brought up Nell, and Mrs. Shedd sucked in her breath big time.

"That doesn't sound good. CeeCee must be very upset," she said. "Be sure and point out Nell next time she comes in." Mrs. Shedd paused before she dropped her voice and added, "That is, if she comes in again." I knew Mrs. Shedd was thinking about Nell getting arrested. I was going to tell her even if that happened, it wasn't as if they were going to put her right in jail and throw away the key. She'd probably get bailed out in no time, making it possible for her to come in the bookstore again. But it wasn't worth explaining so I let it be.

Mrs. Shedd said Mr. Royal had hung around, and between the two of them, they'd managed okay. He'd been a silent partner and out of the picture when I first started working there, and even though they were equal partners and both my bosses, I always thought of her as the one really in charge. Maybe it was because for a long time Mr. Royal had been such a silent partner I'd doubted that he really existed.

I laughed at that concept now. Once I'd gotten to know Joshua Royal, he seemed like the world's most interesting man. It turned out he'd been everywhere and done just about everything during his time away.

"It's already so late, Molly, take a little more time and get something from the café. You look like you need it." I appreciated her concern and took her up on the offer. Mason's coffee and roll had only been a stopgap, and I needed a second round.

Bob had done a double take when I placed my order but didn't say anything about how I looked, though as he pushed the coffee with the shot of espresso across the counter, he'd added several chocolate pieces on a napkin. Facing him made it hard for me to ignore that hair growth below his lower lip. Should I call it a beardette?

"Alain Des Plaines brought the chocolate in," Bob explained, referring to the guy who wrote the cookbook *Melts at Body Heat*, which was the centerpiece of Salute to Chocolate. "He wants to know what everybody thinks about him doing a demo of making these. I've tasted them, and they seem to be just what you need."

Bob watched while I ate one. I bit into strong bittersweet chocolate before hitting something sweet with a smack of heat. "It's chocolate-dipped candied ginger," Bob explained, and I nodded with recognition at the flavor of the inner portion.

Bob was right about it being just what I needed. The kick of the ginger picked me up right away. I took a slug of the coffee and all the flavors blended nicely. "Alain gets a thumbs-up on these as far as I'm concerned."

"Alain wanted me to tell you that he's been getting some strange e-mails complaining that he's only doing a chocolate demo. He said they even sent him a list of alternative recipes," Bob said.

I put up out my hands in a gesture of disbelief. "That's crazy. It's called a Salute to Chocolate."

"That was just about what Alain said," Bob said. "I'll pass along your agreement when I see him."

I was about to leave the counter when Rhoda and Elise came in and dropped their canvas bags full of their crochet supplies on one of the tables. I called out a greeting and they suddenly noticed me.

"What happened to you?" Rhoda said. "We saw you get dragged out of the audience with Adele, and then as soon as the show finished, all these cops came in and started taking down everybody's name. I must have asked five different officers what was going on, but all they gave me was the silent treatment," Rhoda said. She gave off an air of authority, and I was surprised she hadn't managed to get an answer.

Elise seemed a little distraught by the incident. "It was obvious something serious had happened. We decided the best thing to do was come here," she said in her birdlike voice. "Sheila's already back in the yarn department. I saw her when we walked in."

"So, are you going to tell us what happened? What could Adele have possibly done to bring out all those cops?" Rhoda asked. I took my coffee and came over to their table, not wanting to broadcast everything over the café. A number of the tables were occupied and several people had already looked up and were eavesdropping on our conversation. A guy in jeans and boots passed me carrying a coffee mug. I was surprised to see him walk behind the counter and help himself to a refill instead of having Bob get it. But then the café wasn't really my domain, so I didn't know what kind of arrangements Bob had with regular customers.

Rhoda and Elise leaned close over the table as I repeated the chain of events in a low voice. Both of them looked like their eyes were about to fall out when I told them about what happened to the segment producer.

"Poor CeeCee, she takes in her niece and then Nell turns around and murders somebody. And of all times, when her aunt is doing the show," Rhoda said.

"If she really did it," Elise said.

Rhoda snorted. "Like who else could it have been? It was just Molly, Adele and Nell in there."

Elise shrugged uncomfortably. "Remember, somebody is innocent until proven guilty. It's not nice to jump to conclusions." Elise had been on the other side of conclusion jumping and so was ultrasensitive. Rhoda gave her a hopeless shrug, and the two of them went to order their drinks.

The three of us took our drinks and headed for the back of the store. The café might not be my domain, but the yarn department was. At least if I was back there, I would feel like I was working. Ever since we'd added the yarn department and left the table up all the time, it seemed like there were always people around it crocheting. And even knitting, when Adele wasn't around. Though right now, the only one at the table was Sheila. She was hunched over her work, and I was concerned that she was having an attack of her nerves, but when she sat up and I saw her work, I was relieved to see that she had nice even stitches on the heathery blue shawl in progress. Previously when Sheila got tense, her stitches turned into little knots and we'd had to get her a smaller hook to pry them open. She pushed her blunt-cut dark hair behind her ears to get it out of her face.

Her eyes were like saucers when she looked up at us. "I didn't know what else to do but come here," she said. "I couldn't find Adele or anybody when the cops let me go." She said she'd gotten a ride from some other audience member who was headed for Woodland Hills. Sheila held up about a foot of crocheted shawl with skeins of blue, green and purple yarn hanging off it. "I did this while I was waiting," she said. Apparently she had turned her nervous energy into speed, which was more productive than the old tight stitches. She put down her work and jumped up to hug us all. "I was so worried. Where's everybody else?"

Eventually Sheila thought to ask what had happened. I was getting tired of repeating the story and was actually relieved when Rhoda took over for me. The story lost a little in her rendition, but it was close enough. I tried Dinah's phone again and was relieved when she finally answered. I told her we were all gathering at the bookstore and she said she was just minutes away.

I hadn't thought to ask how she'd gotten back, but when she came in, I realized I had the answer. She wasn't alone. Commander Blaine had his arm linked in hers. The slender man with thick white hair shared the same high energy of my best friend. They explained together how he'd come to rescue Dinah when she'd discovered she had lost her ride. His eyes were shining, and it was pretty obvious he had enjoyed playing the white knight. He seemed stuck to Dinah's side like there was glue involved. I was still surprised to see my very independent friend so connected with someone. She didn't like the title boyfriend any more than I did and referred to Commander as her relationship partner. I wasn't so cool on that title, either, but it wasn't really my affair.

Before Dinah even asked, Rhoda was repeating the story of what had happened. Dinah sucked in her breath and looked toward me. I felt a sense of relief. Together, Dinah and I would make some sense out of what was going on. We'd played Sherlock and Watson before. But then I noticed Commander tug her arm slightly, and Dinah sheepishly said she'd just come to find out what had happened and make sure everybody was okay.

I said, "Everybody hasn't shown up yet," but Dinah just averted her eyes and said they had to go.

What? I screamed in my mind. Someone died in front of my eyes and my best friend wasn't going to stay while I tried to figure out what was going on.

Commander took over for her, and as his gaze moved around the group, staying the longest on me, he explained, "We agreed to help with a wine-and-cheese karaoke thing at the Tarzana Senior Center." Dinah started to walk out with him but ran back and whispered, "I'll call you later."

I had mixed emotions. I was glad that Dinah had finally

met a really nice human being. How could you fault someone for volunteering their services to help a bunch of seniors have a fun evening? Commander had learned to deal with his own loneliness by thinking about other people and putting on social events for them. Dinah had an equally big heart. Who else would have had their ex-husband's children with his newly exed wife keep coming back to visit her? I knew it was selfish, but I missed my best friend.

For about sixty seconds, they all sat and crocheted in silence, but then Adele showed up with her hat sitting way back on her head, which was not an improvement. She dropped into one of the chairs with a dramatic sigh.

"They tried their best to get me to confess, but I wouldn't do it," she said before letting out an even bigger sigh.

"What?" Rhoda said.

"They thought because that woman dragged me out of the show, I might have wanted revenge. One of the cops even suggested that maybe I carried a supply of poison in case anybody happened to irritate me." Adele looked around the table at us. "Can you imagine anyone thinking I'd do something like that?"

Adele saw that everyone had taken out their current crochet projects and joined them. I had been hanging back, straightening up stray skeins that were laying around the counter at the base of the bins of yarn. I longed to join them and finally gave in. Like everybody else, I had a bunch of projects in the works. I kept a scarf in progress stashed in the yarn department for times like this. I took out the canvas bag with the apricot yarn from the cabinet and joined the group. It was a simple pattern of double crochets and chain stitches and perfect when I needed something that was repetitive and relaxing.

I'd just settled into a rhythm when CeeCee showed up. She was still wearing the outfit she'd worn on the show and appeared the least discombobulated of any of us.

"I thought I'd find you all here." She stopped at the head

of the table, which was her usual place since she was more or less the leader of the group. "What an afternoon," she said in a breezy tone. "Thanks to this Oscar buzz, everybody wants to do an interview with me. My publicist had set up a bunch for this afternoon. I just sat there as one group after the other came in and we had almost the exact same conversation." She settled into a chair and produced a canvas bag with some yarn and hooks. "I need to unwind," she said with a sigh. "I think the show went very well, except"—she glared at Adele—"I can't believe you made a scene. Thank heavens no one knew I had any crochet connection."

Adele's eyes flew skyward. "I can't believe you'd try to deny your crochet heritage. You should be proud of your talent." Adele picked through the donation box we'd set up to keep all the things we made for different charities and held up a precious baby blanket made in natural-colored organic cotton that CeeCee had made, to illustrate her point.

CeeCee touched the blanket and said she was very pleased at how it had turned out. "I'm certainly a proud crocheter, but I don't have to hit everybody over the head with a hook." She gave Adele a pointed look. "Whatever you did caused all kinds of problems. As soon as the show wrapped, they whisked me out of there so fast I didn't even get a chance to pick up my things. They just said there'd been some kind of trouble. And I think we know who caused it."

So CeeCee didn't know what really happened. Nobody said anything, and the tension was so thick you could have cut it with a knife. For some reason, everybody looked toward me. "You tell her," Rhoda said.

"Tell me what?" CeeCee said, suddenly appearing wary.

"There was an incident when Adele and I were in the waiting room," I began. I just gave her the facts, but she did an excellent job of filling the blanks and appeared stricken. "They can't possibly think my niece had anything to do with it. Besides, how could they tell so quickly it wasn't some sort of seizure?"

"Cop instinct," I said. "Just like they decide who they think did it." I realized what I'd said and wished I could take it back, but CeeCee went pale and pulled out her cell phone. She had her agent on the other end in no time. He didn't know anything about the so-called incident but promised to find out all the details. "I think he knows more than he's letting on," she said to us in a pointed voice as she pushed the button to disconnect. She turned to Adele and me. "When was the last time you saw my niece?"

I explained about them separating us, and then Adele made things worse by complaining she'd been grilled by the cops and they'd tried to pin the segment producer's death on her.

"This isn't about you, Adele," CeeCee said with a worried sigh. "I'm responsible for Nell." She'd picked up her work but wasn't crocheting. She leaned back in her chair with a heavy sigh. I said something about her being an adult, and CeeCee surprised me by snapping at me. "I can't believe you don't understand. You're a mother. What if it was your son Samuel or Peter?"

Okay, I got it. I told her about Mason's offer to help, and she wanted me to call him. "He's at a dinner meeting. I'd only want to bother him if . . ." I couldn't bring myself to say it. I would disturb him only if Nell had been arrested.

Bob showed up with a tray of coffee drinks and more of the chocolate samples.

"Thank heavens," CeeCee said, reaching for two of the papers filled with the candy. "If ever there was a time I needed emergency chocolate, it's now." As CeeCee was working on saving herself with candy, Bob pulled me aside. He'd figured there was some kind of trauma going on—that's why he'd shown up with the drinks and samples—and he wanted to know details.

I gave him the short version and just said a segment producer on the *Barbara Olive Overton* show had died. I mentioned Mrs. Shedd had said she was a customer of the café. When I gave him her name, he gasped softly and went pale. He mumbled something about knowing her.

"There's Nell," Elise said, standing up. We all looked toward the front as Nell walked like a zombie across the bookstore. Her eyes were glazed like she was in some kind of shock.

CeeCee sprang into action as Nell got close to the table. "Get her a hook," CeeCee demanded.

I'm not sure if CeeCee really believed crocheting was a cure for Nell's condition or she just felt helpless and it was the first thing that came to mind. Either way, I wanted to help. Bob took off, saying he'd get more chocolate samples and a glass of water.

I still had Adele's large turquoise hook and yarn in my pocket and offered it to CeeCee. She did a foundation chain and the first row of single crochets before pushing it in her niece's hand.

Nell sank in a chair and CeeCee told her to start crocheting. Whatever objections to crochet Nell'd had before, she seemed to have forgotten them and followed her aunt's orders. Sheila came and stood next to Nell and had her do yoga breathing in time to each stitch.

By the time Bob returned with the chocolate-covered ginger and a glass of water, Nell had relaxed her shoulders and Sheila didn't have to coach her breathing anymore.

Nell set down the couple rows of crochet and took the chocolates and water gratefully. Everyone was staring at her. Rhoda couldn't take the tension anymore and leaned toward her.

"So are you going to tell us what happened to you?"

Nell set down the glass and took a couple more of Sheila's yoga breaths while we all waited expectantly.

She started with what happened to Robyn. Everyone had

already heard the story at least once but listened again since it was obvious she needed to talk about it. "If that wasn't bad enough, these detectives thought that I did it. Me. One of them was called Detective Gilmore, and she kept saying I'd feel better if I just told them the whole story. I did tell them the whole story—over and over. I got Robyn her latte and I went and got the special sweetener. They kept me in a room and keep asking me again and again if I'd poisoned Robyn. I kept saying no, but they didn't believe me. They asked me about Robyn and I told them I didn't know much about her. It wasn't like she shared her personal life with me." Nell stopped, as if considering something. "The only thing she ever told me was that her parents died when she was a kid. And the only reason she told me that was to point out how she'd had to get everything on her own, unlike me, who according to her, had gotten the job just because of Aunt CeeCee." Nell's voice had risen in anger as she got to the end and everyone at the table appeared uncomfortable. It sounded a little too much like she might have done it.

Suddenly it was as if she realized how she'd sounded and she collapsed on the table. "It's lucky the cops aren't here. They might have taken that the wrong way." Nell sat up and appeared composed as she turned toward me. "I told Detective Gilmore that I knew you since you seem to have police connections." Nell stopped and sighed. "She wasn't impressed."

The color had come back into Nell's face. "After I'd told them for the zillionth time I had nothing to do with it, they finally let me go. Thank heavens she realized I was telling the truth and all that is over."

I didn't want to tell her, but I had a feeling it was anything but over.

CHAPTER 6

FOR ONCE I CAME HOME TO AN EMPTY HOUSE. SAMuel had left a note. He'd taken care of the animals and had gone to play backup for some singer-friend. Cosmo danced out the door, and the little black mutt ran around the yard while I watered the flowers. Blondie finally joined us, though the strawberry terrier mix wasn't quite as exuberant. Since it was dark, I made sure Holstein and Cat Woman stayed inside.

To say I was a little keyed up from the day was an understatement. And, well, the three red-eyes I'd had in close succession hadn't helped, either. I thought I was immune to caffeine, but I guess all those shots of espresso had added up.

I ruffled through the refrigerator for something to throw together for dinner. Ha! I shook my head at its empty state, the result of having Samuel, Barry and Jeffrey around. Even what was there wasn't really there. The milk carton had a few drops left in it. The package of Muenster cheese was down to the last two slices, and somebody hadn't closed the package, so those two slices were dried up and inedible. I tossed both items.

It looked like it was going to be ice cream for dinner whether I wanted it or not. Except when I checked the freezer, all that was left of the ice cream was a spoonful at the bottom of the container of vanilla bean.

I was considering my options when my kitchen door pushed open, startling me. The dogs came in, followed by Dinah. She'd gradually been becoming more of an animal person and gave them both some affectionate rubs in greeting. When her kids were growing up, her idea of a pet was, at best, a goldfish.

"Karaoke night over already?" I asked and she nodded.

"Those seniors go to bed early." She sighed deeply. "I'm sorry for rushing off before," she said. Blondie left the kitchen, but Cosmo sat down to watch what was going to happen. Unlike Blondie, who was the Greta Garbo of dogs—she spent most of her time alone—Cosmo liked to be in the middle of the action.

"Commander had planned the evening and I promised to help." She sat down at the built-in kitchen table. "This is all new to me." Her salt-and-pepper spiky hair gave a little edge to her looks. She'd branched out in the scarf department now that she'd started making her own. Instead of long flowing fabric ones that tended to flap in the breeze behind her, she wore a long thin orange one she'd crocheted wrapped around her neck. It was a nice point of color over the beige linen loose-fitting top and matching pants she wore.

"No problem," I said, checking the refrigerator again. "Adele was happy to step into your position of sidekick." I turned toward Dinah and noted her hurt look. "I'm joking," I said, shaking my head. "It's okay, really."

"No, it isn't," Dinah mumbled. "Do you have any idea how hard it is to adjust to being with someone I'm not always upset about?" I laughed and Dinah sighed again. "I don't want to be the kind of person that throws over their girlfriend for a guy," she said. "It was never a problem before.

When I was involved with jerks, they were never around enough to get in the way."

"Forget it. You're here now. And there is nothing to eat in my house," I said, pushing the fridge door shut.

The original plan was to go to the market, but Whole Foods was pulling in their outdoor display of fruit in anticipation of closing and Gelson's was doing the same with their outdoor tables. There were other markets that stayed open later, but we decided to go to a restaurant. As we drove down Ventura, most of them were shut for the night, too. Le Grande Fromage was so dark I could barely see the sign. The only place still open was an Israeli place. We found a table and ordered their special array of salads and freshly made humus that came with a circle of hot bread.

I filled Dinah in on what had happened after she left, and she shook her head with concern. "Poor Nell. I agree with you. Just because the cops let her go doesn't mean its over."

"CeeCee's worried, too. She pulled me aside before they left and asked—well, begged me really—to get Nell off the hook. I think CeeCee is concerned about her own reputation, too."

"In other words, she wants you to find out who really killed the producer—what was her name again?"

"Robyn Freed," I said. The eleven o'clock news had just started on the flat-screen TV that hung over the bar. The anchor went to a reporter in the field. I recognized the street outside the Wolf Brothers Studio. Now the street was deserted and dark except for the camera lights. It was so ridiculous how they had reporters doing live feeds from places where something *had* happened. The overdressed blond reporter said, "Pandemonium broke out earlier this morning at the *Barbara Olive Overton* show when, according to witnesses, an audience member jumped up brandishing a weapon."

They went to tape, and suddenly it was daylight and audience members were trickling out of the exit. There was another shot of people loitering on the street looking at the line of police cars and an ambulance. This short scene kept playing over and over as the reporter continued doing a voice-over. "The woman was escorted from the show and details are sketchy, but apparently paramedics and police were called in."

"Pandemonium?" I said. I started to go on about how ridiculous the newscast was but stopped to hear the reporter.

"Unconfirmed rumors said that Ms. Overton had been taken hostage by the crazed fan. We tried contacting the production offices, but they were being tight-lipped about information and would only say there'd been an incident."

After they'd repeated the scene of the audience leaving for the umpteenth time, they finally went back to the reporter standing in the dark.

"Can you believe they call that news?" I said. "They play a meaningless scene over and over and offer a story I know is absolutely not true. Whatever happened to getting the facts?"

Dinah and I did a knuckle bump in agreement. Apparently somebody else in the restaurant wasn't happy with the news, either, and the station abruptly changed to one of those entertainment news shows.

The waitress brought us another hot circle of bread. I pulled off a piece and dipped it in the garbanzo bean puree. "Look," I said, pointing at the huge screen. The screen had flashed the show's logo before going to a scene that looked similar to the news program we'd just been watching. Pierce Sheraton was standing on the street outside the studio. He was the hottest entertainment reporter at the moment—so hot that the show was called *Pierce Sheraton's Entertainment Zone*. As was his trademark, the tall lanky reporter was wearing a black tee shirt over dark-washed jeans. He'd been known to show up at award shows in the same outfit with a tuxedo jacket thrown on top. He had shaggy hair and a smirky attitude. For a moment, the screen showed the *Barbara Olive Overton* show, and I was curious what his report on the incident was going to be. When the shot went back to the street, he'd been joined by a tall woman with sharp features and a severe, short haircut.

"Rumors are swirling about what happened at the *Barbara Olive Overton* show this morning," Pierce said to the camera, "but once again, *Entertainment Zone* has the real story. This is Talia Canon." He gestured toward the woman standing next to him. "She's an assistant producer on the show and has the inside scoop. Talia, tell us what happened." Pierce put the microphone in front of Talia, and she proceeded to explain that one of the segment producers on the show had died under suspicious circumstances. Pierce asked her for the person's name, but she wouldn't give it. She'd heard the cops were still looking for her next of kin and thought there was some kind of rule about not making a dead person's name public until their family had been notified.

"Thank heavens for that," I said to Dinah. "It would be awful if that was how her family found out."

Pierce kept trying to find out as much as possible about the victim and who might have wanted to harm her. "You were telling me a production assistant is the one who gave the victim the poison."

Talia suddenly appeared uncomfortable. "I said *allegedly* might have given the victim some kind of poison. And please, no names for the victim or the sus—alleged suspect." Pierce tried to squeeze more details out of Talia, but all she would talk about was Robyn's job.

"We call them segment producers to separate them from the other kinds of producers on the show. It's their responsibility to get all the pieces together for the shows. Like, they take care of all the video background pieces we always have. Sometimes it takes a year to put one together if they're following somebody's progress at, say, losing weight." Pierce wanted to know what kind of shows the victim had been working on. She hemmed and hawed and finally would only say she had been assigned two shows—one featured an author and one a celebrity couple.

"And you worked for the deceased woman?" Pierce said and she nodded. "Is it safe to assume that you'll be taking over for her?"

Talia must have realized how cold all of this sounded, and she suddenly appeared anguished or tried to appear that way. She insisted the whole staff was brokenhearted over the loss. "But Barbara can't just stop her show and let all her fans down. I'm going to be doing my best to step into Ms. X's shoes." Talia seemed done, then she looked back at the camera. "And for all you fans out there. Under the circumstances, we're doing a repeat tomorrow, but after that, it's back to our regular schedule."

"Barbara is certainly not letting any grass grow under her feet," Dinah said.

"I suppose it seems that way, but they can't just close up shop," I said. "I sure hope CeeCee isn't watching this. If she hears anything about a suspect, she'll have to figure it's Nell," I said as we got our leftovers packed up to go. I drove the greenmobile, as I called my old blue green Mercedes 190E, back to my house. Dinah pushed me to take all the leftovers and then got in her car and left.

I called Mason as soon as I got inside. He listened as I relayed how Nell seemed to think she was off the hook because they let her go, but then I'd just heard somebody on TV say the cops had a suspect. "Could it be someone other than Nell?"

"Anything is possible," Mason said. "But I wouldn't get too hopeful." He repeated his offer to talk to Nell or CeeCee. "This must be a whole new experience for CeeCee—having to focus so much attention on someone else." He realized that had sounded wrong and corrected his statement. "I didn't mean anything about her personally. It goes with the territory. Lord knows I deal with enough celebrity types to see how they are. They get so used to being the center of attention it's hard for them to consider somebody else." He brought the subject back to me, remembering I'd been pretty worn when he dropped me at the bookstore.

"You sound exhausted, Sunshine," he said in a caring manner. I was agreeing with him when Samuel came in the kitchen door carrying his guitar. I had left the bag of leftovers on the counter, intending to put it in the refrigerator. He opened the bag and pulled out one of the containers and some bread and headed for his room. The door opened again and Barry came in. He was in shirt sleeves with his tie hanging loose. He touched my shoulder in greeting and started poking through the bag of restaurant food. He tried to look intent on the food, but I knew he was listening to my call.

"Do you have company?" Mason asked.

"Yes," I said, feeling inhibited.

"And you can't talk anymore, huh?" Mason said.

"Right."

"You know where to reach me if you need anything. Sleep well." And then he hung up.

I put the phone back in the charger and Barry didn't say anything at first. Like I was supposed to believe that he hadn't noticed that I was off the phone. He had made a plate of food but left it on the counter as he came up behind me and wrapped his arm around my shoulder.

"You okay?" His hand began to massage the back of my neck. "I don't get it. Only you go to a talk show and end up with a corpse. You better let this one go. No investigating. Let the cops handle it," he said.

"You know something, don't you?" I said.

"And I'm not telling," he said.

CHAPTER 7

I WENT TO THE BOOKSTORE EARLY THE NEXT DAY to try to make up for the lost time. I picked up a coffee from the café and headed to the yarn department. Yesterday the group had hung out there almost until closing time, and I'd never gotten a chance to straighten up. We'd arranged the bins of yarn by color, and it was like being surrounded by a rainbow. Once I'd picked up the stray hooks and yarn bits off the table, I began to straighten out the bins so that all the skeins were where they belonged. I heard someone come into the area and turned to ask if they needed help.

"Oh," I said, surprised when I saw that it was Detective Heather. She had walked over to the bins that we'd labeled "Just Socks." She began taking out skeins and feeling the yarn. I had never made any socks and didn't know how much help I could be but offered anyway.

"I don't need any help," she said with just the slightest edge. "I've been making socks for years. I'd like some really soft yarn, like a cashmere blend. You have no idea how sensual a pair of hand-knit socks can be. Men love them."

"Oh," was all I could croak out as she continued on going through our stock of yarn.

"I'm looking for something special for someone special," she said, and then explained she was getting a head start on holiday gifts. On top of everything else, she had to be one of those organized people who probably had all her holiday gifts wrapped and ready to go before Thanksgiving. Not me. The night before Christmas, I would probably be trying to finish a scarf. Something in the way Detective Heather emphasized the phrase *someone special* gave me the feeling she was talking about Barry, but I couldn't really ask.

"I suppose you'd have to be careful who you give hand-made socks to. It might seem a little personal," I said.

She looked at me dead-on. "That's the point. Forget all this nonsense about the way to a man's heart is through his stomach. Make his feet feel good and he's yours." She plucked two skeins out of the cashmere blend in a color called midnight rumble, which was really just black, and began looking at our display of needles.

"Just a heads-up," she said. "You might as well save your sleuthing skills. There's no question—Nell Collins killed Robyn Freed. Several of Ms. Collins' coworkers said Ms. Freed was always picking on her because she thought her aunt had gotten her the job. One of the other production assistants even said Ms. Collins had said she wished Ms. Freed would drop dead." Heather let the comment hang in the air a moment before proceeding. The rest had to do with Nell getting the drink and sweetener for Robyn. All the tests weren't in, but they were pretty sure the cyanide had been in the sweetener. "We checked the rest of the supply, and if you looked closely, you could see where the packets had been slit open at the seam and reglued," Heather said. "We searched Ms. Collins' cubby at the production office and found a glue gun."

I didn't know what to say. I knew Robyn had hassled Nell, and I'd heard Nell say she wished Robyn was out of the picture. And yes, Nell had given Robyn the drink and the sweetener. But the last part? "So, the packets were reglued and Nell had a glue gun. There's no proof the two things are connected," I said finally.

Heather picked up the yarn and two sets of metal circular needles. Before she headed to the front to pay, she turned back to me. "Maybe not yet, but I'll find a connection. The best thing she can do is confess, and then maybe we can get her a deal. I'm just telling you all this so you don't waste your time playing detective."

I had to sit down and pull out the apricot scarf and do a few rows after that. The whole conversation had left my heart thudding. The worst part was I thought Heather really meant it when she thought she was doing me a favor.

By the time the Hookers showed up in the afternoon, I'd decided not to repeat what Heather had said. Well, I would have told Dinah if she'd come, but she had a meeting with a student.

CeeCee was the first to arrive, and when I saw how tense she was, it only reinforced my decision. Since the previous night's get-together of the Hookers had been a little off, we agreed to meet the following afternoon to make up for it. CeeCee sat down at the table and took out a ball of sunny yellow cotton yarn and one of white cotton yarn. In no time, she'd done a foundation and a couple of rows in yellow before she switched to the white.

"I make pot holders when I'm upset," she said. She explained it was just a simple single crochet, then double crochet stitch throughout the whole thing, and then she'd put on a nice edging. For a moment, she forgot her tension. "You know, dear, it's all about the finishing. If I just left this a plain square, it would look so blah, but add a couple of rows of edging and suddenly it's adorable."

She shook her head in dismay and her shoulders sagged as the momentary respite ended. "I've had lots of ups and downs with my life and just rolled with the flow, but this is different. It's happening to somebody I care about, and I don't know what to do," she said. My apricot scarf was still on the table and I picked it up and began to work.

CeeCee put her work down with a heavy sigh. "Did you see the news this morning? The news people couldn't stop talking about it. Murder backstage at a talk show, what could make a better story? Thank heavens they didn't give Nell's name. They just called her *a production assistant*."

Adele left the kids' department and joined us. Her tendency to see herself in the center of everything came through when she started talking about the news report. "Well, at least they finally got it right. The stuff they said yesterday was just ridiculous. I mean, calling a crochet hook a weapon and me a madwoman." She looked toward us expectantly. When neither of us nodded or did anything to show our agreement, she harrumphed and took out her work-in-progress. She was making fingerless gloves for the donation box. "It won't stay warm forever," she said as she picked up the yarn.

CeeCee began to rub her temples. "I tried to get Nell to come with me, but she wouldn't. She appreciated the relaxation she got from the crochet last night, but she kept saying why start something she knew she'd never finish. She's just so impatient. I suppose that's the way it is when you're twenty-one." CeeCee gave up on the massage and searched her purse for some aspirin. She pulled out a bottle of water from her bag and took the two tablets. I said some coffee might help her headache. "If I have any more coffee, I'm going to jump out of my skin. Nell made a big pot this morning. She made a whole production out of it. She even grinds the beans."

Suddenly CeeCee stopped and it seemed like she wasn't going to say anything more. Then she sighed to herself. "They called Nell and told her that, under the circumstances, they thought she should take a leave of absence until everything is settled. Whoever she talked to assured her they believed she was innocent, but still . . ." CeeCee's voice trailed off as she rolled the hook between her fingers. "She's going in to pick up her things. I'm afraid she might make a scene."

CeeCee turned to me. "Molly, I'm worried. I don't think she should go alone. I'd go with her, but it would probably get picked up by some paparazzi. So far the news people don't seem to know the connection between us. If they knew Nell and I were related, it would just bring more of a spotlight to this whole business."

It was hard to figure out who she was really concerned about. Was she worried her name was going to bring attention to Nell? Or was she worried that having a niece suspected in a murder was going to bring the wrong kind of attention to her?

"I'm available to go with," Adele said a little too quickly. CeeCee's eyes flew skyward.

"You caused enough trouble the last time. I want someone to guide my niece, not make a ruckus."

"I wouldn't make a ruckus," Adele protested. "Maybe a hook and some yarn would fall out of my pocket. And maybe I'd mention to whoever that it would really turn around Barbara's life if she learned how to crochet."

"That is exactly what I'm afraid of," CeeCee said. "Dear, you're going to have to wave your hook on your own time; this trip is strictly about my niece." She turned to me. "Molly, would you go with her? You're a mother; you must be used to doing things like this."

The idea seemed to be that since I had experience dealing with uncomfortable situations, it was easy for me. I agreed to go with her but made sure CeeCee understood it wasn't going to be piece of cake for me, either.

"And while you're there, maybe you do a little investigating," CeeCee said. "You're so good at getting at the truth," she added in a hopeful voice.

Though CeeCee seemed relieved I was going with Nell, she still seemed less than her usual cheery self. "This isn't what I bargained for," she said finally. "I thought having Nell stay with me would be like having a daughter. But without all the baggage like arguing about clothes and curfews. I thought we'd be like friends." She turned to me. "Were you ever upset with your sons?"

I rolled my eyes and laughed. "Of course, do you want examples?"

She seemed slightly relieved by my answer. "She's just so difficult." CeeCee went back to crocheting while she talked. "Why couldn't she have gotten along with the woman who died? I didn't know what to tell her or what to do to help. When I was a struggling actress, if a director yelled at me, I just smiled back. I knew there was a whole line behind me anxious to take my place." Then the truth came out. "I should be basking in the glow of my Oscar buzz instead of worrying about Nell."

She must have felt guilty about what she said because she got defensive and tried to explain just what Oscar buzz meant. "My agent is already getting more movie offers. Nothing I'd do so far, but it wasn't like this before. This is my moment." She sagged again. "What am I going to tell my brother? His daughter stays with me, and after just a few months, she's an interesting person to the police."

"That's a person of interest," Rhoda corrected as she joined us. Elise was with her. "Your niece is a suspect?"

"Wow, wait till that hits the newsstand," Rhoda said in her nasally voice. "Oscar buzz and your niece being investigated by the cops."

"It's not going to hit any newsstand. And she's not being investigated by the cops. She was there and they asked her some questions, that's all. And nobody is going to connect me with any of it."

The rest of the group drifted in, and by the end, CeeCee was telling everyone I was going with Nell, was investigating the murder, and had everything under control.

If only that was true.

CHAPTER 8

NELL PICKED ME UP THE NEXT MORNING, AND WE headed across the Valley to the Wolf Brothers Studio and the *Barbara Olive Overton* production offices. I think she was glad I came along, though it was hard to tell for sure. The first thing she'd said when I got in the car was, "You don't need to come. I'm not a baby."

She was dressed in what seemed like a uniform for production assistants—worn jeans, a burgundy red tee shirt with a long-sleeved black flannel shirt layered over it. She had sneakers on her feet and a black-and-white bandana tied over her long brown hair, along with no makeup. As she drove, Nell kept telling me everyone was overreacting. "I'm not a person of interest or a suspect. How could I be? I had nothing to do with it." I didn't want to tell her that what she was saying was pretty much what most suspects said. Not that I believed she'd poisoned the sweetener, but I knew if she gave the "I had nothing to do with it" argument to the cops, it was likely to fall on deaf ears.

I took the opportunity to ask her a few questions about

the sweetener. Where was it kept? Who knew it was there? How did Robyn get along with other people on the production staff? Nell fumed at first, but I explained I was on her side and she finally opened up.

"Robyn seemed to really have it in for me, but she was hard on all the production assistants. I think she figured she'd gone through it when she was a PA and now it was her turn to dish it out," Nell said as we neared the studio entrance. "I just grabbed a packet out of her desk drawer. They're shaped kind of weird, kind of like a pyramid. Robyn made such a big deal about only using Nature's Sweetie. I think it was because it came from some plant grown in the Amazon and you can't just buy it at any grocery store." Nell shrugged. "The one I grabbed looked like all the others."

Nell pulled into the driveway that led to the guard house and entrance. This felt more familiar to me. When I'd gone to any tapings with Charlie, we'd always parked inside the gated area and gone in through the backstage entrance. Nell slowed long enough to let the guard see her parking emblem hanging from the mirror and prepared to glide through, but he held his hand up for her to stop.

She did as requested and opened her window. "Hi, Hank," she said to the uniformed guard. "What's up?"

He muttered, "Sorry, miss," as he reached in through the open window and took the dangling parking emblem. "Here's a temporary one for today," he said, writing the date on a card and handing it to her. "Hang it on your mirror."

Nell started to protest, but he just put up his hands in a helpless gesture and said again that he was sorry. "It's probably just standard policy, like if you go on vacation or something, that they take back your parking pass," Nell said to me.

I just nodded in agreement. Of course, I knew it wasn't true at all, but why make her feel worse. *BOO* productions had their own building within the Wolf Studio grounds. She parked close to the warehouselike building, and I followed her as she walked to a door on the side. She swiped a card and the door opened. Inside, there was a uniformed security woman sitting at a desk reading a book.

"She's with me," Nell said, jerking her thumb in my direction as we walked past. The woman set down the book and came from behind the desk, stopping our progress.

"Just hold on a moment," she said in a friendly voice tinged with authority. She made a call on her walkie-talkie. Nell was ready to protest, but I gave her a discreet shake of my head to discourage her. Of course they weren't going to let her wander around unescorted. A few moments later, a tall woman with short, dark hair approached us. She was only a few years older than Nell, but there was light-years of difference in their expressions and their clothes. Nell looked like she was dressed to go out and play. The woman's clothes were what I'd call business casual. She wore black jeans, a white collared shirt not tucked in and topped with a jacket. Several layers of necklaces adorned her neck and a stack of silver bangles jangled on her wrist. I recognized Talia Canon immediately from the entertainment news show the night before, though I didn't let on.

Nell greeted her and she responded with what seemed like forced friendliness. She looked at me, and I started to introduce myself, but she interrupted. "Are you a lawyer?"

"No, she's not a lawyer," Nell said vehemently. "Why would I have a lawyer? I didn't do anything. Her name's Molly Pink and she's a friend of my—" She had an awkward moment and instead of adding *aunt*, slid the *my* into *mine*.

Talia gave me a dismissive nod in recognition. In person, Talia's features were even sharper and more foxlike and there was a hardness to the set of her mouth.

As we began walking down the utilitarian corridor, Nell explained that Talia was an assistant producer, but Talia cleared her throat, and with a sideways glance, corrected her. "I was an assistant producer, but now I'm taking over for

Robyn." She must have realized she sounded a little too pleased about it and dropped her voice with a serious expression. "At least for now. Robyn was in the middle of working on several shows and they asked me to step in and take over for those."

We passed a series of dressing rooms. Names had been written on placards and slid into holders on the doors. At the end of the corridor, we passed through a door and came out into a reception area. There was a door to the parking lot and a counter with a man and woman close to Nell's age and experience behind it. The glass door to the outside opened and a man came in with a shopping bag and some boxes. "Who are these for?" the woman asked, picking up a clipboard. The delivery guy had already started to leave but came back and picked up each of the packages and read off the names on them.

"I might as well deliver them," Nell said, reaching for the shopping bag. The couple behind the counter and Talia all froze and traded glances.

"No, they have it covered." Talia took the handle of the bag out of Nell's grasp and set it down before giving us an impatient wave to follow her as she crossed the lobby. A door on the other side led to the production offices. The corridor was identical to the one on the other side, but instead of dressing rooms, there were small offices on either side. Talia stopped in an open doorway. My eye went right to the remnant of yellow crime scene tape stuck to the door handle. The door had a name holder just the way the dressing room side had, but it appeared more permanent. The "Robyn Freed" sign had been made by some kind of machine instead of scribbled in marker. Above it, a cardboard strip had been taped with "Talia Canon" written in. It was pretty clear that the show went on no matter what.

"When they say *leave of absence,*" Nell said, "how long do you think they mean? Like maybe a few days but not more than a couple of weeks, right?" Talia didn't respond but had us step into her office. I took the opportunity to look around, knowing this was probably going to be my only chance. Though between whatever the cops had taken and the fact that Talia seemed to have settled right in, I doubted there would be much to see. I noticed a brown cardboard box full of stuff in the corner. I wasn't sure if the contents were on the way in or the way out.

The Average Joe's Guide to Criminal Investigation said that investigating was really about talking to people. Though Talia was acting distant and cold, I figured she had a softer side somewhere. I'd found the best way to get through to even the toughest person was by being sympathetic.

"This must be hard for you," I said to her in a friendly voice. "You must have mixed feelings. Happy for the promotion, but sad how it came about. Is that the dead woman's stuff?" I vaguely pointed in the direction of the box.

Talia regarded me with interest as her expression opened a crack. "You've got that right," she said. "I've been afraid to seem at all excited about my new position for fear people would take it wrong." She was just talking to me now and seemed grateful to be able to express her feelings, though her version of soft was closer to hard than I'd hoped. "I mean, this is my big chance. I've had to step right in, but you have no idea how Robyn left things. There are just cryptic notes for the two shows she was working on. She kept everything under wraps."

"It sounds like she was trying to protect her job," I said, and Talia threw me a shrug, as if to say *whatever*. I wondered if Talia realized that she sounded more annoyed with Robyn than upset that she was dead. She gestured toward the box and finally acknowledged my question. "Yes, that's Robyn's stuff. I barely had time to clear her things out of my desk."

"Is there any of the sweetener in there?" I said, trying to look into the brown shipping box.

Talia shook her head. "The cops took all of it."

"But she kept it in here?" I asked, directing the question to both of them.

Nell nodded first. "She kept it in that drawer." Nell leaned forward and yanked the drawer open. "I swear, I think she counted how many of those weird packets were in there every day. She kept going on about how expensive Nature's Sweetie was and nobody was supposed to touch it except the production assistant who was getting her coffee drink." All that was in there now was an array of Talia's personal items. I saw some nail polish and a mesh bag filled with makeup.

I glanced at the office and adjoining hall. "Anybody could have come in here and messed with her sweetener."

Nell nodded in agreement quickly. "That's right. That's absolutely right. It wasn't as if she locked the drawer or anything."

Any chink in Talia's tough exterior had closed up and she'd gone back to her professional mode as she pushed closer to the desk and shut the drawer. As I stepped back to get out of her way, my elbow knocked into the box and several things on top fell to the floor.

"Leave it," Talia said as she picked up an envelope off the desk. She turned to Nell. "I have a check for you."

It was against my grain to leave a mess, so I bent down to pick up the stuff anyway. I laid the two copies of *Los Angeles Magazine* back on the pile in the box but stopped when I saw the last item was a clear plastic picture frame. I turned it over and examined it.

"What's this about?" I said, looking at the photograph slipped inside. It wasn't the image of Robyn that inspired my comment. She was wearing a paper hat and holding a noise-maker with some people scattered behind her. What got my attention was the hole next to her. When I say hole, I mean actual hole in the picture. Whoever had been in the photo with her had been carefully cut out, leaving a big opening. I held it up and showed it to the two women and asked if they knew who was missing.

Talia seemed impatient as she shrugged off the question and said Robyn didn't discuss her personal life. Nell seemed too distraught about her situation to even care about my question. Talia took the photo from me and laid it back on the box and turned all her attention on Nell as her lips curved in a calculated sympathetic smile.

"I'm sure you probably had nothing to do with the stuff in Robyn's coffee, and if it was up to me, I'd say it was fine for you to be here. But the powers that be just think it's best for all concerned if you take some time off. You're not being fired or anything, and as soon as things get straightened out, I'm sure they'll have you come back," she said. Nell swallowed, clearly not happy with the situation. Nell's face fell when Talia held her hand out and asked for the pass she'd used to come in. "And I'll need the phone we got for you," she added, gesturing impatiently as Nell rummaged through her purse. When Nell finally held them out, Talia quickly took both items.

Only then did Talia hand Nell the check and, in the same move, usher us back out into the hall. Now that Talia had what she wanted, it seemed like Operation Get Us Out of There had taken over.

"Let's get your things so you can be on your way." Talia was smiling as she said it, but it was a cold smile. You could tell because there were no eyes in it at all.

Talia touched us both on the arm and almost swept us toward the big room at the end of the corridor. There were desks scattered about and a bunch of people who all seemed to be talking and rushing around. Not one of them made eye contact with Nell. She was definitely persona non grata. Talia stood with me while Nell went to her cubby to get her stuff.

I was relieved when one of the production assistants stopped playing "you're invisible" with Nell and came up to her and handed her a plastic grocery bag to put her stuff in.

As for me, I was checking out the big wipe-off board hanging on the wall. There were columns with names on top. Talia's had been written in over a smudgy erasure. Below Talia's name *Tribute—Celebrity Golf Tournament* was written in green marker. Beneath it was a list of names in various colors. When my eye moved even lower, I was surprised to see *Shedd & Royal* written in blue marker with a question mark after it. There was just white space beneath it.

Then it came back to me. With all that had happened, I had forgotten all about Robyn calling Mrs. Shedd concerning staging a book signing. The notation must have something to do with it.

"I can help you with this," I said to Talia, indicating the board. Her gaze swept over it and she seemed perplexed.

"You know Becca Ivins and Derek Trousedale?"

"Huh?" I said, confused by her question. Where did that come from? Becca Ivins and Derek Trousedale were like Hollywood royalty. They'd been married forever, both could still open a movie, and they were known for all their charity work and good deeds. My blank look seemed to irritate her and she stepped up to the board and tapped her finger on the line about the celebrity golf tournament. "What exactly is it you can do?" she asked. Then I got it. I shook my head and pointed to the listing below.

"I handle the events for Shedd and Royal." I went on to explain Robyn's request and Talia nodded with understanding.

"Sorry, I assumed you were talking about the show I inherited featuring the celebrity couple. I'm a little consumed with it. I can't afford to have anything go wrong if I want this promotion to be permanent. Becca and Derek are being honored at this event." She explained the board was used for scheduling crews, and a lot of people had been assigned to the golf tournament to get material for the background piece on the couple.

She admitted she was less concerned about the author's show and hadn't even considered why the bookstore was on the scheduling board or, for that matter, even realized that Shedd & Royal was a bookstore. She didn't seem to be paying much attention when I explained how we'd thought it best to have the staged event coincide with a real one. She just wrote down the date and time, erased the question mark and scribbled in film crew.

We exchanged business cards, and she gave out an impatient sigh when she realized Nell was hanging in front of her cubby on the verge of a meltdown. I stepped in and gathered the young woman up.

As we left, I glanced over the board and caught sight of something below another segment producer's name. Written in bold letters it said, *BOO Learns to Knit*, followed by a list of celebrity names. Thank heavens I hadn't let Adele talk me into letting her come along. She would have thrown a fit.

CHAPTER 9

"I'D LIKE A RED-EYE," I SAID TO BOB AND TURNED toward Nell to get her order. She was slumped in a chair, leaning her face in her hands. On top of everything else, she'd found a note in her cubby saying the cops had taken her glue gun as possible evidence. When she didn't respond, I told Bob to make her something rich and delicious.

"Hard time?" Bob asked as his gaze went to Nell. Whenever I saw him, it was hard for me not to stare at that dab of hair below his lip. I just didn't get the look, but then I didn't get a lot of stuff, like why somebody would want to give their hair the color of red velvet cake. He was just a little taller than me, so my eye sort of naturally rested in the spot.

"An understatement," I said before telling him about the events of the morning. He was interested in hearing how the show had more or less just stepped over Robyn's dead body and moved on. I mentioned the picture with the cutout. "You said you knew her. Any idea of who it was?"

Bob shook his head. "She always came in alone. Mostly at the end of the day," he said. He handed me my cup and made

Nell what I called a party drink. "This ought to give her a boost," he said, squirting whipped cream on top of the icy beige mixture.

"I don't suppose Robyn ever ordered one of those," I said, grasping the cold drink.

Bob's eyes went skyward. "With all that sugar. Are you kidding?"

"How well did you know her?" I asked.

Bob seemed a little uncomfortable. "She was just a regular customer, so I knew her drink preference."

"And?" I said, sensing there was something more.

"And she talked to me sometimes." I prodded to find out what she talked about and he claimed not to remember that well. "She was pretty much consumed by her work," he said with a noncommittal shrug before turning to get my drink.

Nell looked up when I slid the drink in front of her. "Thanks," she said, pulling it closer. "And thanks for going with me."

She'd been a wreck by the time we left the studio, and I'd figured she needed a little pick-me-up. In more ways than a sweet drink. I'd called Dinah, who'd called the rest of the group and arranged for the Hookers to join us. There's nothing like the support of a group when you're feeling down.

Not everybody could make it. Sheila was tied up with her new job at Luxe. Eduardo had been keeping a low profile as far as the group was concerned and said he had some kind of meeting. All he'd said to the group was that he was in the process of making some changes in his life, and once it was all together, he'd tell us about it.

Rhoda and Elise came in and offered Nell supportive hugs before getting some drinks and joining us. Both of them had brought their crochet project bags and pulled out their work. Rhoda had some glittery silver yarn and was making an evening wrap, and Elise was making a black-and-white striped afghan. Dinah rushed in, having just finished teaching her class. She threw her arms around me and asked me how I was holding up.

"Managing," I said, grateful for her moral support.

Adele drifted in from the bookstore and started examining what Rhoda and Elise were working on. Finally the door to the outside opened and CeeCee came in, and she wasn't alone.

A man in a baseball cap was trailing her. Next to him, another man was holding a small video camera. The baseball cap put a shadow over the first man's face so that I didn't recognize him at first, but when he got closer, I saw it was Pierce Sheraton, the host of *Entertainment Zone*. More than host, he seemed to act as the main reporter. CeeCee really had made it back into the big time if the host of the entertainment show was following her. In the past, she'd always been worried about being caught by the paparazzi with poppy seeds stuck in her teeth, but those had been independent photographers trying to get a shot they could sell to one of the tabloids. Anything Sheraton got would end up featured on his show.

She was used to being noticed whenever she went out in public, which put a certain amount of pressure on her. She couldn't just throw on any old thing and stick a scarf over her hair to run to the market. Particularly not now when, thanks to her hosting the reality program and the vampire movie, people like Pierce Sheraton had started latching on to her when their paths crossed.

CeeCee had been around long enough to be a true professional. She knew the rules of the game. Entertainment reporters needed her, but she needed them. She was all smiles as she mugged for the camera and talked to Sheraton. But she'd also stopped a good distance away from us.

I could tell by her body language she was trying to end their encounter, and maybe it would have been a success if Adele hadn't jumped in. She saw reporter and camera and her eyes lit up as she grabbed Rhoda's crochet project and joined CeeCee.

With her ample size and naturally loud voice, Adele was impossible to ignore. The outfit didn't hurt, either. She had a lacy wine-colored shawl tied around her shoulders and large earrings crocheted out of black thread that moved whenever she swung her head.

"CeeCee, you're here at last," Adele said in a dramatic voice. "All your crochet buddies are waiting for you." Adele did a grand gesture toward the table, dangling Rhoda's silvery project from her arm. The reporter gave Adele and the crochet stuff a dismissive nod and took a step back. Nell pushed back her chair and rushed up to her aunt and threw her arms around her.

"Oh, Aunt CeeCee, it was awful going to the production office." The reporter suddenly looked at Nell intently. I saw CeeCee's head drop and the slightest of groans escaped her lips as the video camera recorded the moment.

"You're the one from the *Barbara Olive Overton* show. The alleged production assistant who gave Robyn Freed the poisoned drink." He looked at CeeCee and back at Nell. "CeeCee, how does it feel to have your niece be regarded as a person of interest in a homicide investigation?"

This was far worse than poppy seeds in her teeth.

I wondered how Sheraton had figured out who Nell was and made the connection to Robyn Freed. Then I remembered the entertainment report Dinah and I had seen a couple of nights ago. Off camera, Talia must have told him all about Nell and maybe even shown him a photo of her.

I stepped in and reminded him that they were on private property and asked them to leave. I was surprised when the reporter and cameraman did.

Only Adele wasn't happy with the outcome. The rest of the table gave me a round of applause.

CeeCee sat down with what was becoming a characteristic

sigh. "The damage is done, though. Now that they know Nell and I are related, the story is much more interesting." I went to get CeeCee a party drink after her momentary ordeal. Bob knew that CeeCee was always supposed to be concerned about her diet and offered to use a fancy no-calorie sweetener, but I said I thought CeeCee needed the real thing under the circumstances.

By the time CeeCee had drained half the creamy drink, she'd recovered. "Molly, I don't mean to pressure you, but now that Pierce Sheraton is going to hang on to this story like a terrier on a pant leg, you really need to step up your investigation and get the spotlight off of Nell."

I wasn't sure whose reputation CeeCee was more concerned about—hers or Nell's—but either way, she was right. I just wasn't sure how to do it.

Nell finished her drink by using the straw to vacuum up the last smidgens in the corner of the glass. "If it's any help, I know where Robyn lives, uh, lived."

CeeCee's cell phone rang, interrupting us, and she fumbled in her purse to get it. Her ring was something like a royal flourish and seemed completely appropriate. She stepped away from the rest of us and turned her back as she took the call. Even with her facing away, I could hear the little shrieks she was making. An *uh-oh* went off in my head.

A few moments later, a pale CeeCee came back to the table. She put her hand on Nell's for support and then turned to the rest of us. "That was my housekeeper. The police are there with a warrant to search Nell's room. She called to find out what she should do." CeeCee's head hovered lower. "As if there was a choice."

And here I'd been worried about telling her what Detective Heather had said about Nell being in their crosshairs.

CHAPTER 10

I USUALLY LIKED GOING TO CEECEE'S HOUSE. THE stone cottage was set far back from the street in a miniforest and had a fairy-tale-like feeling to it.

But not this time.

I pulled Nell's car behind the two cruisers and black Crown Victoria parked at the curb. Mrs. Shedd hadn't been pleased when I said I had to leave, but when she saw how flustered CeeCee and Nell were and I explained I didn't think they should drive, she told me to go.

We all got out of my car and went through the open front gate. CeeCee's housekeeper, Rosa, was standing outside the front door. Marlena and Talullah, CeeCee's two Yorkies, must have been stationed just inside the door and sounded hoarse from barking.

CeeCee rushed ahead and asked Rosa if the cops were in the house. The housekeeper shook her head. "They only wanted to see Miss Nell's room."

CeeCee tried to hide it, but I knew she was relieved. I followed as she continued on around the outside of the house.

I'd never noticed the garage before or that her property went all the way to the street behind. The garage was a separate building and the driveway went back to the other street.

CeeCee hadn't mentioned the details of where Nell was staying, and now explained there was a small apartment above the garage she'd given to her niece. Nell rushed ahead to a stairway on the side of the building while CeeCee and I followed. Detective Heather and two uniformed officers were coming down the stairs.

Nell appeared wild-eyed and CeeCee had reached new levels of upset as they eyed the brown paper bag in one of the officer's hands. Detective Heather gave me a dirty look and gave Nell a list of what they'd taken. Nell pushed it on me and ran up the stairs and went inside to see what damage they'd done.

Heather said something to the effect that they were done *for now* before they left. I glanced at the list.

"What did they find?" CeeCee sounded agitated.

"Dirty laundry. It says they took some items from the hamper. A denim shirt with something on the pocket."

"Not that shirt," CeeCee said with a sigh. "Nell and I had a big battle about it. The clothes those production assistants wear are so dismal looking and I wanted to give her something special. I bought the shirt and added a subtle round motif to the pocket. Nell protested about the decoration but finally gave in. I don't suppose you had those kind of problems over clothes with your boys."

I said it was true, but I left out that I'd never interfered with their clothes choices, either.

"What do they want her dirty shirt for?" CeeCee asked.

There was no point in hiding the truth from CeeCee. "They probably want to check it for trace evidence to see if there is anything to connect Nell to Robyn." I thought back to that morning in the waiting room and got a bad feeling as I remembered that Nell had taken the packet of sweetener out of her shirt pocket—a pocket with a small blue motif on it.

We went up the stairs and into the large room that served as both her living and bedroom. Thankfully, the cops had been neat and had not tossed the place. The bed was rumpled, but I guessed it had been left that way when Nell left. She was looking around and appeared uneasy. I could understand how she felt. Her privacy had been invaded. It was like having a stranger go through your purse.

"Maybe you'd rather stay in the house," CeeCee offered. Nell accepted before the words were all out of her aunt's mouth. She rushed ahead of us and said she'd get her stuff later.

CeeCee led me inside and we settled into her living room. The windows looked out at the tangle of trees and kept the room shadowy even though the sun was shining.

"What should we do?" CeeCee said.

I directed my gaze at Nell. "You might want to talk to Mason Fields. He's an excellent lawyer and a nice—"

"No," Nell said, vehemently shaking her head before I could finish. "I didn't do anything wrong. I know how it looks. You hire a lawyer and people think you're guilty and trying to hide something. I don't need a lawyer."

No matter what CeeCee and I said, Nell wouldn't budge. I finally mentioned what Detective Heather had said about being confident that Nell was the guilty party.

"Oh, dear," CeeCee said. "I had no idea it was that bad. It's totally ridiculous. They should be out looking for other suspects. For the person who really killed that woman."

I hated to be the bearer of bad news, but they needed to deal with the truth. "I think all of her efforts are just going to build a case against Nell."

"But they can't. I didn't do anything. Aunt CeeCee, do something," Nell wailed.

CeeCee turned to me. "Molly, you have to do something."

"Well," I said, "the one thing we can do—if they won't look for other suspects, we can." I looked to Nell. "You said anyone could have gotten into Robyn's drawer where she kept the sweetener." Nell started to nod, then her eyes widened and she almost smiled.

"Or the poison could have been added before she even got it. How could I have forgotten? Someone sent the box of sweetener to Robyn. I know because I was in her office when she was opening it. She seemed real happy about it and put the whole box in the drawer. I'm probably the only one who knows about it, though."

"Did you have any idea who sent it?" I asked.

Nell shrugged. "Are you kidding? She barely talked to me. But there's a way to find out. We log in every package that comes in and who it's from."

"Well, there's the solution," CeeCee said. "We just find out who sent her the sweetener and the cops will have their real killer." She looked toward her niece and Nell looked toward me.

"I can't call any of the other PAs and ask them to check. You saw how they were, Molly. They all think I'm guilty. You think anybody is going to try to help me. No way." Now they were both looking at me.

"Maybe I can figure something out," I said.

I had to walk back to my house and pick up the greenmobile and drive back to the bookstore. I did my best to make up for all the lost time. I updated Mrs. Shedd on the fake book signing, telling her about the scheduling board and that I'd met the person who was taking over for the dead woman. I thought it might make her feel a little better about me being gone.

"I'm glad you got something accomplished for the bookstore," Mrs. Shedd said. "As far as I'm concerned, the business with the blogoir author is off my plate and on yours. Just remember our aim is to get something that says Shedd and Royal Books and More in the shot."

Just before I left for the day, I went over to the event area and tried to picture where to put a sign. Through the window, I saw that the sky was my favorite translucent blue and still had a hint of light. It had been a trying day and I was glad to be finally going home.

I left the car in the driveway and crossed through my backyard. The orange blossoms were just about finished, but the air was still filled with their sweet scent. Floodlight illuminated the lawn, which thanks to the winter rain was a bright spring green. Pink and red carnation blossoms showed as bright spots in the flower beds. More hyacinths and daffodils had popped up from the bulbs I'd randomly spread around the previous years. The dogs flew out as soon as I opened the back door. Okay, the *flew* related to Cosmo. The little black mutt loved to charge out and run around the yard and check his territory. Blondie followed more slowly and, after a few sniffs, draped herself on a chaise lounge.

I'd left the house in a hurry. Nell had just honked and I'd run out. I was surprised to find the coffee mug I'd left on the table was in the dishwasher. Someone had brought the mail in and set it on the kitchen table. I was pretty sure it must have been Barry, because his flannel shirt was hanging on the door handle. I checked on the shelving unit and it was definitely closer to being finished.

During my afternoon at the bookstore, I'd thought about the best way to deal with who had sent the sweetener to Robyn. I was sure the cops could do a more efficient job than I could, but I didn't think Detective Heather would appreciate my suggestion. More than not appreciate it, I was pretty sure she'd ignore it. But if it came from someone else—

I picked up the phone and called Barry's cell. Expecting to get his voice mail, I had my message all worked out. I was caught off guard when he answered and barely croaked out a hello.

"Babe," Barry said with a lift in his voice when he realized it was me. "You found the brochures I left about a condo development in Simi Valley. Don't you agree it would be perfect for us?"

He sounded a little disappointed when I said I hadn't seen them yet, though as I was talking, I found them on the counter and promised to look them over. I told him about my morning at the studio and about Nell's remembrance about the box of sweetener. "I was just thinking maybe you could tell Heather about it. Nell said they log everything in. Whoever sent it has to be the real killer."

There was silence at Barry's end for a moment and then a tired sigh. "Molly, I can't suggest anything to Heather. I'm sure she's already checking on who had access to the sweetener and where it came from." He paused a moment. "Doesn't it seem awfully convenient that Nell suddenly remembered that the sugar substitute was sent to the victim and that only she knows about it?"

"Barry, she's CeeCee's niece, and even though she barely crochets, she's one of the Hookers. She's not a murderer."

I heard Barry breathe for a moment before he spoke, which is what he usually did when he thought I wasn't going to want to hear what he had to say. As usual, he was right. "Murderers have families and hobbies. Just because you know someone, doesn't mean they're innocent." Before I could protest, he continued. "I did hear it was confirmed the poison in the drink was cyanide and it was the cause of death." He told me more than I wanted to know how cyanide worked and finished with, "It acts so fast. Once she drank the coffee, it was already too late."

I tried to tell him that Heather was so sure Nell was guilty, she wasn't checking anything else.

"Molly," Barry said with a frustrated sound. "You know I can't get mixed up in Heather's case. Let's talk about something else like that I'll be finished soon and I was planning to stop by for a while." His voice was heavy with suggestion.

"We could look over those brochures together, among other things." There was a short pause. "Should I pick up some Chinese?"

I wasn't happy with his answer even if I understood. Just when I was going to agree to the Chinese food, someone started talking to him and abruptly he said he had to go. So much for any plans. I sat down at the kitchen table and glanced through the condo brochure. It showed off a nice-looking town house with a small yard along with listing all the amenities like the pool and clubhouse. I understood why he wanted us to start with a new place, but I wasn't sure I agreed. In any case, there was lots of time to think about it. It wasn't like he'd put a down payment on a place. I left the pamphlet on the table. I was sure if Barry hadn't gotten off the phone so quickly, he would have repeated his usual admonition for me to stay out of the investigation. It was pretty much a given, just the way it was a given I wasn't going to listen.

If he wouldn't get Heather to check out who had delivered the package, I'd have to figure out a way to do it myself. I already had an idea.

I pressed in Mason's number. He answered on his cell, but he was home. "What's up, Sunshine?" he asked.

I started to tell him about the whole scenario from the morning, but he stopped me. "I was just going to go out. I was going to pick up some dinner. Join me, and you can tell me all about it on the way," he said. Why not? Mason said he'd be by in a few minutes.

"I was just going to get some food to go," Mason said as I got into his black Mercedes, "and take it back to my place. Does that work for you?"

"I interrupted your plans," I said with a shrug, "so, sure, whatever you were going to do is fine." Mason said something about being glad for the company and the next thing I knew, he'd gotten on the 101 freeway.

"I hope you don't mind a ride. I have to pick something up from my office first," he said. He got off at Coldwater Canyon and headed toward the mountains. I barely noticed the twisty ride and the lights of the houses on the hillside as I gave him the whole unvarnished story from the morning.

"Nell should really call me," he said. "She needs to have somebody advising her on what to do and say or not say."

"She thinks because she's innocent that that's enough. She thinks getting a lawyer makes her look guilty."

Mason made a tsk sound. "I hate to say it, but she's right about the general feeling that someone who hires a lawyer when they haven't even been arrested is guilty. Not that I'm saying she shouldn't get one anyway. But think about it. What kind of reaction do you have when you see some guy's lawyer speaking for him on a morning talk show."

"Yikes, now that you mention it, you're right. She's right," I said. I thought back to watching the news and seeing some lawyer doing the talking while his client mutely stood by. My first thought was, what's the guy afraid of saying. And my second thought was that he was guilty of whatever he was being accused of.

"She doesn't need any help looking guilty," he said "We know it, and I'm sure the cops do, too, that she had the perfect storm of motive, means and opportunity."

"Geez, when you put it that way, it really does look bad for her."

"Are you sure she didn't do it?"

"Yes," I said. "I can't explain why I know, but I just know she didn't."

Once we reached the city side of the Santa Monica Mountains, he drove to Century City. At one time, it had been part of a film studio, but then had been developed into office buildings, luxury condos, a hotel, and shopping and entertainment centers. He pulled in front of a high-rise, made a call and a moment later, the security guard came out carrying a briefcase.

Mason thanked him and put it in the backseat. "Okay, business taken care of, now for food. I was going to pick up some wrap sandwiches and side dishes."

I told him it sounded good to me. Actually anything sounded good to me. Somehow in all that had gone on, I'd forgotten to eat. I was always up for serendipity in the food department anyway.

The small café was getting ready to close, but the owner seemed to know Mason. I let Mason do the ordering, and a few minutes later, we left with shopping bags of delicious-smelling food.

"One more stop," he said, heading for Melrose. I knew where he was going before he pulled up to the curb. I didn't get there often because it was in the city, but it was my favorite cake bakery. Their berry cake was probably my favorite cake in the world. We both went inside and looked at the glass case of cakes sold by the slice. They all looked good, but I still went for a slice of the berry cake. No surprise, Mason got devil's food.

Driving home, I felt naughty, like being out late on a school night, but at the same time it was fun. Mason lived in the flats of Encino. His house was huge, particularly for one person and a small dog. He'd bought out his wife's share of the sprawling ranch-style house when he'd gotten the divorce and seemed to enjoy having so much space. I'd actually only been there a couple of times. It seemed like he mostly came to my place or we went somewhere.

Spike was patrolling the door when we came in from the garage. The tiny toy fox terrier seemed to have no concept of his size and took his job as watch dog very seriously. He ran around my feet, keeping me in the doorway until Mason laughed and told him it was okay.

Then he followed us into the kitchen as we carried in the food.

I felt guilty. Although I'd told Mason all about what was

going on with Nell, I'd gotten distracted and never brought up finding out about the package. Wasn't that why I went along in the first place? I quickly mentioned that Nell had remembered that the box of sweetener had been sent to Robyn. Mason picked up on it right away.

"So, you think whoever sent it is the real killer," he said. "Very good, Sunshine. And it must have come pretty recently," he added.

"How did you figure that?" I asked.

"Elementary, my dear. Because if the packets were tainted, as soon as she used one she'd . . ."

"Die," I said, and he nodded.

"Even if they hadn't all been tampered with, my guess is the ones with the poison would have been positioned on the top," Mason said as he put everything out on the counter and we made up plates. He'd gotten several kinds of wrap sandwiches, pasta salad, green salad, roasted potatoes and fruit salad. We took our plates of food into the den that overlooked the pool. Mason's yard was landscaped beautifully, complete with a waterfall cascading into the free-form pool. Lights had been strategically placed to illuminate the lush foliage.

"It happens you're right about the time frame. Nell said the package had come in the last week," I said, salivating at my plate of food. I'm sure the food tasted delicious, but I was so hungry, I practically inhaled it. Of course I had room for dessert. I enjoyed every mouthful of the yellow cake covered with whipped-cream icing, along with strawberries, blueberries and raspberries.

"So you want to find out who sent the package," Mason said with a grin. "Barry wouldn't help you, would he?" Mason said, and I nodded. "Let me make some calls in the morning."

I thanked him profusely and he did a little mock bow. "Glad to be of service."

I was shocked when I saw how late it was and quickly helped him clean up and then he took me home. I hadn't noticed, but Mason had gotten an extra piece of the berry cake for me to take with me. "I'll call you in the morning, hopefully with an answer," he said as he pulled in front of my house. I looked for my keys and was about to get out of the car when I saw my front door open.

"Uh-oh," Mason said as Barry jogged down the path to the street.

"Where were you?" Barry demanded. "You didn't answer your cell phone."

"It's my fault," Mason said, leaning across the seat. "I had to pick up something from my office and then we got some food." He handed the white box to me. "Don't forget your cake."

I got out of the car and fumbled for my BlackBerry. Somehow it had gotten set on silent.

"You can leave now," Barry said to Mason in an angry tone, and to punctuate it, he closed the front door of the sleek black car.

I knew Barry well enough to understand his seeming anger was a cover for worry.

"I told you that I was going to come over and bring Chinese," he said when we got inside. I could smell the food as soon as I got in the door. "You could have at least called and told me you were going out."

Just then the door opened and Samuel walked in. He nodded a greeting to both of us and sensed trouble. Whether it was nosiness or some thought of protecting me, he hung around instead of going into his room. Having an audience made it awkward, and in a stilted tone, I reminded Barry of the interruption during our phone call. "You know how it is. Something comes up with work and all bets are off," I said.

Barry blew out his breath a few times. He knew what I was saying was correct. Still, he wasn't happy. "You couldn't have just stayed home?" he said.

"I wanted to talk to Mason about something," I said. Before Barry could start asking more questions, I just told him he wouldn't want to know what the something was.

"What are these?" Samuel said, picking up some condo brochures on the living room coffee table.

Before either of us could answer, Samuel's cell phone got his attention and he went into his room to talk. Barry picked up the brochures where Samuel had left them. "Everything will be different when we have our own place," Barry said.

I was too tired to even tell him about my concerns. I took the path of least resistance and just apologized for everything. Who knew the word sorry would have such an aphrodisiac effect? I was too tired to fight, but not to make up.

CHAPTER 11

"I'VE GOT GOOD NEWS AND BAD NEWS," MASON said when he called the next morning. The morning was overcast, with a silvery sky and flat light. There wasn't a shadow to be found. I was leaning on my arm, nursing a cup of coffee. It was just regular brew, but what I really needed was the jolt from an added shot of espresso.

Barry and I had spent a lot of time making up, and then he'd gone home and I'd fallen into a dead sleep. This was my second cup of coffee and it still hadn't cut through my sleepy fog. I yawned and Mason laughed. "Did the detective keep you up all night interrogating you about where you'd been and what you'd been doing?"

"More or less," I said, reaching for my coffee.

"Hmm," Mason said in a less happy tone. "Maybe I don't want to know what was going on. Now for the news. The bad news is my calls about the package came up empty, but the good news is I have a plan for how we can get the information you want. I have everything worked out. I think you're going to like this. Do you have a suit or something?"

He proceeded to give me instructions on what to wear and we arranged to meet in Encino on a street corner. It was all very cloak-and-dagger and frankly kind of exciting. The only problem was it had to be today.

I stopped at the bookstore first just when I was supposed to start for the day. I found Mrs. Shedd putting out some new releases in the mystery section. When I said I needed to take a couple of hours off, her face stiffened. "You need to take more time off?" Mrs. Shedd said, sounding a little frantic. "I've always let you make your own hours because I always came out ahead. You spent more time here than I paid you for. But lately . . . Are you trying to make up for it? You know it doesn't work that way. It's not like you were putting hours in the bank." She caught herself. "Oh, Molly, I'm sorry. I know you work far more than I pay you for. It's just that I was hoping the bookstore would be back in the black by now and I'm worried."

I assured her the Salute to Chocolate event would be a big draw and that, one way or the other, I'd figure out how to get a sign in the fake book signing. Then when I explained the time off was to help CeeCee's niece, she totally backed down. "We're all like family," she said. "Go on."

"ACTION," I SAID UNDER MY BREATH. THIS TIME I really did wish I had one of those chalkboards to clap. Mason and I were standing outside the glass door that served as the public entrance to the *BOO* production offices. I had done what Mason had requested and gone into the back of my closet and found a Chanel-style suit with a boxy jacket and a pencil skirt. I'd pulled out heels and a white blouse. Finally I'd taken my shoulder-length hair and put it in a low ponytail and put on much more makeup than I ever wear.

Mason took a last look at the result of his suggestions and shook his head in disbelief. "I barely recognize you," he said.

"Let's do it." He pushed the door open and walked in brusquely, with me rushing after him. "I don't know what I'm going to do with you, Sally. You're supposed to follow up on things."

"But I did, Mr. Fields. This is where I sent the package." I gestured toward the reception counter.

"But did you check to see if it got here?" he said as though he was pushing me in a corner.

"I'm sure it got here." I tried to say it with a wail in my voice and to look like I was about to cry.

Since it was Saturday, there was only a skeleton staff. Mason had chosen the day deliberately, figuring there was less chance anyone would recognize me as having been there before and more chance we'd be able to get what we were after.

The counter was manned by a young woman dressed the way Nell did, and it seemed a safe bet she was a production assistant. She didn't seem happy to see us. Who could blame her? We looked like trouble.

It had been no problem to get a pass into the studio. Mason's connections made that a breeze. All the way over, we'd gone over our story. Mason kept grinning and saying how much fun this was. He'd dressed in his work clothes: a beautifully tailored suit in midnight blue, a creamy white dress shirt and subdued silk tie that probably cost a fortune. Mason had thought out our style of dress. Thanks to dealing with defendants, juries and judges, he knew how clothes altered an impression.

"Think about it, Sunshine, a defendant with a few teeth missing, dressed in baggy jeans and an old tee shirt versus the same guy with a full smile, wearing a suit and tie," Mason had said. "Our suits give off an air of authority. Watch, nobody will question we are who we say we are." Now, I saw that he was right.

"What am I going to do with you, Sally?" Mason bellowed. "The client insisted that he was told the package never arrived. And now you're admitting that you never really followed through." He slammed his fist on the counter in supposed anger. Both the girl and I jumped. Then he continued to berate me. I began to slump as if the weight of his words were pushing me down. I stole a glance at the girl behind the counter. She gave Mason a dirty look, and when she glanced toward me, her expression said she felt sympathetic.

"Can I do something to help?" she said. I looked up at her as if she'd just thrown me a life preserver in the middle of the ocean. Mason had coached me on how to react. I stepped closer and dropped my voice, giving the impression she and I were now a team and he was the enemy.

"Look, I just need to prove to my boss that a package arrived here. Otherwise he's going to fire me."

She gave Mason another dirty look. "How'd you send it? Messenger or mail?" She held up the clipboard that I knew listed the things delivered by messenger. A little *uh-oh* went off in my head. We hadn't considered this. I struggled to think of what to say, but my cohort didn't hesitate. He took the clipboard from her hand and fluttered through the pages for a moment, then dropped it on the counter.

"It's not on here." Then he looked skyward as if this Sally was just too incompetent for words. "Don't tell me you mailed it."

Mason was doing too well at being obnoxious, and I wondered if there was a whole side of him I'd missed. But then he caught my eye and winked. I remembered that among Mason's other talents, he could speed-read. I picked up on his cue.

"You said you were trying to cut expenses," I said in my wailing voice. For a second I thought Mason was going to lose it. His mouth had started to quiver and slide into a grin, but he forced back the grim expression.

The girl leaned across the counter and whispered to me, "You can check the log in the mailroom."

I threw her a grateful nod and she took me back into the inner sanctum. Mason, still in character, gave off an impatient snort and started to cycle through the messages on his BlackBerry.

I recognized the corridor that led through the offices from my previous trip. Most of the doors were closed and it was very quiet. Talia's office still had the temporary sign. The large room the production assistants worked out of was almost empty. There was just one person off in the corner working on something. Just beyond was the mailroom. I felt my heart beating faster as we went inside. She handed over a clipboard with a stack of papers attached. I knew the window of time I was looking for and went right to those sheets.

My eye moved down the first page and found nothing. Ditto for the next couple. Then saw Robyn's name on the following sheet. But when I looked at who sent it, it listed Crown Apothecary. Not exactly what I'd been hoping for. I was about to thank her and leave when I noticed there was a *p* next to it. Maybe it meant something helpful, as in the package came from someone named Paul.

I didn't want the girl to see the entry I was looking at, afraid it might stir things up if she realized it was connected to Robyn, who had been murdered. I scanned the list quickly and found something with a blank in the spot for return address and a *p* next to it. I pointed to it enthusiastically and said that must be the package I'd sent. Then I asked what the *p* meant.

"The *p* means it was marked personal. No wonder they didn't confirm they'd got it from you." She pointed to the asterisk in the blank spot for a return address. "The asterisk means there was no return address," she scolded. "Did you at least include a card?"

I shook my head and the girl gave me a disparaging shrug. But her mention of a card made me wonder. Would a murderer have put a card in the package? Maybe some little clever message like, *Hope you enjoy this sweetener; it's to die for.* Or what if the store had included some kind of packing slip that listed the sender. Would Robyn have even kept it? I decided it was worth a shot. I thanked the girl for all her trouble and said it was all my fault. I glanced toward the way we'd come and said something about being anxious about facing my boss.

"Could I use the restroom?" I asked, and she nodded with understanding. Who wouldn't want to stall a little before having to tell their angry boss about their carelessness. She pointed me down the hall and quickly headed back to her station.

Maybe Mason's ability to think on his feet was catching. The lack of a person's name on the return address was devastating, but then I'd gotten a ray of hope when she'd brought up the idea of a card. And maybe a card or packing slip was in the box of Robyn's stuff I'd seen in the office. I was hoping that Talia hadn't been too efficient about getting it out of her office. As soon as I heard the door to the lobby click shut, I turned away from the restroom and hurried down the corridor. Talia's office door was unlocked. I slipped inside quickly and turned on the light. The box was still there.

My breath was choppy and my heart was jumping in my chest. I had to hurry. I fumbled through the carton and started taking things out. If there was a card or sheet of paper, it would most likely have fallen to the bottom. I glanced at the photo of Robyn and the hole and set it on the desk with the other stuff. It was just the usual hairbrush kind of stuff. One thing did surprise me. A small crocheted cactus complete with a crocheted terra-cotta-colored pot was stuck in the bottom. I looked it over and was impressed by how nicely done it was. On the bottom, there were two initials done in surface crochet. I couldn't quite make them out because they were so small, but the first one definitely wasn't an *r*.

I snapped back to reality and realized I was wasting time and began to feel around the bottom. A stray paper clip got under my nail and poked me. I pulled out my hand and was examining it for damage when I heard voices. I quickly put everything back as it had been.

It sounded like a woman and man, and the voices were getting louder. Then I heard the man say, "Talia." Oops, I was in trouble. I looked around the small office frantically. There was no closet, only a tall narrow metal cabinet, which looked like it served as one. I doused the lights, pulled open the cabinet door and got in, grateful for small favors. Half of the cabinet had no shelves and I was able to stand upright in it.

I pulled the door shut just in time as I heard them come in. The couple moved their conversation into the small room.

"Robyn promised me an advance on a big story," the man said. "You took over for her. Any idea what the story is?"

"Whatever it was, she never told me. But she did have something up her sleeve. I had to connect the dots myself, though. It seemed like she'd figured out a way to shake things up. Some big surprise that would show a whole other side of Barbara and push the ratings up during sweeps," Talia said. "It doesn't matter. I'm in charge now. And don't worry, I'll give you any hot info I get."

I hoped after that they'd leave, but instead, they seemed to settle in. The cabinet was hot and stuffy and I had the horrible feeling I was going to run out of air. I was really in trouble now.

CHAPTER 12

MASON AND I KEPT UP OUR DEMEANOR AS ANGRY boss and errant employee until we drove through the studio gate and were back on the street. Then we both began to laugh so hard Mason had to pull over and park.

"You were so convincing as the mean boss," I said. "That girl really felt sorry for me." I wiped a tear of laughter off my cheek.

"You have to be dramatic when you're in front of jury and need to stir their emotions," he said. "Besides, it would have been a little hard to explain if you'd gotten caught in the closet."

I leaned back in the seat, realizing a lot of the laugher was release from the buildup of tension. "Thank heavens for my BlackBerry," I said.

"And thank heavens that you thought to use it," Mason said with a grin. I seemed to be having an endless battle with the smart phone, and for once I had come out the winner. As I was getting close to panic at the idea of running out of air, I had remembered my BlackBerry in my pocket. It was hard to type on the tiny keyboard in the dark, but I'd managed to send Mason an e-mail with enough misspelled information for him to figure out my situation.

"Ah, but you deserve the credit for knowing what to do with the information," I said.

"It was all improv, Sunshine," he said as he began to recount what he'd done when he saw my e-mail.

"That poor girl behind he counter," Mason said. "You should have seen her jump when I started bellowing that Sally was taking too long and I barged through the door to the office area. She came running after me, telling me I couldn't go in the ladies' restroom and said she'd check on Sally."

"I heard you charge into Talia's office, saying you were looking for your assistant," I said, picking up the story.

"Luckily I made such a ruckus, I caught Talia and the guy with her off guard and they didn't have time to think. Before any of them knew what was going on, I'd herded them together with the girl from the reception counter, all the while ranting on about my terrible assistant and how I was going to fire her as soon as I found her."

"That's when I opened the door a sliver."

Mason nodded. "I saw you, which is why I upped my rant. I don't even think they realized I had moved them so their backs were facing the cabinet. I hoped you would figure out my plan."

"Great minds think alike," I joked. It had come to me in a flash, he'd positioned them so I could slip out behind them and get into the corridor. "And when I got in the hall, it looked like I was coming from the restroom."

"I must have sounded like a lunatic," Mason said. "But I had to get you out of there quickly before they got a good look at you."

"You were more like a whirlwind," I said. "You just flew out of the office, yelling at poor Sally that it was about time.

I wonder what they thought when you grabbed my hand and we started running toward the lobby?" We hadn't stopped until we got to his car.

"Probably good riddance, Sunshine. We make a good team," Mason said as he put the car in gear and pulled away from the curb now that our giggles were spent. "I don't know about you, but I need a coffee after that. Maybe even one of your famous red-eyes." He drove to someplace called The Coffee Shack and parked.

"I'm afraid the production assistant lost her sympathy for me," I said as we took our coffees to a small table by the window. "But luckily Talia didn't recognize me, thanks to you." I took a sip of my red-eye and was surprised at the red stain on the cup. At first I thought it was blood, but then remembered my red lipstick.

Mason set down his cup. "I have lots of experience of hustling clients past the news media so that no one sees their face. I just had to be a little more creative this time."

It was only then that it registered who Talia's companion had been. Pierce Sheraton.

"What was she doing with the entertainment reporter?" I said.

"They seemed pretty cozy. Maybe they're a couple," Mason offered. He drank down his coffee and made a face. "I don't know how you drink these. The espresso makes it a little too coffeeish for me."

"There's only one problem with our adventure," I said. "It was all for nothing. I found the package listed, but the return address was just some store."

"I don't care," he said. "I haven't had so much fun in a long time."

His mention of time made me think of the real time, and I shrieked when I looked at my watch. "I have to get to work. Mrs. Shedd wasn't happy about me missing this morning."

"But it's Saturday," Mason said.

"And just another day at the bookstore."

Mason thanked me again for our playdate when he dropped me in front of Shedd & Royal. With all our giggles, we'd forgotten that my car was still parked near the corner where Mason had picked me up.

I got a few strange looks as I walked in because of my clothes. I never wore skirts to work, let alone a Chanel-like suit. The red lipstick was now long gone, left on the coffee cup, and my low ponytail was undone. I'd pulled off the scrunchy in the car.

I dropped off my purse in my cubby and was glad I'd left a pair of plastic flats there. My feet said a big thank you as I went back into the store.

"Hey, Pink," Adele called as she stepped out of the children's area. "The Hookers are getting together in the back. Something about CeeCee's niece." My coworker stopped talking and looked me over. "Are you going for a kind of new look?"

Adele mumbled something about how my jacket would look a lot better if I added some crochet trim, and then she marched toward the yarn area of the store.

Mrs. Shedd was relieved to see me. I told her I was just going to check on the yarn department and then I'd handle the information desk.

Was there ever a time that some of the Hookers weren't at the table? I could understand Rhoda and Elise practically living there. It was a way for them to get out of their houses, but I was surprised that lately CeeCee always seemed to be there, too. Then I got it. She was looking for moral support in handling her niece.

The whole table looked up when I approached. If they were trying to hide it, they all failed. I have never been so aware of being looked over. "If you're after a new look, you might want to contact my stylist," CeeCee said.

"Lose the suit," Rhoda said in her usual straight-on manner. Elise tried to be diplomatic and said I looked good in a skirt. Adele repeated her advice about adding crochet trim.

"Why are you wearing a suit?" Dinah asked. There was hurt in her voice. I hadn't had a chance to tell her about the plan and I knew she felt out of the loop. Nell came back from the café carrying drinks. She set them down and slumped in her seat, though when I started to talk about where I'd been, she sat upright.

I mentioned what Talia had said about Robyn having some secret plans for the show. "Do you know anything about that?" I asked.

"Are you kidding? Robyn barely talked to me, let alone told me about her plans. All I know is she seemed to work twenty-four, seven. Everyone said she was set on getting ahead. I heard that both she and Talia were up for the segment producer job, and who knows what Robyn did to get it." Nell stopped and reflected for a moment. "I guess it doesn't matter anymore; Talia ended up with the job after all."

I brought up the photo of Robyn with the piece cutout again. Nell started to dismiss it, then said she vaguely remembered looking at it on Robyn's desk. "It was whole then. The other person must have seemed like a boyfriend, because I remember wondering how she had time for one.

"What about the return address? Did you find out who sent the package?" Nell asked expectantly.

"It's not exactly good news," I said. I mentioned finding the listing on the log, but the return address was a store—the Crown Apothecary. When I explained exactly how I'd gotten the information and had to escape the cabinet, there were a few gasps. Dinah looked upset when she realized Mason had been my wingman.

Nell popped out of her chair. "Well, let's go to that store now. We have to do something to find the real killer." Nell's eyes grew watery. "If that police detective starts questioning me again, I don't know what I'll do."

I tried to distract her by mentioning seeing the entertainment reporter with Talia. "Do you think there's any connection—"

"I'll tell you what the connection is," CeeCee interrupted. "I've been thinking about the whole situation, dear, and I think it is all about me. Think about it: That woman was killed while I was doing the show. An appearance where the Oscar buzz about my performance was mentioned. The suspect turns out to be my niece. And that entertainment host shows up outside the bookstore. I've had paparazzi snapping a photo when I come out a restaurant, but not someone with a video camera looking for me. I think somebody is trying to frame Nell to get at me. Somebody who hopes this will leave people with a bad taste about me, and when it comes to nomination time . . ." Her voice trailed off, but we all got her drift.

I shook my head with disbelief. I knew CeeCee was used to the idea that the universe revolved around her career, but this was too much even for her. "So you think this was all about someone trying to discredit you so you won't get an award nomination?"

"It's a cutthroat business. You'd be amazed what people will do to try to get ahead." CeeCee's voice had a musical quality, and even though the meaning was tough, it came out sounding bubbly like something in a sitcom.

Nell ignored her aunt's comment and repeated that we should go to the Crown Apothecary right away. I had to remind her that I *worked* at the bookstore and had already missed the morning trying to get her off the hook. Finally, we arranged to go when I was entitled to take a break. It would give me a chance to pick up my car as well.

"I'm coming, too," Dinah said. "I'm taking back my position as sidekick."

Several hours later, the three of us headed to Encino. The Crown Apothecary was in a bank of old stores near Encino park. I'd passed it before and been curious about the name and the fact the sign gave the impression of an old-time drugstore.

As we approached the entrance, I noticed the window of the store next to it was covered with brown paper and had a sign on it that read, "Coming Soon: Apothecary Annex with Soda Fountain." The store lived up to my expectations. As soon as we stepped inside, I felt like I'd just stepped back in time. It was much smaller than the superstores that called themselves drugstores these days. The walls were lined with shelves holding the usual stuff like bandages and aspirin, along with various sundries. The middle of the store had glass display cases with fancy soap and things like silver shaving equipment. Toward the back, a framed piece of stained glass said "Pharmacy" above a wood-paneled partitioned-off area. I saw the white-coated pharmacist inside his area as he passed by the customer window. Next to the opening, I noticed black metal letters that read "Ty Holzer, Pharm. D."

"Look at this," Dinah said, pulling me to a wooden counter along the wall that was lined with glass jars of candy. Everything from Mary Janes to Red Hot dots. Each jar had a scoop, and a supply of clear bags sat at the end of the row. We both laughed at the sign that proclaimed "Penny Candy" and then listed the price in dollars.

Nell didn't seem nearly as entranced with the place as we were and had started tapping her foot impatiently as Dinah and I looked into a doorway that had been cut into the wall. Though it was still awaiting finishing touches, it was an old-fashioned soda fountain.

A clerk had been watching us and, when she saw us looking in the addition, stepped next to us. "It'll be open soon. The new owner wants to make this a full-service nostalgia trip. Is there something I can help you with?"

Nell nudged me. "Molly, do your thing," she said under her breath.

"I'm trying to track down a package," I said with my

friendliest smile. The story had worked before, so why not stay with it with a slight variation. "It was sent to the *Barbara Olive Overton* production offices." I didn't say I worked for the show, only implied it. "It had the return address of this store. It was a box of Nature's Sweetie."

Her expression clouded as she led us back to the display of boxes of sugar substitute next to a basket filled with boxes of assorted kinds of tea. "We don't ship packages. It couldn't have come from us." She looked at me intently. "Who did you say you were?"

Before I could stop her, Nell launched into her story how the cops were sure she'd killed somebody with a packet of sweetener and I was this amateur detective who was trying to help get the cops off her back. She looked over her shoulder at me. "Molly, I appreciate that you're trying to help, but personally I think Aunt CeeCee ought to hire a real PI."

Dinah almost choked and gave her a dirty look. "I can't believe you said that. Do you have any idea how many murders Molly has solved?"

Nell suddenly appeared uncomfortable and grabbed my arm. "I'm so sorry. I'm just so worried."

The clerk appeared uneasy about our interchange and started gradually easing us toward the front. She pointed to a basket of cards with the logo of the store and address. "Maybe someone bought the sweetener here and just used one of those as the return address and mailed it themselves."

We were almost to the door and I stepped away to stop the clerk's progress. "Do you keep any kinds of records of who you sold the sweetener to?" Now the clerk really wanted to be done with us.

"We just got the supply in a few week ago. We don't keep those kinds of records, only how many we've sold for inventory purpose."

I opened my mouth to ask about that, but she beat me to the punch. "Personally, I only had one customer." The three of us leaned closer to the woman as I asked if she remembered their name or what they looked like.

"A lot of people go through this place," she said, starting to shrug off my question, but then she stopped. "I do remember it was a man and there was something odd about him. He had this ball of hair growing below his lip. I don't even know what that's called."

The three of us traded glances. Bob?

CHAPTER 13

NELL, DINAH AND I MARCHED INTO THE CAFÉ ready to confront Bob, but we all deflated when we looked at the counter and saw Mr. Royal was acting as barista. He'd pulled his shaggy multicolored hair into a tiny ponytail and wore an apron over his long-sleeved green shirt and jeans. He moved with the agility of a much younger man, and I noticed he had a wooden bead meditation bracelet wound around his wrist. Nell got to the counter first.

"Where's Bob?" she demanded. Dinah and I almost crashed into her. I think the three of us came across as a little frantic.

Mr. Royal looked up from the metal pitcher of milk he was foaming for a cappuccino. "Don't worry, ladies, I am an excellent coffee mixologist. Any drink you can name, I bet I can make." I'm sure he was right, too. Mr. Royal had been everywhere and done everything. No doubt tucked in all the other jobs he'd had, he'd probably served up espresso drinks in Rome or something.

When it was clear the question really concerned Bob's

whereabouts, Mr. Royal said he'd be back in a couple of hours. I told Nell not to worry, and that as soon as Bob returned, I'd talk to him.

"C'mon, Nell," Dinah said, putting her arm around the girl's shoulder. "Molly has to work." As a community college instructor, Dinah was an expert at dealing with hysterical people Nell's age. Dinah gave me a wave and then escorted Nell to the yarn department.

When I looked back there, I saw that some of the group was still around the table.

I started to go back into the bookstore, but Mr. Royal stopped me.

"I wonder if you could give me an update on the Salute to Chocolate event." He poured the steamed milk expertly into a mug with a couple of shots of espresso, then spooned fluffs of foam on top and finished by swirling a pattern with it. The customer waiting took it and walked away. Was he worried because I'd been missing so much time lately?

I told him all the books we were going to feature had been chosen and I'd been hearing from the different stores in the area. The plan was they would do their own setup. All we had to do was provide them with tables. "Alain Des Plaines is going to have a demo dipping things in his special chocolate blend." Mr. Royal nodded and then asked me to check the signs around the store.

"There seems to be some graffiti on them," he said. I promised to check it out first thing and left him to his drink duties.

Sure enough as I checked the free-standing signs we had spread around the store, they all had something scribbled on them. Right next to the photo of Alain Des Plains holding a handful of chocolate bars like they were a fan, someone had made a couple of lines next to a stick figure holding up one of its arms. I glanced toward the kids' department. Somebody must have escaped Saturday-morning story time and gone wild. But they obviously didn't know about permanent ink. A little wipe with a damp paper towel and all that was left was a smudge.

Mrs. Shedd saw me working on the signs and gave me a nod of approval. I couldn't help it, I kept looking toward the table longingly. Finally, with the excuse to myself of needing to straighten up the yarn department, I headed back there.

Adele was standing at the end of the table with a piece of bright quilted material in front of her.

"Hey, Pink," she said, waving me over. "You have to see these hooks I got on eBay." I stepped closer and realized the material was actually a holder for the hooks. I'd never thought too much about hooks and had just used the metal or plastic ones that every craft store sold. These were like a different species.

Adele was savoring the spotlight as she took the hooks out one by one and showed them off. They were all made of wood. Some were dark and had fancy shapes on the nonhook end, and some were plain except for the hook. She started rattling off the different kinds of wood they were made out of. Rosewood sounded lovely, but bloodwood?

"Dear, your hooks are lovely," CeeCee said in a dismissive tone before turning to me. "Molly, if Nell said anything to hurt your feelings, I'm sure she didn't mean it." From across the table, Dinah did a tiny nod. She must have spilled the beans about Nell's desire for a real PI.

Nell hung her head. "It's my life on the line here. That blond detective is out to get me. She's going to find something, and then bam, I'm arrested." She got up like she was thinking of leaving and directed her next comment at me. "I decided if that happens, I'm calling your lawyer-friend."

"Dear, you need to calm down. Molly will figure out something." Adele kept making loud sighing noises to get the attention back on her hooks. Well, really, on her. I didn't look, but I'm sure she wasn't smiling when Rhoda and Elise arrived. Before they'd even reached the table, Rhoda was already taking something out of her bag.

"Girls, I'm glad you're still here." She stopped between CeeCee and Nell. "I know you want your niece to get into crochet," she said, looking toward CeeCee. "And I know you keep resisting." Rhoda was usually very matter-of-fact, but this time she was literally flushed with excitement. "Wait until you see what I've come up with."

She urged everyone to sit down. It was a hard sale with Adele.

"Rhoda, I know you mean well. I know you all mean well, and I really like the way you all care, but like I told you before, why should I start making something when I know I'll never finish it?" Nell said.

"This is different," Rhoda said. "I call it impatient crochet."

Nell actually smiled when she heard the title. "Well, that sure describes me." CeeCee nodded in agreement.

Adele was practically jumping out of her seat. She and CeeCee still hadn't worked it out about leading the group, and she was upset that Rhoda was directing all her comments to CeeCee. "You should have explained it to me before you brought it to the group," Adele interrupted.

CeeCee sighed. "Adele, will you stop making a scene. None of us need an okay before we bring something for the group."

Rhoda thanked CeeCee and continued. "My Hal thought it was a great idea. The whole point of this kind of crochet is not to make a big production out of it." She emptied her canvas bag on the table, and a bunch of small colorful items fell out. Everyone started to grab something and look at it.

"Not only will this work for Nell, but for the things we're making for the donation box. These items would be great to give for a Hearts and Barks bazaar." She held up an eyeglass holder. It was black with a bright orange fabric lining and a multicolored yarn corkscrew as decoration. There were cell phone holders and some small change purses. "The key is in the finishing." Rhoda pointed out the silver heart-shaped button on the coin purse. It *made* the purse, as did the flower with a bead in the center on the cell phone holder. "They all start out the same." Rhoda explained she was going to demonstrate with a big hook so we could see how it worked. She made a chain of large loops with some terra-cotta-colored yarn and then went back across them, making single crochets in the front loop. When she got to the end, she held it up. "Here's where the trick is, girls." Instead of going back over the row she'd just made, she made an extra single crochet in the last chain and, starting with that same chain, made a row of single crochet stitches in the other side of the chain stitch foundation. When she reached the end, she made two single crochets, saying that the extra stitches on both ends gave it shape. Then she kept going around. In no time, she began to make a tube.

Personally, I was mesmerized and couldn't wait to try it. Something about the terra-cotta tube jostled my memory and I blurted out that it made me think of something I'd seen in the box of Robyn's stuff.

"What was in there?" Nell asked. Rhoda stopped her lesson and everyone turned to me. Well, not Adele. She'd taken out one of the wooden hooks and some cotton yarn and was trying to mimic what Rhoda had started.

"She had a crocheted cactus. It even had a pot that was that color," I said, pointing to Rhoda's yarn.

"She did?" Nell said. She thought it over a moment and I described how it had white flowers on the top of the cactus.

"There were some kind of initials on the bottom," I said.

"Somebody was signing their work," Adele said, holding up what she'd done. She seemed distressed that everyone was paying more attention to the talk about the segment producer's yarn plant.

Nell's eyes suddenly showed some recognition. "I remember the cactus now. I made some joke about it once since she didn't have a window, it was the only kind of plant she could have. She didn't even crack a smile. That was crochet?" Nell sounded genuinely impressed. "I guess making something like that wouldn't be as fast as this, huh?" she said, pointing at Rhoda's demonstration piece.

"Don't worry about making anything that complicated yet." CeeCee pushed a hook and a ball of cotton yarn toward Nell, while Rhoda handed out sheets for everybody with instructions and patterns for the pieces she'd brought in. She'd added suggestions for ways to personalize each piece.

I took some extra. I knew Sheila and Eduardo would both love the idea. Eduardo had been missing so many of our get-togethers I was really beginning to wonder what was going on with him. I knew he was trying to branch out from modeling. He'd been concerned about the kind of offers he'd been getting. Sheila said she'd heard Eduardo asking the owner of Luxe for some advice about owning a business.

"I spent the afternoon with Rhoda," Elise said, showing off the cell phone sock she'd made. "I call it the Anthony," she said, referring to the vampire who crocheted. It was black with a red corkscrew hanging off it. She handed it to CeeCee. "I was hoping you could give it to Hugh Jackman next time you see him." There was swoon in Elise's birdlike voice.

Everybody started working. CeeCee watched her niece and helped her with the first row and took out a stitch marker and stuck it in the last stitch so she'd be able to see where a row ended.

I started on a change purse. The group became silent as our hooks flew and objects grew right in front of our eyes. For the first time since the incident, the worry disappeared from Nell's face. I would bet money that, at least for a moment, she'd forgotten all about being a murder suspect. I, however, couldn't forget and, while I was working, kept my eye out for Bob.

CHAPTER 14

"SIMI VALLEY?" DINAH SAID. "HE WANTS YOU TO move to a condo in Simi Valley?"

"It's not exactly the ends of the earth," I said. "And he just had some info on a couple of condo developments. It's not as if he put down a deposit or anything."

Dinah looked at me with concern. "Are you so sure?" She mentioned a trip to Hawaii Barry had planned to the point of buying nonrefundable tickets without consulting me. "He just seems to act on things," she added.

"He wouldn't," I said. I hoped the tinge of doubt I suddenly felt didn't show in my voice.

When the group had broken up, Dinah and I had gone to the café. Mr. Royal was still manning the counter and I was determined to wait for Bob. I assured Nell I'd let her know as soon as I talked to our barista about his sweetener purchase. She and CeeCee left to go shopping for buttons and beads to put on their impatient crochet creations. Adele rolled up her fancy wooden hooks and went back to the kids' department. Rhoda couldn't wait to tell her Hal about the success of her crochet idea. I think Elise went to the movies to see *Caught By a Kiss* again.

"We might as well have a coffee while we wait," I said. I wasn't totally brokenhearted that Bob wasn't back yet. I was glad to have some time to catch up with my friend. The whole condo concept was new to her. Ever since she and Commander Blaine had become a couple, it seemed like she had less and less time to hang out. Was I jealous? Jealous that she didn't have time for me or that the man in her life made plans and kept them? Commander was his nickname. I never got it straight where it came from other than his real name was Sylvester. You could say he was the other extreme from Barry. Commander always seemed to have something planned, usually involving doing something nice for other people, like the senior karaoke event. But then it was easier for him to figure his time. He owned the local Mail It center and had regular hours.

It wasn't Barry's fault. It was part of being a homicide detective that dead bodies, clues and runaway suspects came up when they came up, with no regard to convenience. Still, it was hard to deal with and even harder now that my best friend wasn't around as much.

I was truly happy for Dinah. After a long line of jerks, she'd finally connected with a winner. It showed in her face, too. Her eyes were always animated but seemed even brighter now. The way she wore her short hair gave her a playful look, and the way she'd swirled the pink-and-brick-colored scarves together added a rakish touch.

The café was busy, which was a saving grace for the bookstore. It had been genius on Mrs. Shedd's part to come up with the idea of having freshly baked cookies. Bob had come through by being a fabulous baker. He might write about aliens in his spare time, but his baking was definitely down to earth. The trays of cookies in the display case were almost empty.

I noticed Dinah surreptitiously glancing at her watch as we discussed Barry's plan for our future together.

"Do you have to go somewhere?" I asked finally, and she looked up with a guilty smile.

"Commander volunteered our services at the square dance and ice-cream party at the Tarzana Park Recreation Center, and I promised to help set up. You ought to come."

I started to automatically say no, but she worked on me until I said I would try to make it. Why not? It sounded like fun. Right? Saturday night was when people went out and did fun things or at least stayed home together and did fun things. Not like Barry and me. More often than not, I'd end up crocheting in front of an old romantic comedy and he'd end up at the morgue.

Dinah sat back and said she still had time before she was supposed to meet Commander. "It was so different when I was just involved with jerks. They all seemed to always have one foot out of the door. Commander actually wants to spend time with me, and he wants me to be part of the things he does." Dinah rolled her eyes as if even she couldn't quite believe what she was about to say. "He even likes to talk. And talk about us."

We both laughed. Wasn't that the universal complaint about men? As much as they didn't want to talk to their girlfriends, they wanted to talk about their coupleness even less.

"Men, go figure," I said, throwing up my hands.

"Who's talking about us?" a male voice said. I looked up, and a man with an impish smile and tousled brown hair leaned on the chair back next to me. "Can't live with us or without us," he said with a good-natured twinkle in his eye.

"Something like that," I said.

"Sorry for jumping into your conversation. I have a bad habit of eavesdropping and then adding my comments. I don't think we've met. I'm D. J. Florian," he said. "Molly Pink, right? Mr. Royal pointed you out. He said you're the

one to talk to about the setup for the faux book signing."
He'd caught me off guard, and instead of explaining the
whole thing about Salute to Chocolate, I just asked him for
his phone number. Nobody could find a piece of paper, and
then he pulled a scrap out of his pocket and wrote his information on it. He smiled at Dinah and said he didn't mean to
ignore her, and they introduced themselves as I slipped it in
the pocket of my suit. He looked around as he turned the
chair he'd been leaning on and straddled it, facing us.

"I've gotten to love this café. It's certainly a lot better than
the donut shop I hung out at when I was on the skids. What
a great place to do my blog." I noticed a laptop set up on a
table near an outlet, and I realized I'd seen him in here before. I just hadn't known who he was. "Any idea of when Bob
will be back?"

"Soon, I hope," I said before explaining to Dinah about D. J.'s
blogoir.

Dinah, forever the English instructor, made a face at the
word, and D. J. rushed in to explain that he'd coined the
word to describe a new literary form.

"I describe my book as a blog mixed with a memoir," he
said. Dinah was curious what it was about. I tried to be diplomatic and say that he'd turned his troubles into something
good, but he laughed and took over. "Molly is being too kind.
I was a mess. There's a reason I call the book *Back from Hell*.
Because that's where I made it back from." He explained how
he'd lost everything and hit bottom, but the blog and the
comments he'd gotten from people had helped him turn his
life around. "I turned it into a book that I hope is inspira-
tional. Something like, I did it, so you can, too." He looked
toward the entrance to outside. "And there's Bob."

Bob was wearing a suit and he looked about as comfortable in it as I was in mine. I got up and blocked his path. "I
need to talk to you."

"Be there in a minute," he said, nodding toward Mr.

Royal, who seemed to be perfectly happy making coffee drinks.

"Well?" he said to me in a worn voice.

Dinah had joined me and I was all set to grill him about the sweetener, but first I had to find out what was wrong. The obvious opener was to ask about his attire.

"I went to Robyn's funeral," he said. Not what I expected.

"You did?" D. J. said from the table. "Sorry, my eavesdropping habit," he said. He got off his chair and joined our little circle. "I still can't believe she's dead. I just talked to her last week about my appearance on the talk show," the author said.

I asked Bob for details about the funeral. For some reason, I'd thought it would be small and poorly attended. Maybe it had something to do with Nell's complaints about her and what I'd seen with my own eyes. It turned out to be just the contrary.

"The chapel was full," Bob said. "Barbara Olive Overton was there. I'm not sure who everyone else was, but I think they probably worked for the production company."

"Was Talia Canon there?" D. J. asked. "I know the show must go on and all, but she certainly stepped into Robyn's shoes quickly." The author ruffled his hand through his dark hair. "I admit I was concerned with thinking how Robyn's death was going to affect my appearance, but when Talia called to tell me she was in charge, I expected her to sound more distraught somehow."

Bob didn't know who Talia was and couldn't say if she was there or not. I asked about Pierce Sheraton. Bob knew who the entertainment reporter was and nodded.

"Did he try to interview Barbara?" I asked.

"No," Bob answered. "No cameras, no sticking his face in the middle of things. He didn't even bother the movie-star couple. I almost forget they were there." He thought a minute. "Becca Ivins and Derek Trousedale."

I was surprised about the celebrity couple being there, but

then I remembered the big board in the production office. Robyn was in charge of their appearance on the show. They must have come out of respect.

D. J. hung his head. "I probably should have gone, too."

Bob looked toward the counter and started to separate himself from us, apparently assuming I had finished with whatever I wanted to talk about. Dinah and I exchanged glances and I followed behind him, while she stayed at the table. I heard her reassuring D. J. that it was okay about not going to the funeral.

Mr. Royal took off his apron and handed it and the counter back to Bob. As they made the transfer, Bob looked sideways at me, apparently assuming I was there about a drink. "Give me a minute and I'll make you a red-eye."

He looked at the empty cookie trays and opened the refrigerator. He'd left rolls of butter cookies ready to be sliced and baked. He set the oven and pulled out the cookie sheets.

I didn't want to think he had anything to do with anybody's death, but there was the glaring fact that the clerk had described him as the customer who bought a box of Nature's Sweetie, and the store was the return address on the package. He could have picked up one of those business cards in the store and stuck it on the package as a return address.

I must have been breathing funny, because Bob looked up from his slicing. "Is something wrong?"

"I'm surprised you went to Robyn's funeral. I guess you were more involved with her than I realized."

He kept slicing the cookies and laying them out on the tray. "I wouldn't say I was involved with her. When she started coming in, she noticed me typing on my laptop and asked what I was working on. I showed her a scene from my script." Bob picked up the cookie sheet and slid it into the oven. "She really got the concept of a werewolf planet. She even suggested I might want to add some other kinds of aliens. Whenever she came in, I showed her another scene. She made some good suggestions, and I was hoping when I finished it, she might help me get it in front of the right set of eyes. I wanted her to keep coming in. So, I . . ." His voice trailed off and he looked guilty.

"So, you what?" I prompted.

"You won't tell Mrs. Shedd, will you? I gave her free drinks."

"I know about the Nature's Sweetie," I said finally. He put up his hands defensively.

"I bought it with my own money. It was the only kind of sweetener she would use." He leaned behind the counter and pulled out the box to show me. He even handed me one of the weird little pyramid-shaped packets.

"How many boxes did you buy?" I asked.

"Just one. Are you kidding? That stuff is expensive," he said. If he'd only bought one box, and it was here, then he didn't send the tainted box to Robyn's office. That is if he was telling the truth. I really wanted to believe him. Yes, I wanted to get Nell off the hook, but I didn't want Bob to be a murderer. I hugged him and thanked him for the information.

He seemed uncomfortable with my sudden show of affection, and I certainly wasn't about to explain. I let go abruptly and stepped back. I was still holding the packet.

"Keep it," Bob said. "Try it in your red-eye." He'd filled a cup with the day's brew and pushed the button on the espresso machine.

"No, thank you," I said, dropping it back in the box. "I only drink my coffee straight."

As it turned out, it was a lucky choice.

CHAPTER 15

DINAH HAD VAMOOSED WITH AN APOLOGETIC WAVE as I picked up my coffee. I noticed that D. J. had retreated to his computer as I headed into the bookstore. Mrs. Shedd and Mr. Royal were standing over the best-seller table rearranging books. His hand brushed hers and she looked up at him. The look they exchanged was out of a romance novel and spurred me to action. Maybe I could stir up a little romance for Barry and me. I tried to avoid making personal calls at work, but I called Barry and told him about the square dancing Dinah had talked me into. "I thought it would be fun. Would you like to go?" I asked.

He laughed—in a good way. "Babe, I'm on the way to Santa Barbara to talk to somebody." He didn't have to say more; I got it. He was gone for the duration, and if I wanted to go, it would be alone. Or almost. I called Barry's son and asked if he was interested. Jeffrey was, but there was a hitch. OMG, Jeffrey/Columbia had a girlfriend. Yes, I used the text talk I was always making fun of. What can I say—you have to move with the times.

When I stopped home, I finally got out of my dreaded suit

and into a pair of khaki slacks and a white shirt. I folded up the jacket and put it into a shopping bag. Did I need my head examined? I'd agreed to let Adele add some crochet edging to it.

I took care of the animals and I was off to pick up Jeffrey and then his date. I tried to keep a straight face as I acted as chauffeur. I knew Barry had no idea about Autumn. That was her name, and they were just too adorable sitting in the backseat of the greenmobile. Jeffrey was so unlike the other boys his age. He was gentlemanly and sweet. He'd actually brought a flower for her, though I think he picked it out of a neighbor's yard. I'd barely parked near the playground when he jumped out and came around to open the door for her. I was pretty much old news as he took her hand and they walked toward the recreation building.

They were already clear of the entrance as I got inside. It was hard to believe this was technically part of L.A.; the setup in the multipurpose room felt strictly small town. Bales of hay were spread around the edges for display and someplace to sit. There were streamers and balloons and a whole ice-cream setup at the back. Dinah and Commander were handling ticket sales at a table by the entrance. The small price of the tickets was going into a fund for the kids' basketball team uniforms. Commander's thick white hair stood out in contrast to the new-looking jeans and a red and white checked shirt. He even finished the look with a bolo tie. I think Dinah was a little embarrassed when she stepped from behind the table. Gone were the slacks and scarves she usually wore, replaced by a light turquoise dress with so many crinolines under it, it almost stood straight out. Her spiky hair made a funny contrast.

She apologized for rushing off and wanted to know what Bob had said. She was relieved to hear the explanation for his box of sweetener. "Look who I convinced to come," she said, pointing toward the sundae station. D. J. Florian, the blogoir author, was looking over the ice-cream offerings.

"Good," I said as I began walking toward him. "I didn't get to explain how we're doing his book signing bit when I met him in the café. Telling him in person is better than a phone call." Dinah called after me not to spend my whole time talking shop. It was a dance after all.

D. J. was just paying for his ice cream when I joined him. I passed on the treats but sat on one of the hay bales with him while he ate his.

"Dinah sold me on coming when she told me there'd be homemade ice cream," he said, wiping some fudge off his lip. "Though who knows," he said, looking toward the several squares of dancers. "Maybe I'll join them."

"I don't know if Talia told you about how we're going to handle the pretend book event," I said. It was impossible to hear in there, so he took his ice cream and we walked outside and sat down on the steps. I explained about tagging it on to a real event and gave him the date and time.

"I guess it'll be fine," he said in a voice that implied he wasn't sure. "This is a big moment for me," he began. "Being on the *Barbara Olive Overton* show is every author's dream. I hope this doesn't sound cold, but I just hope that Talia doesn't mess anything up. What about the books I'm going to be signing? Who's taking care of that?"

He was a little on the scruffy side, with the jeans, tee shirt and worn leather jacket. The only part of his attire that seemed to go with the square dancing were the cowboy boots. But there was something definitely likeable about D. J., and I tried to reassure him that she seemed very capable and I was sure she was on top of getting the books.

I asked him how well he'd known Robyn.

"It was just a business relationship. Since she was in charge of my appearance, we talked over the background piece they were putting together. She wanted it to show my story with the worst and the best. We filmed a piece downtown in the area where I'd hit bottom. The piece at the bookstore is supposed to show how far I've come." He wanted to know why I was so interested.

I told him about being there when she died and how Nell was the cops' chief suspect and I was trying to help.

"So you're one of those amateur sleuth types," he said. "Since you're talking to me, does that mean I'm one of your suspects?" His tone was joking, and a friendly smile danced in his eyes.

"Hmm, maybe you should be. Did you have something against Robyn?" If he could joke, so could I.

"Believe me, I wish she was here. I'd feel better about my appearance going well." He looked toward the inside. "Maybe I will try one dance." He got up and picked up his empty sundae cup.

"One thing before you go. Did you notice a photograph on Robyn's desk? A photograph with someone cut out of it."

"You saw that?" he said surprised. "She told me she was going to throw it away."

"So, you knew who was in the picture?" I said, feeling the excitement rise in my voice.

He shifted his weight a few times. "Right after I first met her, she broke up with her boyfriend and decided to cut him out of all her photos. When she told me about it, I thought she was giving me a little too much information but figured maybe she had nobody else to talk to. So it's her ex who was in the picture." His eyes lit up. "If you're looking for a hot suspect, I'd check him out."

"Do you know his name?"

D. J. shrugged with a smile. "Afraid not. She just referred to him as *the jerk*." He gave me a little good-bye salute and headed back inside.

I sat on the step for a minute thinking about Robyn's ex. There was no point in even mentioning it to Barry. I thought about calling Heather myself and realized it would be a waste of time. I'd have to find him on my own.

I could feel the cold concrete through my khaki pants now. While I was talking to D. J., it had gotten dark and chilly. I dusted myself off and went inside.

A man in a cowboy shirt and jeans was in the middle of the crowd, calling the dance. D. J. was already do-si-do-ing around one of the squares. He looked like he was having fun. Jeffrey and Autumn were in another square and were all smiles, too. There were Tarzanians of every size, age and shape.

I was admiring the dancers when my cell phone started to go off. I would have never heard the "ring" over the din, but somehow it had set itself to vibrate and I felt it jump around in my pocket. I picked up and said hello.

"Hello?" Mason said. "What's all the noise?"

I explained the noise and he explained the call or tried to, I could barely make out what he was saying, though apparently he could hear me just fine. I mentioned being at the dance alone.

"Be there in a few minutes," he said in a loud voice. "We can talk then."

I half expected Mason to show up in some cowboy shirt, but he didn't. He was wearing jeans and a Hawaiian shirt and a big smile.

"Okay, what were you saying?" I said as he looped his arm in mine. It was between songs and some of the squares were reforming. Before I could protest, Mason was pulling us toward one of the squares.

We took two vacant spots and waited for the music to begin. I repeated my question and Mason leaned close. "I had a thought about the Crown Apothecary. We ought to check it out."

Before I could tell him I already had, the music started and the caller began to call the dance. No surprise, Mason, a man of many talents, was adept at square dancing, and all of a sudden I started to have fun.

The evening went by in a whirl of dances, with a few glasses of punch and a shared caramel sundae. In between it all, I told him about my trip to the drugstore and the ultimate dead end. He wasn't so sure about letting Bob off the suspect list so quickly.

"But it's Bob," I protested. "And he showed me the box of sweetener."

Mason wasn't convinced. "Sunshine, just because you know him doesn't mean he couldn't kill somebody."

Jeffrey and Autumn stayed on their own far away from me throughout the evening.

Finally the square dancing ended and they began winding down the evening with some slow songs. I was going to sit down on one of the haystack benches, but Mason pulled me on the floor with him. It officially felt strange. Square dancing was one thing. You were really dancing with all the other people in the group. This was up close and personal. Most of Mason's and my contact was mental, and this was definitely physical. I didn't know where to look or how to hold myself. My breathing seemed a little off, too.

I sensed a presence near us and saw a hand tap Mason on the shoulder none too lightly. In fact, the fingers seemed to almost dig in his shoulder. Mason let out a disappointed sigh and stepped away. We were both surprised at who was cutting in.

"Barry? What are you doing here?" I said. He took over and danced us away from Mason.

"I sensed this was important to you," he said. "I got through my interrogation and then I lead footed it back here." He pulled me a little closer, and I could smell the leftover scents of his day, coffee mixed with car freshener.

"I'll take it from here, Mason," Barry said in an alpha male tone when the song ended and Mason rejoined us. I started to tell Barry that Mason and I were discussing the situation with Nell, but then he saw Jeffrey sitting on one of the haystacks with his arm around Autumn.

I thought his eyes were going to pop out of his head. Mason and I each took one of Barry's arms and steered him into the corner, while I mentioned my chauffeuring duties.

"He's got a girlfriend?" Barry sputtered. "He didn't tell me. Why didn't he tell me?" I figured it probably had something to do with how Barry was reacting and Jeffrey knowing that's how it would be. "This means I have to have *the talk* with him."

Mason laughed and said, "I guess you don't remember being fourteen. Your son seems like a pretty smart kid and probably knows whatever he needs to know." Barry answered him with a glare. Barry the homicide detective, who could pin a suspect against the wall with his endless questions, was coming undone over the news that his son was on a date.

In the end, Mason drove himself home, I drove the greenmobile alone and Barry acted as chauffeur for Jeffrey and friend. Oh, to be a fly on the car wall.

CHAPTER 16

I WAS GLAD TO HAVE SUNDAY MORNING OFF. I'D certainly packed a lot into my Saturday. I'd gone from the charade at the production office to the square dance and ice-cream social with no time to catch my breath. But a good night's sleep had done wonders. The two dogs and two cats trailed me across the house. I was surprised at the scent of brewing coffee and to find Barry working on the shelving unit. He looked up from his work when I stuck my head in. Instinctively, I felt my hair and checked my outfit. The hair felt like a mess, but the gray knit pajama pants and the long rose-colored tee shirt were fine.

"I hope I didn't wake you. I was just hand sanding," he said, putting down the sand paper and coming to join me. He laughed at the parade behind me. I opened the door in the kitchen and the menagerie took off outside.

"I thought we could spend the day together," he said.

"Can't do it. I have to work this afternoon." With all the time I'd been away from the bookstore, I'd fallen behind in the final prep for the chocolate event. Sundays were always pretty peaceful, and I was planning to get caught up.

The coffee finished brewing and I poured us each a cup and we took it to the built-in table. Barry seemed disappointed, but recovered. "You don't have to be there until late afternoon, right?" I nodded. "No problem then. We can do what I planned, just end it a little early." He told me to finish my coffee and get dressed, so we could get going. He wouldn't give details.

My hair was still wet when we left. And he still wasn't telling where we were going as he backed the Tahoe out of my driveway. He headed north on Corbin Avenue. I thought at first he might be heading to Porter Ranch, but then he got on the 118, heading west. By the time we were passing through the barren rocky mountains in Santa Susana Pass, I knew where we were headed even before I saw the Simi Valley sign.

Our first stop was the new outdoor mall, where we had brunch at a restaurant with a patio. I had to admit it was very pleasant. Though it seemed Barry was trying too hard and kept pointing out all the shopping options.

"Okay, I agree, it is a very nice mall," I said. "And your plan has us looking at a condo after we eat, right?"

He stopped with the sales pitch. "Sorry for tricking you, but I knew if I asked if you wanted to go, you'd never say yes. All I ask is that you look at the development and give the place a fair chance."

"Sure," I said. We weren't really that far away, but it looked foreign. This valley was much smaller and the mountains surrounding it were drier looking and more barren. I missed the green of the Santa Monicas. The whole area seemed rawer, with smaller trees than the San Fernando Valley.

The condo was in what they called a gated community, which meant it was surrounded by a fence. Inside, there were streets with cute-sounding names and different types of dwellings that had the same kind of architectural design. People were already living there, but a lot of it still seemed vacant. Someday I was sure the little slips of trees along the streets would be tall and shading, but for now, the light was blinding.

There was a grassy area in the middle of the community with swimming pools, a playground and a clubhouse that featured a restaurant, a small theater and rooms for different activities. "It's got everything," Barry said brightly. He had his arm around me in an affectionate manner. "If there isn't a crochet group already, you could start one."

Finally we looked at the town house he had his eye on. Inside, it smelled of new carpet and plasterboard. We walked through the living room, the deluxe kitchen and the eating area attached to a small den. Upstairs, there were three bedrooms and two baths. Barry pulled me inside the master bedroom and showed me the view of the mountains.

"This could be our place. We could fix it up just the way we want it. Think about all the memories we could make." I knew he really wanted me to like the place. It was nice, but he was just moving too fast.

"Have you talked to Jeffrey about the condo?" I said, moving on to look in the room Barry said would be his.

"Not yet. I wanted your okay first. But I checked it out for him. The schools are nearby and they have a drama club," Barry said. Barry was less than thrilled with his son's aspirations to be an actor, so if he was finding out about the drama club, he was pulling out all the stops.

"What about Jeffrey's girlfriend?" I asked, and Barry threw up his hands.

"He went on one date," he said.

"That you know of. You're gone a lot."

"He'll adjust. I'm sure there are plenty of girls around here." The saleswoman had left us alone to discuss. "So, what do you think?" Barry said as we headed back downstairs.

"I don't know," I said with a noncommittal shrug. Barry's face fell and suddenly I remembered what Dinah had said. "Did you put a deposit on this condo?"

"Of course I didn't," he said. We walked outside and stopped on the perfect little street while he tried to qualify me. Was it the particular condo, the development or where it was located that was a problem?

"It's just not a good time to make such a big change," I said. "Samuel is still living at my place. And I'm so close to Shedd and Royal and my friends." He looked so disappointed that I felt terrible. I hugged him to try to smooth things over and then said I'd think about it.

He knew better than to keep talking up the place on the way back. I knew he was really trying to win me over when he didn't even object to the line of conversation when I asked him if he thought Bob could be a murderer.

"Babe, anybody could be a murderer. But Bob—the big question I'd ask is why."

Barry said he wanted to finish sanding the unit when we got back to my place. I just picked up my car and went to the bookstore.

As expected, it was quiet. The vendors who'd agreed to take part had left information on what they were going to offer and what they were going to need. We were certainly going to have a variety of chocolate things. Luxe, the lifestyle store where my fellow Hooker Sheila worked, was providing chocolate tea. Caitlin's Cupcakes was bringing in vampire cupcakes, also called red devil's food. Trader Joe's was offering a tasting of single-origin dark chocolate. They all just needed display space. Only Alain Des Plaines needed access to an outlet for his hot plate.

I went to check on the signs around the store. "I can't believe it," I said out loud. The graffiti from before was back. I wiped it off again and went to the kids' area to talk to Adele.

She was sitting at one of the tiny tables crocheting a flower

to put on the purse she'd made using Rhoda's impatient crochet method.

"Adele, the kids were at it again. I found scribbles on the
signs."

"Pink, I handle story time. I'm not the bookstore police. I
don't know what the kids do when they're not in here." She
gestured around her area. "As you can see, nobody did anything here." She was right. The only thing that seemed out of
place was some red thing that looked like a strawberry sitting
on the table. I picked it up and asked her what it was.

"I'm supposed to wear it when I read the Strawberry Patch
books. The publisher sent it, but I don't know. I think it's a
little too much." She finished the flower and held it against
the cream-colored purse. "Wait. It gets better. I'm going to
put this in the middle of the flower. She reached in her pocket
and emptied her hand on the table. A pink pearl rolled toward me and a small red tube hit the table. I grabbed the
pearl just before it fell off. Adele picked up the red thing.

"I didn't mean to grab this, but as long as I did, you've got
to see it," Adele said, pressing something on it and pointing it
at the table. A heart with the word *love* in the middle was projected on the dark wood. "It's a flashlight." She stared at me until
I seemed duly impressed and then she dropped it in her bag.

She picked up the pearl and set it in the middle of the
flower. With the flower and the pearl, the purse went from
ordinary to adorable. It was all in the finishing touches.

I went back to the main part of the bookstore, and a few
minutes later, Adele came out and said she was leaving. It
looked like it was just going to be me and our cashier, Rayaad, along with the few customers wandering the store. Even
the café was slow. Bob was at his computer, probably cooking
up an alien battle.

I was surprised when CeeCee and Nell came in the door.
Nell pointed toward the back and said she was going to be
looking for some yarn. CeeCee joined me.

"Dear, I thought you were going to call us after you talked to Bob," she said. I apologized and said in all that went on, I'd forgotten about calling.

"There wasn't much to say anyway. He bought a box of Nature's Sweetie, but he brought it here."

CeeCee acknowledged it by sighing. "I was hoping it was him and you'd have it all wrapped up. You have no idea what a trauma this is. Ever since the police did their search, Nell has been a wreck, and she never wants to stay home because she's afraid the police will come again. She has no friends because everyone she knows works on Barbara's show and now wants to stay away from her." CeeCee sighed again. "So, I'm it." She seemed a little desperate. "You've got to get her name cleared so she can get her job back. My show goes back in production in a few weeks, and there might be more press to do for the movie. And my brother still doesn't know anything. What am I going to say? That he entrusted me with his only daughter, and she's a suspect in a murder case and has been put on a leave of absence, which seems to me to be a politically correct way to fire her?"

We walked back to the yarn department together. Before Nell could ask, I told her Bob didn't do it. "Or at least, I don't think so."

"But maybe he knows something," Nell persisted.

"I don't think so. He just told me Robyn had been looking at his script."

Nell made a disbelieving *hah* sound and put down the skein of yarn. "Do you really think he would have gone to her funeral just because she looked at his script. Let me talk to him."

CeeCee and I followed behind as Nell went to the café. I watched her go up to Bob and start talking to him. He responded differently to her than he had to me. I remembered how when I'd hugged him, he'd seemed to have felt awkward. I didn't think a hug from her would have gotten the same reaction. She flipped her long hair off her shoulder, and his face became animated as he talked. Was he flirting with her? Bob with the puff ball under his chin? D. J. came in while they were talking and set up his computer on one of the tables. Bob started to get up, but the blogoir author gestured for him to stay seated. D. J. got his own cup of today's brew and left some money on the counter.

Nell seemed like a changed person when she rejoined her aunt and me. The hangdog look had been replaced by some enthusiasm. "I was right. There was more to their relationship. It turns out baristas are like bartenders. People dump their troubles on them. Bob said Robyn was always telling him about stuff. Like how she broke up with her boyfriend and she had some plan for the show. He said he never gave him the details. Just that it was a risk, but she was willing to take it because it could pay off big time for her career and it could settle some kind of score."

"That must be what Talia Canon was talking about," I said, remembering overhearing Robyn's replacement talking about some kind of plan Robyn had that sounded similar. "What else did he say?" I was a little miffed that she seemed to have done a better job interrogating him, but there were extenuating circumstances. She was young and cute and I'd joined the age of the invisible woman. Instead of thinking you looked cute, men just looked through you.

"I think Bob liked her. I mean really liked her," Nell said. "He seemed to be glad she broke up with her boyfriend. I think he was hoping to be a replacement." Then Nell sagged a little. "But I think you're right. There doesn't seem to be any reason he would have wanted to kill her."

We went back to the yarn department. Nell started to check through a bin of fancy cotton yarn. Rhoda had used what she called kitchen cotton, but Nell wanted to try something a few steps up. CeeCee sat down in one of the over-stuffed chairs. She asked if there were any more of the chocolate samples from the other day. All the things with her niece had left her in need of some medicinal chocolate. I had some samples from Trader Joe's in the office and got her a hunk of dark chocolate with a hint of orange.

"I feel like I've hit a wall," I said. "The sweetener could have been sent to Robyn by anybody. Who knows if they even bought it at the Crown Apothecary. Other places sell the sweetener. The killer could have just stuck the card with the return address on the shipping box. Nobody knows who her ex-boyfriend is. She had some plan, but what?" I mentioned the crowd Bob said had been at the funeral. "I don't know who those people are. Suppose one of them is really Robyn's killer."

"Maybe if you took a look at her house, you'd find something there," CeeCee offered, then laughed at herself. "I can't believe I'm getting involved with solving this case."

Nell had taken the sample skein and cut off a length to try it.

"Who better than you? You love your niece," I said as CeeCee and I watched as Nell headed for the table.

CeeCee nodded and took another chocolate sample. Nell sat down and began to make a foundation chain with the black yarn. The impatient crochet had been a godsend to her. It had finally turned her on to crochet. And now the rhythm and repetition were helping her release all her pent-up emotion.

I was surprised to see that Dinah had joined us. "I had a nice talk with Commander. He understands I need girlfriend time. What's up?" I brought her up to speed and mentioned CeeCee's suggestion. It seemed to me my friend's smile dimmed a little even as she was saying it was a good suggestion. Someone else was trying to be my sidekick.

"Nell knows where Robyn's house is," CeeCee said. She turned toward her niece. "You said you did the other day."

She looked up and nodded. "Yes, I had to deliver something there once."

CHAPTER 17

"OKAY, LADIES," DINAH SAID MONDAY MORNING when we all met in the café. "Time to go." We'd all agreed that Sunday night was not a good time to go check out where Robyn had lived. We also agreed that it was best to take Nell's car. The white Ford Focus blended in better with the surrounding cars. And since Nell knew where we were going, best to let her drive. We all had our coffees and headed out.

Bob was curious where we were all headed as he handed us our drinks. I didn't want to tell him where we were going and just said we were off on an investigation.

"Wish I could go with," he said. "You guys always seem to have so much fun, and it would be good research for my script."

"I thought it was some kind of outer-space thing," I said.

"Yeah, but investigating is investigating, whether it's on earth or the planet Zumeria."

I promised to tell him all about it.

When I saw how close Robyn's house was to the book-store, it made sense why she had stopped by the café a lot for coffee. It seemed silly to have driven. The house was all of two blocks from Shedd & Royal. Nell parked her car and gestured across the street to a small light blue stucco house and announced it was Robyn's.

"Well, not exactly hers," CeeCee said, pointing at the "For Rent" sign stuck in the front lawn.

"They sure didn't waste any time," Dinah added. "Not even a week has gone by since she died."

Dinah and I got out and Nell and CeeCee stayed in the car. CeeCee was convinced she might be recognized and it would be a distraction, and Nell didn't want to take a chance of getting herself in more trouble.

I didn't think there was a name for the style of the house. The closest thing I could think of was *starter house*. In other words, small. The front yard had a small, neatly trimmed lawn, no doubt due to a gardener who was still caring for the yard despite Robyn's absence. Just before the house, there were a few bushes and some white flowers that contrasted nicely with the blue color of the walls. A driveway ran along the side and ended in a one-car garage.

"Well?" Dinah said as we stood on the sidewalk in front.

"Let's have a look around. The 'For Rent' sign is a perfect cover." I walked along the front of the house, looking into the windows. Though I couldn't see details, it was obvious that the house hadn't been cleared out. Feeling bolder, I went up the driveway toward the back, with Dinah following.

"Hey, there. What are you two doing?" a threatening voice demanded. Dinah and I stopped abruptly and turned. A woman was standing at the edge of the property next door. She held up her cordless phone like it was a weapon. "I've got nine-one-one on speed dial. I push one button and the cops are on the way."

Holding the phone like it was a gun, she backed down the driveway toward the street. It hadn't registered before, but the garbage cans were lined up against the curb for pick up.

Robyn's were still in the driveway since there was no one to take them out. Still with her eyes locked on us, the woman flipped the lid on her big blue plastic can meant for recyclables. She grunted when she looked inside.

"Okay, you two, where are they? You know scavenging is against the law. I put a whole sack of bottles in my blue can and now they're gone. Put them back and I'll let you go."

It took a moment for me to get what she was talking about. I realized we were standing in front of Robyn's blue can and she apparently thought we were working the neighborhood.

I held out my hands to show they were empty and Dinah did the same. The woman let out a disappointed grunt and stepped closer to us. She was older, wearing a bright magenta gauze dress and flip-flops. Her blond hair was pulled back into a ponytail. She looked us over a few more times. "We've been having a problem with scavengers going through the recyclables." She narrowed her eyes and said, if we weren't after bottles and cans, what were we up to? She waved the phone around for effect, and reminded us about the 911 on speed dial.

I pointed toward the "For Rent" sign on the lawn. Suddenly her expression relaxed.

"You looking to rent the place, huh?" She made no pretense of looking us up and down. "I hope you're not into wild parties. This is a nice street. Just remember—" She waved the phone at us in what was becoming a redundant threat.

I finished the thought for her. "You have nine-one-one on speed dial. Got it," I said. I looked back at Dinah and winked and turned back to the woman. "You're just the kind of neighbor we'd like. These days nobody seems to care anymore." The woman's face lit up with the compliment. "I bet you know all about everybody around here," I said in a friendly voice.

"Miranda Baker," she said, holding out her hand. "And

yes, I pride myself on being the eyes, ears and conscience of this street. Let me tell you, nobody TPs the trees around here on Halloween. And by the same token, every house gives out candy."

She started to go off into the details of the neighborhood, and I waited until she stopped for a quick breath. I took the opportunity to jump in and bring the conversation back to the house. "Of course, you probably want to see the inside." She told us she'd get the keys; the owner had left them with her, figuring she'd do a good job at screening potential renters.

She opened the front door and let us walk inside, then stuck to us like glue. "You know you look kind of familiar," she said, peering at my face. Since the bookstore was close by, I thought she might be a customer. This could be trouble if she figured out where she knew me from. I didn't want her to show up in the bookstore and keep asking why I wasn't renting the house or, worse, find out that all along I owned a house. I tried laughing it off and said I got it a lot. "I have one of those faces that looks like everybody."

We stopped in the middle of the living room. As Dinah and I glanced around, Miranda said the owner ought to have gotten the place emptied before he put up the sign. "But you know what they say, time is money."

The room looked like what it was, a place where someone had gone to work fully expecting to come home. We glanced through the kitchen and then on to the bedrooms. There were two. One she'd used to sleep in. The double bed was unmade and the closet door open. I walked in, pretending to be curious about the size of the closet, but really was more curious about the photo on the nightstand. It seemed to be a beach scene. She was in the picture and whoever was next to her had been cut out.

"Is this the person who lives here?" I asked, holding up the picture frame. Miranda appeared uneasy.

"The owner didn't want me to bring this up. He said it might make people feel funny about renting the place. But you two look like you've got both feet on the ground and know what's what. It's not like she died here."

I feigned surprise. "How terrible. She looks so young."

Miranda stepped closer and dropped her voice to a whisper. "Murdered. Right in the middle of work. The cops came by and talked to me. They were having a hard time finding her next of kin and wondered if I could help them with that."

Neither Dinah or I spoke or even breathed, afraid she'd stop talking just when she got to the important part.

I'd learned long ago when I first started using *The Average Joe's Guide to Criminal Investigation* that one piece of advice the book offered really worked. Dead air. It made people nervous and it made them keep talking. Miranda was no different.

"I told him about her boyfriend." She hit the hole in the picture with her finger. "That's him. She went through all her pictures and cut him out. Kind of symbolic, I guess. She was cutting him out of her life."

"What happened?" I asked.

"They broke up," Miranda said like I was an idiot for not getting it. "Not that I miss him. He used to park his BMW so it just barely cleared my driveway. I couldn't even call the cops on it, because technically he wasn't blocking it." Miranda knew that he smoked because she'd often seen him sitting outside at night smoking. She knew what brand of beer he drank. Apparently she taken it upon herself to check Robyn's trash for evidence of scavengers, but she didn't know his name. "Oh, please," she said as if it was an absurd thought that she would know his name. "I'm not that kind of nosy neighbor."

We'd moved into the other bedroom that functioned as Robyn's home office. She had one of those wipe-off boards hanging on the wall. Robyn had written in D. J.'s name, but most of the space was devoted to Becca Ivins and Derek Trousedale. She'd written in *the perfect couple* and then, underneath, things like *wedding footage, what happened to their family, awards, a happy ending.*

"She worked on that *BOO* show," Miranda volunteered. "When I found out that's what she did, I asked her to get me some tickets. One of the shows where they give the audience something, like a car." Miranda kept on talking about how Robyn hadn't come through yet, then caught herself and said it was hard to think of her as dead.

"What's this?" I said, noting a girl and boy doll made out of yarn sitting on a shelf in the wall unit. They stood out from the rest of the house, which was all clean lines, bare floors and impersonal. The soft-bodied dolls looked as if they were a remnant from childhood and as if they'd been well loved. "They're crocheted," I said to Dinah after examining the arms on the girl doll. Miranda started to scowl, and I quickly explained that I was a crocheter and that was why I was so interested in it.

"Personally, I'm a knitter," she said with just a touch of disdain. "I never did get the hook business." I picked up the doll's foot and noticed something on the bottom. If there was such a thing as scribbling in crochet, that's what it was. It seemed like initials, but I couldn't make them out.

Suddenly Miranda seemed to notice that we were spending more time looking at the things in the house than the house itself. She took the doll from me and put it back.

"Don't worry, the place will be cleaned out next week." She asked if we wanted to put a deposit down. Dinah and I hemmed and hawed; meanwhile, she seemed to be studying our faces.

"That's it. I saw you at the square dancing event. You," she said, pointing at me, "were dressed in a getup all wrong for dancing." She made a sound as if she was astonished. "Who goes square dancing in pants unless you're a man?" She turned to Dinah. "Now, missy, you had it right. All those crinolines."

We'd begun edging toward the door, realizing we'd gotten all the information we were going to. Dinah came through and said we wanted to look at some more places first. Miranda did a little sales pitch. Apparently we'd done too good a job at selling ourselves as potential neighbors, but she finally let us go. We hung on the sidewalk long enough for her to go back to her house. I was glad Nell had parked a distance away. Imagine the fuss Miranda would have made if she'd seen us getting into a car with CeeCee Collins.

When the coast seemed clear, Dinah and I ran down the street and jumped into the backseat of Nell's car.

"We've got to find out who Robyn's boyfriend was," I said as I pulled the car door shut.

CHAPTER 18

"A CROCHETED DOLL? WHO'S MAKING A CROCHETED doll?" Adele said as she came in at the end of the conversation. Almost all the Hookers were gathered around the table, and I was telling them about what Dinah and I had seen inside Robyn's house. The group had felt protective of Nell before, but now that she'd started crocheting with us, they were even more so. Everyone wanted to see her get her life back.

Dinah was a no-show. She had a freshman English class to teach. But the rest of us were working on one of Rhoda's impatient crochet projects.

"Nobody is making a doll. I was just telling them about what I saw when I went into Robyn's house. It isn't about the dolls so much anyway, but what they mean."

I had all their attention now. This was my big moment to bring out something I'd read about in *The Average Joe's Guide to Criminal Investigation*. According to the book, when checking out someone's surroundings, everything tells something about them. I called it the Sherlock Holmes effect. What could you deduce from things.

"The point is that Robyn's house was utilitarian and sparsely furnished. Her office was similar, or at least I think so from what I saw in the box of her belongings. So why would she have a crocheted cactus in her office and keep a couple of worn-looking dolls in her house?"

"Because they meant something to her," Elise said in her wispy voice.

"I can't imagine anything meaning much to her," Nell said. "She seemed hard and cold."

"All the more reason those two things say something important about her," I said. "And there's something else to consider. The dolls look worn and seem like something from her childhood. The cactus appears newer and as though it was made for her office. Both of them had similar initials on the bottom, though I'm afraid I couldn't read them. I think it's safe to assume the same person made all of them, which means it's somebody she'd known when she was a child but she was still in touch with."

"Ooh, that's good," Sheila said. She had taken a short break from her job at the lifestyle store, Luxe, to join us. Even though it was literally the next store to the bookstore, it was hard for her to get to the group. Not that she couldn't take off time, she didn't want to. She'd had enough bad jobs to treasure a good one.

"Maybe it is someone from her family?" Eduardo said. His voice was so much deeper and masculine than the rest of ours, everyone did a little double take when he spoke. "My gran made a lot of toys for me." The comment got an extra double take from Rhoda. She didn't know Eduardo as well as the rest of us since she was relatively new to the group. You truly couldn't judge Eduardo by his cover-model looks. He had learned how to crochet from the grandmother he'd just mentioned.

He'd been missing a lot of our get-togethers and seemed like he had something on his mind. When I asked him if everything was okay, he assured me it was. When I asked for details, his almost-too-handsome face broke into a broad smile and he said all would be revealed in good time. . . .

"I heard Robyn's parents died when she was young. Maybe she kept the dolls because they gave them to her," Nell offered.

"I don't think finding out who made the doll is going to be any help in finding out who killed her. I think it's a waste of time," CeeCee said. "You said she cut her boyfriend out of some photographs. Well, I still think he might have decided to cut her out of his life."

Without missing a beat, CeeCee took out a box of buttons and spoke to her niece who had begun decreasing to make the flap on the envelope-shaped purse she was making. "Next, dear, you should think about what you're going to use as a closure. The button choice can make or break it." CeeCee took out a handful and spread them on the table. If it was up to me, I'd have voted for the silver heart with a design etched in black.

"Aunt CeeCee is right," Nell said. "I bet her boyfriend is the killer." Everybody looked at me.

"I'm working on it," I said, hoping no one asked for details. I agreed finding his identity was important; the trouble was all I had reached were dead ends. I was relieved when Mrs. Shedd came by the table carrying a stack of books and broke the chain of conversation.

"I found some more books with a chocolate connection," she said, setting them down next to me. "See what you think." As she was about to leave, she commented, "There was some more of that graffiti on the signs for the Salute to Chocolate." Both of us looked in Adele's direction.

"I'm responsible for the kids' department, not the kids," she said. Mrs. Shedd didn't seem happy with her comment. I started to get up to clean off the pen marks, but she said she'd already taken care of it.

I set down the cell cover I was making. It was my first attempt at impatient crochet and was actually for my phone. I thought the cream-colored cotton might make it easier to fish out my BlackBerry from the dark cave of my purse.

I looked through the books she brought and had to chuckle at the titles. I wondered how Tom Clancy would feel about *The Hunt for Chocolate October*. She'd found a cookbook that just had recipes for chocolate chip cookies, and one that featured chocolate drinks. There was a paranormal romance called *The Clairvoyant Chocolatier*, and a mystery called *Bittersweet Death*. The last book was *Felix and the Fudge Factory*. As soon as Adele saw me holding it, she jumped up and came around the table.

"Why did Mrs. Shedd give that to you?" Adele had backed off a little from trying to take over my domain as event coordinator, but heaven help anyone who touched anything related to the kids' department. She repeated to the group that it wasn't her fault if kids were marking up the signs in the store.

CeeCee was craning her neck to get a better view of the covers of the cookbooks. "Are you going to have samples?"

"Luxe is providing chocolate tea," Sheila said. I was pretty sure that wasn't what CeeCee was thinking about. I mentioned the exotic chocolate bars and that Caitlin's Cupcakes was bringing in bite-size pieces of their vampire cupcakes.

CeeCee was practically drooling. The sweet tooth must have run in the family because Nell was gazing at the chocolate chip cookbook with a hungry eye.

"I don't know why Caitlin doesn't just call them Anthony cakes," Elise said. She almost had a swoon in her voice as she said the name of the vampire known for his crocheting. I saw Rhoda rolling her eyes. She'd softened a little about the vampire character but still thought he was too foofie. Elise had been over the top about Anthony from the books, but when the movie came out, it had only gotten worse. Now she had a real face to put to the character. I had expected to hear that she was stalking Hugh Jackman.

I started looking into the bookstore, picturing how we should set up the chocolate festival so we could use it for the fake book signing as well. Someone walking through the area caught my eye. Barry? He was carrying a bag of something and looking for something. Me, maybe?

I left the table and walked toward him. As soon as he saw me, his face opened into a warm smile.

I was glad for the smile. Usually when he just showed up at the bookstore, it was because there was some kind of problem.

He held up the bag. "I brought lunch." He asked if I could leave and suggested we take the food to the park. I must have looked surprised at his impromptu plan.

"I thought it would be fun, babe," he said. "I had some time before I had to go to the morgue." Fun and morgue so close together seemed a little odd, and Barry did sound like he almost choked on *fun*, but he certainly got credit for trying. Even though I had to believe it had something to do with my adventures with Mason.

Mrs. Shedd was okay with me taking my lunch break then. I left my crochet project and grabbed my purse.

The May gray clouds had burned off and the sun was shining. We went to the Los Encinos State Park, which was like an oasis in the midst of busy Ventura Boulevard. We ignored the old ranch house that had been turned into a museum and found a bench that faced the guitar-shaped minilake that was fed by a natural underground spring. The ducks and geese saw the promise of food and gathered around us.

Barry sat down with a sigh and I knew he was tired. It made me appreciate this gesture even more. He'd gotten wrap sandwiches and some containers of different salads that we shared.

"This is nice," he said. He sat so we rested against each other. We passed the containers of salad back and forth, and I tossed bits of my sandwich to the visitors at our feet. After his initial comment, Barry was suddenly silent, which was like a neon sign saying there was something on his mind. It took a few minutes of listening to him breathe before he finally got it out.

"So, have you thought any more about the condo?" he said. He didn't leave a space for me to answer, but described his plans for the place. The shelves he was making for my yarn would fit in the third bedroom. He would make built-in cabinets for the den to make it seem roomier. And he realized he'd forgotten to show me the space for a laundry setup in the garage.

All I could do was to tell him the truth. The condo was very nice, but it wasn't the right time for me to make that kind of change. Barry didn't say anything. I just heard a little grunt of displeasure. Of course, I felt the need to smooth things over and started telling him I was so distracted because of Nell. I mentioned going to the dead woman's house and Barry sighed and shook his head.

"No breaking and entering," I said before explaining the place was for rent. Barry surprised me by chuckling. I was expecting some kind of admonishment about keeping my nose out of things.

"I know I have to accept that my son wants to be an actor and has a girlfriend, and I have to accept your sleuthing."

I seized on the opportunity. "What would you think if you saw your victim had a bunch of photographs with someone cut out of them?" When he didn't answer, I answered for him. "The obvious question is why not just toss the photos. I think she was trying to tell herself she didn't need him in the picture of her life. Did I mention the missing someone was her boyfriend? Don't you think he'd be a likely suspect?"

"I said I needed to accept it. I didn't say I would help." He started to pack up the food items and tossed some leftovers to the ducks. "I heard they had some trouble notifying next of kin. Heather found the boyfriend. If he's a legitimate suspect, I'm sure she's on it."

"I don't suppose you know his name."

He squeezed my shoulder in an affectionate manner. "No one can say you're not persistent. I don't know the guy's name. Remember, it's not my case and you don't need to know it anyway. Have you ever heard of the charge for interfering with a police investigation?" Barry said. "Heather would just love to pick you up for that."

From deep in his jacket, Barry's cell phone began to ring. No hotsy-tots musical rings for him. His was just no-nonsense and jarring. As soon as he answered it, he moved to the edge of the bench, and I could see the change in him. It was like doors closing everywhere and he was back to a homicide detective. I gathered from his end that whatever was going on at the morgue had been pushed up and he had to hurry.

I finished gathering up the food items, and by the time he hung up, we were already walking toward the gate. A few minutes later, he dropped me back at the bookstore. Disgruntled that I still didn't know the identity of Robyn's boyfriend, I got out.

CHAPTER 19

A WEEK WENT BY AND DETECTIVE HEATHER talked to Nell twice. Supposedly it was just to clarify something, but we all knew Heather was hoping Nell would confess. The good part of that was it meant Heather still didn't have strong enough evidence to make a case. But even if she never got strong enough evidence to arrest Nell, it would hang over Nell's head forever and ruin her future. What could she put down as the reason she left her job—that she didn't do it but was a suspect in the murder of one of the people she worked for?

On the positive side, the donation box was filling up. Everyone was in love with impatient crochet. It was the perfect take-along kind of project. Most of the finishing touches were done with the group, though. We had fun picking out buttons and flowers to add or some kind of trim. My cell phone cover was done and in use. At least now, if I heard the frantic voice Mason had recorded as a ring, I could find the phone in my purse.

CeeCee came in when I was straightening up the yarn department. I was surprised to see her alone.

"Where's Nell?" I said, trying to keep the panic out of my voice.

CeeCee put a reassuring hand on my arm. "Don't worry, Molly, she wasn't arrested. She went out with Sheila." CeeCee seemed relieved. "I feel guilty for saying this, but I'm glad to have some time off." I could see her point. Nell had been pretty needy and CeeCee wasn't used to that kind of giving.

"Tony's with me," she said, gesturing to the almost-too-handsome man looking over the new-release table. She referred to him as her boyfriend, but I wouldn't. But then I don't think *manfriend* sounded any better. "I'd like to take my time looking at yarn. You know men. They say take all the time you want, but all the while, they're looking at their watch and tapping their foot. If I stay until you close, could you give me a lift?"

I told her of course and she rushed off to tell Tony he could leave. He sent me a thank you wave.

CeeCee had a field day with our try-before-you-buy policy, and by the time I was shutting off the lights, she had amassed a pile of yarn.

It was after ten when we pulled out of the parking lot. "Do you mind if we take a short detour," I asked. Then I explained I'd been driving by Robyn's house almost every night, to see what was going on. So far it had been nothing.

We drove onto the residential street and I had to dodge the trash cans that had been put into the street for pick up the next day as I pulled up to the curb across from the house. I was surprised to see lights on and a car in the driveway.

"I'm getting out," I said.

"I'm coming, too." She pulled off her seat belt and got out on the passenger side. I had to laugh when I looked over at her and she was crouched next to the car in some stealth mode straight out of a TV drama.

Down the street, I heard the rattle of some kind of cart and I saw some shadowy figures. CeeCee straightened to see what I was looking at.

"It's nothing. Just some people out walking," I said as we crossed. I slipped up to the living room window with CeeCee practically touching me. I was stunned by what I saw. The room was completely empty. A moment later, I heard the front door open and someone came out and walked around to the driveway and got in the car. As it backed down the driveway I got a look at it in the streetlight. The BMW things on the front reflected in the light, and I remembered that the neighbor had said that Robyn's boyfriend drove a BMW. I locked my eyes on the license plate, trying to memorize the number while I struggled to find a pencil and scrap of paper in my purse.

As I was scribbling in the dark, I stepped back and almost tripped over a trash can. It was so full, the lid was flipped back and stuff was sticking out. Since it was in front of Robyn's, it wasn't hard to figure that it must be her stuff from the house.

"Is that one of the dolls you were talking about?" CeeCee said. The streetlight illuminated the crocheted girl doll lying on top of the overflowing garbage can.

"It seems wrong somehow to throw away something like that," she said. I agreed and pulled the doll out. I stuck it under my arm and started feeling around in the can for the other one. "I wonder what else is in here?" I pulled out the other doll and peered into the can.

"Saving the dolls is as far as I go. I'm not going to start sifting through trash cans," CeeCee said. I heard a noise and turned as someone flipped the lid of one of the cans down the street. I strained to see in the darkness and saw maybe five people in dark clothes were spreading across the street looking in the blue recyclables can. They were tossing the bottles and cans in a kid's stroller that had been outfitted with a large plastic bag.

It had barely registered what was going on when Miranda flew out of her front door and trained a powerful flashlight on the street. The people began to blink and back off. I was waiting for her to do her speech about having 911 on speed dial. Then I realized why she didn't say it.

Lights flashing, cop cars appeared out of nowhere from both directions and squealed to a stop, boxing all of us in the middle of the street. The thwack of the helicopter almost drowned out CeeCee's squeal.

"That's them," Miranda yelled, pointing at all of us. "I warned you scavengers," she said. "But you wouldn't listen."

Other neighbors came outside, and I heard her telling them how, thanks to her, the gang that was stealing the bottles and cans had been caught.

"We better get out of here," CeeCee said, grabbing my hand and heading across the street toward my car.

"Freeze," a voice called from behind us.

"They don't mean us, do they?" CeeCee's face registered shock when I nodded.

"But don't worry. I've been in situations like this before. They'll let us go as soon as I explain." With that, I turned back to face the two male officers. I was surprised to see they had their guns drawn. "Isn't that overkill for a bunch of bottles and cans?" I said. I made the mistake of pointing at them, which I realized too late was dangerous. In the dark it was hard to tell that my hands weren't holding a gun. "On the ground, you two," one of them yelled.

"I don't think your plan is working," CeeCee said. We both laid down in the middle of the street, and the uniforms came up behind us and handcuffed us and patted us down.

"You don't understand," I said. "We're not part of that gang," I said. "Do you know who she is?" I said, nodding my head toward CeeCee. "She's probably going to get an Oscar nomination for her role in *Caught By a Kiss*."

CeeCee heard me. "Well, it's not certain yet, but there is a lot of buzz going around about it," she said.

I heard the two talking among themselves. One of them had heard of the movie, one hadn't. The one who had gave details and the other one groaned. "Oh yeah, the vampire movie."

Unfortunately being a celebrity was no guarantee of any special treatment these days. Once London Omni spent thirty days in jail, despite being a wealthy heiress and actress, all bets were off. CeeCee, sensing that they didn't like vampire movies, brought up her reality show.

"Yeah, yeah," one of them said as he helped her up. "*Making Amends*. Looks like that's what you two are going to be doing." The uniform hanging on to me pushed my head down before he put me in the backseat of the cop car. CeeCee came in from the other side. No one could say she was silent about it, either.

"I demand that you call my attorney immediately," she said as the doors shut on either side of us.

She kept saying it, but with the Plexiglas panel between us and them, I don't think they heard.

"How does my hair look?" she said to me. It wasn't exactly what I was expecting her to say. The passing lights of Ventura Boulevard illuminate the backseat, and I caught a glimpse of her. Laying down in the street isn't good for your appearance. CeeCee's hair was always perfectly coiffed. Thanks to her newfound place in the spotlight, she never went anywhere without considering that she was going to be noticed. Right now she had a smudge on her cheek and the officer must have smushed her hair when he helped her into the car. Lucky for her, she'd chosen to wear black pants and a black loose top, which hid all the dirt marks from the street.

CeeCee read my silence. "That bad, huh?" She sighed a few more times. "And I was worried about being seen leaving a discount store with a case of toilet paper. You've seen what they do with celebrity mug shots. They post them on the Internet and put them on the news. They never die. Those awful photos keep showing up again and again." CeeCee was trying to maneuver her shoulder to fix her hair. "I don't suppose they'd let me put on some lipstick."

There was both good and bad about the short ride to the police station. Good because we got out of that awful backseat. Bad because they handcuffed us to a bench.

CeeCee had given up on me handling things and she'd taken over. She kept up a rant about calling her attorney. "I'm not saying a word until my attorney is here," she yelled every time anyone passed. Lucky for us, one of the officers who had seen her on the *Barbara Olive Overton* show was sympathetic to her comeback-kid story and agreed to call Mason.

By now it was late, but who knew how late. With my hands in handcuffs, I couldn't even check my watch. I figured Mason must have arrived and pulled some strings because out of nowhere, they uncuffed us and handed us back our stuff.

Mason was just coming in as we came out into the lobby. He looked a little surprised when he saw us. "You're out already?"

"Thanks to you, Mr. Super Attorney," I said, rubbing my wrist and doing shoulder rolls.

"I wish I could take the credit. I just got here," he said.

Worried that they'd made a mistake in letting us go, the three of us hustled out of there in a hurry. Only later did I find out that the gang of can and bottle thieves thought we were up to some kind of bigger crime, and the whole time they were dealing with the cops, they kept insisting they had nothing to do with us.

"Thank heavens, no mug shot," CeeCee said as we walked outside. She realized she'd spoken too soon; a bevy of photographers were hanging by the door. When they saw Mason, they started shooting. I don't think they even knew who they were shooting at first, assuming if they were with him, they had to be somebody. I was surprised to see Pierce Sheraton in the crowd. You would think that as the host of an entertainment show, he'd be above hanging outside the police station in the middle of the night, but what set him apart from the others was that he got down and dirty to get a story.

CeeCee immediately started finger combing her hair and trying to stay behind Mason. That is until she realized they weren't after her. They had focused in on Mason and wanted to know if he was there because the starlet Valerie Vancouver had been picked up on her third DUI.

As soon as she thought she wasn't in the spotlight, she wanted it, and CeeCee stepped from behind Mason and started talking to the photographers about her false arrest.

It was a lot nicer getting into Mason's Mercedes than it had been the cop car. It smelled much better, too. CeeCee took the backseat and sighed as she slipped in. "It's so good to be free again." She leaned toward the front seat. "Molly, do you have any of those chocolate samples in your purse? I'm feeling a little weak from our ordeal."

"Don't worry, ladies, I have it under control." The streets were as close to empty as they got in the Valley, and after a fast ride on the 101, he pulled into Du-par's parking lot. "I always say the best thing to have when you get out of jail are pancakes."

There was just one other table of customers in the landmark coffee shop. Their pancakes were legendary and came soaked in a puddle of melted butter.

Insisting she was just trying to keep herself from fainting at the memory of our evening, CeeCee polished off a short stack with barely a crumb left over. Personally, I was too unnerved to eat. I kept wiggling my hands to make sure they weren't restrained. Mason thought it was all too funny.

He dropped CeeCee off at her place first. The lights were on at my house as he drove up. He pulled into the driveway and his headlights illuminated Barry's taupe Tahoe parked in front of the garage.

Uh-oh. Not again.

CHAPTER 20

"I MISS ALL THE EXCITEMENT," DINAH SAID AS WE walked into the bookstore café.

"I'm not sure that CeeCee would qualify it as excitement," I said, thinking back on how she'd looked when we finally exited the police station.

There was a low din of conversations and the air had a strong enough scent of coffee. Just breathing it in made me more alert, which I sorely needed after everything that had happened the night before.

Bob started drinks for us—a red-eye for me and a café au lait for Dinah—while we found a table. Most of them were full. Interspersed with the people hovering over their computers, there were a few people actually talking to each other. I noticed that D. J. Florian was one of the computer hoverers. No doubt writing his blog. When we were situated, I opened my tote and took out the girl doll that had started the whole fiasco with the cops. The cops had taken both dolls, along with my purse, and then, since they weren't bottles or cans hoisted from somebody's trash, had given them back when we were released.

I didn't even want to consider what they must have thought about me carrying around a couple of dolls.

Lying across the table, she looked like a doll corpse, with her rosebud mouth and embroidered eyes staring vacantly at the ceiling.

"Okay, so what happened when you got home?" Dinah said. I'd told her everything up to finding Barry's Tahoe parked in my driveway when Mason brought me home. I was glad when Bob brought over the drinks. I fortified myself with a sip of the strong coffee drink before I recounted what happened when I got home.

"My front door opened before I could get out of the car. Barry sure keeps in shape. He was across my lawn in a flash." I took another long drink of coffee before continuing how Barry had reached the car just as I was opening the passenger door. To say he looked unhappy was an understatement. Why hadn't I answered my cell phone? The phone got e-mails, did I ever look? What was my story this time?

I was the first to admit I didn't have a very good record with my cell phone. Something always seemed to happen. I forgot to charge the battery and the phone was dead, or it somehow set itself to silent, or I just didn't hear it ring. Though with Mason's custom "ring," I didn't think that was going to happen. How could you not hear a voice crying *get me out of here* coming from your purse? As for the other stuff the phone did, I wasn't much for squinting at the small screen and pretty much ignored it.

"I didn't exactly have it," I said.

"You lost it?" Barry asked.

"Not exactly. More like it was confiscated."

I guess Mason was used to speaking for his clients because he took over and explained my trip to the cop shop. He did a much better job than I would have done. He made it sound like CeeCee and I were just crossing the street and suddenly had been surrounded by the gang of bottle thieves.

Barry ranted on about being worried. I was sympathetic to a point. I guess it didn't occur to him that when he was off chasing suspects, disappearing and reappearing without a word, that I might feel the same. Mason must have realized his presence wasn't helping and, with a wave, left.

When Barry and I went inside, Samuel came out of his room. "You were out kind of late. Everything okay?" he had said.

"It was a weird feeling being on the other side of a comment on what time somebody got home," I said to Dinah. She wanted to know what I'd said and I told her I did just what he and his brother had done when I said something similar about their late arrival. I just nodded and gave no details.

"And?" she prodded.

"Samuel went back into his room and then Barry wanted to hear all the details. He did a lot of head shaking and finally laughed when I described CeeCee's disreputable appearance when she met the photographers hanging outside. After he took me to pick up my car, he left; he had to drive carpool."

"So you never found out who was driving the BMW," she said. I started to nod my head in dismay and then began scrounging in my purse.

"How could I have forgotten? I wrote down the license plate number." I found the scrap and waved it around.

"Are you going to ask Barry to find out the name that goes with it?"

I rolled my eyes. "Are you kidding? He said he accepted my sleuthing activity, not that he would help with it. You have no idea how upset he was when he heard about our almost arrest. Well, upset, until he started to laugh. He might have said something about when you stick your hand in the beehive you shouldn't be surprised when you get stung." Besides, I figured with all Mason's connections, he could probably find out and be willing to do it.

Dinah looked at the doll and lifted its crocheted skirt to see how it was made. "Oh, look, she's wearing undies," Dinah said. Not only did she have underpants, they had a little pink rosebud sewn on them.

Just then, CeeCee came in, or more correctly, made an entrance. She couldn't help it, really; she seemed to automatically make a stir. She was wearing sunglasses and looked like she had a hangover.

She sank into one of the chairs with a loud sigh. "Going out with you is quite an adventure. I hope Nell appreciates what I did for her," CeeCee said, looking over the top of her sunglasses at me. She made a weak gesture toward the counter as if she didn't have the strength to get up and go place her order. One of Bob's gifts as a barista was he knew how to cater to our clientele. He didn't wait for CeeCee to even say anything before he was on the way to our table with a lemon bar.

"You're a dear," she said, extracting it from his hand. She savored the scent and took a big bite. She sighed with delight at the flavor. "There, better already."

"Your usual nonfat double cappuccino?" Bob said before he went back to the counter.

"I think you better use whole milk today," she said. She turned to us and assured us it was for medicinal purposes.

I started to apologize for the previous night, but she held up her hand to stop me. "If you want to know the truth, I haven't done anything nearly as exciting for a long time. Of course, when it wasn't clear what was going to happen, I wasn't quite so sure."

I mentioned the press people hanging by the door when we left. She took off the sunglasses, and I could see her eyes had lit up. "It turns out that was a good thing. I talked to my publicist about trying to kill the story, but she was thrilled when she heard I got photographed leaving jail." CeeCee appeared sheepish. "Maybe I embellished a bit. I had us in a cell with all sorts of lowlifes. Anyway, my publicist said that she'd already been getting all kinds of requests for my story. I kind of hate to have to say it was all a mistake. I'd get better street cred if I'd said I was researching a part and had been part of the bottles and cans gang."

Bob brought her the foamy coffee drink. When he set it on the table, she noticed the girl doll for the first time. "You're why we almost went to the pokey?" she said, picking it up. She lifted the skirt and there was a small burst of her musical laugh when she saw the underpants. "Look at all the details," she said, indicating the tiny pink flowers crocheted out of fine thread along the hem of the moss green full skirt. She showed us how it was made and commented on the high quality of the workmanship. All the while, she looked like she was thinking of something but couldn't quite grasp it. She finally set the doll down.

"I've seen a doll like this before. Not exactly, but the flowers, the underpants with the rosebud."

I lifted the bottom of one of the doll's black Mary Jane–style shoes and showed CeeCee the scribbles on the bottom done in surface crochet.

CeeCee sat forward suddenly. "I know where I saw a doll like it before."

Adele interrupted CeeCee's thought as she stood next to the table. "Where'd the doll come from?"

We all ignored her as I cajoled CeeCee into continuing. "It was a sale we had for Hearts and Barks. All the things were made by celebrities. You know how that can jack up the price we get."

"That was made by a celebrity crocheter?" Adele said, her voice quaking with excitement. "Who? We have to get her to join us. Nothing personal, CeeCee, but I knew you couldn't be the only other celebrity crocheter besides Vanna White."

We all looked at CeeCee expectantly, waiting for the name, though for different reasons. I was looking for clues into Robyn's life and Adele was after publicity.

CeeCee said she didn't know offhand and would have to ask around the charity group. She picked up her drink and then set it down with distaste. "I think my cappuccino needs some sweetener."

I volunteered to get it for her. When I went behind the counter, I saw the box of Nature's Sweetie that Bob had bought for Robyn. I grabbed a packet and asked if it was okay if I gave it to CeeCee.

Bob gave me the go-ahead and said I might as well leave the box on the counter. Just as I was about to hand it to CeeCee, out of left field, D. J. came bolting over from his computer and grabbed it, yelling, "Don't!"

I let go at the same time he did and the packet fell to the floor. Before I could retrieve it, the author had picked it up by the tiniest edge. He dropped it on the table and told all of us to stay away. Then he brought over his laptop and pointed out the news story he was reading. In big letters, it said, "Nature's Sweetie Recalled After Another Tainted Box Found."

CHAPTER 21

I'M NOT SURE WHOSE IDEA IT WAS TO CALL 911. WE could have just taken the box back to Crown Apothecary where Bob got it. It wasn't like it was going to blow up or anything. As long as nobody used it, it seemed like we would be safe.

Three cop cars squealed to a stop in front of the café and two officers came in, guns drawn, and ordered us all to freeze. Okay, I also don't know what whoever called had said, either.

When Bob pointed with his head and said, "It's over there," and they saw that it was a pyramid-shaped sweetener packet in the middle of the table, the two serious-faced uniforms cracked a smile.

The arrival of the police brought a sudden surge of attention to the café. I think the fact the cruisers had their lights and sirens on had something to do with it.

The extra officers held back the lookie-loos who'd drifted in from the bookstore, while D. J. explained the problem with the box of Nature's Sweetie by showing one of the uniforms his computer screen.

The cops did a bunch of conferring by radio. The lookie-loos left after a few minutes once they saw the source of all the action and realized they couldn't even order a drink. Mrs. Shedd and Mr. Royal came in and had to fight through the exiting crowd like fish swimming upriver.

A police supervisor showed up after a while and looked over the situation. She, in turn, put in a call to somebody else. That's when things got really strange. She decided they should move everybody outside and hustled us out the door. Not even the cops stayed inside.

An awkward-looking black truck rumbled in front of the cop cars and parked directly in line with the café. I waited to see who was going to get out. After what seemed like forever, two people exited the truck. I say *people* because no way could I tell if they were men or women, or one of each. They were totally suited up in white space suits complete with their own air supply. They didn't so much walk in as lumber. One of the cops stood at the glass door and pointed out the packet of sweetener and the box on the counter. The suited-up pair went inside, and I watched as one of them picked up the packet and the other the box. Once the packet was back in the box, they lumbered back to the door and onto their rein-forced truck.

One of the officer's radios squawked and he bent his ear toward it. "Okay, folks, we have an all clear, you can go back in."

Mr. Royal pulled me over. "Do something. The last thing we want is for people to connect the café with people in hazmat suits." I saw his point. Everyone had sort of stunned expression and seemed reticent about going back inside.

The obvious answer was to give something away. Nothing like free stuff to cheer people up. I found Bob and the three of us worked it out. Bob and I went on inside, and Mr. Royal apologized to the crowd and said we'd be giving out free party drinks to make up for it.

"Wait for me," Adele called, threading through the people

until she caught up with us. We worked out an assembly line. Bob manned the blenders. I poured the drinks into small cups, Adele did whipped cream and set them out on the counter. Dinah stepped in and handled crowd control. CeeCee was our first customer. She seemed a little unnerved by what had just happened.

"That's it. From now on, it's only real sugar for me."

Finally Bob made drinks for us and seconds for CeeCee, and we all collapsed around one of the tables. D. J. pulled up a chair and joined us. The doll was still laying on the table and I went to pick it up. CeeCee sucked the last of her drink through a straw and got my attention.

"I made a few calls while we were stuck outside. I described the doll, and one of the Hearts and Barks directors remembered it. More than remembered it; she'd bought it for her granddaughter. When she told me who'd donated it, I was surprised I hadn't remembered myself. Ariel Rose made it. Get it?" CeeCee said, pointing to the rosebud on the underpants.

Adele reacted first. "Ariel Rose," she repeated in a loud voice. "The Ariel Rose. She crochets. Wow, we've hit the jackpot." The donation was from several years earlier before Ariel Rose had become the current *it* girl. Since then she'd been in a rash of romantic comedies—*Always the Bride, Penny and the Spy, The Girl with the Zirconium Tiara* and *Hearts and Harriet.*

D. J. listened with a confused expression. Dinah was sitting next to him and told him the whole story of the doll in the garbage and why we were so interested in it.

"Pretty clever," he said. "Also pretty interesting. It doesn't exactly go with the image I got of that producer. She seemed all aggressive-career-woman to me."

Bob pulled a chair up and joined us. "It looks like Robyn was just what they call collateral damage. Someone is out to discredit Nature's Sweetie. The whole pitch for the product is how it has almost no calories but is safe and natural. You think anybody is going to want to buy it now?"

"That's wonderful news," CeeCee said and stopped herself. "Dear, that came out wrong. It's not wonderful news that nobody is going to buy that sweetener. It's wonderful news that as soon as the dust settles, I'm sure they'll give Nell her job back."

Now that Adele had heard that Ariel Rose crocheted, she said we had to meet her and talk her into being a cheerleader for the yarn art. "Just think of it, if she wore a little caplet over her evening gown on her next red carpet event and said she'd made it."

"Hold on, dear," CeeCee said to Adele. "If Nell is not on the hot seat anymore, the whole investigation is over with. It doesn't matter about the dolls."

"Here's something weird," I said. "This doll is obviously from when Robyn was a small child. Ariel Rose is in her late twenties and can't be more than a few years older than Robyn. Unless she was some kind of child prodigy in the crochet department, it seems a little odd. Are you sure the doll in the past sale and this doll were made by the same person?"

"I know my crochet," CeeCee said, "and the underpants with the rosebud is like a signature. Plus you said there was the surface crochet markings on the bottom of the shoe, and the person I spoke to said there were yarn squiggles on her doll, too."

"I think we should talk to her. Even if we're not investigating Robyn's murder anymore, I'm really curious about how Ariel, the crochet items and Robyn are all related. Besides it feels a little anticlimactic to just drop everything."

"If anybody is going to talk to her, it should be me. We talk the same language, besides I'd like to get her involved with Hearts and Barks again," CeeCee said. "And Molly should go with me. She's the professional here." Adele's eyes bugged out in response to the comment.

"I'm as much as a professional as Molly Poirot Pink is," Adele protested.

"Let me see if I can put something together," CeeCee said, pulling out her cell phone. I knew where she was headed. She'd call her agent and publicist, who in turn would get in touch with Ariel's agent and publicist and try to set something up.

People outside the entertainment industry thought everyone knew each other, but it was far from true. Personally I thought the idea of setting something up would never work out, or if it did, it would take too long for it to happen.

"I think we should find out where she's going to be and just show up," I said.

"We can't ambush her," CeeCee said. "Then she'd never agree to help out with Hearts and Barks or even talk to us. Let me think about it."

I stepped away from the table and called Mason. Really for two reasons. To see if he knew how we could get in touch with Ariel Rose and to find out if he could get a name to go with the license plate number I'd gotten. Even if the investigation was technically over, I still wondered who Robyn's boyfriend was. I got his office, and instead of being put through, his assistant came back on the line and said Mason was tied up and offered to take a message.

By the time I went home for the day, I still hadn't heard back from Mason.

In the meantime, I found another way to get to Ariel Rose. It happened by chance. Dinah and I had arranged to have a girl's night out. It seemed like it had been forever since the two of us had an evening together. I made a brief stop home to take care of the animals, but it turned out to be unnecessary. Barry was working on the shelves and Jeffrey was in the den doing his homework. They had let the dogs out and fed them and the cats.

"Trouble sure follows you. I heard there was some excitement at the bookstore," Barry said. He hadn't changed out of his work clothes, which meant that he was probably expecting to leave. He'd merely taken off his tie and jacket and rolled up the sleeves of his dress shirt. "So, CeeCee's niece should be off the hook," he said. I asked what he knew and he gladly shared this time because he thought it would end my skulking around.

"The crime lab found several packets in the box from the bookstore café that appeared to have been opened and glued shut. It was like playing Russian roulette with sugar substitute. Lucky Bob didn't put the sweetener out sooner." I shuddered when he said this, remembering that Bob had offered me a packet. I'd almost been curious enough to try it.

"The packets looked just like what they found in Robyn Freed's desk drawer and the box that somebody brought into the Van Nuys station. There was a note inside of that one from someone who seemed to have a beef with the product. They said all their claims were lies." He explained they were all at the crime lab being checked for cyanide, but everybody seemed confident that it would be the same in all of them. "Then they'll look for trace evidence that occurs in all three boxes and hope it connects them to somebody. So you see your work is all done." I didn't say anything, but until Nell was in the clear and actually had her job back, I wasn't considering this case closed.

I asked him who had brought the box of sweetener to the Van Nuys station.

"It doesn't matter," Barry said, turning back to his work. I stared at his back as he went back to filling in the nail holes. Did he really think I would accept that answer?

"It does matter, a lot," I said. Barry went on with his work. I saw his shoulders drop just a little, a subtle indication that he'd figured out I wasn't going to let it go.

"Molly, I can't tell you. Heather doesn't want the information to get out." He put down the can of wood filler and his tool and held both my shoulders in a tender manner. "Telling you would get us both in trouble." The look in his eyes made it clear that was all the information I was going to get. He took his jacket off the back of the dining room chair and put it on before slipping his still knotted tie over his head and tightening it. He looked at me and cocked his head. Ever the detective, he noticed that I still had my purse in my hand.

"I just stopped here to take care of the animals. I'm going out." I was going to leave it at that but realized it sounded kind of short, and it wasn't like I had anything to hide. I mentioned meeting Dinah for a girl's night out. He called to Jeffrey and said he'd drop him off at home, and the three of us walked out together.

I let him pull out first and then drove over to Dinah's. She had the door open before I even walked up the few steps to her front porch.

When I went inside, I was surprised to see Sheila sitting on Dinah's chartreuse couch. She looked up and smiled at me. Her new job at the lifestyle store next to the bookstore had done wonders for her confidence and made it possible for her to have just one job rather than several.

She was so happy with the job, she gladly spent her evenings at the store. It seemed like forever since the three of us had gone out together. "I hope you don't mind that I invited Sheila to join us," Dinah said.

"Mind? I'm glad you did." I went over and hugged Sheila. She looked really good. The owner of Luxe had her wearing pieces from the store. Tonight she had on a peasant blouse with apricot-colored flowers embroidered on it over skinny black jeans and boots. "It'll be great to catch up with each other." Dinah and Sheila got ready to go. I pulled out my cell phone to see if I'd missed any calls. There was nothing. How odd that Mason still hadn't called back.

We went to an Italian restaurant on Ventura Boulevard that had a patio surrounded by trees and illuminated by a string of globe-shaped lights. Even though it was practically on the sidewalk, it seemed like a separate world.

We ordered pasta dishes, salad and garlic bread. Sheila said she was doing better in the nerve department, but she still carried her emergency crochet hook and string. She pulled it out to show us. But working in the store had made such a difference for her. She started chatting on about the customers and how they'd begun to get some celebrity clientele. She'd talked to her boss about putting up photos of their well-known clients, which was common practice. Every restaurant and dog groomer had pictures of some of their famous customers posted on the wall.

Our food came, and since it was served family-style, we began to pass around the plates as Sheila continued. "I told Nicholas that if we were going to have photos, they ought to be unique rather than just head shots." Sheila smiled broadly. Whenever she spoke about her boss, her face seemed to brighten, and we all thought she had a thing for him, though she denied it. "He listened to what I said and he agreed. So now when someone famous comes in, I take a digital picture of them with whatever they bought. Instead of hanging the photos on the wall, we put them in frames we have for sale and spread them around the store."

Dinah complimented her on the idea and started talking about her students and getting ready for finals, but then went off into talking about Commander. "This probably sounds stupid, but he's so nice to me, it's making me nervous." My normally chipper friend hung her head. "He's making all kinds of plans for the summer."

"Don't you like what he's planning?" Sheila asked.

"It's not what he's planning that's the problem. All the things are lots of fun and help people. He has us volunteering at the next Hearts and Barks carnival." She handed me the pasta in pomodoro sauce. "You should understand," she said to me. "Look how upset you are that Barry wants you to move to Simi Valley when you get married."

"Married?" Sheila said. "You're getting married?" She knew about the ring in the drawer and my lack of an answer.

"I'm not getting married," I protested.

"Sorry," Dinah said. "I should have said *if* you get married. But Barry is almost living at your house." She explained the condo concept to Sheila.

"It sounds to me like he's trying to take you away from your old life," Sheila said.

As much as I was against the condo idea, I found myself defending Barry. I argued that he wanted us to have a place that was fresh for both of us. And Simi Valley was more affordable. "With Barry's ego and all, he wants to buy the place." I made excuses, but what Sheila had said registered. I didn't want to think it was true.

The pasta was delicious, and when they brought the dessert menu, we ordered a chocolate soufflé and shared it. Sheila had seen the cop cars and hazmat team and heard some vague details but wanted the whole story. She shuddered when I told her about the Nature's Sweetie problems. "You know we sell coffee and teas. We almost were going to sell that sweetener as well. I'm glad now we didn't. So what's the next step for you?" she asked.

"Barry thinks I should drop it, but then he never thinks I should investigate anything. But he said now that it seems the problem is with the sweetener rather than Robyn being a target, Nell should be exonerated and get her job back. But it feels strange to me." I mentioned the no-name boyfriend who'd been cut out of the pictures, and the crocheted items that seemed at odds with the kind of person she was. Then I brought up the doll and how CeeCee was sure that this actress had made it, and I explained why it didn't make sense. "The doll is definitely old and been through a childhood. If Ariel Rose made it—"

"Ariel Rose?" Sheila said. "She's been in the store. I just took her picture. She has young kids and she likes it because we have the whole kids' area."

"She does?" I said. Far better than anything CeeCee could

set up would be just running into Ariel and starting up a conversation. I asked Sheila if she had any idea when she'd be in the store again.

"How about she's going to be there tomorrow afternoon," Sheila said with a smile. "She ordered some hand-painted cereal bowls and is coming in to pick them up." We finished our dessert and coffee. Sheila insisted on picking up the check and said it was her thank-you for all the times we'd taken her out.

I didn't say anything to Sheila as we said our good nights, because I didn't want to put her on the spot. But I'd already decided that one way or another, I was going to just happen to be in Luxe when Ariel Rose came for her bowls. I discussed it with Dinah, who suggested we just keep a watch for the young actress from the bookstore and then just happen to show up in Luxe when we saw her go in.

It was late when I finally got home. I checked all the phones and had no return call from Mason. Even though it looked like I might not need the information, Mason didn't know that. He didn't even know why I was calling. Now, I was officially worried.

CHAPTER 22

THE THING ABOUT CELEBRITIES WAS THAT AT LEAST some of them had regular lives. When they weren't being pampered on the set, they went to the grocery store, stopped at a Starbucks for coffee, and shopped at the bookstore. So the idea that Ariel Rose shopped at Luxe didn't seem that strange at all. But how to approach her in a way that didn't freak her out was a different story. Who wouldn't be creeped out if someone just came up to them and pushed an old doll in her face and asked her if she'd made it?

When I called CeeCee to tell her where Ariel Rose was going to be, she insisted on being there and even offered to be the lookout, tracking her arrival. When Dinah heard CeeCee was coming, she bowed out. We decided to say nothing to Adele. It would just stir up trouble if I told her about the plan and then said she couldn't come. Ignorance was bliss. Right, her ignorance was going to be our bliss.

"She's coming. She's coming," CeeCee said in a stage whisper, finding me after she rushed into the bookstore. "I saw her pulling into the parking lot." CeeCee started back toward the door, and in some move she must have picked up from some role she'd had, jerked her head as a signal to go. Adele was busy in the kids' section. She was working on something for Salute to Chocolate and was being very secretive. I told our cashier, Rayaad, I was just going next door for a few minutes if Mrs. Shedd asked for me.

CeeCee and I walked next door to Luxe. As we went inside, as always, I was struck by the exotic smell that came from the combination of coffees, teas, spices and fragrances they sold. It was no wonder Ariel Rose shopped there. With the whole world gone to chain stores, Luxe was one of a kind. And most of the merchandise was, too.

Sheila was in the center of the store behind a counter that held small items like the silver dessert spoons and jewelry. The top had a display of items crocheted by Sheila. She had refined her style but still kept true to the impressionist appearance of her mixtures of greens, blues and lavender yarns, which she crocheted together into shawls, scarves and throws. Much to Adele's chagrin, Sheila had knitted some of them.

The store was empty of customers, and Sheila offered us samples of the tea of the day. They always had catchy names and claimed some sort of cure. Today's was Afternoon Slump Begone. It sounded good to me, and I took a sample cup from the pot.

"Try to act nonchalant," CeeCee said, adding some sugar to her tea as the bell on the door tinkled and we all looked up. Even dressed in jeans and a white shirt, Ariel Rose stood out with her long blond wavy hair and lilting smile. Two little girls dressed similarly rushed ahead of her to the kids' section. A woman trailed them to the table hand-painted with a pretty design, surrounded by small chairs. There was a toy box of things to play with and nonmessy art supplies. It was obvious the woman was there to take care of the kids, and she stayed next to the table.

Ariel turned her smile on Sheila and said hello. Sheila had

figured we were up to something, and the old tension began to show around her eyes. She looked back and forth between the three of us and seemed at a loss what to do.

I covered the awkwardness by telling Sheila that CeeCee and I were in no hurry and to go ahead and wait on the new customer.

This was one of the odd things about seeing some actor type when you were out and about. You were really strangers, yet you knew way too much about them. On the other hand, they knew nothing about you.

The good thing about this time was CeeCee had every reason to know that Ariel crocheted, since CeeCee was heavily involved with the Hearts and Barks charity.

Still, how did you go from smiling and nodding at someone to asking them about some doll they crocheted a while ago?

We were hemming and hawing when I noticed something zip by the window. The door opened and the bell went into a frenzy. When I looked toward the sound, Adele was standing in the corner with a stormy expression.

"Nice work, Pink. Slipping out without telling me." Adele's voice was naturally loud, but when she got upset, it got even louder.

If it was possible, Adele had outdone herself in the clothes department. She'd taken a black tee shirt and cut off the short sleeves and then used bedspread-weight thread to crochet elbow-length lacy ones. She had a necklace made of crochet motifs and a beanie with a flower. Any one of them would have been lovely alone. Together, they were overkill but a conversation opener.

Ariel walked over to Adele and looked at her shirt. "Do you sell these here?" she said to Sheila.

"Sell them here, no way. This is a one-of-a-kind piece. I made it myself. It's CROCHETED," Adele said, raising her voice for emphasis when she got to the yarn art, then she viewed Ariel with an expectant expression. Ariel touched the sleeves with an admiring gesture, but that was it. Adele seemed frustrated. I guess she was expecting Ariel to get all excited about it being crocheted and then say that she crocheted, which would give Adele the opening she was looking for.

"It's a great look," Ariel said, and then looked away.

CeeCee took the opportunity to introduce herself. "You're involved with Hearts and Barks, aren't you?"

Of course Ariel knew who CeeCee was but seemed a little surprised by the Hearts and Barks question.

"*Involved* seems like the wrong word. I take my kids to the carnival every year," she said. "Anything I can do to help the animals," she said with genuine emotion. "I want them to care, too," she said, glancing toward her daughters.

Ariel turned to Sheila and asked about her order. Once she got it and paid, she wasn't going to hang around.

"Wasn't that terrible about that producer on the *Barbara Olive Overton* show," I said ostensibly to CeeCee. "What was her name, Robyn something?" It was a bit of a non sequitur, but there wasn't time to ease into the subject.

"Freed," CeeCee said with a nod. "And to think she was murdered right in front of you." I watched Ariel for her reaction. None.

Now it was getting strange and I began to think that the board member that CeeCee had talked to must have been mistaken about who made the doll she bought. Adele was getting upset, too. Her first shot at a celebrity seemed to be slipping away. While CeeCee and I were trying to be subtle, Adele finally just lost it and stepped closer to Ariel, backing her into a corner. "We want to know about the doll."

Ariel tried to move away and gave us all a perplexed look. A moment later, her lips curved into the smile so familiar from all those romantic comedies. "I know, this has to do with your reality show. Right? But I don't get what the point is. A scavenger hunt maybe. You have to get a doll or something." She glanced around the store.

CeeCee's eyes flared. "My program is called *Making Amends*. It has nothing to do with scavenger hunts and everything to do with correcting some wrong in someone's past."

I'd brought the girl doll with me, and I whipped it out of my bag. I waved it in front of her and pulled up its skirt and showed off the pink rosebud.

"It looks like this one," I said.

Ariel's eyes got big and her smile vanished. "Oh my God," she said as her mouth fell open. She slipped out of the corner and made a move toward the door, waving at her girls to follow. "How did you find out? I didn't mean any harm." She swallowed hard and had pulled out her cell phone. "But isn't it awfully late to be coming out about it. I'll reimburse the money if she wanted a refund. I just wanted to help the animals."

"What exactly did you do?" Adele demanded.

"I know the doll you're talking about now. Okay, I lied and said I'd made it. The rule for the auction was that the items had to be made by a celebrity. I don't know how to thread a needle. The kids' nanny made the doll."

We all looked toward the woman with the girls.

"That's not her. Annie doesn't work for me anymore."

"What happened?" I asked. It was more out of curiosity than anything else.

Ariel seemed to consider what to say for a moment, then she shrugged to herself as if to say, *Why not?* "She was a nanny with an agenda." It seemed like that was all she was going to say, but as I've mentioned before, dead air has all kinds of benefits. It makes people uncomfortable, including me, and they attempt to fill it. I struggled with myself to keep silent.

Finally Ariel broke. "We have a fabulous playground set up in our yard. All state-of-the-art equipment. There's a tree house and a rope ladder, swings and more." Ariel's tone changed to irritation as she continued. "The nanny didn't think it was good for children to be isolated from the real world. So, even though we had everything you could ask for, I found out she was taking the kids to the park." When she said *park*, there was a definite *ick* sound to it.

"I just wanted to dip the kids in hand sanitizer when they came back. They had sand in their shoes from the sandbox." She wrinkled her perfect nose with distaste.

I didn't say it, but I was thinking that they probably had much more fun at the park with all the kids than in their pristine yard of perfect equipment.

There must have been something in my expression, because suddenly she got defensive. "I gave her a great reference and didn't say anything about the park. Her name is Annie Hoover." She had sunk into a chair by now. "Okay, I admit it, I didn't tell Annie what I was doing with the doll. I'm sure she wouldn't have approved."

"Do you know how I could get in touch with her?"

Ariel seemed distraught. "Why tell her what I did now? What possible difference could it make?"

I had to explain I wasn't looking for the nanny to turn Ariel in. I started to tell her about Robyn, but as soon as she realized it wasn't about her, she gave me the information.

"She's in her forties and has brown hair. She took my kids to the park Tuesday and Thursday morning around ten. She's probably doing the same with the family she works for now. They live up in the hills, so she's probably still taking them to Tarzana Park." I noticed that Ariel's eyes were filling with water. "What I did was wrong. But please don't say anything to him." We all glanced toward the window. Pierce Sheraton and Talia Canon were walking by toward the bookstore. "I'm sorry if it caused some kind of trouble." She took out a check-book and wrote a check and handed it to me. "Please give this to the Hearts and Barks people to make up for any problem."

She'd begun edging toward the door and waved to her daughters and the woman to join her. Then she was gone.

"Well, I guess there was some benefit out of all that,"

CeeCee said, taking the check from me. "Her guilt payment is going to help a lot of dogs and cats."

As we walked back to the bookstore, Adele was sulking and mumbling about losing out on a celebrity crocheter. I was more interested in trying to find the nanny.

No time to think about it. Adele went back to her area and Mrs. Shedd waved me over. Talia Canon was standing with her.

"Molly is the one who handles all the events," Mrs. Shedd said. "You should talk to her." Mrs. Shedd took off and I sensed there was some kind of problem. I was still holding the crocheted doll. Talia gave it an odd look. I had it under my arm nestled against my body like I was cuddling it, and I suppose it must have looked a little strange.

"It belonged to Robyn," I said. Luckily Talia didn't ask me why I had it. It would have sounded too weird to say I fished it out of the trash. D. J. Florian came out of the café and joined Talia. I noticed that the entertainment reporter was following him out of the café and carrying a coffee drink. Pierce eyed the doll and gave me a strange look. One that didn't improve when I mentioned who the doll had belonged to. I began by apologizing for asking him to leave the café a while back.

He laughed. "I've been chased out of lots of places. It goes with the territory. Don't worry, I didn't take it personally." He looked at the doll in my arms. "What are you doing with Robyn's doll?"

"It's a long story," I said with a dismissive wave. "Did you know her very well?"

"I like to think I know everybody in the business. Too bad about what happened to her."

I asked him if she passed along information to him.

"What are you, some kind of amateur detective?" he said, suddenly noticing that I was asking him a bunch of questions. "You're not trying to make me one of your suspects, are you?" He laughed at the absurdity. "Maybe you haven't heard, but the cops are just considering her a random victim now that other tainted sweetener has shown up."

"I heard someone brought in a box of it to the Van Nuys police station," I said, and Pierce got his trademark smirk.

"Not exactly brought it in," he said. "The cops are trying to keep a lid on it. They want to give the impression they know who dropped off the tainted box."

"But you know what really happened?" I asked.

"I get the scoops on everything," he said with a certain amount of cocky pride. "I heard from my source that the box of sweetener was actually left outside the door in the middle of the night."

"They must have some kind of surveillance cameras," I said.

"Very good," Pierce said, seeming impressed. "But it didn't do them much good. Since it was drizzling that night, the person was carrying an umbrella and used it to block the camera's view. Personally, I think the whole tainted thing is a diversion. To make it look like Robyn wasn't the target," Pierce said. I got a sinking feeling that the cops might be thinking that, too. Specifically Detective Heather. Maybe poor Nell wasn't off the hook after all.

Talia made a loud *ahem* noise and seemed irritated at being kept standing there.

"We're not here to discuss Robyn," the segment producer said. Any hesitation about stepping into Robyn's shoes seemed to be gone. "I happened to be in the area and stopped in to look over the place for the piece on D. J." The blogoir author nodded to her and she continued. "He's concerned about being stuck on to the chocolate event."

She was carrying a folder and began to thumb through the pages. "Robyn left some notes about the kind of shots she wanted." A sheet slipped out and she grabbed it. "What's this?" she said, holding it out to D. J. I got a glimpse of it. It seemed to be blank except for *Insert NY*.

He handed the sheet back to her. "We already filmed that. She wanted to recreate when I hit bottom."

"I'm glad somebody can make sense out of her notes." Talia found another sheet that had *bookstore* scribbled on it. She struggled to read the handwriting and then ignored the sheet altogether. "The point is, we want something to show off how far D. J. has come. We want something serious."

I tried to be diplomatic and explained that there would be no horde waving chocolate bars. We would set D. J. up before the event actually began. "It's much more efficient and cost effective for us," I said.

Talia cut me off, shaking her head. "Maybe that's true, but it really won't work for what I have in mind. Is there any way I can get you to reconsider. I'm sure when Robyn set this up, that isn't what was agreed on."

I will usually try to please someone who asks so directly, but she was rubbing me the wrong way. Shedd & Royal was only getting a small fee and a promotional consideration out of all this, and it wasn't worth a whole separate setup.

"Now if you'd like to reconsider and rent out the store for the day, you could shoot it any way you want," I said, pleased with how I stood up to her.

Talia's mouth slipped into the mixture of a sneer and pout. I got the feeling spending more money wasn't in her plan.

"I'll say it again. This just won't work for us. If you can't accommodate us, I'll use a different bookstore."

I called her bluff and told her to go ahead.

CHAPTER 23

"GOOD FOR YOU, MOLLY," DINAH SAID THE NEXT day when I told her how Talia had tried to steamroller me into doing a whole separate setup for D. J.'s fake book signing. In the end, Talia had sputtered a lot and then given in. We were sitting at my kitchen table and were so busy catching up, I hadn't even thought to make coffee.

I shared what Pierce had said about the box of sweetener, and Dinah shook her head. "I debated what to do with the information," I said. Then I guiltily admitted that the first thing I'd done was to check where Nell was when the box was dropped off. "CeeCee assured me Nell was at her house the whole night. She knew because Nell had slept on the couch in her living room. Apparently Nell had gotten fearful of sleeping in the guest quarters since Detective Heather had done her search."

"Did you tell CeeCee you think Nell might still be a suspect?"

"I had to tell her what I heard. I had hoped to talk to Mason first, but—" When I stopped talking abruptly, Dinah looked up.

"And?" she said. My friend knew me too well not to figure there was something wrong.

"Mason has been hard to reach lately," I began. "More than hard to reach. He hasn't been returning my calls. So, I called his house, late, figuring he'd answer." I paused for a moment. "Let's say I got more than I bargained for."

Dinah was all ears as I recounted the phone call. I told her how it had rung a long time and I'd been about to hang up when he had answered.

"Mason," I said. "Finally. I have so much to talk to you about."

"Molly, this isn't the best time," he said. There was something in his voice I'd never heard before. He sounded awkward, distracted, and then I got it.

"Is someone there?" I said. I waited hoping he'd dismiss my concern with some other explanation, but he just cleared his throat a few times. Suddenly I felt embarrassed and uncomfortable. "Sorry, if I interrupted something."

"We'll talk another time," he said, and then he'd hung up.

"I guess I knew it was inevitable that he'd meet someone eventually," I said, "but it just seems so sudden." Dinah came over and put her arm around my shoulder as I continued talking. "I'm still going to call him about Nell, but I'll call his office."

Dinah tried to change the subject. "In the meantime, you asked if I was up for some investigating," she said, reminding me that I'd called her and asked for her help. She had no classes and no plans with Commander and had jumped at the chance to be back in the middle of things.

I repeated the story about Ariel Rose and her nanny with an agenda.

"We want to meet the nanny," I said. "In fact, let's go now. The time is perfect," I said, checking my watch. I got up and she followed. I was glad to have Dinah with me again. She was decked out in her best dangle earrings and had gone back to her long-scarf look. This one was white and gauzy and wound around her neck with a long tail to blow in the breeze. Dinah looked contemporary and fun. She was both.

"And why is that again?" Dinah asked as she got into the passenger side of the greenmobile.

I explained that the way Ariel Rose had recognized Robyn's doll made it pretty certain Ariel's former nanny had made it. The crocheted cactus I'd found in Robyn's office had been made by the same person. We knew because the initials crocheted on the bottom of both the doll and cactus had looked the same. Since the doll was old and the cactus relatively new, it seemed pretty obvious the nanny had known Robyn when she was a child and was still in contact with her.

"She probably knew a different side of Robyn," I said. "I think if we find out more about who Robyn was, it might point us toward who killed her."

"Sounds good to me." Dinah pulled the door shut and I started the motor.

I had a plan. It might have seemed like a lame plan, but it was the best I could come up with. According to Ariel Rose, Annie the nanny had taken her kids to the park on Tuesday and Thursday mornings around ten. I was hoping she'd kept the same schedule with her new charges. It was a little after ten as I steered the greenmobile toward Tarzana Park.

We didn't know what she looked like besides having brown hair and being in her forties. It was certainly not enough of a description to pick her out of a crowd. So I'd come up with the other part of the plan.

I parked not far from where I'd parked when I went square dancing. Neither of us wanted to have to worry about our purses, so we left them in the trunk, but we both took our totes with our crochet supplies.

How funny, I hadn't been to the park in years and now in the space of a few days, it was my second trip. I glanced toward the recreation building and thought back to the square

dance. I got a warm feeling thinking about how Barry had
made such an effort to get there. That evening had made up
for the times when things went the other way and our plans
got trashed.

We got to the playground and picked out a bench. Being
there brought back memories. My boys had played there
when they were little and later moved on to play baseball in
the sports field. I looked at the playground equipment.

"It's not exactly the state-of-the-art stuff that Ariel Rose
said she had in her backyard," I said. Dinah nodded in agreement. The equipment was utilitarian and well used, but the
kids in the sandbox and on the merry-go-round and swings
all seemed to be having fun. I searched the mostly women
sitting on the benches that ringed the play area. It was easy
to eliminate most of them as possible Annie Hoovers. They
were too young and too busy texting and talking on their cell
phones. I had decided that a professional nanny would be
more likely to keep a constant eye on her charges.

There were several older women in the group, but there
was no way to tell if any of them was Annie.

"If we can't find her, let her find us," I said, taking out my
crochet project in progress. Dinah got the idea and took out
hers, too.

We both were working on cell phone socks using Rhoda's
impatient crochet method. Dinah joked, if all else failed, we
could probably sell them there. She gestured toward the array
of potential customers with their naked cell phones. I noticed
a woman on the other side of the play area watching us. Was
she Annie? I didn't want to stare, but out of the corner of my
eye, I watched as she checked on a couple of kids playing on
the edge of the sandbox and then came over toward us. I forced
myself not to look up until I sensed her standing in front of
me. When our eyes met, we exchanged smiles.

"What are you making?" she asked in a friendly voice.

I held out the cell phone sock and told her about the impatient crochet idea. She seemed very interested and asked if she could look at mine. I invited her to sit and she joined us. After looking over my project, she handed it back and pulled her own crochet things out of her pocket.

"I always carry a ball of cotton and a hook and make washcloths," she said, showing off a half-finished square. I told her about the Hookers and invited her to join us.

"It sounds nice," she said. She stood to check on her charges. The kids waved to her and she sat down again. I introduced myself and mentioned story time at the bookstore. She fit Ariel's description and I was ninety-nine percent sure she was Annie. I pulled out the long soft girl doll from my bag and showed it to her. That took care of my one percent of doubt. Her reaction to the doll said it all. Her eyes got round and sad.

"Where did you get this?"

"It belonged to someone named Robyn Freed."

Her voice was almost a whisper. "I know. But how did you get it? Who are you?"

I decided the best thing to do then was to tell the truth and explain everything down to Ariel Rose giving a hint about where we could find her.

When I explained about Nell and that I was trying to find out what really happened to get her off the hook, she asked me if I was some kind of private investigator.

"Not exactly. More like a concerned friend. I was hoping you could tell me something about Robyn that would help me figure out who might want to kill her."

Annie thought it over a moment and then agreed to help. "The first thing you should know is that Robyn was living a lie," she said. As she told me the details, I struggled to listen as I heard the whine of sirens in the distance. They were definitely getting louder. When a police helicopter flew overhead and began to circle low above the park, it all but totally drowned her out. Between the thwack of the helicopter and the shrill sirens, I only got the bare bones of the story. I caught a glimpse of flashing lights as two black-and-whites zipped into the parking lot.

"For once, it isn't anything we did," I said to Dinah with a laugh. But even so, we were like lemmings and followed the crowd to the parking lot to see what was going on.

When we got closer, I grabbed Dinah's arm. A group of people were standing around the greenmobile pointing at the trunk as the cops approached. One of the uniforms had his nightstick in hand and was about to smash in the window. I pushed through the crowd to find out what was going on. Then I heard it. A voice was calling from inside the trunk.

"Hey, get me out of here. Help me, please! Somebody, pick me up. Hurry before it's too late." It stopped for a moment than began again with the plaintiff cry.

I dove through the crowd and grabbed the police officer's arm just before his tool hit the glass. Not a good move. His partner had my hands behind my back and cuffs on before I could blink.

"I have the key," I said, trying to point toward my pocket with my elbow.

The officer who'd handcuffed me stuck her hand in my pocket and snatched the key. She fumbled a moment, realizing it was an old-fashioned key and not some clicker device before using it to unlock the trunk. She jerked it open and started rummaging through the assorted junk back there. Did they really think there was a person hidden under my recyclable grocery bags?

A moment later, a black Crown Victoria drove over the sidewalk into the parking lot. Barry was out of the car with the motor still running. I don't even think he even saw me before he pushed through the crowd to get to the open trunk. Just as he did, my phone started again. His expression went from tense to rolling his eyes in a split second as he found my purse and pulled out my whining BlackBerry.

When the crowd realized what was calling for help, they started to laugh. Even the cops joined in. They took the cuffs off and I reached for my phone, but Barry held on to it.

"I don't know why Fields even gave this phone to you. It's nothing but trouble," Barry said with a dark look. He reprogrammed it to have a regular ring. "That should keep you out of trouble until we can get you a new phone."

When I looked back toward the playground, Annie was gone.

CHAPTER 24

DINAH AND I HAD LEFT MY HOUSE WITHOUT SO much as a cup of coffee. After all the excitement, we both needed something for sustenance, so we headed for Caitlin's Cupcakes. Recently Caitlin had branched off into savory items. She called them cupcakes because they were that size, but they were more like mini quiches and popovers. As soon as we got there, I called CeeCee to tell her what I'd learned from the nanny, but as soon as she heard the word *bombshell*, she insisted I come directly to her place to talk because she was worried about who might be listening. Frankly, it was just a bunch of hungry Tarzanians who seemed more concerned that someone might butt in line, but I saw her point.

"Come in, come in," CeeCee said, holding back the two yipping Yorkies as Dinah and I slipped in the door. Once we were inside and the Yorkies released, CeeCee looked at my empty hands. "I thought you were at Caitlin's," she said. "You didn't bring anything with you? I'm dying to try the new items. I heard the popovers are heavenly and no sugar added," she said. CeeCee was suddenly trying to curb her sweet tooth now that *Making Amends* was close to going back into production.

"I thought you were so anxious to hear what I found out. You should have seen the line." Dinah nodded in agreement. CeeCee let out a disappointed sigh as we stood in the entrance hall.

"I'd offer you coffee, but Rosa is off today. You know me, I'd burn water." She gestured toward the living room. "We might as well go in there."

"I could make the coffee," I offered and CeeCee immediately brightened.

"And," she said expectantly. I looked at her blankly and she rolled her eyes. "Dear, nobody has just coffee. There has to be something that goes along with it."

Dinah and I were hungry, too, since we 'd now missed breakfast and Caitlin's, so after seeing that Rosa kept the place stocked with the basics, I offered to make a baked pancake, which was really close to a giant popover.

"How wonderful. We can talk as you cook. Let me get Nell." We went into the kitchen, and she called Nell on the intercom. I started on the pancake while we waited for CeeCee's niece. When she came in, I was struck by the change in her. She looked exhausted and it was the kind sleep wouldn't help.

She greeted us and then looked at me with tense eyes. "Aunt CeeCee told me you said the cops are just pretending they know who dropped off the box of Nature's Sweetie at the station. I'm guessing that's why Detective Gilmore called and wants to talk to me again. She's going to try to pin it on me?"

CeeCee put her arm around her niece's shoulder but spoke to me. "I had to tell her. I thought it was better that she be forewarned." CeeCee's tone brightened. "But Molly has some bombshell information that will probably fix everything.

I wasn't sure if it would fix anything, but it would certainly shake things up. Dinah put on the coffee while I turned on the oven to preheat and cut some butter into a heavy cake pan. I began to beat the eggs with a whisk.

"Well," Nell said before leaning against the counter in a depressed slouch.

"You remember that Robyn said her parents were dead and how she resented your so-called connections?" I said and Nell nodded.

"How about this—her parents aren't dead. And you'll never guess who they are."

All eyes were on me. Even though Dinah knew what I was going to say, she'd still gotten caught up in the suspense. "Her parents are Becca Ivins and Derek Trousedale."

Nell looked shocked. "You mean the whole orphan thing was a scam." There was more life in Nell's face than I'd seen in a while as the information sank in. "That's too weird. You know she was working on the show that featured them? The title was 'Enduring Hollywood Couples' or something." Nell shook her head with disbelief. "And she was on me for having help getting the job."

"Well, the part about Robyn doing it on her own is true. Becca and Derek weren't really interested in being parents. They were totally involved with their careers and with each other. Robyn was brought up by the nanny until she went to boarding school. She wanted nothing from her parents, not even their name. She's been on her own, making her own way, since she got out of college. She even worked as a nanny herself. She worked for someone who works on the *Barbara Olive Overton* show. That was her in."

Nell was stunned. While I finished putting together the rest of the ingredients, she went and got her laptop. I put the pan in the oven to melt the butter and she powered up the computer. A few minutes later, I pulled out the pans and poured in the batter. I returned them to the oven and set the timer.

Nell started to search online. She found a Web site for the

couple and clicked through everything, but there was no mention of any children. It did, however, speak glowingly of their charity work, describing them as being Hollywood's sweethearts even after all these years, who selflessly used their celebrity status to help those less fortunate. Nell went through a bunch of other sites and finally found something that mentioned the couple had chosen to protect their family by refusing to talk about it.

"No doubt some publicist thought of that," I said. My late husband, Charlie, had been in public relations, and he'd talked about how to put a spin on things so that a negative became a positive. Nell kept looking and finally found an old picture.

"Look," she said, holding it where we could all see. There was a photo of Becca and Derek with a little girl in a sundress. The caption said, "Star couple at the beach with children." "It says *children*," Nell said, studying the picture. A little boy was crawling on the sand toward the water. "Robyn must have a brother."

"If he didn't drown," Dinah said. "Even in the photo, you can see they're not involved with the kids." I studied the body language and realized Dinah was right. Becca was holding Robyn's arms, but it was stiff and posed rather than loving. The actress seemed to have a much stronger connection with the camera than her daughter.

CeeCee nodded at the screen as if the picture confirmed some thought of her own. "Now maybe you understand why I didn't have children. At least I was honest enough to acknowledge that my career came before anything and that I might be a little self-absorbed."

Nell went and hugged her. "I love you anyway, Aunt CeeCee."

CeeCee appeared shocked. "Oh, then you agree that I'm self-absorbed. I thought one of you would at least try to argue with that comment. Think about all my work for Hearts and

Barks. I help out at the women and children's shelter on holidays." Her gaze moved over us and she seemed genuinely concerned. "And there's the crochet group. If I was so self-absorbed, I'd just turn it over to Adele and say the heck with it."

"You're right. You do spend lots of time thinking of others," I said. CeeCee still looked a little fragile. I nodded to Dinah and we all stepped in for a group hug.

"What would I do without my friends and niece," CeeCee said, regaining her good humor. She sniffed the air. "I might not know how to cook, but I know how things are supposed to smell, and that pancake smells done."

I popped it out of the oven and the fragrance was even more intense and more delicious. Nell got plates and we all sat down at the kitchen table and divided it up.

"Do you know them?" Nell asked after downing her last piece.

CeeCee laughed. "People think all celebrities know each other. The real truth is, Becca and Derek are on a different level than I am and have always been. They're stars and I'm an actor."

"You're a star. What about the *CeeCee Collins Show?*" Nell protested. "And *Caught By a Kiss?* There's even Oscar buzz. What have those two done?"

"They've both won Oscars, honey. But what they don't have and I'm grateful for, is a niece like you who wants to stick up for me."

I interrupted the mutual admiration society and got back to the real issue at hand.

I told Nell that Pierce Sheraton has mentioned that Robyn had promised him some kind of scoop. I'd also heard Talia mention something about some plan Robyn had for a surprise on the show. Nell's eyes got big. "What if it had to do with her parents?"

"What if she was going to ruin the tribute to them by

revealing what they were really like as parents?" CeeCee said. "Like in the middle of the show come forward and confront them."

"And what if they found out?" Dinah added.

CeeCee nodded. "Something like that would tarnish their image forever. Knock them off their pedestals."

We all looked at each other, and I know we were thinking the same thing. How far would they go to protect their image? Would they murder their own child? Finally CeeCee spoke.

"I've heard of wanting to kill to get a part. . . ."

CHAPTER 25

I GOT TO THE BOOKSTORE AROUND NOON AND went right to the yarn department. No surprise, Elise and Rhoda were hanging out at the table. Elise seemed stuck on turning out black cell phone covers with red decorations. Though Rhoda had talked her into letting go of the vampire connection and she'd started adding things like red heart-shaped buttons. I began putting out some new yarn we'd just gotten in, which was dangerous. It was all I could do not to set some aside for myself. Barry's shelves would be overflowing before they were even finished.

As soon as I had time for a break, I went into the café. CeeCee had pulled me aside before Dinah and I had left and asked me to talk to Mason. Even if Nell didn't want a lawyer, maybe he could offer some advice.

As soon as I sat down at a table by the window, I tried calling him at his office. I was sure it would work out better than when I'd reached him home and not alone.

"What's up, Sunsh—Molly?" he said. Hmm, so my nickname was dead. No doubt this other woman was his sunshine now. He was polite but distant as I told him about the sweetener drop off and CeeCee's concern.

"Just tell her to say nothing," he said. Then I brought up who Robyn's parents were. I thought for a moment that he was interested.

"I had no idea Becca and Derek had any kids," he said, then his voice flattened and he asked if there was anything else. I thought there probably was, but I was so unnerved by how he was acting, I couldn't remember, and we hung up.

Bob dropped off a red-eye just in time. I needed something to perk me up because the call had totally bummed me out. I could deal with Mason meeting someone but not losing him as a friend. Dinah had said that Mason had probably faced I was more or less engaged to Barry and he decided to move on.

"I'll just have to get used to it," I said to myself, feeling my lip tremble. I swallowed back my tears and told myself I had to be a big girl. I'd taken to sticking a hook and wad of yarn in my pocket for times like this. I took it out and started working on another cell sock. Bob had his computer on the counter and, after delivering my drink, went back to hammering away, no doubt on his screenplay. I glanced around at the tables and nobody was talking—everybody seemed to be hovering over a computer or reading a book. I hadn't even noticed D. J. before.

The quiet ended abruptly when the door whooshed open and Pierce Sheraton came in. *Came in* sounds a little tame. He rushed in and surveyed the area and focused in on Bob.

"Hey, there," he said. "Did you find a little black notebook?"

Bob must have been lost in tales of the werewolf planet. He glanced up at the sound, but it took a moment before he realized who was there. Bob's eyes lit up and he straightened.

"Sorry, I was just taking a moment to work on my script." There was heavy emphasis on the word *script*, and Bob waited

expectantly for Pierce to pick up on it, but there was no response. While Bob checked behind the counter and handed
over the lost notebook, he kept talking about his screenplay.
He was doing a good job of pitching it by likening it to other
hit movies. He said it was like *Star Wars* with fur, and I noticed a flicker of interest from Pierce. Bob upped the ante by
offering Pierce a coffee drink. The entertainment reporter
could be a good connection for Bob, and I was curious to see
how it was going to play out, but I got interrupted.

Just then Rayaad come up to me and jostled my arm.
"Here she is," our cashier said. I was surprised to see Annie
the nanny was with her. Rayaad went back to her station.

"I'm sorry to disturb you while you're working, but I
didn't know any other way to contact you," Annie said. She
explained she was on an errand for her employer and only had
a few minutes but accepted my invitation to sit. She picked
up the cell sock I was working on and admired it.

"I don't know if you know, but Robyn has a brother," she
began. "Miles is nothing like her. He took all the rejection
from his parents badly and was a cliché of a Hollywood kid
with too much money and too much time." She shook her
head with dismay. "He struggled with a drug problem for
years." Her face brightened. "But he's doing okay now. He
used to be a resident at the halfway house, but now he's a
counselor." She digressed and said she didn't normally stay
this connected with her charges, but seeing how their parents
had shut them out had left her with a feeling of responsibility
for them. She wanted me to know that Robyn had a soft spot
for her brother and had done what she could to help him. I
was still processing the information she'd given me when she
asked me for a favor.

"I go to the halfway house once a month to teach a crochet
class. I'm sure I don't have to tell you about the tranquilizing
benefits of it. It's good for them to keep their hands busy, too.
I'm sure this impatient crochet would appeal to them. The

idea they could make something fast might encourage more of the residents to join us, and maybe they could even use the items for a fund-raiser." She paused and smiled. "I know this is all last minute, but the class is in a few days, and I was wondering if you would be willing to come along and show them how to make one of these." She held up my cell sock.

My brain was clicking. Robyn's brother was another piece of the puzzle and talking to him seemed like an excellent idea. And I didn't mind spreading the word of crochet. I told her the impatient crochet wasn't really my idea, but I'd be happy to go with her and help show the group how to do it. I could bring patterns for some small items and everything. Annie seemed pleased and we set a time to go there together.

I mentioned the boy doll I'd rescued from the trash. "Did that belong to Miles?" Annie seemed surprised.

"I didn't know Robyn kept it. Yes, I made them each a doll when I was taking care of them. I do it for all the kids in my charge."

"Should I bring it for Miles?" I asked.

Annie nodded. "I think he'd like that."

As she was getting ready to leave, I threw a few more questions at her about Robyn, but all I managed to find out was that the celebrity couple knew about their daughter's death and that was why they were at the memorial service. But they had decided it was best for everyone not to publically acknowledge their relationship. I suspected the only ones it was best for was them. I wanted to ask if she thought the couple capable of murder, but she looked at her watch and rushed off.

The rest of the day went by in a blur of books and yarn, and it was dark when I drove home. As I pulled into my driveway, I saw Barry's Tahoe parked on the street in front of my house. Barry and Jeffrey were walking toward me when I got out of my car.

"We're just coming from open house at school," Barry said

as an explanation. I was glad that Barry had made it to the event, though the expression on his son's face made me wonder if he felt the same. We all walked into the backyard together just like a regular family.

"Any more problems with your cell phone?" Barry said. I was relieved to see he was smiling. If we were going to be together, he had to have a sense of humor. I asked how he'd happened to show up and he laughed.

"Babe, all I had to hear was the color and make of the car. How many blue green 1993 190 E Mercedes, do you think there are?" He unlocked the back door with his key and slipped on the lights. Cosmo was waiting by the door and ran outside. Jeffrey went on ahead, saying he would feed them.

"Have you eaten?" I asked. Barry said he'd taken Jeffrey out after the school thing.

"Sushi," he said with an unhappy face. "I can't believe my kid wants to eat raw fish."

When we were out of earshot of Jeffrey, I asked Barry if he'd had the "talk" with him yet.

"I'm waiting for the right time," he said, obviously uncomfortable. "And some noisy restaurant with the tables on top of each other isn't the place." As we passed the hall that led to Samuel's room, I noticed a stack of moving boxes against the wall.

I went to check them out and Barry followed. "I wonder what this is about. I told Samuel not to worry about getting a place. Better for him to take his time than move in with the wrong people," I said.

"He's an adult. I'm sure he can figure it out." I detected a note of pleasure in Barry's voice and called him on it.

"Of course the idea that he's moving on sets well with me. Then we can fix your house up and put it on the market."

"Hey, hold on," I said, suddenly feeling like I was being rushed into a decision.

Barry's voice got a tired sound. "I know you still haven't

officially said yes. You know you are going to. We're good together." He was hesitant to act affectionate in front of Jeffrey, concerned it would make him feel uncomfortable. He hesitated to act affectionate when Samuel was around because of the way Samuel looked at him made him feel uncomfortable. But here in the hallway away from everyone, he put his arms around me and held me against him.

I started to tell him about the rest of my day. It was fine until I told him that I wasn't buying the tainted sweetener to discredit the company theory, and I explained why I thought Becca Ivins and Derek Trousedale were valid suspects in Robyn's murder.

He listened, but I could tell by the way he was breathing he didn't really want to hear about it. But he still got an A for effort. He also didn't tell me to stay out of it. It would have been nicer, though, if I could shoot ideas around with him, and if he'd share information.

Jeffrey called out that he was finished with the dogs and then said he'd forgotten he had homework. Reluctantly Barry left my side and went with him. "If we were married . . ." he said with heat coming off his eyes.

Once they'd gone, I realized I hadn't eaten and made myself a salad out of whatever was in the crisper. It was the one part of the refrigerator that didn't seemed to get ravaged by Samuel, Barry and Jeffrey. The house seemed quiet without Samuel there and with Barry and Jeffrey gone.

I thought about Mason. He'd be interested in hearing about my potential meeting with Robyn's brother. He'd be interested in who I had for suspects. Or he would have been. I knew I'd said I'd only call his office from now on, but I punched in his cell number anyway. When it went to voice mail, I hung up.

CHAPTER 26

As soon as the group heard about the plan to teach crochet at the halfway house, they all wanted to help, but since it was short notice, not everyone could come. Dinah had a class, Sheila had to work, CeeCee had a meeting about the new season of her show. Oscar buzz might be nice, but she was concerned about keeping her paycheck. Nell said her reason for not going was that she felt like too much of a beginner to be much help, but I knew the truth was she didn't want to meet Robyn's brother. It wasn't a secret that the cops had their eye on her in the death of his sister. How friendly would he be, even if she was there to help.

The one person I was hoping wouldn't come, of course, did. When Mrs. Shedd heard Adele wanted time off to help at a rehab place, she was all for her going. Our boss was very generous when it came to any kind of charity or good deed. So the three of us headed over the hill and to the beach town of Venice. I was always struck by how the light was totally different by the ocean than in the Valley. All the moisture in the air caught the sun and made it iridescent.

The building appeared to be an old hotel or rooming house. Annie signed us in, and we went to a large room on the first floor.

Annie had brought balls of cotton yarn and had a cup full of hooks. I took out a wad of papers and set them on a coffee table. Rhoda had been all for the plan and agreeable about me making copies of her directions to hand out. Adele staked out the middle of the room as the participants came in. The four women and two men situated themselves on the couches and chairs around the room. A young man, holding a clipboard, came in last. He hugged Annie, and before she introduced us, I knew by his resemblance to Robyn that he was her brother, Miles.

On the drive in, Annie had told me more about him. He'd kept the last name Trousedale and was still hoping for some kind of relationship with his parents. Annie confided that she knew Miles' problems had shut the door forever on that. It was a Pandora's box they weren't going to open. Robyn had stuck by her brother through everything and had found the halfway house for him.

Though he appeared to be putting on a good face, Annie said Robyn's death was devastating to him, and he was very angry that the police hadn't arrested anybody. She was concerned about him backsliding. "But I can only get involved so far. Don't get me wrong, I care about Miles, but I'm not family." Finally, she admitted that she was still being paid by their parents to stay in touch with them, though Robyn and Miles had never known.

I watched the young man in loose jeans and a blue polo shirt with the collar up perch on the arm of the sofa. He appeared to be there as a supervisor.

I was happy to give Adele center stage when it came to a demonstration. No matter what our differences were, I never denied that she was superior at crochet. And it meant so much to her to be the center of attention. Once she'd given them all the idea how to do impatient crochet, Adele supervised while Annie handed out supplies and I gave them each a copy of the directions to make a cell sock.

The three of us helped the six of them get started. Then we just watched as they worked. I took the opportunity to talk to Miles and immediately noticed that he was much softer than his sister. Something about him tugged at my heart. He seemed very needy, like someone who longed to be hugged and reassured. But at the same time, he was aware of being in charge and responsible for the residents in the room. It was as though he was handling his need by helping others. Knowing everything I did, my heart went out to him.

I took the crocheted boy doll out of my bag and offered it to him.

Miles' eyes got round when he saw it, and then instinctively he picked it up and held it to his chest. Both dolls had been dressed in moss green crocheted clothing. Robyn's doll had a dress with a pocket and pink flowers along the hem. Miles' had overalls in the same color with a tiny pink hankie sticking out of the pocket on the front. A moment later, he set it down as if he'd suddenly remembered where he was.

"What were you doing with the doll?" he asked. His demeanor had changed and he seemed wary.

I didn't give exact details about where I'd found the doll, but I mentioned I was investigating his sister's death. I explained I was an amateur sleuth and my real job was working at the bookstore. I gave him my card as a visual aid. I was surprised when his expression hardened.

"I don't know what they're waiting for. Why don't they just arrest that production assistant and lock her up?"

He didn't want to let go of Nell as the prime suspect, but while the group continued on their project, I worked on him. I explained I'd been there when Robyn died and that I knew Nell and was sure she'd had nothing to do with it. "I have reason to believe that your sister had a plan for one of the shows she was working on. Do you know anything about it?"

He took a moment to think. "I know Robyn was worried about someone she worked with. Another person had been up for the job as segment producer. Robyn thought the woman hadn't taken it well when she got it. Maybe it had something to do with that."

I took a moment to absorb what he said. I had to admit that Talia hadn't seemed very broken up about Robyn's death. And it was impossible to ignore that Talia now had the job she'd been passed over for before. As I was thinking that she certainly could have sent the box of sweetener, Miles said something else.

"Robyn said a bunch of things about her job. I can't remember it all. Just that she was working on something that would either make Barbara Olive Overton look really good or get Robyn fired."

I asked him if he knew who the guests were on the shows Robyn was working on. I wasn't really surprised when he claimed ignorance. No doubt telling him his star-couple parents were being featured would have been awkward for Robyn since the siblings' feelings about their parents wasn't the same.

"I asked my sister if she was sure she knew what she was doing, taking a big chance like that." He looked me right in the eye. "I tried to get her to tell Barbara Olive Overton about what she had planned."

"Did she?" I asked. His eyes burned with intensity and he made an uncertain shrug in response. Silence hung between us. Was it possible that the talk show host was involved in Robyn's death? "Well, if you think of anything else." I pointed to my cell number on the card. I started to move away, but he stopped me.

"I forgot. The last time my sister came here, she gave me a weird framed photo of herself."

I asked if I could see it. He seemed a little hesitant at first but agreed to get it. He left and came back as Annie was winding things up with the crocheters.

When he handed me the photo in a flowery silver frame, I almost choked. It was similar to the picture I'd seen in the box of Robyn's things, as if it had been taken at the same time. She was in the funny hat, and there was a hole next to her. "She must have said something when she gave it to you," I said. He thought for a moment and finally spoke.

"She did, but I can't remember exactly what. Something like she couldn't tell me about it then, but she'd explain it later." He hung his head. "That was the last time I saw her." His voice trailed off, and the sadness in it touched my heart. No matter what Robyn had been to anyone else, her brother had definitely loved her.

An hour later, Adele and I were trooping through the café on the way to the bookstore.

"Pink, why were you hanging out with the guy with the clipboard? He wasn't even crocheting," Adele said. Apparently, Adele had been listening to her MP3 player on the drive in and missed Annie's whole story. When I explained who Miles was, she got all huffy.

"You should have told me you were investigating. I could have helped. You know, we could have played good cop, bad cop or something."

I said a silent prayer that she hadn't known. "Thanks for the thought, but I doubt it would have gotten me any more than I got. He said something about his sister's job, and then he showed me a photo similar to the one I saw before with Robyn's ex-boyfriend cut out of it. I'm hoping he thinks of something else."

"Who's the ex?" Adele asked. When I shrugged and said I didn't have a name, she put her hand on her hip and looked toward Bob for agreement. "If I were Sherlock Pink, I'd be looking for Mr. Missing."

Bob seemed to ignore her comment. He was up to his elbows in brownies for Salute to Chocolate. D. J. was standing at the counter with his empty mug, and Bob stopped cutting the squares long enough to give him black coffee and make me my trademark drink.

"Pink, you're a caffeine addict," Adele said with a snort before she rushed on to the bookstore.

Thankfully, most of the preparations for Salute to Chocolate had been taken care of, but still I knew once I walked into the bookstore I'd get snagged into doing last-minute stuff, so I let Adele go on ahead and I found a private corner and called Mason's office. Adele's comment had reminded me of what I still hadn't been able to ask Mason. His assistant answered, and when I asked to speak to Mason, he hemmed and hawed and asked what I wanted. Mason had left instructions that he was to take care of anything I needed. I could feel my face falling. This was worse than when I'd called and he wasn't alone. When I told the assistant I wanted the name connected to a license plate number, he sounded doubtful but took the information. If I couldn't get one kind of information, I thought I'd try for another.

"I guess a lot of stuff has changed now that Mason has met someone," I said. "Do you know anything about her?" I asked.

The assistant took a while to answer. "You mean like a girlfriend? Not that he shares that kind of information with me, but I don't think he's got one. He gave me his tickets to the U2 concert at Staples because he had no one to go with."

"Well, then, if he hasn't met someone, why is he being so strange? Is he mad at me?"

The assistant seemed suddenly uncomfortable. "He didn't seem angry. He just said, if you called, I should take care of anything you needed."

I asked if I could speak to Mason directly to straighten things out. He hesitated and finally said he couldn't put me through. When he said Mason had been specific about that, I felt like I'd been punched in the gut. How could I straighten out whatever was wrong if he wouldn't even talk to me?

A bunch of thoughts went through my mind. Was Mason sick? Had I done something to offend him? I was definitely going to find out. Just not now.

I ended the call and went on into the bookstore. Mrs. Shedd and Mr. Royal were waiting for me in the event area.

"Look what Joshua made," Mrs. Shedd said as he carried in a cardboard cocoa bean tree and set it up. Some of the vendors had already brought advertising materials and their chocolate offerings. The main table was clear except for a perfectly centered calligraphy placard with the bookstore name. There was no way the camera could miss it.

D. J. wandered in from the café and checked out the preparations.

"Nice," he said, touching the cardboard tree. No matter how casual he was trying to appear, I knew he was trying to make sure all the arrangements for him were in place. "So what's the plan?"

"We start off with Eduardo reading from *Hot, Hot Chocolate*, since he was the cover model for the book, to loosen up the crowd. Then we'll bring you up, and the crew from the *Barbara Olive Overton* show can film what they need. When you're done, we'll clear out your books, and Alain Des Plaines will do his chocolate-dipping demo," I said.

"Between a cover model and being dipped in chocolate," he said with a grin. "Sounds good to me. By the way, thanks for doing this. I was afraid Robyn's death was going to mess things up." He caught himself. "Sorry, I didn't mean that as cold as it sounded. This bookstore and the café have become like home to me now, and I just wanted to say how much I appreciate everything."

Throughout the rest of the day, even as I finished the setup for the evening, my thoughts kept going back to Mason.

As Mr. Royal and I set up extra folding chairs since free chocolate was likely to bring in a big crowd, I decided that I was going to get to the bottom of the thing with Mason when the evening was done. Making the decision made it a little easier to focus on the event in front of me. Just as I was roping off the event area to keep customers out until the appointed hour, a local food artist rushed in with a fudge sculpture of an open book, along with a brochure showing off centerpieces for everything from weddings to sweet sixteen parties.

As usual, there was more to do than I'd expected, and I had worked straight through without even going home to change. I'd called Samuel to make sure he took care of the animals.

There was a lull in the store around dinner hour, and I rejuvenated with a red-eye and checked out what Adele had done for the kids' department. She wasn't big on the idea of a bunch of kids running around with sticky fingers, so she'd set up games. Leave it to Adele to get something crocheted in it. She'd made a yarn checkerboard with milk chocolate and dark chocolate colored squares. Even the games pieces were yarn circles. She had a number of Candy Land games out, too, and a display of the Chocolate Cookie Man series.

Talia and her crew came in and set up their lighting and put up the notification of filming signs.

People began to filter in and fill up the seats. D. J. had changed into a corduroy sports jacket over his jeans and looked very much the writer. He hung around the front of the area, talking to everybody. Even though this was really just a run-through, I could see it was a big moment for him. People seemed to know who he was and were disappointed when he said they couldn't buy his book yet, since it wasn't officially out for another few weeks. He seemed personable and knew how to work the crowd. I was glad things had worked out.

One of Talia's people brought in a box of D. J.'s books. I'd seen the advance copies, but these were the first with the actual covers. *Back from Hell* was written in jagged letters, and the artwork was dark and murky on the bottom and then it changed to a bright scene above.

Talia still wasn't happy about the staged book signing being patched onto a real event. I was hoping to keep her discontent from spreading to D. J. "Don't worry, it will be fine," I said to both of them.

"Whatever," Talia said with an impatient groan. "Let's get started."

I didn't like her pushiness, but I wanted to get D. J.'s part done with. I was about to step to the front of the crowd when Rayaad, our cashier, threaded through the people and got my attention.

"There's a phone call for you. Someone named Miles said something about a photograph," Rayaad said over the din of conversation. When I made a move to follow Rayaad, Talia put her hand on my arm.

"You're kidding, right? You can't seriously be taking a call now," Talia said, gesturing toward the film crew.

"It's important," I said, but Talia rolled her eyes in disbelief. It didn't make any difference even when I explained who Miles was and what information he might have. I had no choice but to tell Rayaad to give him my cell number and tell him to call back in an hour.

I moved in front of the table we'd set up and started things off by welcoming everyone and introducing Eduardo. He warmed up the crowd with his reading. When he was done, I introduced D. J. and explained the filming. The only thing more appealing than free chocolate was the chance to be on TV. The whole audience began smoothing their hair and sitting up straighter. I stepped aside and let Talia take over. She positioned D. J. and a stack of books before giving directions to the audience. Once she was satisfied, the actual filming began.

D. J. started to do his spiel and I was only half listening, planning how we'd move the books out and Alain Des Plaines things in. I could tell D. J. had gotten to the dramatic part by the way his voice dropped. Just as he was saying something about stealing from a blind musician, there was a rush of noise from the front of the store.

Out of the corner of my eye, I saw a crowd come in, but there was something odd about them. When I turned to get a full view, I saw that they had some kind of antennas on their heads and they were all wearing cream-colored shirts with brown speckles. They ploughed through the bookstore toward the chairs. Now I could see they were spraying something and hear that they were chanting.

Everybody turned around in their seats toward them and even the camera crew stopped filming D. J.

"Vanilla, vanilla," the head guy said. "We demand a voice in the flavor world."

I realized what I thought were antennas were actually *v*'s and they were spraying vanilla scent.

The vanilla people marched to the front of the group and stood right in front of D. J., holding up their fists and chanting, "Vanilla power, the other bean." Now I got all the scribbling on the signs. It had been a bad rendition of a *v* and a fist. Everybody but me and my bosses thought the vanilla-chocolate standoff was planned, and the audience began taking up sides. I saw a bunch of hands go up with their fingers in a *v*.

I should have noticed that Adele was being too quiet in all this. All of a sudden, she came out of the kids' department. She'd wrapped herself in a red shawl and pulled on the Strawberry Patch hat. "Don't forget strawberry," she said. The kids were following her, chanting, "We love strawberry, we love vanilla, we love chocolate."

"Can't we all just get along and make Neapolitan," Adele said, waving the little flashlight around that projected the word *love* on the carpet and then on my shirt.

Mr. Royal rushed up to the front. He took Adele by the arm and waved to the kids around him. "Let's give it up for the strawberry-ice-cream dancers and the vanilla fans." He gestured toward me to get them out of there.

Talia gave us all a dirty look and said she hoped they'd gotten what they needed. I tried to apologize to D. J., but he was following Talia, trying to talk her into waiting until things calmed down and doing the whole thing over again. She shook her head and said something about no overtime in the budget.

Adele and the kids went back to their area, and Mr. Royal and I quickly changed the table over to the cooking demo. Once Alain Des Plaines came up and started doing his chocolate-dipping demonstration, nobody paid any more attention to the vanilla protestors. I noticed some of them ended up finding seats and hanging around for the samples.

The rest of the event was a big success, and when Mrs. Shedd and Mr. Royal checked the sales at the end of the night, they were both smiling as we all closed the store together.

But as soon as I got into the greenmobile, I started thinking about Mason again.

CHAPTER 27

OKAY, I COULD UNDERSTAND HIM BEING DISTANT if he had a girlfriend. I might not like it, but I could understand it. But if he hadn't met someone, why was he cutting me out of his life? I couldn't let it be. I knew I might end up really embarrassed, but I was willing to risk it to find out what was going on. He could dodge me on the phone, but not in person.

It was after ten and Ventura Boulevard was quiet as I drove to Encino and turned on his street. I parked in front of his large ranch-style house and looked past the low fence and lights that showed off the soft hills in the front yard beautifully landscaped with pungent rosemary, white-barked beech trees, and rosy-flowered azaleas. The lights were on in the house and I was sure he was home.

It's Mason, I told myself as nerves made my heart thud against my chest. Mason who'd come through for me countless times. Again I wondered if he was sick or that something terrible had happened. Whatever, I wanted to know. I marched up the walk and rang the bell. From deep in the house, I heard Spike go into a barking frenzy. I stood there for a moment and suddenly had a fear that Mason would see it was me and simply not answer the door.

The barking got louder, and as I heard the handle turn, I choked as I tried to swallow. And then there I was, face-to-face with Mason. He was wearing gray sweats and his face looked flushed.

His lips began to curve into a smile, but he seemed to force them back into a straight line, and he narrowed his eyes. Not a good sign. "Hello," he said finally in a flat tone.

"Aren't you going to invite me in?" I said. When he hesitated, I lost it. "Tell me what's wrong." I tried unsuccessfully to keep the panic out of my voice. "I thought you met someone. I could understand that. I really could, but your assistant said you hadn't. Are you sick? Why won't you talk to me? What is it? Just tell me what's wrong and I'll leave." I hadn't meant to, but by now I was crying.

Mason's head dropped back in exasperation and he took my arm. "C'mon in," he said, pulling me inside. Spike wasn't sure what the story was and yipped behind me as Mason walked me back to the den. "Sit," he said, pointing at the soft leather couch. He went out and came back with two glasses of red wine. "I was on the elliptical," he said by way of explanation for the sweats. "But I guess that's done for now." He handed me one of the glasses of wine and took a sip from the other. He sat down on a chair across from me. "You better drink some of that," he said, nodding toward my glass.

"That bad?" I followed his orders and took a sip of the wine. I have no tolerance for alcohol and the mouthful went right to my head. "Well . . ." I said

There was a long silence. "You're not going to like this," Mason said at last.

"I don't care. Tell me," I demanded.

Mason sighed. "Barry talked to me. He said if I cared about your happiness, I'd get out of your life. He's convinced the reason you won't commit to him is because of our friend-

ship and because Samuel moved back home. I'm just guessing, but I bet he had a similar conversation with your son."

For a moment, I was speechless. Now I understood the
moving boxes Samuel had brought in from the garage. "Why
didn't you tell me?" I said, still processing the information.

"Barry made me promise to say nothing. He said if I told
you, it would just make problems."

"For who?" I asked.

Mason shrugged. "Probably for him."

I got up and started pacing. "I can't believe you listened to
him. I can't believe he said that." I was half talking to Mason
and half mumbling to myself.

"I only did it because he said it was about your happiness,
which I'm all for, even if I don't think being a cop's wife living in a condo in Simi Valley is exactly the key to it." Mason
paused. "You can't blame him. If you and I were engaged, I
wouldn't want you hanging around with him."

"He told you about the condo in Simi Valley?" I said.
"We're not engaged." I waved my bare hand and Mason shook
his head.

"But he thinks if he gets rid of me and Samuel, you will
be." Mason watched me as I walked around the room. "I was
kind of hoping you'd do something like this." He was trying
to keep his lips from grinning. He knew I was fuming.

I pulled out my cell phone and called Samuel and told
him no matter what anyone had said, he didn't have to worry
about moving out until he was ready. Then I called Barry. I
got his voice mail and left a message for him to call me
ASAP, no matter how late.

I was about to put my phone away when I noticed there
was a voice mail and realized I'd turned my phone to silent
during the bookstore event and never turned it back to a
ring. The message was from Miles Trousedale. Oh no, in all
the fuss with the chocolate event, I'd forgotten about telling
him to call back. He didn't give details, but said he wanted

to tell me something about the photo we'd been discussing and would call back the next day.

I got up to leave, but Mason shook his head and extracted my car keys from my purse. "Friends don't let friends drive drunk," he said, closing his hand around the keys.

"I had a half a glass of wine," I protested

"For you, that's enough to be impaired."

My smile might have been a little loopy, and I was actually glad to sit down again on the pillowy sofa. "Well, at least you said we're friends again." Then I looked at him intently, but half joking. "But don't get any ideas about taking advantage of me; it was only a half a glass of wine."

Mason chuckled. "Don't worry, Sunshine, if anything ever goes on between us, I want you to be one hundred percent present so you know exactly what's happening." Even the chuckle couldn't hide the intensity of his voice, which only added to my rubber-leg feeling.

He sat back and abruptly changed the subject to something with less heat. "As long as you're staying, you might as well tell me about the message you were so upset about."

I think we were both relieved and I began to talk about the case. I told him about meeting Robyn's brother and the missed phone call and what he'd said in the message.

"I can't wait to hear what he has to say about that photograph. Did your assistant tell you why I called? It would really help if I could find out the identity of the missing head," I said. Mason said he'd take care of it the following day. Then he asked me how my investigation was going.

"This case is so confusing. Just when I think things are going one way, something else shows up. There's the issue of Mr. Missing. Who knows how he reacted to the breakup. Maybe he decided to cut her out of life in general. Then from what Robyn's brother said, she was worried about Talia Canon's reaction to her getting the promotion to segment producer. Talia certainly seems happy to have taken over. Really anybody could have sent the tainted sweetener. There are these peripheral people like Pierce Sheraton, D. J., Bob and even Barbara Olive Overton. It sounds like Robyn had taken something about the show in her own hands. Maybe the host found out and wasn't happy about it. But then the whole issue of Robyn's parents showed up. I don't know if they knew she was the segment producer working on their appearance. Suppose they found out and figured out she was going to ambush them?"

"I just saw something with the celebrity couple's name on it," Mason said. He excused himself to go look for something. A few moments later, he returned and handed me a thick invitation for a charity celebrity golf tournament in Palm Springs. It was an all-day affair, with a banquet and auction capping it off. Becca Ivins and Derek Trousedale were the guests of honor.

"Hmm, interesting, Barbara Olive Overton is one of the sponsors," I said. Then it rang a bell in my brain. Hadn't the golf tournament been listed on the wipe-off board in the production office? I asked if he was going.

"I know where you're headed," he said with a knowing look. "You think it would be an opportunity to meet Becca and Derek." I nodded in agreement. "I know for sure I'm not going. I have a family thing. But the firm will probably buy a bunch of tickets. I'll see what I can do."

By now the wine had worn off completely and Mason gave my keys back. He walked me out to my car while Spike protested at being left behind. The temperature had dropped to somewhere in the fifties and I shivered. Mason pulled off his sweatshirt and handed it to me. As soon as I put it on, I was enveloped in his scent and the remnants of his body heat.

He waited while I started the motor, and when I opened the window, he leaned in. "I'm glad we're friends again. Call me after you talk to Barry. No matter what time." He ruffled my hair and then stepped away from the car. As I drove away, I saw him wave before he went back to his house.

Now to deal with Barry.

CHAPTER 28

The phone ringing woke me and I sat up with a start. The lights were still on and I'd fallen asleep in a chair in the den. As I reached for the phone I looked at my watch. All I saw was the hour hand and it was on the four. It had to be Barry.

He was calling from his car. There was concern in his voice as he asked if everything was okay.

"You're not in jail again or anything?" he said. I wasn't sure if he was joking, trying to lighten the moment, or he really thought I was.

"I need to talk to you in person," I said once I'd assured him there was no emergency.

By now I was no longer angry. The thing was, I understood what he'd tried to do, but just because I understood didn't mean it worked for me. He said he'd be right over and my heart began to thud in anticipation.

I was sitting on the couch in the living room when I heard his key in the lock. Barry was a good detective, so of course, he'd figured out something bad was up. He held out a bouquet of mixed flowers, saying he'd gotten them at the all-night market. He looked exhausted, but he forced his face into an upbeat expression. "So what's up, babe?" He glanced around for the animals. Blondie was asleep in her chair and the cats were sacked out somewhere. Cosmo woke up when he heard the door, but just like Barry, the black mutt had figured something was up and sat across the room, staring at us.

"I saw Mason," I said. "And he told me everything."

Barry's expression darkened. "He's a lawyer, I should have figured I couldn't trust him to keep his word." He laid the flowers on the coffee table and I made no move to get up and get a vase.

"I don't want to move to Simi Valley," I said. "I don't want to make a fresh start." He'd flopped on the couch next to me and I turned to face him. "You can't just cut people out of my life and think suddenly everything will be different. And you can't assume you know what makes me happy."

Barry blew out his breath a few times but didn't say anything. "It's not that I don't love you," I said. "Can't we just keep things the way they are?"

Barry seemed to be considering what to say. He sat forward. "They can't stay the way they are because I want us to have a life together. I want us to live someplace that isn't filled with memories and where I feel like a guest. I want someone who is committed to me, not hanging out with a bunch of troublemakers raiding garbage cans in the middle of the night. I don't want to have to share you with everybody." He didn't say it, but I knew he meant Mason.

It was my turn, and I had a hard time saying it, but I spoke my piece. "I understand what you think goes with getting married. But I don't want to give up the life I've made for myself. I love my job and my friends and even raiding garbage cans in the middle of the night. I don't want to get married. It's not you. I don't want to marry anybody right now." I paused and looked at him "Why can't we just keep things the way they are?"

"You can't have it both ways. Either you're committed to me or you're not."

For a few moments, we sat there in silence as the gravity of the situation sank in. We had reached an insurmountable impasse, and there was only one thing left for me to do. My body felt heavy and worn down as I got up and went in the other room. I came back with the little blue box and held it out. He stared at it for a long time before standing up and finally taking it. Then he walked to the door and left without a word.

I sat on the couch, stunned. It wasn't the same as when we'd had arguments and broken up. There was no anger, no heat, just resignation. This time, I knew it was really over. I felt like a piece of my heart had been ripped out and all the implications sunk in. I'd never find out what happened with Jeffrey and his girlfriend. With no one keeping an eye on maintenance, my house would fall apart. No more coming home to find Barry working on something. No more Barry. Just like that, gone.

I couldn't seem to get myself off the couch and then the phone rang. For a moment, I thought Barry had reconsidered. That he'd realized something was better than nothing. But it was Mason. I heard him blow out his breath when I told him what happened.

"I didn't think he'd be so all or nothing," Mason said.

"Neither did I," I said as my eyes began to water.

CHAPTER 29

DESPITE THE LACK OF SLEEP, THE NEXT MORNING I dragged myself to work, though I only made it as far as the café. The place was quiet. Two women were talking softly in the corner, and D. J. was hovering over his computer at a nearby table. I went over and told him I was sorry about the vanilla people and their interruption. He looked pretty annoyed, but then finally let it go. "It wasn't your fault," he said. "I talked to Talia this morning and she said they'd gotten enough for the clip."

Bob took one look at me and said he was making me a black-eye. I was glad for the pampering and gratefully accepted the cup of coffee with two shots of espresso when he brought it to the table. I was hanging over the brew when Dinah came in a few minutes later to pick up a cup of coffee before she went to the Hooker meeting.

"Molly, you look awful," she said.

"Geez, thanks," I said, trying to force myself to sit up straight.

"I'm sorry. I didn't mean that the way it sounded. I was saying it out of concern."

"When I tell you what happened, you'll know why I look this way." I smiled weakly. "You might even wonder why I don't look worse."

"Spill," Dinah ordered. I began with meeting Robyn Freed's brother and the vanillites storming the Salute to Chocolate. Then I told her about Barry. She almost choked as I told her. As bad as my news was, it was nice to have Dinah there for support.

"You broke up with Barry." Dinah jiggled her head as if she was trying to make sense out of everything. "I can't believe you told me that part last. I think it rates higher than Robyn Freed's brother and a bunch of flavor freaks." Bob set her drink down. "I'm sure Barry will come around. Is he nuts? You're offering him every guy's dream, a relationship with no strings."

"Not his dream, apparently," I said. Then I explained what had caused my showdown with Barry.

"I can't believe he went behind your back." She stopped a moment to think. "Though I do kind of get why he was trying to push Mason out of the picture. You guys have way too much fun together." When I told her about Mason's late-night phone call, she smiled. "I bet Mason wasn't exactly brokenhearted at the news."

"He was very supportive."

Dinah laughed. "I just bet he was. I still say don't count things being over with Barry. You two have broken up before and then made up."

"Not this time. I'm sure it's really over. He already made arrangements to pick up his tools and the things he and Jeffrey had left at my house. He wanted to take Cosmo, too. But he accepted that the little black mutt is better off with me. He has Blondie for a friend and now the two cats, too. I have a nice yard and I'm dependable about taking care of him." I took a drag of my coffee drink, hoping the caffeine would finally kick in and I'd be able to open my eyes all the way. It was tiredness mixed with crying. "It was awful. If he'd slammed the door and been angry, it would have been different. Then I would have thought we could work it out. He was just quiet, with that inscrutable cop face."

CeeCee came in and saw us as she headed toward the counter. She detoured to the table and waved at Bob that she wanted her usual. "Dear, you look awful. Is something wrong?" I leaned on my elbow for support and waved to Dinah to fill CeeCee in. Nell was dragging a few steps behind CeeCee and she finally slouched in one of the chairs.

"That police detective showed up again. She gave me this whole number how they knew I was the one who had dropped off the sweetener. She said they had it on videotape. Then she had the nerve to try to get me to dress up in a hooded sweatshirt and carry an umbrella to see if I matched it." She looked at me and mumbled something derogatory about the speed of my detective skills, but both CeeCee and Dinah gave her dirty looks and explained I was in the middle of a personal trauma.

"That's okay," I said, taking a deep breath and sitting upright. The caffeine at last was beginning to make me feel a little more alert. "I'd rather think about murder than breaking up."

Rhoda and Elise came in and I waited to start the update until they joined us. But then the door opened again. This time it was Sheila. Everyone looked at her and began to talk among themselves about the change in her. She walked taller and her eyebrows were no longer permanently knit together. Now that she had one job instead of a bunch of little ones, she was actually thinking about moving out of the room she'd rented in a house in Reseda and getting an apartment with a roommate. Did I mention that Adele was trying to convince her they should share a place?

Sheila took one look at me and pulled out her emergency crochet stuff. "What's wrong, Molly? You look—"

"Terrible," I said, finishing for her. "I know. Everyone's been telling me."

Adele whooshed in from the bookstore just as Dinah began to tell Sheila about the breakup. I was really tired of hearing the story over and over. It was bad enough going through it.

But as much as I was tired of hearing my own tale of woe, I loved the support everyone gave me. Even Adele's.

"Pink, I'm here for you. We're sisters of the hook. Musketeers in mystery solving." She squeezed me so tightly I could barely breathe.

"Molly was just going to bring us up-to-date on what she's found out investigating Robyn's murder," CeeCee said. Everyone had found chairs and pulled them up to the table. Bob was in the process of bringing drinks over. Without even looking down, the whole group had taken out their crochet projects and begun to work on them.

I didn't know who knew what so I threw all the information out there. "Robyn's parents aren't dead." When I mentioned Becca Ivins and Derek Trousedale, Rhoda started to swoon.

"I loved them in all those comedies with the great dialogue. Remember *The Sailor and the Debutante*, *Mr. and Mrs. Jones*, and *Two Weeks in Geneva*?"

I brought up Miles and the phone message. "I tried to call him this morning but got his voice mail. I'm hoping whatever he remembered is some kind of amazing information that points to Robyn's killer," I said. Nell was incredulous that not only did Robyn have a brother, but she seemed to have cared about him.

Bob came over with a tray of drinks just as I told them about the charity event. Nell let out a loud groan.

"I forgot about that. I was supposed to be there," Nell said, her tone drooping. "It's supposed to be fabulous. It was going to be my chance to go to Palm Springs. Everyone was getting hotel rooms and everything. I heard from the other production assistants that it's really an event for the show. Since Barbara Olive Overton is one of the sponsors, she gets to look like a good guy, she gets a big tax write off, and she has a lot of her upcoming guests there and gets clips to use in their background pieces, which again point out what a good guy Barbara is. Everybody is going to be there but me," she said with a pout.

"Who is everyone?" CeeCee said. "I wasn't invited."

"That's because you already were on the show. They don't need any film on you."

"Mason said his law firm was probably buying a block of tickets," I said.

"Does that mean you're going?" Dinah said.

"Mason isn't going, but maybe I can get a couple of tickets," I said to Dinah. "It would give us a chance to talk to Robyn's parents."

"I bet they're super-VIP tickets," Adele said. "Like right by the head table where Barbara will be sitting." I saw Adele's mind working. "Pink, I have to go, too. It's my big chance to get her to see the light about crochet. We have to do something before she does the knitting show."

"I'm not even sure I'm going," I said by way of an excuse.

Nell sidled close to me. "If I could talk to Barbara herself, I bet I could get my job back. She's always talking about injustices. How about my getting forced into a leave of absence is really a big one." She took my arm. "I know you said you don't have the tickets for sure, but if you do, can I go with?"

I was trying to think of a nice way to tell her it was a bad idea when D. J. came up to the table. He smiled at Nell in a flirty manner and reminded her that they'd met before. "Sorry for eavesdropping," he said, "but I couldn't help but overhear. I didn't realize why I got the invite from Barbara for the golf thing, but I'm sure you're right. It's all about getting another clip for my background piece. They said I could bring a guest." Nell was all set to accept, but CeeCee gave her one of her cease-and-desist shakes of her head.

At the same time, a woman at the counter recognized CeeCee. I'd seen it happen before. People always stared a little too long. A moment later, the woman left her ice tea sitting on the counter and walked over to the table.

"Oh, Ms. Collins, I've been watching you since I was a girl," she said, eyeing her with reverence. CeeCee changed her expression in a split second and smiled sweetly, despite the *since she was a girl* comment. The woman meant well, but it made CeeCee sound older than dust.

"Did you make that?" the woman squealed touching the small purple purse CeeCee was holding. She had just attached a tiny white flower with an iridescent crystal in the middle.

Eduardo came in from the bookstore. "Are we meeting here now?" he said, looking over the overflowing table.

Adele stood up and grabbed her work. "No, c'mon, everyone, let's go to the yarn department where we have some room." CeeCee gave her an annoyed flick of her eyes. Even after all this time, Adele was still trying to take charge of the group.

The coffee had done its job and I felt like myself again. Just as I prepared to get up, Mrs. Shedd came in and looked around.

"There she is," she said as Annie Hoover stepped from behind her. If I had looked awful, the nanny looked worse. The two kids I'd seen her with at the park trailed her.

"It's Miles," Annie said. "He's dead."

CHAPTER 30

I HADN'T NOTICED AT FIRST THAT ANNIE HAD more with her than the kids. Then I saw the man and woman in dark suits. They flashed badges and I told the rest of the Hookers to go on without me. It turned out to be without Adele as well. The man glommed on to Adele, not that she seemed to mind. I watched as she puffed up with importance and wondered if he knew what he was in for. The woman introduced herself as Detective Henderson and explained she was an investigator with the sheriff's department. She was all friendly as she led me outside and said she'd like to ask me a few questions to clarify things. She opened the passenger door of her sedan and gestured for me to get in. The door shut almost before I'd cleared it. She got in the driver's seat and took out her pad. She asked me about the previous day.

"I went to the halfway house with Annie to help teach a certain crochet technique," I said. "What happened to Miles?" She ignored my question. Not a surprise, I knew by now that the law enforcement people tried to keep all the questioning in their hands.

"Ms. Hoover said you were interested in talking to Miles. Why is that?"

I dreaded telling her I was investigating Robyn's death. Along with not wanting to answer questions, law enforcement people weren't all that fond of amateur investigators. The detective just stared at me, waiting for an answer. Finally I just told her the truth. It didn't go over very well, particularly when it was obvious I was investigating to try to prove the cops were wrong.

She had her notebook open and was scribbling down notes. I asked again what had happened to Miles. She was getting impatient and must have realized she might have to give some information to get some.

"He ODed," she said curtly. "We're trying to find out how he got the drugs. Ms. Hoover mentioned that you'd given him a crocheted doll. We found it in his room. The back was cut open as if something had been stashed inside."

"What?" I said in an incredulous tone. This wasn't good. I suddenly felt vulnerable. Had I been set up? "I don't know anything about anything," I said. The detective gave me a disbelieving look and said nothing, and I knew she was using the dead-air technique. But two could play that game. I just sat there and let the silence hang like a stone in the air. She finally cracked.

"Where'd you get the doll? Why did you give it to him? When did you put the drugs in?"

"I don't have anything else to say," I said.

"I'm just trying to clear things up," she said in a friendly voice. When I held my ground, she excused herself and went back into the café. Through the window, I watched as she waved to the detective who was questioning Adele to confer with her.

She doesn't know who she's dealing with, I thought. This was all a ploy and I knew exactly what she was going to say when she came back. She didn't let me down, either. "You might as well just tell me the whole story. Your friend just gave you up," she said with a triumphant air.

For a split second, I wondered if it was true. But then when the detective claimed that Adele had said I'd put drugs in the doll and given Robyn the poisoned sweetener, I knew it was just a detective's trick. Her partner probably said something similar to Adele. There was something wrong about them being able to lie like that, but I knew they did it.

"You're not going to deny that you were present when the victim's sister was poisoned are you?" she said. I admitted to being there, but that was all. She tried to work me some more, but I just stonewalled her. I'd learned enough about how cops worked from Barry to know that saying nothing was my best defense, but I also knew that this wasn't going to be the end of it.

Finally Detective Henderson left. Annie was sitting in the café with her charges. She looked worried. Adele was sitting with her and gave me a suspicious look as I sat down.

"Pink, I can't believe you fingered me," she said.

"I didn't. That's just a detective's trick to try to get confessions. I didn't finger you any more than you fingered me," I said. Adele suddenly avoided my eye and looked down at the table. "You did finger me, didn't you?" I said incredulous.

"I'm sorry, Pink, that detective got me in the corner. I might have mentioned that you were there when Robyn died. He said they were going to arrest me and there'd be no judge to set bail and I'd be stuck in a cell for days."

"Arrest you for what?" I threw up my hands. "Nobody gets it, the cops don't have to tell the truth."

Adele threw herself across the table and almost tackled me with her hug. "Can you forgive me, Pink?" When I took a moment to answer, she got hysterical. "You have to, we're like sisters."

Finally I let her off the hook and she left the café to go back to the yarn department. Annie said she had to get the two kids to some kind of event and gathered them up, along with their chocolate milk. I watched them go out the door as I pulled out my BlackBerry

"Sunshine," Mason said in a happy voice when he picked up the call. No delay this time, as soon as his assistant heard it was me, he put me through. "How are you doing? Do you need some consoling?" he said.

"Not exactly, more like legal help." I told him about Miles and my visit from the sheriff's investigator. I could practically hear Mason sitting taller on the phone as he told me what to do. Basically, if the sheriff's people came back, I was to say nothing and call him. I knew it wasn't a matter *if*, it was more like *when*. Before he signed off, he suggested we get together to talk strategy, maybe over dinner.

When I finally got back to the yarn department, the group had scattered and only Dinah was still there. "What happened?" she said, reading my expression.

If only I'd been able to take Miles' call. A thought went through my mind. What if somebody didn't want me to hear what he had to say?

CHAPTER 31

AFTER THE WHOLE THING WITH BARRY AND NOW being almost accused of providing drugs to Miles, I did the only thing I could do, which was totally put it out of my mind and focus on work. I stayed late at the bookstore to make up for all the lost time. There was plenty to do. We were still cleaning up from Salute to Chocolate. The vanillites had turned out to be peaceful enough, but after they left, I'd begun to notice they'd left bits of vanilla beans everywhere. It was both good and bad. The good part was the bits of bean smelled better than any air freshener you could buy and added a gentle fragrance to the whole place, but the bad part was people had started complaining about being startled when they came across some little brown things they thought were bug parts.

There were books to be put back as well. At least the evening had been a success. Mrs. Shedd and Mr. Royal were both still smiling about the money the store had taken in. If we kept these events happening, maybe we could pull the bookstore back from the brink of disaster. I was running on autopilot by then and was relieved when I got home.

When I walked in, Samuel was in the kitchen grilling a cheese sandwich for himself. The scent of browning butter reminded me that I had forgotten all about eating again. Spatula in hand, he turned toward me.

"I'm not planning on staying here forever," he said.

"I know," I said. I wanted to give his sandy hair a reassuring ruffle, but he was too big for that. "There's no reason to move out until you find the right situation."

He flipped his sandwich on a plate and offered to make me a cup of coffee. He didn't have to say it, but I knew what the offer meant—that I looked like a zombie. He was a professional barista, and making a cup of coffee was an art for him.

I might have been coffeed out from the black-eye and subsequent red-eyes I'd had at work, but I knew if I said no, it would hurt his feelings. I sat down at the kitchen table and watched as he set up a cone filter over a mug and poured in freshly ground coffee and boiling water. The fragrance of the brewing drink overrode the buttery smell of his sandwich.

"Barry came by," he said. I could hear Samuel swallow from across the room, a sure sign he was uncomfortable about the subject. "He said he'd forgotten some stuff." Samuel left the statement hanging as if to ask if it was okay that he'd let Barry go through the house. I told him it was fine. "He left that," Samuel said when he brought the cup of coffee to me. I hadn't noticed the key sitting on the table until Samuel pointed it out. It was all alone, no note. Somehow more than anything else, seeing the key meant *the end*. Tears clouded my vision.

"I'm sorry," Samuel said in a low voice, seeing how I was staring at the key. It was an odd feeling having him trying to console me. I'd always been the one offering sympathy when he'd had a setback.

The doorbell interrupted us. Samuel went to answer it,

and a moment later, he returned with Mason. He took one look at me and appeared concerned.

"Don't even say it. I know how bad I look."

Mason had a supportive smile. "You look fine, just a little tired. No worries. I'm here to take care of everything." He appeared too refreshed, too happy. He eyed my coffee and Samuel offered to make him a cup. There was definitely something different in Mason's vibe. He hugged me in greeting and then joined me at the table and started talking about dinner.

I saw Samuel glance over from his coffee preparations. There was disapproval in his expression. I suppose it did look like one guy out and another one already taking his place. Samuel brought over Mason's coffee and sat down with us. He began to eat his sandwich while Mason launched into how to handle the sheriff's detective.

"What happened now?" Samuel asked, clearly distressed. Mason answered for me and told Samuel what he needed to know—that there was nothing to worry about. "They're just rattling cages, looking for someone to blame. I don't know how that halfway house is run, but I'm pretty sure if he was a counselor, he wasn't a prisoner of the place. If they were going to try to pin it on anybody, I'd think it would be the nanny." He told me again that if they contacted me to refuse to say anything until I talked to him.

I was too tired to mention my thought that someone might not have wanted me to hear what Miles had to say.

In the midst of it, my other son arrived. Peter surprised me by giving me a hug. He was usually more standoffish. He was older than Samuel and so wrapped up in his career as a talent agent that I'd barely seen him lately. I realized Samuel must have called him. I noticed Peter hadn't brought his girl-friend with. He'd brought her over once and I don't think I made the best impression.

"Sorry about the detective," he said. His comment sur-

prised me because Peter had been so open about not liking
Barry. His somber expression disappeared when he held out
his hand to Mason. If Peter had been rooting for me to be
involved with anybody, it had always been Mason.

The three of them began talking, and even with the coffee, their words began to swim in my tired mind. Somewhere
in it all, I put my head down on the table and went to sleep
on my folded arms.

I awoke in the dark and for a moment didn't know where
I was. Then my room came into focus. I was still dressed, on
top of the covers, with an afghan draped over me. Cosmo was
cuddled next to me and the two cats were on the pillow next
to my head. Blondie was in her chair. Vaguely, I remembered
the three of them helping me across the house. I rolled over
and went back to sleep.

By MORNING, I FELT ALL BETTER. NOW THAT MY
mind was clear, all kinds of issues surfaced. I realized I had no
idea what had happened to Miles beyond that he was dead. I
kept thinking about his phone call to me and wondering if it
was related to his death. I shuddered when I realized that when
I'd called him back, he was probably already gone. Were Miles'
and Robyn's deaths related? Since they were brother and sister,
it seemed likely. It also seemed likely that if their deaths were
related, there was a good chance their parents were involved.
Hadn't Annie said Miles was still hoping for a relationship
with his parents, but it was a Pandora's box they weren't going
to open. Maybe they or someone acting for them had decided
to make sure that box never got opened.

I was sure the nanny had more information and regretted
that I hadn't gotten a phone number from her. But then I knew
where she would be that morning, I thought, getting up.

After a quick shower and a fruit smoothie, I was out the
door on the way to Tarzana Park. I left my car in the parking

lot and headed for the playground, hoping she hadn't varied her schedule. Sure enough, Annie was on the bench with her crocheting out and the two kids were busy in the sandbox with trucks and pails. As soon as she saw me, she started to apologize. She hadn't meant to sic the sheriff's detective on me. All she'd done was answer their questions about seeing Miles. As soon as they'd heard Adele and I were with her, they wanted to talk to us. I shrugged it off. Getting questioned was no longer a big deal for me. Now it was my turn to talk.

"What happened to Miles?" I said as I sat on the bench next to her.

She'd been keeping an upbeat demeanor, but she let it down as she began to talk. She'd gotten a call the morning after we'd been there. The director of the halfway house had been concerned when Miles didn't show up for breakfast. They checked his room and found him unresponsive and called the paramedics. She said they'd found the crocheted doll I'd brought. Annie hesitated. "The doll's body was cut open and there were some pills hidden inside it. The director wanted to know where the doll came from. . . ." She let it hang in the air.

"You can't think I put drugs in the doll."

"I don't know what to think. I just told the detective what I knew—that you'd helped with the crochet group and had brought him the doll."

"I certainly didn't put anything in the doll, and the Hookers checked out the doll to see how it was made. If it had been cut open and sewed up, one of us would have noticed," I said. "I think someone tried to make it look like there were drugs in the doll. I wonder who else had access to his room."

"The director admitted that although they try to keep track of visitors, it's possible for a counselor to bring somebody in without signing in." Annie stopped to regroup, and it appeared she was having a hard time keeping it together. "I know he was upset about his sister, but he has been doing so well. I don't believe he threw away all his hard work and went back to drugs, even though the detective told me they are treating it as a self-administered accidental overdose."

"Overdose of what?" I said and she shrugged.

"They wouldn't say. Maybe they don't know until they do all their tests. They did say if they find the person who gave him the drugs, they're going to charge them with something."

I sat down on the bench beside her. I didn't know Miles other than seeing him during the crochet group, but I had to agree with her that he seemed to be doing okay. "He did seem to have a purpose helping the other residents. But if he didn't backslide, what happened?"

"I don't know," she said. "Oh, there was something else the director told me. He said he'd found a bunch of broken picture frames on the floor. The photographs seemed to have been removed and cut up in confetti."

I felt a shiver go through me and told her about the photograph he'd shown me. "Miles said Robyn was strange about it. Then he called me and left a message that he'd remembered something about the photograph." My voice dropped as I said how sorry I was I had missed his call. I stared at her intently. "Do you know who was in the photos that got cut up?"

Annie took a moment to think. "Miles was very sentimental. He kept thinking his parents would wake up one day and realize they wanted him in their life. He had some pictures with them from when he was small. Robyn was the one who really acted like family, so he had a number of pictures of her. Some alone and some with her boyfriend." Annie stopped and swallowed. "And he had a picture of me."

"Why would he cut up the photos?" I said. "Unless—somebody else did. Was there something in those pictures somebody would want to hide?" Annie started to shrug as an answer, then her face lit up.

"The director told me something else. One of the residents thought they saw a stranger in the hall."

"Did they give any description?" I asked, but Annie said she didn't know. This time it was my face that lit up. "Maybe the stranger in the hall was the person who shredded the photographs and they did that because they were in the pictures but didn't want anyone to be able to identify them."

I mentioned the picture Miles had shown me with the hole next to Robyn and said it was similar to one I'd seen in Robyn's former office. "It seems the person cut out of the pictures was her boyfriend—or ex-boyfriend," I said and then asked if she thought it was the same boyfriend who was actually in the other photos Miles had. She nodded, saying they'd been going together for a while.

"Do you know who he is?" When she nodded again, I wanted to kick myself for not thinking to ask her about him before.

I heard her suck in her breath. "You don't think it was him?"

I took a deep breath and asked for his name.

"His name is Ty Holzer."

Why did that name sound familiar?

CHAPTER 32

I CALLED DINAH AS SOON AS I LEFT THE PARK. IF I
hurried, I figured Dinah and I could meet and do some sleuthing and I'd still be to the bookstore on time. "So what do we do? What do we ask him? Who is Ty Holzer anyway?" Dinah sounded excited and happy to be included in the adventure.

It hadn't been until I was getting into my car that I put Robyn's boyfriend's name together with a face. Not a face really, more like a white jacket and a placard that read, "Ty Holzer, Pharm. D."

"He's the pharmacist at Crown Apothecary," I said to Dinah. "Think about it. Crown Apothecary was the return address on the box of sweetener sent to Robyn. Who better to get drugs than a pharmacist? I'll be at your place in a few."

Dinah was waiting outside when I got there. Pulling her long yellow scarf behind her, she got in the passenger seat and shut the door of the greenmobile. "What if Ty got rid of all the photos because someone could identify him as the guy in the hall if they saw them?" she said, continuing our conversation.

"That's what I thought, too. What's that cliché about great minds thinking alike?" I said. "So, all we have to do is take a picture of him and show it around to everyone at the halfway house." Dinah nodded in agreement. "That should be easy," I said with an expectant smile. I should have known, nothing ever is.

We drove to the Crown Apothecary in Encino. We might have opened the door a little too enthusiastically and the bell rang with a frenzy. Workmen were painting a sign on the glass door that led to the soda fountain. I had hoped it would be busier so we could blend in with the crowd, but there were just a few customers in the store. Someone was waiting by the pharmacy and the others were browsing. The clerk I'd seen before stepped forward and asked if we needed help. I was relieved to see she didn't seem to recognize us, and I quickly said we were just looking. "This place is so wonderful, I could look for hours," I said, hoping she would go away and leave us alone.

How do you take a picture of someone without their knowing? Even if I used my BlackBerry, I still had to hold it up, and I wasn't always so good at finding the button to push when I wanted to take a picture. I was more likely to hit it by mistake. It wasn't an issue anyway, because the pharmacist was in the partitioned-off area and only visible when he passed the customer window.

When I saw him move from his work area into the consultation cubicle, I held up my phone, but I couldn't get a shot of his face.

"What about if we take a picture of a picture of him?" Dinah suggested. Next to the shelves with jars of penny candy, there was a framed newspaper article about the store with a photo of Ty. The clerk gave us a hard look, and I was concerned if she looked long enough, she might recognize me from earlier. As a distraction, I grabbed one of the clear plastic bags they had for the penny candy and began to shovel

Red Hots into it. When that was full, I took another and began to fill it. Dinah nudged me when the woman walked away.

"Don't ditch the candy," Dinah warned as I started to drop the bags near the jars.

"Right, it'll look better if we buy something anyway." Since I needed my hands free, I set the bags of candy in the top of my purse. Someone walked by us, and I stepped into the aisle and pretended to look at the array of natural-bristle hairbrushes.

Dinah poked me and pointed to the consultation cubicle. The door was open. "Maybe you can get a shot of him from in there." We slipped up the aisle and went into the wood-lined enclosure. It was set up so the pharmacist could come in through a glass door that led to his work area in the pharmacy. I noticed that door was ajar and someone was moving in the work area. Assuming it was him, I stepped into the doorway and stuck my arm out with the BlackBerry, hoping I was hitting the right button.

"You can't go in there," a voice said in a clipped tone. The clerk had come into the consultation area. "Is there something I can help you find?"

"Sorry," I said, backing away from the open door. "I was looking for the powder room." I'd found that saying you're looking for the restroom was a great catchall for snooping. She apologized and said the restrooms were still under construction. As soon as we got back into the main store, I checked the photo on my BlackBerry. It was just one of the clerks, and it looked like she was putting away stock in the pharmacy.

"This isn't working. Maybe I'll try coming back when they close and try to get a shot of him when he leaves," I said.

"What are you going to do, hide behind his car?" Dinah said with a laugh.

"Well, at least I know which one is his," I said, thinking

back to the night I'd seen him leave Robyn's. We started toward the front of the store, but before we'd taken more than a few steps, one of the clerks stepped in front of us. "You can't leave without getting a sneak peak at the soda fountain," she said in a forced friendly voice. She didn't wait for an answer, but ushered us toward the entrance. The sign painter had finished and left the door propped open.

Inside, she pointed out the authentic small white octagonal tiles with an occasional green one thrown in. She demonstrated how the stools at the soda fountain really spun.

"Try them," she said. She left us and went behind the soda fountain. "We're still waiting for the ice cream, but we have phosphates. Let me get you each a complimentary one." She grabbed two tall glasses.

She rambled on about how Crown Apothecary was more than just a drugstore. "We want our customers to feel at home here," she said. I asked for a cherry phosphate and Dinah a lime one. The woman handed us the drinks and started talking about all the services the store offered.

Ty came in and greeted us and he started pitching their pharmacy. "We do compounding," he said. "Great for kids. We can take the ick out of their medicine with their flavor of choice.

"Come, ladies, bring your drinks," he said. He nodded to the clerk and she walked away. "Let me show you our consultation cubicle." Seizing upon the opportunity, I told him the store was so fabulous I'd really like to get a photo of it, and did he mind?

He walked us into the cubicle and the door shut behind us with a click that sounded like a lock. He invited us to sit down in the wooden captain's chairs and then asked us if we thought there was anything they'd missed in the design of the soda fountain. We both said it seemed they had everything covered and the drinks were great and we thought it'd be a big success. We set down our glasses as we both stood and started toward the door. I stopped and asked about taking the picture. He was agreeable, and I took several. I checked and they'd turned out. Mission accomplished.

This time, I walked to the door and pulled on the handle, saying both Dinah and I had to get to work. "The door won't open," I said. I heard Dinah make a noise behind me. When I turned back toward the pharmacist, he had something in his hands. Before it could register, he'd pulled my hands behind my back and put plastic ties on them. I saw he'd already gotten Dinah. A moment later, I heard the clerk outside the door say, "They're on their way."

"Who's on their way?" I demanded.

"The cops," he said, pointing toward my purse. The clear bags of Red Hots were visible.

"It's just a misunderstanding. I was going to pay for them before we left."

Ty was unmoved, and both Dinah and I started straining against the plastic ties and making noise. Then it hit me maybe this was a good thing. I could show them the photo in my phone and tell them to show it to the director of the halfway house.

"Donna remembered you came in here before," he said, nodding toward one of the clerks. "Was that just a chance to case the place?"

"Case the place? Yes, I came in here before because this place was the return address on the box of sweetener that poisoned Robyn Freed. That package was sent from here—by you—wasn't it? I know who you are. You're her boyfriend."

"Was. Was her boyfriend," he said with a sigh. "What's it to you anyway? You're not trying to tell me you're some kind of cops or PIs?"

He realized what he said and laughed. "No, you're definitely not cops. I don't think LAPD is that hard up. You're more like *Agnes and Casey*," he said referring to a comedy cop show about two detectives who were also friends. "Cancel the part about private investigators, too. So what are you?"

"It doesn't matter," I said. "We're just after the truth. So why'd you kill your girlfriend and her brother?"

"Miles is dead?" he said. It seemed like pretty genuine shock. "What happened?"

"I'll ask the questions," I said, trying to act intimidating. It would have helped if I'd had a badge or a gun and hadn't been handcuffed. "Just wait until the cops come and I show them the photo of you and they take it to the halfway house. Ha, you thought making all those photos disappear would get you off the hook."

"I don't know what you're talking about. What pictures?"

"You also have access to all kinds of drugs," I said, narrowing my eyes, "and probably stuff like cyanide, too. What was it? You were angry because she broke up with you and you cut yourself out of the pictures to hide the evidence."

"She didn't break up with me; I broke up with Robyn. We'd been going together for a long time. She cut me out of the photos because she was angry. Robyn was always aggressive, but once she got the promotion to segment producer, she was impossible. The job consumed her, along with her desire to go even further. You can't have a relationship if you never see each other. She worked twenty-four, seven."

"Geez, just like dating a detective," I said, feeling a pang as I thought of Barry. "Did you know who her parents were?"

"Yeah. At first she told me they were dead. Then she told me the truth, which was that they were dead as far as she was concerned. When I heard she was handling the Barbara show they were going to be on, I got concerned. Even more so when she started talking about going outside the box and doing something really flashy without telling anybody. It's on live in some cities, and whatever Robyn set up couldn't be edited out. She thought if she could do something that would catch everyone, including Barbara, off guard, the show would make a splash, and they'd make Robyn a higher-level producer. It was all she talked about for the last couple of weeks. Then I snapped. I thought there had to be more to life than a TV show. She didn't take the breakup well. I think anything close to rejection brought her right back to the relationship with her parents. She told me when she was a kid, they were never there. Either they were off making movies somewhere or they were just busy with something else. It bugged her because they gave off this image of being such caring humanitarian types."

I heard the bell go crazy as the front door opened, and somebody said, "Back there." A moment later, the cubicle was unlocked from the outside and a handful of uniforms came in.

"I detained them for you," Ty said. He stepped over to two of the uniforms and started explaining something. I saw him pointing to the pharmacy area and heard something about us having a meth lab. They had separated Dinah and me and someone grabbed our purses, and the next thing I knew, I was getting into the back of a police car. Again.

Mrs. Shedd was not going to be happy when I didn't show up for work.

CHAPTER 33

MASON WAS LAUGHING WHEN DINAH AND I WALKED out from behind the counter of the police station. A couple of the cops were laughing, too. I half expected Barry to pop up somewhere, but he didn't. Though I was sure he'd hear about it somehow.

"You'll be hearing from us about false imprisonment," Mason said, putting on his serious lawyer face. He was laughing again before we got out of the door.

It was all a big mix up. Here's what happened. Ty Holzer saw me walk through the open door into the pharmacy. Unbeknownst to me, inside there was a box of cold tablet packets one of the clerks was putting away. They were not prescription, but they were kept behind the counter and you could only buy a limited amount and had to show ID, all because people were using them to make street drugs. I mean, really, could anybody think Dinah and I were drug queenpin masterminds?

The clerk who'd been doing the stocking saw the Red Hots in my purse and thought they were the red cold pills. All the drinks and such were just stalls and tricks to get us in the consultation cubicle. Needless to say, when the cops took a really good look, or should I say *sniff*, of the "cold pills," they realized the mistake.

On the drive back, Mason shared some information he'd gotten. The medical examiner had determined that Miles had died from a drug injection, not from the pills in the doll, which turned out to be aspirin. No syringe had been found in the room, leading them to speculate that someone else had given him the drugs. They were still waiting on results of what was in his system. Lastly, he'd given me a piece of paper. "Sorry it took so long," he said. When I unfolded it, it had the license plate number and Ty Holzer's information. It turned out he lived in Tarzana, too.

Mason dropped Dinah off at her house and me at the bookstore. "Should I give you a note, or do you want me to come in and explain?" he asked.

"I'm a big girl. I can handle it myself," I said, getting out of the car.

Rayaad handed me a package when I passed the front counter. On top it said *I'm Sorry* in big letters, and inside was a selection of things from the Crown Apothecary, along with lots of coupons for complimentary hot fudge sundaes and a note saying he'd called the director of the halfway house and offered to go there in person and let the residents look at him to prove he wasn't the one who had been there the day Miles was found dead. Ty had also called Mrs. Shedd and said the new owner had suggested that instead of just a rack of books from some distributor, that Shedd & Royal could have a rack of books for sale along with a sign advertising the store.

"He must feel very bad," Mrs. Shedd said. She looked at me and suggested that after what I'd been through, I might want to take a crochet break before I started dealing with work. It sounded perfect to me and I headed to the back table. No surprise, there was a group of people around it, including Adele. She looked up as I approached.

"Pink, I heard you got arrested again," Adele said. "How many times does that make? Let me see," she said. I rolled my eyes. She made it sound like I was a regular at the police station.

"Before any ridiculous stories start to circulate, this is what happened," I said and told them about the Red Hots being mistaken for cold pills.

"And you were worried about ridiculous stories circulating. What could be more ridiculous than that?" Rhoda said. Elise was sitting next to her, and in her birdlike voice, said she was just glad that Dinah and I were all right. Sheila appeared to have gotten nervous just thinking about us in plastic handcuffs. Eduardo shook his head. "Somebody is an idiot." I was surprised at his anger. Eduardo was usually so mellow.

CeeCee was speechless until she began talking about her own stint in jail.

"Everybody is missing the point. Who cares if this Ty guy didn't kill Miles? The cops still think I killed Robyn. They're closing in. I don't want to end up a *Dateline* story about how an innocent woman got sent to jail," Nell wailed, and I could see her point. Just because we hadn't seen Detective Heather lately didn't mean she'd forgotten about Nell. Who knew what kind of case she was building. Once the prosecutor thought they had enough, they'd arrest her in the middle of the night. And who knew what a jury would believe. Nell could end up in jail for years, not minutes like I was.

Dinah got a round of applause as she made a grand entrance and joined the group. Sheila surprised all of us by standing up and telling us we would all feel better if we'd focus on making something with one of the impatient crochet patterns for the donation box.

"Crocheting will calm your nerves," she said. "And thinking about making something to help somebody else will make you forget your own problems."

Nobody could argue with that.

"Mom," a voice called. Don't they say that a mother always recognizes her kid's voice? I knew it was Samuel before he'd said the second *m* in *mom*. He'd been trying to call me and only getting voice mail. He left text messages and e-mail messages. He'd gotten an out-of-town gig at the last minute and wanted to make sure I knew. As he was about to leave, he gave the group a dismissive glance until he saw Nell. She looked up at the same moment and their eyes met. Uh-oh. Samuel, who could care less about crochet, was suddenly so interested in what she was making. She wanted to know about his gig. The next thing I knew, they were headed toward the café. Well, at least it had gotten her mind off her troubles.

I took out another cell sock I'd started. This time I'd tried some glittery silver yarn with the idea of making an evening cell sock. It was much thinner than the cotton yarn, and I was surprised how different the same stitches looked done in it. Though I tried not to, I started thinking about Barry. I knew without a doubt that he had to know about the episode in the afternoon. I thought he would call or something, but there was just silence. It still seemed so odd how everything had turned upside down in a couple of days.

I worked until closing, still trying to make up for lost time. When I was turning off the lights and Mrs. Shedd and Mr. Royal were shutting everything down, I saw Mason standing outside. He remembered my car was still by the Crown Apothecary. When I came outside, I could see the effect of my presence on his face. He seemed very happy to see me.

"Hmm, this is interesting. We don't have to pretend this is a legal-defense dinner. We can just do it for fun." Mason caught my expression. "I know you're still adjusting, but the best way to do it is get out there—"

"And get back on the horse," I said, finishing the cliché. "I need some time to just walk along the path for a while first," I said. "Besides, until Nell is cleared and has her job back, I can't worry about my social life. It's her whole life we're talking about."

We went to a busy sushi restaurant in Encino. While we were waiting for a table, Mason brought up his plan, apparently undaunted by my comment.

"Okay, but once everything is settled, after all that you've been through and are going through, don't you think a change of scenes would be good? I was thinking we could both take a few days off and drive up north. So many great places to choose as a destination. Personally, I love Carmel. Lots of cozy little inns and interesting little restaurants. But my favorite thing to do is to take a cappuccino to the beach and watch the sunset."

Hmm, it sounded nice.

CHAPTER 34

A WEEK WENT BY AND NO WORD FROM BARRY. IN the past when we'd split up, he'd still driven by at night to check that everything was okay. But now there was no Tahoe driving by in the middle of the night, at least that I saw. There weren't any stops in the bookstore, either. There was just the big silence.

Mason did his best to keep from looking too happy about the situation, but he didn't succeed. He kept pointing out how he showed up when he said he would and never rushed off in the middle of a meal because he had to go chase down a lead. It was hard to feel glum with him around.

Dinah and Commander included me in their plans to run karaoke at the senior center. I had to admit it was fun. In short, I barely had time to notice how quiet my house had become. Maybe it was because I was getting older and had been through Charlie's death, but after the week with nothing, I began to really let go and stopped looking for Barry to show up.

Mason found out the results of Miles' autopsy and toxicology screens. He'd died of an overdose of heroin, but they'd also found Rohypnol in his system. Commonly known as roofies, the drug has the effect of knock-out drops. They traced it back to a bottle of fruit punch in Miles' room. They surmised someone had knocked him out with the fruit punch and then administered the heroin. But the question was why. When they checked Miles' cell phone records, they noted the call to me.

Detective Henderson from the sheriff's department got in touch with me and wanted to know why he'd called. She caught me off guard and I forgot about giving her the silent treatment and answered. "He wanted to tell me something. I'm guessing he thought it might help me find out who killed his sister," I said. Big mistake. Apparently Detective Henderson called Detective Heather, and the next thing I knew, Heather got in touch with me.

"You're doing it again, Ms. Pink," she said. "Interfering with a police investigation. If Miles had some information that pointed to his sister's killer, it seems pretty clear who killed him. If you want to help Nell Collins, get her to tell us the truth."

It didn't make me feel any better to realize the spotlight was off me.

The next day, I broke the news to CeeCee and Nell as they came into the yarn department. "Oh, this can't be," Nell said. "Now they think I killed two people?"

"Dear, we really should get you a lawyer," CeeCee said. Both of us had been saying it all along, but Nell had continued to insist it made her look guilty. This time, she nodded in agreement.

"Everybody thinks I did it anyway," she said in a forlorn voice.

I called Mason, and we made arrangements for her to come to his office. Nell wanted CeeCee and me to go with her. I could see that CeeCee was squirming. All of this made her very uncomfortable, but she said she would go. I wasn't sure of the exact proportions, but the balance had changed. CeeCee was more concerned about her niece than her career— even with the Oscar buzz.

I'd never been to Mason's office before. Only to the building the time he'd picked up his briefcase. This time we parked and rode to the fortieth floor in one of the primo Century City office buildings. The law firm had half the floor. Mason had a corner office with a west-facing view. I could see the sun reflecting off the ocean as I stepped inside. I was surprised to see Spike. The toy fox terrier had his own area, complete with water, toys and his own blanket. He barked when we came in and gave us all the once-over before going back to his blanket and watching us. You had to love a man who would take his dog to work with him.

It was odd seeing Mason at work. He was more formal than I was used to. Everything in the office was big. Big desk, big windows and big comfortable chairs. You could almost smell the power in the air. His assistant came in and offered us refreshments. We're not talking coffee that's been sitting in the pot for hours, either. They had an espresso machine, imported bottled water, any kind of soda you could think of and finger sandwiches. CeeCee said all this had been such a drain on her, she needed to keep her strength up. The assistant came back with the works.

Nell insisted that she wanted CeeCee and me in on everything, so there would be no problem for him to discuss her case with us.

"I think that whatever evidence they have against you is too easy to blow away. But that doesn't mean they won't keep showing up and questioning you. In this situation, the cops' best chance is getting you to confess," Mason said.

"But I didn't do it. You have to believe me," she said, suddenly worried.

Mason got up and walked around the desk and stood next to her.

"I know you didn't. No worries. If the cops or the sheriff's investigator show up, don't say anything, just have them talk to me." He put a reassuring hand on her shoulder. "I have a daughter your age. I'm not going to let anything bad happen to you." I wanted to hug him for being so sympathetic.

Nell and CeeCee went out into the reception area and I hung back.

"The first time you've seen me in action," he said with a grin. "What do you think?"

I glanced around the office and at him in the dark gray power suit. "Pretty impressive."

Spike took the opportunity to come over and sniff my shoes. "Thanks for making Nell feel better, though I'm still worried. Even if the cops never arrest her, it doesn't clear her name or get her job back," I said.

"Hmm, you're right," he said. "You haven't by chance figured out who really killed the two of them? It would help if we had somebody else to throw to the cops."

"Not exactly," I said with a wince, "but let me roll out my list of top suspects." I mentioned Talia Canon. "She had the big three—means, motive and opportunity—at least for Robyn. She certainly gained from Robyn's death." I shrugged. "Maybe what Miles remembered was something about her. But I keep thinking about Becca and Derek. Being their parents, they certainly had a connection to both Robyn and Miles. It seems pretty clear that Robyn planned some kind of ambush on the show." I shuddered. "If they were cold enough to cut their children out of their lives, is it so hard to imagine that they might have had them killed to save face?"

Mason put a hand on my shoulder in a supportive move. "I can understand how you'd have a hard time with that with the way you feel about your sons." His phone started to ring and I knew CeeCee and Nell wanted to get going, so I quickly went through the rest of the list.

Something was up with Pierce Sheraton. The guy seemed

to show up all the time, though I had no idea why he'd want to kill either Miles or Robyn. Barbara Olive Overton had to be included. Ty Holzer had done a good job of getting himself out of the running, but I still wondered about him. Then there were the people like the production assistants, D. J., Bob and even Annie Hoover, the nanny, who couldn't be totally counted out.

Mason let out a world-weary sigh. "I'd put the parents at the top of the list. Everybody thinks they're Hollywood's sweethearts—the perfect couple known for all the humanitarian gestures. It sounds like Robyn was out to ruin them. It's a cold world, Sunshine."

"I wonder how they'd react if I showed them Robyn's doll?"

Mason took an envelope out of his desk. "Here's your chance to find out. I told you the law firm was buying a block of tickets for the benefit Barbara Olive Overton is putting on in Palm Springs. Becca and Derek are going to be there. I wish I could go, but I have a family thing—my daughter's engagement party." He seemed a little wistful. "Geez, father of the bride, what's next, grandpa? I'm not sure I'm ready for that."

"I bet you'll love it," I said as I looked inside the envelope.

"Enough talk about my future in a rocking chair. The tickets will get you into the golf tournament and the festivities afterward. There's even a room for the night included. I assume you'll being sharing it with Dinah."

I gave him a thank you hug for everything. "Palm Springs, here we come."

CHAPTER 35

MASON WAS RIGHT, MY FIRST THOUGHT FOR THE other ticket was Dinah. I caught her the next morning as she went back to the yarn department. She looked at the ticket longingly. "I wish I could, but Commander bought tickets for us to go whale watching." Her brows were knit together in concern. "You know I love being your Watson. I'm still trying to work out a balance." I promised her I understood and wouldn't let anyone permanently replace her as my wingman. We were just starting to think of who else I should ask when Adele interrupted.

"Pink, you have to pick me," Adele said. "Don't you see, it's destiny. It's my chance to show Barbara the wonders of crochet." She suddenly appeared uncomfortable. "I wasn't deliberately eavesdropping, but you two were talking kind of loud."

It turned out Adele won by default. I had already nixed the idea of Nell going. I think CeeCee was afraid she might end up getting arrested again. Sheila had to work. Weekends were busy at Luxe. I couldn't picture going with either Rhoda or Elise. Eduardo? Not a chance.

* * *

PALM SPRINGS WAS ONLY ABOUT ONE HUNDRED and twenty-five miles away from Tarzana, but to me, it looked like another planet. The desert community sat at the base of the San Jacinto Mountains, but until you got close to the town, all you could see was beige.

Adele and I had both worked the morning at the bookstore, and when we left Tarzana, the sky was white and the air chilly, so typical for May. Once we hit the Mojave Desert and started to pass all the wind farms, the sky was clear blue and the temperature near ninety. I was glad I'd worn something light. The loose linen pants with a matching beige tunic top seemed perfect for the desert. I matched the sand. It must have been a challenge for Adele to find crochet items to wear that wouldn't cause her to overheat, but she'd done it. She'd worn an open vest made of pale blue light-cotton yarn. It worked well with the white capri pants and white loose cotton top. But, of course, Adele couldn't leave it at that. She'd added a granny-square bracelet, big circle earrings crocheted in thread, and a wide-brimmed sun hat, she'd made in cotton yarn.

Palm Springs was one of the older desert communities and had been the playground for Frank Sinatra, Bob Hope, Elvis and lots of others. The air was so dry it made the outlines of the landscape show up in crisp detail.

We drove through the main drag with all the small shops and restaurants. The town had kept its charm, thanks to all kinds of rules that outlawed billboards and neon signs.

I found the entrance to the resort hosting the event and turned into the driveway. It was odd after all the sand to have the rich green of golf courses on both sides of the curving driveway before I pulled in front of the two-story hotel. We'd decided to check in first.

Once we'd stowed our stuff in our room, we headed out

again. Just past the low building, the setup for the event began. We passed the crowd of spectators watching the game on the golf course. Beyond there was a parking lot and an encampment of open-air tents. All the media trucks were parked together. There were also RVs that appeared to be used as dressing rooms, and the large white trucks I'd seen when there were TV or movie shoots in my area. They were called honey wagons and were portable restrooms. I'd seen the inside, and they had nothing in common with Porta-Potties beyond their basic function. They had porcelain fixtures and running water. Nothing but the best for this crowd.

One of the tents had been set up for registration. As we walked toward it, I saw people dressed in jeans, tee shirts and sneakers—or the unofficial uniform of production assistants. *BOO* productions must have brought their whole staff. It made me think of Nell and how much she said she'd looked forward to working this.

"Where's Barbara?" Adele said, shading her face with her hand and scanning the area. Adele had a messenger-style bag strapped across her chest. "I'm ready for her." To make sure I understood how ready, she opened the bag and showed me the contents. "I brought the fancy hooks," she said, showing me her hand-carved wooden ones. "These are my pride and joy. Who could possibly turn down crocheting with these?" She had cotton yarn as well. "And I'm going to get in a picture of her with the hooks," she said, checking the battery level on her camera.

I had been hearing her plan over and over since we'd left the bookstore. I had my own agenda, but I hadn't battered her eardrums with it. Mine was much simpler: show the doll to the celebrity couple and ask a bunch of questions before they had a chance to think about it. I patted my canvas bag to make sure Robyn's doll was still in it.

There was a throng of people at the registration table as we approached. Talia Canon went by and seemed all business.

D. J. was with her. She stopped short when she saw me. "I didn't expect to see you," she said, sounding surprised. "What are you doing here?" While I was thinking of how to answer, Adele opened her bag and mouth at the same time. I gave Adele one of CeeCee's famous cease-and-desist looks when she started to speak. If Adele said anything about what she'd planned to do, we'd be out of there before we got in.

"We're here for the festivities," I said and explained a friend had given me the tickets. Pierce Sheraton joined Talia, but barely seemed to notice Adele and me.

I was so nervous that Adele was going to say something about her plan to snag Barbara and show off her hooks, I dropped my bag. I'd tried to incorporate everything in the cloth tote. D. J. gave me a friendly smile and scooped it up but grabbed the bottom instead of the handles. Everything fell out, including the doll.

They all looked at the doll and gave me a strange look. I ignored their expressions and went to retrieve my stuff. It had scattered all over. It was going to be the last time I tried to use a canvas tote bag as a purse. While I chased down rolling coins, Talia picked up the doll by its feet and the green dress flew over the doll's head. She saw the underpants with the pink rose and pulled at them. Something that looked like a piece of gum dropped out and hit the ground next to me. "What's that?"

Adele had taken offense at Talia manhandling the doll and grabbed it from her and snatched the fallen object. "Pink, you've got to get caught up on your technology. It's a media card." I just wanted to pick my stuff up and get it back in my bag, but instead of helping me, Adele took out her camera and removed the media card. I heard her mumbling something about New York and then a disappointed comment about there only being a blue screen.

At least D. J. helped me retrieve my things. I picked up a handful of dusty coins, and D. J. got my wallet and the other odds and ends of stuff. We both straightened.

"D. J., let's go," Talia said. "The film crew is waiting." He dropped what he was holding back into my bag and said they wanted some more snippets to put in his background piece and made a joke that he hoped the flavor protesters wouldn't show up again.

"I'm sorry about that, I really am," I said, putting the coins back in my bag, but my BlackBerry fell on the ground. He retrieved it for me and I stuck it in my pocket before wiping the dust off my hands. "I'm glad there is one thoughtful person in the crowd," I said with a grateful nod. I grabbed the media card and doll from Adele. I didn't know what else to do with the card but stick it back in the doll's underpants. Pierce, Talia and D. J. took off. Only D. J. had the courtesy to wave and say something about seeing us later.

Adele started to say something, but a young man who looked like a production assistant brushed past us, waving for a group of people to follow him. As we went to get in the registration line, he took his group in front of us.

"Sorry, folks," he said to those of us in line, "but we've got to get them in now." His crowd dripped of money and I guessed they were big-time donors. There were always different-priced tickets at events like this. I had to grab Adele before she made a scene.

We finally got our turn to register and exchanged our tickets for plastic badges, which we put on around our necks. Then we were directed to the *BOO* Two Pavilion.

Adele was so busy looking for the actual BOO, I had to grab her arm to keep her from wandering off. The pavilion was a huge open-air tent with a large number of white-clothed round tables on a floor that had been laid over the sandy soil. A band was setting up next to space for dancing. Uniformed waiters were setting out baskets of rolls and filling the glasses with water. I noticed a woman who looked like some kind of supervisor. I went and asked where Becca and Derek would be sitting.

She laughed. "Not in here." She picked up my badge and pointed out the *B* on it.

Adele figured out that meant that Barbara wasn't going to be there, either, and started looking stormy.

"C'mon," I said. "Maybe we can catch them at the golf tournament." We backtracked out of the tent and went back toward the registration area and the entrance for the spectators. It wasn't much help. There was a roped-off section for the A-list and we B people couldn't get in.

"Pink, what are we going to do? Who cares about sitting in a tent eating rubber chicken. I came to get Barbara."

"And I came here to flash Robyn's doll at her parents," I said. We both blew out our breath in disappointment.

I saw D. J. coming out of the spectators' area and he came over to us. "What's wrong?" the blogoir author said. "You two look upset."

I told him about our predicament, and he thought it over for a moment before his face broke into a big smile. "This is perfect. I finally get to play the hero." He held out his badge, which said "All Access." "The dinner for Barbara and all the celebrities isn't even here." He grabbed my hand. "C'mon, I'll get you both in with my badge." Adele rushed after us, her hat flapping in the breeze.

I was surprised when he led us to the parking lot. "You won't believe where they're having it. Those celeb types are so jaded, they had to come up with something bordering on ridiculous."

We got in his black Scion and he drove out of town and turned onto a road that said Palm Springs Aerial Tramway. I'd heard about it but never been. Neither had Adele. Both of us said we'd always wanted to go.

The mountains were already cutting off the late-afternoon sun and the parking lot seemed dark after the brightness of the desert floor. The cool shade felt good. Even though it was dry heat, ninety degrees was still hot. D. J.

walked ahead and said he'd use his badge to get us passes on the tram.

By the time we caught up with him, he had tickets and ushered us into the waiting area. There were only a few people waiting to go up. When I seemed a little uncertain, he smiled. "I told you it bordered on ridiculous."

I followed the wires that carried the tram up the mountain with my eyes. They seemed to go almost straight up.

Our tram arrived and the small crowd got on. As we began our ascent, there was a running taped commentary talking about how the tramway was built and how everything that went up or down the mountain, including trash, went via the tram. The gondola kept turning, giving us a view of the desert floor below that looked golden in the fading afternoon sun, and then the changing vegetation on the mountain side.

It was amazing; in the short ride we'd gone up to 8,900 feet above sea level. The tram door opened and we walked directly into the station. D. J. led us through it quickly, and I barely noted that there were a few shops and some busy food places. I got a brief view out the window and saw that the station was situated on the edge of the mountaintop and there was a panoramic view of the desert below.

We had to rush to keep up with D. J., and Adele's hat flew off, but luckily she had attached a tie to it like those on cowboy hats, and it hung on her back. D. J. opened the door, and we stepped out onto a concrete deck. What I saw totally surprised me. Snow! He waved for us to follow. I looked at my linen top and slacks and hesitated.

"Don't worry, it's not that cold up here now. They have tents set up with heaters and sweatshirts on every seat." He wore only jeans and a dress shirt himself. "What kind of gentleman am I?" he said, taking my tote bag. I'd stuffed everything in there and it was kind of heavy and a relief to let it go. He offered to carry Adele's as well, but she insisted the way it was strapped across her chest, it was easy to carry. My bag grazed his fanny pack as he slung it on his shoulder.

We went down a zigzagging concrete ramp and then out onto the snow. It was a little chilly, but we were moving so quickly, we built up body heat. I guessed it was close to sixty degrees. Still, I was looking forward to the heated tents he'd promised. We passed some other people dressed in open jackets, heading in the opposite direction, and they nodded in greeting. Two kids lagged behind, stopping to throw snowballs.

Walking through the snow wasn't easy. It appeared to have frozen and melted and frozen again so it was packed down but still slippery. Occasionally we hit a soft spot and snow got in my shoes.

I questioned the lack of a path and wondered about the pampered celebrity types walking through the snow.

"They're ferrying them up by helicopter. I thought it would be easier to sneak you two in if we came up this way." I noticed he'd glanced at his watch a number of times, and I supposed he was trying to get there before the crowd started arriving and security might be tighter.

I glanced around as we rushed on. In one direction, the land sloped up to a peak and it was covered with snow and pine trees. I looked back, expecting to see the tram station, but all I saw was snow, more pine trees and an occasional boulder.

"Are you sure you're going the right way?" Adele said, stopping for a moment to catch her breath. "This doesn't seem like a very good plan."

I leaned against a boulder, my feet were wet, and even with the built-up body heat, I was getting cold. The sun had disappeared behind the mountain and the temperature was dropping quickly. "Maybe we should just go back," I said.

D. J. stepped next to me. "I'm sure we're almost there. Why don't I run up ahead and pick up a couple of sweatshirts for you," he said.

I turned to Adele to say something, and when I'd turned back, he had disappeared in the trees ahead.

"Why did I ever listen to you, Pink" Adele said, hugging herself to keep warm.

"Listen to me? You thought it was a great idea."

"Right, when we were down in Palm Springs and it was warm and sunny. Nobody said anything about snow."

I stepped closer to Adele and she stepped closer to me until our arms were touching. The snow made it seem brighter than it was. I was pretty sure the sun had gone completely down by now. "I say we give him five minutes and then we head back," Adele said with a shiver.

I suddenly regretted not having my bag but was glad when I felt my BlackBerry in my pocket. I wasn't so glad when I saw that the battery meter was down to two bars. The cord had fallen behind something and I'd forgotten to charge it overnight. Adele rummaged around in her bag and found some mints. Just what we wanted, something to cool our breath.

She asked for my BlackBerry and started fiddling around with it. "Pink, technology is so wasted on you."

She showed me the screen and on it was a picture of one of the trams we'd be on. Then she took it back and began reading and making little squeals as she read.

"Okay, what's the matter?" I asked.

"Nothing," Adele said in a tone that said it was anything but nothing. "Except that it says at least once a month somebody gets lost up here. Some couple got lost up here for three days. But that was summer, no snow and it was much warmer." I heard her suck in her breath. "But some other guy died up here. All they found was his skeleton and his backpack," Adele said as her teeth began to chatter. We both looked in the direction we thought D. J. had gone and there was nothing.

"Something doesn't feel right about this," I said. "You

don't think that D. J. got us up here with the plan of ditching us?"

"Don't say that, Pink." I could barely make out Adele's features in the low light. She looked like she might cry. Not a good idea, because it was getting colder fast and I thought her tears might freeze. She still had my BlackBerry and was online.

"Give me that. You used up most of the power," I said, grabbing the BlackBerry. "Okay, let's look at this logically. Why would D. J. ditch us?"

"Maybe because he wanted your tote bag," Adele said, pointing out that he'd taken it supposedly to ease my way.

I went over what was in it. I couldn't imagine why he'd want any of it. "What would he want with Robyn's old doll?" I said. "Unless it was the media card stuck in her undies. He was standing next to us when we found it."

"Yeah, Pink, that has to be it."

"But I heard you say there was nothing on it."

"No, I said all I got was a blue screen. There could be something on it my camera couldn't read."

"What could be on it that could be so important to him?"

"Sherlock Pink, and you call yourself a sleuth. How about Robyn had some secret information on him?"

I hated to admit it, but I realized Adele had something. I'd been so busy thinking Robyn's plan had to do with the show her parents were on, I never thought about D. J.'s program. What if he was the one she was going to reveal something about? "What information could she have had?"

"News flash, Pink, whatever it was, he killed her over it."

"Oh my God," I said as I began to remember things. I thought back to Salute to Chocolate. "D. J. was right there when Miles called the bookstore." I wanted to kick myself as I remembered how I'd told Talia who Miles was and said he might have some information about who killed Robyn. And D. J. was standing right next to her. He could have been worried about what Miles knew." I stopped while it sunk in. "And he could have been the person someone saw at the half-way house. If anybody would know about drugs, it would be a former addict."

"Great that you figured it out, Pink. I think it's a safe bet he isn't coming back, and in case you haven't noticed, we're in the middle of nowhere, and I mean nowhere. When I looked online, I saw there isn't a road up here for miles and miles and that people use cross-country skis to get to them.

"By the way, the reason people get in trouble up here is because, like us, they come up unprepared for the wilderness. I mean, who expects snow when you're coming from the hot desert?" Adele added. None of it was reassuring.

I took my BlackBerry and punched in 911, but nothing happened.

We argued about who to call. Adele thought we should look up the number for the ranger, and I didn't want to waste the last of the power on trying to find it. Adele took out her cell phone, but it was useless up there. She was with Fred's Friendly Mobile Service, which was cheap, but you only got a signal if you were practically in their store.

"Pink, do something. I don't want to be a human icicle." Typical Adele. As soon as there was trouble, Miss Know-It-All expected me to fix it.

I suggested we try walking back the way we'd come. She had the idea we could follow our footprints, but between having walked on packed down snow and the darkness, we couldn't find them. "We can't just stay here, Pink," Adele said, picking a direction and starting to walk. She brought up how the mountain ended at a ledge, and if we could find that, we could follow it back to the tram station.

Adele stepped on something and skidded. I tried to grab her and we both fell into the snow. Great, now we had wet feet and wet clothes. Adele felt around for what she'd stepped on and picked up something round and metal.

"It's one of those flying saucer sleds. Somebody must have left it," I said. Adele dropped it and we stood up, looking around for some little hint of the right direction. "We've got to keep on going," I said, trying to keep the panic out of my voice. I picked a direction and we started to walk toward some trees. A few minutes later, Adele slipped again, though this time I caught her. We both gasped when we saw that the cause was the same sled. We had walked in a circle.

"It's hopeless. With no path, nothing to orient ourselves with and nothing as far as I can see but trees and snow, we'll never find our way," I said. "Maybe we can make a snow cave or something. If we can make it until morning, at least we'll have the sun."

Adele had my BlackBerry again and had gone online. She shrieked. "You can have hypothermia if your body temperature goes down to ninety-five degrees." She felt her forehead. "I think there's frost on my forehead. Pink, we can't go to sleep, no matter how tired we get. That's what happens just before you die."

I pulled my phone back. How could I have missed it? "We can send an e-mail." But the idea didn't go any further when I realized I'd never gotten around to putting in any e-mail addresses and my one big move had been to clear the mailbox, so I couldn't even reply to one. The power was dwindling. I thumbed through the contacts. I'd been meaning to put in everyone's phone number but not gotten around to that, either. I was embarrassed to admit that I still relied on a paper address book. And my mind blanked when I tried to think of the numbers I called all the time. Hallelujah! Mason must have put his number in when he gave me the phone. I pressed call and hoped for the best.

I heard the phone begin to ring. I crossed my fingers he would answer. Just when I thought it was going to go to voice mail, I heard him say hello. As soon as he heard it was me, he started to joke about me missing him. The low battery warning started to beep and I had to interrupt him.

"We need help," I yelled. "We're stuck in the snow at the top of the Palm Springs Aerial Tramway." I waited to hear him respond, but there was only silence. Somewhere as I was talking, the battery had gone out and the phone cut off. There was no way of knowing how much he'd heard.

I lost it and told Adele if she hadn't been playing around online, the battery would have lasted longer. "He was our only hope," I said.

Adele looked down as what I had said sank in. "We're going to die. We're going to die," she shrieked.

I had to calm her down, which was hard because I was feeling a little panicky myself. I was hoping that even if Mason didn't hear everything, he'd heard enough. But who knew? We leaned against a huge bolder and tried to share our body heat. Adele got the idea we should keep moving, so we started jiggling and shimmying.

"This could be the last night of our lives," she said. As we kept gyrating around, she talked. "Pink, I have a confession to make. You probably never realized this, but I was pretty upset when you got hired as event coordinator. I thought I was going to get the job. I might have been a little mad at you and tried to make things difficult," she said. If I hadn't been shivering and so cold that it hurt, I might have rolled my eyes.

"But, the thing is," Adele continued, "you turned out to be okay. And you might be my best friend," When she said that, my eyes got watery and I had to pinch myself to keep from crying. I should have waited. "But the reason I only said might be, is because you've never invited me over to your house. A real best friend would have invited just me over to brunch or something." She turned to look at me with a question in her eyes.

I jiggled my arms as I put them up in capitulation. "I promise, when we get back, we're on for French toast." I made a point of saying *when* rather than *if*.

"Pink, you shouldn't have mentioned the French toast. It made me think of food and that I'm hungry." She rummaged in her messenger bag and came up with an open bag of almonds that seemed to have a higher ratio of lint. I was touched when she offered it to me first. We huddled together and tried to share our body heat as we blew white bits off the stale nuts.

It seemed to get darker and colder, and every breeze that rustled the trees made us shiver more. I thought I heard something in the distance, but I was afraid it was just my imagination. Then Adele heard it, too. As it got louder, there was no mistaking the thwack of a helicopter. It was so cold now it burned, but with the hope of being rescued, my heart felt lighter.

It was too soon to celebrate. The helicopter began making a sweep and shone its powerful light down, but it was nowhere near us. I jumped up and down and waved my arms as if it would help, but the helicopter didn't alter its course.

"We have to do something to get their attention. I don't suppose you have any reflective tape in your bag or a flashlight."

Adele rummaged around and came out with the tiny flashlight that projected a heart and the word *love*. "That's not going to help," I said.

"People always make fires to get attention," Adele offered.

I was going to mention the fact that any wood on the ground was wet and wouldn't the snow just put a fire out anyway, when I had an idea.

The saucer sled was sitting where we'd left it. "We could make a fire in this." The helicopter seemed even farther away now.

"Give me your bag," I demanded. Adele held back and said something about me being jealous because I didn't have mine.

"Are you nuts? We could die here and you think I want your bag because I don't have mine?"

"I'm sorry, Pink. Me saying that was just a symptom of hypothermia. It's supposed to make you irrational." I rolled my eyes to myself and thought maybe Adele was always suffering from hypothermia.

She handed over her bag and I started to take out all the receipts and scraps of paper. I piled them in the sled. I went through her crochet stuff and took out the wooden hooks.

"You can't take those," Adele protested. "They're handmade and one of a kind."

"You think your skeleton is going to be crocheting with them?" I said, taking them from the bag. I found a couple of skeins of cotton yarn and the pad of Post-it notes she used to keep track of her work.

Adele started to say she needed the yarn to show Barbara how to crochet, but even she realized she was being ridiculous and stopped herself midsentence.

"Now we just need to light it," I said.

"Isn't there something about rubbing two rocks together," she offered.

"Give me that little flashlight you have. Maybe I can use it to find some rocks, though I'm not sure just any rocks will do." She took out the love light. Seeing a heart with the word *love* projected on the snow was pretty, but not helpful.

"Give it to me," I said. For the first time, I noticed the other end. "Adele this is a lighter."

"Really?" she said, completely surprised. I flicked it, and we both jumped up and down before I touched the flame to the pile of stuff. The paper flared and then the cotton yarn and finally the wooden crochet hooks caught. Then we hugged each other and crossed our fingers the helicopter would see the fire.

I was afraid to look. This was our only chance. If the fire went out, we'd have nothing else to burn. Was it my imagination or was the thwack getting louder? Then I was sure. Adele and I looked up and were bathed in the spotlight. We started jumping up and down again to make sure they saw us. It circled and lowered and set up a huge wind. Finally it hovered just above the ground. I saw someone in a bright-colored helmet leaning out. I didn't stop to think about being scared, but just grabbed Adele's hand and we ran toward it.

I felt a pair of arms pull me inside. Adele came in after, and we both fell into seats. A voice barked for us to buckle in and the helicopter took off.

You could say we'd been saved by a hook.

They dropped us off on the desert floor. Several police cars and an ambulance were waiting. They wanted to take us to the hospital, but I insisted we were fine and had to get to the benefit. I told the cops about D. J. abandoning us and the doll with the media card in her underpants that I was sure had some crucial evidence in a murder. I was pretty sure I convinced them we weren't delirious from the cold. Reluctantly, two of the officers agreed to give us a lift.

The real A-list benefit was taking place right next to the tent where we'd been in the first place. There was no problem getting past security since Adele and I had two cops with us.

We might have looked a little worse for wear, and the shiny Mylar blankets we were wrapped in might have given a slight impression that we were aliens. I could only imagine what my hair looked like from seeing Adele's before she put her big hat back on.

There was some kind of toast going on, but it stopped when we came in. Along with our escorts, we walked up to the table where D. J. was sitting. For a split second, he looked shocked to see us, then he recovered. He got up and ran toward us.

"There you are," he said in an angry tone. He told everyone, but mostly the cops, that we'd wanted to see the aerial tramway and he'd gone with us, but we'd rushed off and left him. He'd finally found his way back to the tram and thought we'd gone down before him. Luckily for him, he had a compass on his watch and a windbreaker in his fanny pack. He walked back to his seat. "Here's you stuff," he said, pushing my tote bag on me. I immediately took the doll out and checked its underpants. No surprise, the media card was gone.

CHAPTER 36

"PINK, IF ONLY I'D HAD THOSE HOOKS," ADELE SAID. We had finally made it to our room. Both of us had had a hot shower and we were dressed in hotel robes. We'd splurged and ordered room service.

"You didn't really think Barbara was going to invite us to stay at the banquet and let you give her a crochet lesson?" I said. Once the doll had come out, everything got crazy. Becca saw it first and left her chair to rush up to us. What were we doing with Robyn's doll? she had demanded. Derek joined his wife and I didn't have a chance to answer before D. J. did it for me. I, he explained, was friends with the woman who everybody thought was responsible for Robyn's death and I was trying to help her beat the wrap.

"She came here because she thinks you people killed your own daughter and son," he said to the celebrity pair. Becca started to cry, Derek looked angry, and everyone else seemed confused.

Barbara Olive Overton stepped in and strongly suggested we leave.

Needless to say, nobody wanted to hear our side of the aerial tramway story. Who would believe that the nicely dressed author would try to kill two women wearing shiny blankets. Even the cops who'd come in with us gave us dirty looks. We'd made the top celebrity couple cry.

What could we do but take our silver blanket capes and go. Talk about personas non grata.

At least, now we were warm, dry and working on dessert. "Pink, you might as well just give up," Adele said as she picked off one of the strawberries on her cheesecake. "You might be sure that D. J. killed Robyn and her brother, but where's the proof? Where's even the motive?"

"On that media card," I said with a sigh. "And he probably has cut it up in little pieces and scattered them in the desert by now."

"Now that we've been saved," Adele said, "are you still going to invite me over?" She reminded me that just as she'd offered, she had added the crochet trim to my Chanel-style jacket. She had me there. To my surprise, the embellishment she'd added was actually tasteful, and instead of stuffing it in the back of the closet with clothes I never wore, I'd put it in the front.

As soon as I said yes, she tried to pin me down to a date. I said I'd have to check my calendar. "Pink, if you knew anything about your BlackBerry, you'd realize you could keep your calendar on there."

I had already vowed that if we got off the mountain, I was going to learn how to do everything possible on the Black-Berry. I turned on the TV instead.

It must have been a slow night in Palm Springs; our rescue made the news, though they used only stock footage and never showed us. They interviewed a ranger who repeated what Adele had said about people getting lost up there about once a month and getting in trouble because they didn't understand how much colder it was up there. I shuddered when he talked about the bones picked clean they'd found in the past.

I had just started on my cherry cobbler a la mode when there was a knock at the door.

"Mason," I said in surprise when I opened it. His face went from tense and worried to a grin in a split second, and he hugged me tight. Adele called out a greeting from inside.

"I started driving as soon as I got in touch with search and rescue," he said. He'd kept calling me and had gotten voice mail. "I remembered the tickets included a room. I was hoping you were here." He hugged me again, saying how relieved he was to find us.

"What happened with your BlackBerry now?" he said.

"Dead and nothing to charge it with." I invited him in.

"I'm getting you a bunch of cords. You can keep them everywhere," he said as I shut the door.

I shared my dessert with him as I told him the whole story down to how D. J. had turned the tables on us and made it look like we'd lost him, along with how he'd made the media card disappear. "I'm sure whatever is on it implicates D. J., not that it matters anymore."

"Maybe not, Pink," Adele said from across the room. She stood up and did a little cocky strut. "Who's the detective now? Maybe I'll change my name to Adele Poirot."

CHAPTER 37

ADELE AND I SAT DOWN IN THE FIRST ROW WITH Dinah. It felt like déjà vu, at least sort of. It had been barely a month ago when we'd sat in almost the same seats when all of this began. This time CeeCee was in the audience, along with Nell. Rhoda, Elise, Eduardo and Sheila were in the row behind. The booing started and Barbara Olive Overton came out and greeted the audience.

In the week since the golf tournament, I'd had to pull every string and get help from Mason, Detective Heather and even my talent-agent son, Peter, to make this happen. Adele had talked me into wearing the black Chanel-style suit jacket she'd embellished. I had to admit it: The red trim she'd crocheted on the sleeves and down the front had added some pizzazz, and it looked much better paired with the black jeans I was wearing than the skirt it came with. Over the top as usual, Adele was taking way too much pride in my wearing it, and along with pointing out her work to everyone, was acting like a wardrobe mistress. More than once, she'd adjusted the jacket so it hung just right, even pushing the tissue I'd stuck in the pocket out of sight.

"Our guest today is D. J. Florian, author of *Back from Hell*," Barbara began. She sounded fine, but I wondered if she was nervous, knowing what was going to happen. "For those of you who don't know his story, D. J. started to write a blog as his life was falling apart. He chronicled what it was like to hit the bottom and the hard road back up. Now it's been turned into a book he calls a blogoir." She smiled at the audience and explained the word was coined by combining *blog* with *memoir*. "A reviewer for the *Los Angeles Post* called it 'a book filled with grit, dark humor and hope.' There's talk of a movie deal and more books. He's currently working on a self-help program that will help everyone, whether their problem is drugs, potato chips, smoking or nail biting," she said, holding up her own hands, "which I personally would like to hear about."

Adele nudged me and made a harrumph sound. I knew she was itching to pull out a hook, but for once, Adele behaved.

A video piece began to play on a large screen behind Barbara and D. J. The first scene showed D. J. walking down Cahuenga Boulevard and talking to the camera. He pointed out the Hollywood Hills dotted with houses and the TV- and movie-production-related businesses he was passing and explained his frustration at working as a clerk in an electronic store instead of being part of the entertainment business. He'd always expected better things for himself. So to escape his disappointment, he'd gotten into drugs. Just recreational, at first, with the guys he worked with. Then he had moved over to heroin and everything changed.

The background scene changed to night. "And then I began to lose pieces of my life," he said. "My friends, my apartment and my job all got lost as the sole focus in my life became getting that next fix." The scene faded into a dark downtown street. The stores were closed and mostly covered by pull-down metal doors. The only light came from a small store with a tiny bar-covered window. "I started living on the street. Thanks to a kind guy at a convenience store who let me use his laptop, I was able to keep on with my blog."

Here the scene changed again to a freeway underpass and a motley encampment. D. J. pointed to the upslope under the concrete bridge and said that was where he'd kept his sleeping bag and described in graphic detail about the rain, rodents and outbursts from the other denizens. The picture cut to a downtown street near a sports arena. A blind musician with no shoes was playing a bluesy piece on a guitar. Next to him, a guitar case sat open with some money in it. D. J. stood back from the scene as some well-dressed people passed by and dropped some money in the case. D. J.'s voice faltered. "This was where I hit bottom. It was New Year's Eve of 2008 and just a few minutes before the clock was going to strike midnight. Jerome had collected a nice stash from the people coming from a concert. As I was bending over to steal it, I knew I had hit bottom, but I didn't care. And then it was as if a hand reached out and tapped me on the shoulder. I heard a voice in my head tell me not to give up, that there was hope. From that moment on, my life started to change."

Suddenly the picture cut to a close-up of the still photo of Robyn and Ty wearing silver top hats that said "Happy 2009." They were hugging and both pointing to her watch. It said five minutes to midnight. The view moved back so that the whole picture came into view. There were some people in the background, and one of them came into focus. He was wearing a tuxedo with the tie pulled loose and holding a champagne glass as he tipped his party hat. It was D. J. Florian.

The picture froze on the back screen and the lights came on in the studio. Barbara looked at D. J. and glanced down at the paper in her hand. "What do you have to say about that?"

A hush of anticipation went through the audience. D. J.

was still looking at the back screen. I imagined he was in shock. He was so sure he'd gotten rid of the media card with this photograph. Adele nudged me and gave me a knowing smile. She was taking all the credit, though it had really been my mistake. I'd grabbed the doll and the media card in her hand at the golf tournament without looking at them. In all the confusion, I'd taken the media card with Adele's own photos. At the time, Robyn's card from the doll was still in Adele's camera.

The media card had only appeared empty because Adele's camera couldn't read the program it was in. When we'd put it into a computer with the proper program, we'd been able to see everything Robyn had left.

When D. J. turned back toward the audience, he appeared calm. "Somebody faked the picture," he said. He said it must have been taken the year before. He even walked back to the screen and pointed at the nine in the year and claimed it had been altered from an eight. He started to go off on people who might want to derail his career, but Barbara interrupted.

From the audience, I could see the beads of perspiration on her nose. The talk show host was used to nonconfrontational interviews. This was a first for her, and she was nervous.

The photo on the screen changed to a bunch of photos of the party, with D. J. similarly dressed in the background. "Are you going to try to claim that all of these photographs were altered?" Barbara was finding her sea legs at being a push-the-envelope interviewer. "So, instead of wandering the streets of skid row that New Year's Eve, you were actually at a party in a tuxedo, weren't you?" She waited for him to an-swer, but he said nothing.

Barbara picked up a sheet of paper and explained to the audience who Robyn was and what had happened to her. She said that in addition to the photos, Robyn had left notes for a script she'd planned to add as a voice-over to the photographs. "I'd like to read it in her place," the talk show host said. D. J.

swallowed so loud, I was pretty sure the people in the last row heard it.

"'I asked D. J. to speak to my brother, Miles, who has been valiantly fighting an addiction to drugs and winning for the past year. I thought it would encourage Miles to see how D. J. had turned his life around. But Miles seemed uneasy after he met D. J. My brother said addicts had antennas that pointed up a fake, and that was how he felt when he met with D. J. I was sure my brother was wrong. Nothing would have happened if I hadn't broken up with my boyfriend at that time. I know it might seem childish, but I started cutting him out of all the prints of the photographs I had. If I hadn't, I probably never would have really looked closely at that New Year's Eve photograph.

"'Ty's and my first date was that New Year's Eve. I was living in a building in Studio City owned by a man who loved creative types and offered a low-rent haven for struggling actors, writers and people like me who wanted to work in production. Every year, he gave a party for the tenants. After I saw the picture, I checked back, and though I had never known him, found that D. J. Florian had had an apartment on the floor above me and had been paying his rent on time the whole time he'd claimed he'd been living on the street.'" Barbara paused to let it all sink in before she continued. "'I did more checking, and there were more and more holes in the story. I didn't want to tell my brother the details until the show aired, but I gave him one of the photos with D. J. in the background and told him that it looked like he was right.'"

So that must have been what Miles remembered, I thought, feeling a deep sadness that I hadn't gotten the message in time to save him.

Barbara had a take-no-prisoners look when she turned to D. J. "Is any of it true?" she said.

"I created a hero. People come up to me and say they have

hope from reading my blog. They think if I did it, they can. What's wrong with that?"

"What's wrong with that is that it isn't true. You didn't do anything," Barbara said.

"I almost did. I had the idea of writing a nogel. That's a novel in blog form. But when I started posting the blog, people believed it was real. So, I let them keep on believing, and then it got a life of it's own. I based it on a guy I worked with. I just made it more dramatic, with a better ending. In my version, he comes back from his personal hell and starts a new life. The real guy did drugs, got caught and went to jail."

D. J. began to sweat and move toward the edge of his seat. As Barbara brought up Robyn's death, he took off. But he didn't get far. Detective Heather was waiting off-camera, and I saw her lead him away.

When the show ended, we went backstage. The door was open to the green room, and I saw D. J. and a contingent of cops. "You've got nothing on me," D. J. said. "I had nothing to do with any deaths." He glared at them as he made a move toward the door, and I realized Heather was going to let him go.

And I was powerless to stop him. Until the lucky sneeze.

From behind me, Adele achooed with such force, she fell into me. "Pink, a tissue," she wailed and I imagined something embarrassing had happened. When I reached in my jacket pocket and pulled out the tissue, something else came with it. It must have been left from the last time I'd worn the jacket.

The strip of paper had a telephone number written on it, and I remembered I'd marked it down the first time I'd met D. J. in the café right after Mason and I did the improv at the production office. While Adele mopped up with the tissue, I unfolded the strip. My mouth fell open and I rushed into the green room and grabbed Detective Heather.

She had a now-what look on her face, and I explained that

I'd needed a piece of paper to write D. J.'s phone number on. "He pulled this from his pocket," I said.

She looked at the paper with a dismissive shrug, but her demeanor changed when she saw what it was. It was actually two strips of paper, both receipts. One was from a general merchandise store and listed Nature's Sweetie and a shipping box as the items sold. The other receipt was from the post office and showed a package sent and gave the zip code, which I bet was the production office's.

She signaled one of the uniforms, who grabbed D. J. before he slipped out. She pointed to the receipts in my hand with an expectant expression. "What do you have to say about these?"

D. J. shrugged it off. "Nothing. There's nothing that ties those receipts to me." I started to slump as he pulled free of the uniform, but when I lifted my thumb and looked at the store receipt again, I yelled, "Wait."

It only took a few minutes to confirm the string of numbers my thumb had been hiding, and Detective Heather eyed D. J. with a look of triumph. "How about you used your credit card?"

D. J.'s eyes darted around and he appeared panicky. Then he glared at me.

"If you had just stayed out of it, everything would have been fine."

"For who?" I said, standing in front of him. "For Robyn and Miles, who are both dead? For Nell, who never would have gotten out of the shadow of suspicion?" I glared back at him.

"I saw the photograph on Robyn's desk," he said. "When I realized I was in it, I knew it could ruin everything. I thought Robyn might not have noticed, but then I overheard her telling someone she had a plan to ambush somebody in the middle of their TV appearance. I knew she meant me, and I couldn't let her do that. Finally, I had gotten my shot at the big time. So what if it wasn't true. It was a great story and it inspired people. I could have helped so many more people with the self-help plan I was developing. I had to stop her. I had met with her a few times and knew about her obsession with the sweetener. All it took was a razor blade, some cyanide power and a glue gun to fix the packets. Then to make it look like she wasn't really the intended victim, I added some of the tainted packet to the box in the bookstore café and brought in the other box to the police station.

"When I overheard that you'd talked to Miles and he'd remembered something and had a photo, I couldn't take a chance. I didn't have a lot of time to prepare." D. J. seemed almost in a trance, as if he didn't know what he was saying anymore. I understood now how Barry and the other detectives got so many confessions. No matter how they tried to defend themselves, most people who had done horrible things had guilty consciences, and when they were cornered, let it all out. D. J. knew that Miles' room was on the first floor and had gone to his window. Miles had let him climb in when he'd said he needed to talk to him about something.

He knew the fruit punch was Miles' favorite and had brought it as a treat. To cover that it had already been opened and the roofies added, he opened the top before he'd handed it to Miles. Then, when Miles had passed out, he'd given him an overdose. D. J. had done enough research that he knew how to get drugs and what to do with them. He thought it would look like Miles was despondent about his sister and had gone back to drugs. He'd simply gone out the front door after.

The guilty-conscience part seemed to fade when he got to talking about our trip to the mountains. It was more like anger that he hadn't succeeded. "You should have frozen on that mountain." It had been an impromptu plan, and he regretted that he hadn't had some roofies to give Adele and me to ensure we froze to death.

I hadn't realized Adele and the other Hookers had come up behind me until I felt the group hug.

Detective Heather took us out of the green room and shut the door behind her. It was hard for her, but she apologized to Nell for accusing her. She even promised to get Nell's glue gun and the shirt back to her. It was even harder for her to thank me for my help. She threw in something about it had turned out well, but I had still interfered with a police investigation before she went back into the room.

Word had spread about D. J.'s confession. Talia walked down the hall with Barbara. Talia gave me a thumbs-up and Barbara hugged me in gratitude. "If there's anything I can do for you," Barbara said.

"Well, now that you mention it," I said and pulled Nell out of the group. "How about giving her her job back?"

"Done," Barbara said, getting ready to walk away.

"There's something else," I said. I gave Adele a nod.

We all crowded into Barbara's dressing room, but I let Adele do the honors. Adele was so discombobulated at getting the opportunity she'd been waiting for, she had to wave for CeeCee to take over. At first, anyway. Just as CeeCee got through demonstrating how to make a foundation chain, Adele found her voice and took over. It turned out that unlike the knitting someone had tried to teach Barbara for the upcoming show, she was a natural at crochet and absolutely loved the idea of impatient crochet.

She waved Talia over. "I insist that we change the upcoming show to knitting and crochet. I want CeeCee and Adele on it, too," she said. Uh-oh, I wondered if Barbara Olive Overton realized what she was getting into.

The show had gone live in several markets, but before it aired in the rest of them, Pierce Sheraton played a snippet in his daily broadcast. The ratings for the *Barbara Olive Overton* show were over the top, and she was hailed as turning over a new leaf in her interviewing style. The timing was crucial because it had come during May sweeps, which had to do with advertising revenue for the show. It was all as Robyn had hoped.

I found out that Talia and Pierce were together so much because they were a couple, though it was based more on a mutual advantage to aid their careers than a love match.

Becca Ivins and Derek Trousedale went ahead with their appearance on the show with a change. Instead of the tribute to their longevity as a couple and all their charitable works, they let their hair down and told the truth. By the time they explained all their regrets, they, along with Barbara and the whole audience, were in tears. I admit, I was, too.

When I finally got home after D. J.'s downfall and Barbara's crochet lesson, the dogs and cats were waiting for me. The Hookers had all scattered. Dinah had gone home to grade papers and I suspect spend a little much-needed alone time. Adele had floated off to plan for her big debut, but not without locking down a date for her French toast. Rhoda had rushed off to meet her husband. Elise decided to go home and reread *Caught By the Hook* and dream about Anthony. CeeCee and Nell had had a hugathon and were talking over each other about their excitement. At last, CeeCee could get back to concentrating on her Oscar buzz and Nell was going back to work. They were off to a fabulous restaurant that the paparazzi staked out, both ready for their close-ups.

Sheila was anxious to get back to Luxe and the job that had changed her life. Eduardo had held up the group before they dispersed. He had an announcement. Due to being cast as the father of the pirate instead of the pirate on an upcoming book cover, he'd faced that his cover-model career was on a downslide and was turning his attention to a new endeavor. He handed out invitations to the grand opening and explained he was the new owner of the Crown Apothecary and Soda Fountain.

I set down the red-eye I'd picked up at the bookstore. Bob

was recovering from the shock that his new regular customer had turned out to be a murderer. In the meantime, he'd found a new critique partner for his screenplay. Along with all his other experiences, Mr. Royal had worked with a small movie company in Oregon.

Cosmo ran out and Blondie reluctantly followed. The cats ran to their food bowls. I was still getting used to coming home and finding my house as I'd left it. I went back to the kitchen door and watched Cosmo run around the yard as the phone began to ring.

It was Jeffrey in tears. At first I couldn't understand him, just that it was something about Barry. I finally got him to slow down and he repeated what he'd said.

"Somebody shot my dad," he said. "He wants to see you." I heard him begin to choke up again. "You better hurry."

Impatient Crochet

BY RHODA KLEIN

So, you want to crochet, but you don't have lots of time and you don't have the patience to work on a project forever. Impatient crochet is for you. It's easy, the projects work up fast, they are small and easily portable, and they don't even take much yarn. Did I mention they also make good gifts and bazaar items? Did I sell you yet?

Before I give you the patterns, I want to tell you the basic idea of it. You start with a foundation chain, then starting with the second chain from the hook, make single crochets in each of the chains, adding an extra single crochet to the last chain. The trick comes when you get to that last chain. In your regular crochet, you'd go back over that row of stitches for the next row, but in impatient crochet, you keep going around. So, you work single crochet stitches on the opposite side of the foundation of chains, making two single crochets in the last chain.

You don't join the rounds but rather work in a spiral, which gives the stitches a diagonal look. Oh, and you need to put a stitch marker in the first stitch you make, and then keep moving it up as you complete each round to keep track of where one round ends and the next one begins.

Try it. I'm sure you're going to like it.

Cell Phone Sock

Supplies: I-9 (5.5 mm) hook or any size to obtain the right
                  gauge for sock
                  F-5 (3.75 mm) hook for flower
                  1 skein of Peaches and Creme 4-ply worsted-
                  weight 100 percent cotton yarn; 98 yards (89.6
                  meters) (2 oz.) (enough to make 2 or more)
                  Approx. 9 yards of Peaches and Creme 4-ply
                  worsted-weight 100 percent cotton yarn in
                  another color for the flower
                  Stitch marker
                  Tapestry needle for finishing
                  Needle and embroidery thread to sew flower and
                  bead or button to sock
                  Large bead or button for the center of the flower

Stitches: Chain stitch, single crochet, double crochet, triple
                  crochet, slip stitch
                  Dimensions of the cell sock: approx. 3¼ inches
                  by 5 inches

Gauge for cell sock:

> 6 stitches and 7 rows = 2 inches

With I hook, chain 9.

Round 1: Single crochet in the second chain from the hook, mark with stitch marker, single crochet in each chain, with an extra single crochet in the last chain, turn. Working on the other sideof the chain, make a single crochet in each chain, making two single crochets in the last chain. Do not join. 18 stitches made.

Round 2: Single crochet in the stitch marked with the stitch marker, move the stitch marker up to the stitch just made, and continue around, making a single crochet in each stitch.

Repeat Round 2 until it's approx. 5 inches tall. On the last round, end with a slip stitch into the marked stitch and fasten off. Weave in ends.

FLOWER

With F hook, chain 10 and join with a slip stitch.

Round 1: Chain 1 and make 18 single crochets in the ring. Slip stitch to the first single crochet.

Round 2: Chain 1 and single crochet into the first stitch from the round below. *Chain 3, skip the next 2 single crochets, and single crochet in the next stitch.* Repeat from * to * 4 times. Chain 3, skip 2 single crochets, and slip stitch into the first single crochet.

Round 3: Slip stitch to move the yarn into the next chain-3 space. *Single crochet, double crochet, double crochet, triple crochet, double crochet, double crochet, single crochet in the chain-3 space.* Repeat * to * in the 5 other chain-3 spaces to make the petals of the flower. End with a slip stitch to the first single crochet. Fasten off and weave in ends.

Sew the flower onto the body of the cell sock and sew on the bead or button in the center.

Eyeglass Case

Supplies: I-9 (5.5 mm) hook or any size to obtain the correct gauge
1 skein of Filatura Di Crosa Lovely Jeans yarn
100 percent cotton (50 grams) (enough to make 2 or more)
3 yards of yarn for corkscrew
Stitch marker
Approx. 4½-inch by 14-inch piece of cotton fabric for lining
Tapestry needle for finishing
Needle and thread for sewing lining

Stitches: Chain stitch, single crochet, slip stitch

Dimensions: approx. 3½ inches by 6½ inches

Gauge: 8 stitches and 8 rows = 2 inches

Chain 9.

Round 1: Single crochet in the second chain from the hook, mark with the stitch marker, single crochet in each chain, making an extra single crochet in the last chain, turn.

Working in the other side of the chain, single crochet in each chain, making 2 single crochets in the last chain. Do not join. 18 stitches made.

Round 2: Single crochet in stitch marked with stitch marker and move stitch marker up; single crochet in each single crochet.

Repeat Round 2 until it's approx. 6½ inches tall, then slip stitch in each single crochet. Fasten off and weave in ends.

LINING
With right sides together, fold fabric in half so the fold is at the bottom. Leaving approx. a ½-inch seam, sew up sides. Put inside the case, fold the top down, and stitch to the case.

CORKSCREW
Chain 12, make 3 single crochet stitches in the second chain from the hook, make 3 single crochets in each of the other chain stitches, fasten off, and weave in ends. Sew on the eyeglass case.

Small Purse

Supplies: K-10½ (6.5 mm) hook or any size to obtain the correct gauge
1 skein Peaches and Creme 4-ply worsted-weight 100 percent cotton yarn; 98 yards (2 oz.) (89.6 meters) (enough to make 2 or more)
Stitch marker
Tapestry needle for finishing
Needle and thread
Button

Stitches: Chain stitch, single crochet, single crochet 2 together, single crochet 3 together

Dimensions: approx. 5½ inches by 5 inches with the flap folded

Gauge: 6 stitches and 8 rows = 2 inches

Chain 16.

Round 1: Single crochet in the second chain from the hook, mark with stitch marker, single crochet in each chain, making an extra single crochet in the last chain, turn. Working in the other side of the chain, single crochet in each chain, making 2 single crochets in the last chain. Do not join. 32 stitches made.

Round 2: Single crochet in the inside loop of the stitch with the stitch marker, move stitch marker, single crochet in the inside loop of each single crochet (gives a ribbed pattern).

Repeat Round 2 until it is approx. 5 inches tall. If the marked stitch isn't on the side, continue single crocheting, ending at the side. These 16 stitches are now the back of the purse. Do not finish off.

ENVELOPE-SHAPED FLAP

Row 1: Continuing with the body of the purse, chain 1, turn and single crochet across the back 16 stitches only. Turn.

Row 2: Repeat row 1.

Row 3: Chain 1, single crochet 2 together, single crochet across until the last 2 stitches, single crochet 2 together. Turn. 14 stitches.

Row 4: Chain 1, single crochet 2 together, single crochet across until the last 2 stitches, single crochet 2 together. Turn. 12 stitches.

Row 5: Chain 1, single crochet 2 together, single crochet across until the last 2 stitches, single crochet 2 together. Turn. 10 stitches.

Row 6: Chain 1, single crochet 2 together, single crochet across until the last 2 stitches, single crochet 2 together. Turn. 8 stitches.

Row 7: Chain 1, single crochet 2 together, single crochet across until the last 2 stitches, single crochet 2 together. Turn. 6 stitches.

Row 8: Chain 1, single crochet 2 together, chain 1, and skip the next two stitches (for button hole), single crochet 2 together. Turn. 3 stitches.

Row 9: Chain 1 and single crochet 3 together. Fasten off and weave in ends.

Sew button on to use as closure.

The Collins' Family
Apple Bumble Crumble

6 golden delicious apples, peeled, cored and sliced into approx.
    ½-inch pieces
3 tsp. vanilla extract
2 tbsp. white sugar
2 tbsp. brown sugar
1½ tsp. cinnamon
½ cup raisins
½ cup salted butter cut in pieces
¾ cup flour
¾ cup brown sugar
¾ cup old-fashioned oats
¾ cups chopped walnuts

Generously grease the bottom and sides of a 9-inch by 13-inch pan. Spread the apples evenly in the buttered pan. Pour the vanilla over the apple slices. Mix the white sugar, 2 tablespoons of brown sugar and cinnamon. Sprinkle it over the apple slices, then mix. Sprinkle the raisins over the apples.

In a mixing bowl, cut the butter into the flour using a pastry blender. Mix in brown sugar, old-fashioned oats and walnuts. Spread the mixture over the apples. Bake at 425 degrees for approximately 40 minutes, until the apples are tender. Can be served with ice cream or whipped cream. Serves about 6.

Molly's Baked Pancake

4 eggs
⅛ tsp. salt
½ cup flour
½ cup milk
2 tsp. sugar
1 tsp. vanilla
3 tbsp. butter

Beat eggs until light, add salt and flour and then milk, sugar and vanilla. Heat the oven to 425 degrees. Put butter in a heavy 9-inch round pan. Put the pan in the oven until the butter is melted. Take the pan out and carefully pour in the batter. Return to the oven and bake for about 25 minutes. Can be served with syrup or cut-up strawberries. Serves 2 for a meal, 4 for a snack.

Turn the page for a preview of Betty Hechtman's
next Crochet Mystery . . .

IF HOOKS COULD KILL

Available in hardcover from Berkley Prime Crime!

I HAVE DONE A LOT OF EMBARRASSING THINGS, BUT this morning I topped even myself. . . .

I watched as the detective walked out of the small blue stucco house down the street from my best friend Dinah Lyons's house. Everything about him gave off the vibe of somebody who'd been up all night chasing down evidence. His face featured a day-old beard, his tie was pulled loose from the collar of his pale blue dress shirt, and he gave out a weary sigh as he sauntered down the three steps to the front walk and moved toward the black Crown Victoria parked at the curb.

He was almost to the street when a man in a hooded sweatshirt with a baseball cap on top of the hood darted out from behind a large red oleander bush. The morning sun glinted off the gun in his hand. As he raised his arm and took aim, something triggered in my mind, really someone, namely Barry Greenberg. I'd given up trying to find the right title for Barry. It was enough to say he was my ex boyfriend, he was a homicide detective and he'd recently been shot. I wasn't about to let that happen to someone else.

Without a second of hesitation, I rushed up behind the guy with the gun. If all the adrenalin hadn't been pumping I never would have had the force to knock him over. And maybe I would have noticed a few things like the detective's shirt had no wrinkles. And he was definitely wearing makeup. And there were cameras, lights and lots of people standing around.

"Cut," a tall man in black jeans and a loose taupe-colored tee shirt yelled as he rushed onto the grass. He glared at me and waved to the uniformed officer hanging by the curb. "Get her out of here," he muttered, pointing to me as I rolled off the presumed assailant. The man I had tackled got up and dusted himself off, and the throng of onlookers surrounded me as I got back on my feet. But they parted for the officer who came through the crowd, linked his arm with mine, and pulled me to the edge of the sidewalk.

"Pink, what have you done now?" Adele Abrams rushed up behind me as Dinah Lyons started explaining to all who would listen why I had done what I'd done. No, this wasn't some kind of bad dream, though at the moment I was wishing it was and hoping I'd wake up twisted in the sheets of my own bed. I admit to often finding myself in trouble, but usually it's for something real. This was all make-believe.

It was summer in the San Fernando Valley and the area had become a backlot for TV and film productions. Caravans of white trucks were on streets all over the Valley. Street corners had yellow signs with arrows to direct the cast and crew to the location. They always disguised the real name of the production with some cryptic phrase, so no one would have guessed by the sign on Ventura Boulevard that the area around Dinah's house had become the set for *L.A. 911.*

If this were a TV show or movie, it would freeze frame right now. Then I'd step forward and explain that my name is Molly Pink and that after my husband Charlie died, I'd started a whole new chapter in my life that included getting a job as the event coordinator at the bookstore Shedd & Royal Books and More, which was just up the street from all this activity. I might mention that I was also in charge of the yarn department we had recently added.

You might wonder about a yarn department in a bookstore. The yarn department was added because the local crochet group, the Tarzana Hookers, met at the bookstore and quite frankly the owners, Mrs. Shedd and Mr. Royal, were looking for more revenue streams. I think that's the right term. Actually, with a crafting table and available yarn, the Hookers didn't just meet at the bookstore—they almost lived there. Mrs. Shedd liked to joke that if we had cots, the group would probably sleep there, too.

Adele Abrams, the person who just called me Pink, worked at the bookstore, too. There was a little tension between us. She thought she should have been promoted to event coordinator instead of Mrs. Shedd hiring me. As a consolation prize, she had been given the children's department to oversee. Adele didn't really like kids, though she did like to dress up in costumes for story time.

Then, when the yarn department was added, Adele thought she should be in charge of it. Adele, Dinah and I were all part of the crochet group, and no one would dispute that Adele was far superior with a hook, but she had this small problem. All of the Tarzana Hookers thought crochet was the best of the fiber arts, but Adele took it a step further. If you so much as showed her a knitting needle she would throw a hissy fit. Personally, while I know she had a real reason for being nuts about knitters (she'd had a bad stepmother who was a needle head, as Adele called her), I thought it was time she accepted a world where hooks and needles could get along.

Having a needle hater running a yarn department wasn't a good idea—not if you wanted knitter's business. So, even though I was somewhat of a novice at crochet, Mrs. Shedd wanted me to handle the yarn department.

But none of that explained what I was doing hanging out at a TV shoot. Actually it wasn't planned. Adele, Dinah and I were on our way to one of the newer Hooker's houses to pick up some crochet stuff. Her house was around the corner from Dinah's and we'd had to pass the caravan of trucks and trailers to get there. Even though seeing a set on the street wasn't new, I still found it exciting. It was fun to see what they'd done to the front of the modest stucco house they were using for a location. They'd carted in trees and bushes and arranged them so that the other houses on the block weren't visible and so you couldn't see the open-air tent set up down the street that was acting as a dining room for the cast and crew. A catering truck was parked in the street and the smell of the barbecue wafted down the block.

This is where the freeze frame would end and the action would pick up again. The uniform who'd grabbed my arm had gotten me to the edge of the crowd. Adele followed close behind. "Pink, you'd better thank my boyfriend Eric for saving your skin." Now that we'd reached the sidelines, Eric let go and apologized if he'd been too rough.

"It was fine," I said to the barrel-chested man who towered over me. Eric Humphries was a LAPD motor officer and was using his vacation time to work security on the production. In case there was any doubt, he was also Adele's boyfriend. "Thanks for saving me from the angry mob," I said looking back at the crew as they tried to set up the shot again. Adele glanced around, saw that no one was watching and touched Eric's arm in a possessive manner. He responded by beaming a big smile her way. It was embarrassing to watch them making googie eyes at each other. But at least this time the romance wasn't all in Adele's imagination.

They made an unusual pair. Adele, with her wild clothes and say whatever attitude, was a sharp contrast to the very proper and polite motor officer. He rode his motorcycle with ramrod straight posture and took his security work at the set very seriously. "Cutchykins," he said, winking at her. "I'm glad you stopped by. You look lovely as always."

My eyes started to roll on their own. Didn't the man have eyes? Adele was wearing a one shoulder sundress made out of multicolored granny squares with a red crocheted flounce at the bottom. She looked like she was wearing an afghan. And Adele had crocheted herself a big brimmed cream-colored hat. It had turned out to be a little too floppy in the brim area, and kept dipping down and cutting off her line of sight.

Dinah rejoined us and Eric went back to his post. "Don't worry, I took care of everything," she said. I had no doubt she had. Dinah was a community college English instructor and her specialty was freshman English. She knew how to take charge of an unruly group, no matter who they were. I figured she'd done the same with the production group. "As soon as I explained about your connection to Barry and how he was a homicide detective, and that he'd been shot, and that you were still so sensitive to the whole thing that you'd lost your mind temporarily, they all understood. That North Adams was particularly nice," she said sending back a glance to the seasoned, tall, dark-haired actor who played the homicide detective I'd tried to save. "He even offered to talk to you and help you with 'this difficult time,' as he put it. And the guy who played the shooter seemed to take it as some kind of compliment to his acting ability."

"You said I lost my mind?" I said, skipping over everything else she'd said. "Great, now they think I'm crazy." Normally I might not care what strangers thought of me, but I was probably going to see these people again. The bookstore was just up the street and even though the production was self-contained, providing meals and snacks, the cast and crew still drifted up to the bookstore to hang out, buy books, get coffee drinks and scoop up our barista's great cookies.

"We better go," I said. "We've still got to pick up Kelly's crochet items."

"We don't all have to go," Adele said, reminding us that she was more or less in charge of the crochet group. It was more in her mind and less in reality. CeeCee Collins was technically the leader, but her acting career was so busy right now it was hard for her to handle the group as well. So Adele had jumped in as de facto leader.

"Well, none of us really has to go," I said. "Kelly doesn't know we're coming and we can just wait until she comes to one of our meetings."

Adele snorted. "Maybe you can wait, Pink, but CeeCee and I have our doubts about Kelly's crochet ability. She keeps saying she's going to come to a meeting and she keeps saying she's going to make things for our booth at the Tarzana fair, but I haven't seen anything to make me believe it's true."

"What about the scarf she showed us that she was making?" I said.

"Okay, so she can make a scarf, and so she came to a couple of meetings, and so whenever we see her at the bookstore she says she's been making stuff at home for the fair. But I want to see proof."

It was useless to argue with Adele, so Dinah and I traded nods and kept silent. It was just a short walk up the street to Dinah's house, which was on the corner. Kelly lived around the next corner on the street that paralleled the one the production company was using. As soon as we got on the other street, it was much quieter. The houses were set on orderly little plots, close to the street. This part of Tarzana had sidewalks and seemed more like a neighborhood than where I lived.

"I don't know why Kelly has to be so difficult," Adele said with a harrumph in her voice. It was all Dinah and I could do to keep from laughing. Adele practically wrote the book on causing a ruckus. Apparently immune to our stifled laughs, Adele continued. "If she's going to be one of the Hookers, she ought to follow the rules."

"Rules?" Dinah repeated with surprise. "What are they, the ten commandments of crochet?"

"I don't know if there are ten, but there should be something that says if you join the Hookers, you have to go along with the group, and show up to the meetings," Adele said as the breeze caught the brim of her hat and pushed it down, covering her eyes. She flipped it up and tried to make it stay. Go along with the group? Did Adele hear what she was saying? She never went along with anything.

As we continued down the block, I noticed that the street was crowded with cars and commercial vehicles. Generally it was empty at this time of day. But then I realized they were all part of the production and probably just being kept there until they were needed. I noticed a truck with open slats up ahead, parked in Kelly's driveway. The back of the truck was filled with greenery in pots and two men in jeans were standing next to it.

Since Dinah's house was just up the street from Kelly's, which made them neighbors, my friend knew more about Kelly's business than the rest of us. "She's got her hands full," Dinah began. "You know both she and her husband have kids from previous marriages. It's always a changing cast of characters in that house. His kids, her kids, no kids. You can't just pick up and hang out at the yarn table when you have kids out of school for the summer, and you have to cart them around to activities."

Adele spent some more time fighting with her hat as we got closer. She didn't seem impressed with Dinah's explanation. "And there's her husband's business," Dinah continued. "Maybe she helps out at his store."

The store was Hollar for a Dolllar, Tarzana's first dollar store. Dinah had heard that Kelly's husband was hoping to make the one location into a big success, so he could develop it into a chain. "He went up and down the block and gave us all goodie bags of merchandise and ten-percent-off coupons to entice us to go into the store."

I'd seen the goodie bags. The specialty factor of Hollar for a Dollar seemed to be that it had almost name-brand stuff. Dinah's goodie bag had contained Uncle Len's rice, Suckers strawberry jam and Wiggly's spearmint gum.

As we got closer, I noticed a woman standing on the sidewalk, watching the action with the truck. She had her hand on her hip and you didn't have to be a body language expert to know she was annoyed. As soon as she saw us, her expression sharpened and she stepped toward us.

"Coming to complain, aren't you," she said focusing on Dinah. "Well, I'm with you. It's not enough that we have that production company around the corner, but thanks to Kelly Donahue, its going to be on this side of the block, too. That is, unless we do something to stop it."

I knew not everyone found having a production company on their street exciting. To some it was nothing but a nuisance. Apparently this woman was one of those.

Dinah nodded a greeting at her. "Hi Nanci. I don't think you've met Molly Pink and Adele Abrams." Nanci's angry expression broke for a moment as she acknowledged us, and Dinah told us that Nanci Silvers was Kelly's next-door neighbor and PTA president-elect at Wilbur Elementary.

Nanci definitely acted the part of PTA president. In all the years my sons had gone to school, the names and faces of the PTA presidents had changed, but the personas had stayed the same. The words bossy and controlling came to mind. Nanci's champagne blond hair was cut severely short with asymmetrical long dagger-shaped strands on the side that did nothing to soften her sharp features. There was something businesslike in her attire. The black slacks and short-sleeved jacket seemed like a suit. The jacket was embellished with a cluster of bloodred crocheted flowers. I noticed she'd started tapping her toe as one of the jean-clad men pulled a palm tree in a big black pot out of the truck. He nodded a greeting at our little group before continuing down the driveway toward Kelly's backyard.

"Kelly rented out her yard to the production company." Nanci went on to explain that Kelly's yard was directly behind one of the houses they were using on the other block. "Not only that, but she's signed her house up with a location service." Nanci gritted her teeth. "She's got dollar signs in her eyes. This isn't her first marriage, you know. And I think it won't be her last. That woman will do anything to make a buck. And she didn't even consult her husband. I want to take up a petition to stop her before our street becomes like that one." She gestured toward the street behind us.

"Kelly just doesn't get it about rules," Adele interjected.

Nanci nodded in agreement. "Kelly doesn't understand about being part of a group or neighborhood. It's all about money with her."

I knew what Nanci was talking about. Renting out your house to a production company could bring in a nice profit. Sometime back when Charlie was alive, someone had tried to hire him to do PR for their house. Yes, a house. It had become quite a star because it was Todd Jenkins's house in the family saga *The Jenkins*. It had also been used as the home of the matriarch in *Our Family and Friends*. Though a family lived there when it wasn't being used for a show, it had been built with the idea of renting it out to productions, so the interior was designed with an open plan which made camera setups easy. Charlie had shown me the house and I had laughed when I saw the kitchen. It was designed for cameras, not for cooking. I mean, you practically needed a golf cart to bring the dishes from the dining room to the sink.

After getting an assurance that Dinah wasn't thinking of listing her house with the location service and being noncommittal about signing any sort of petition, Nanci let us go, but I noticed she followed us as we walked up to Kelly's house. Kelly's place had been given an overhaul since it was originally built. Someone had taken the basic stucco house and

added a second story. To me, it looked like a cream-colored
box with a red tiled roof.

Kelly answered the door with a cordless phone to her ear.
I guess she was used to people just showing up at her door
because even though we hadn't called ahead she didn't seem
surprised to see us. Whenever I saw her, I thought of the
phrase *cute as a button*, though the saying didn't really make
much sense. How was a button cute? But Kelly definitely
was. She smiled at us and the two dimples in her cheeks appeared and then quickly disappeared when she saw Nanci
lurking in the background. Kelly put her hand over the
phone as Nanci fussed about the truck in the driveway and
insisted that it was ruining her view. Kelly listened with a
tired sigh; clearly she'd heard this before. "It *is* my driveway,"
Kelly reminded Nanci in a pointed tone.

Nanci made a huffing sound, turned abruptly and left.
The cuteness came back into Kelly's face, and while she apologized for the interruption to whoever she was talking to on
the phone, she gestured for us to come in. Her chestnut
brown ponytail swung from side to side as she led the way.
The beige capri pants and loose ivory linen top were casual,
but something in the fit and the texture of the fabric said
expensive. Still listening to the phone call, she pointed to
some small brightly colored blocks in a box and mouthed
watch out.

Not only did Adele watch out, she picked up the box and
examined the side. She pushed it on me with a knowing nod.
The front had the words LUGO Blocks printed in big letters
and showed some scary looking pictures of things you could
build. Whoever had written the copy clearly wasn't too good
with English. Did anyone really say, "One thousand and one
funs," or "Let's block"?

As Kelly hung up, she saw me reading the box and made
a disparaging sound. "Sorry about the blocks. My kids were
here last week and Dan brought the blocks home from the

store for them. He doesn't understand that kids care about brands. LUGO?" she said with a snort. The phone rang in her hand and she went to answer it. "Go on into my workroom. I'll be in there in a minute." She put the phone to her ear as the three of us went in the direction she'd pointed. Adele pressed ahead mumbling something about wanting to see if there were any crochet supplies.

Dinah pointed at the "No Kids Allowed" sign on the door and gave me a quizzical look. Dinah was all about teaching kids and young adults how to behave, not excluding them. We passed through the door into a large room at the back of the house. A sliding glass door looked out on the backyard, and there were the men we'd seen before, walking around the yard measuring things.

"Hmm, let's just see what she's got," Adele said as her hat brim flopped in front of her face. She lifted it away from her eyes and quickly began to look around the room.

I was less concerned about finding proof that Kelly really crocheted than with checking out the whole room. We all loved seeing each other's craft rooms, hoping they'd be as messy and yarn filled as our own.

Kelly's was neither a mess like mine, with bags of yarn all over the place threatening to trip anyone who walked in without watching their step, nor super perfect looking like the ones I'd seen that were set up like yarn stores. Kelly seemed to favor plastic bins over shelves or cubbies. There were piles of them along the wall and Adele rushed toward one to check the contents. She seemed disappointed when the first one she opened contained yarn. And not just any yarn. When Adele held up a handful of skeins, I recognized the labels as high-end expensive yarn.

The room had a different feeling than what I'd gotten in the rest of the house, where the furniture seemed modest and utilitarian. The living room couch and chairs were plain and could probably live up to the abuse of the assorted kids who stayed there. But Kelly's crafting room was filled with nice things. There was art work on the walls and all the furnishings were tasteful and eclectic. Her computer sat on a beautifully refinished library table and the Victorian dining chair pushed into it had a dusty rose cushion to soften the back. A Victorian style love seat was covered in the same dusty rose material. An old trunk served as a table in front of the love seat and held a silver tray with a silver tea service. I guessed that the Mission style easy chair was Kelly's seat of choice judging by the facedown magazine on the small table next to it and the full spectrum floor lamp arranged to illuminate it. I was admiring the doll-size figure of a knight next to a small silver bowl of dried rose petals when Kelly came in the room.

"You found my knight in shining armor," she said with a smile. Adele let go of the lid of the plastic bin she was snooping in and turned quickly, no doubt to hide what she'd been doing. The brim of her hat flapped down over her face blocking her view, and Adele suddenly lost her balance and whirled across the room. The burst of wind from her movement flipped the brim back up and Adele reached out to steady herself and almost knocked over a lamp with a leaded glass shade sitting on the end of the computer table. I grabbed the brass base just in time to steady it and knocked a small book to the floor instead. I replaced the book, noting it was some kind of guide to coins.

"That glass shade wouldn't have taken a tumble well," I said. When I asked about the Tiffany-style lamp, Kelly laughed and said it was just a copy. "Just like everything else in here," she said, making a sweeping gesture with her arm. "Is there a reason for your visit?"

I noticed that one of the men had set a potted feathery palm tree in front of the sliding glass door. The other man looked at it and shook his head. The first man pulled it away.

Before Adele could stick her foot in her mouth, I told Kelly we'd come to pick up anything she'd made for our booth at the Jungle Days Fair. Kelly's phone rang, interrupting us. She answered it and listened for a moment before turning to the group.

"I have to go pick up my kids and take them to their father's house. I still have a little finishing to do with the pieces I made. I'm really coming to the group meeting tomorrow. I'll bring everything in then." She ushered us toward the door. "I promise."

When we got outside, Adele gave Dinah and me a knowing glance. "I'll believe it when I see it."

Betty Hechtman

A STITCH IN CRIME

·A CROCHET MYSTERY·

Molly Pink and her crochet group friends are packing up for a creative weekend away. But with danger following them, trying to solve the latest mystery might just prove trickier than a back post double crochet stitch . . .

Summer's wrapping up—and it's time for the annual creative retreat hosted by the bookstore where Molly works. This year, her boss has dropped out at the last minute, dumping the responsibility all on Molly. But even with the stress of organizing, it should be an exhilarating weekend out on the Monterey Peninsula, complete with crochet classes and campfires. Unfortunately for one teacher, though, the breathtaking scenery is where she'll take her last breath . . .

It's Molly who stumbles over the dead body of crochet teacher Izabelle Landers. Now Molly will have to solve a murder *and* find a replacement instructor. Fortunately her pals from her crochet group, the Tarzana Hookers, are around to help her untangle this tightly twisted yarn . . .

PRAISE FOR THE CROCHET MYSTERIES

"Get hooked on this great new author!" —Monica Ferris

"Readers couldn't ask for a more rollicking read."
—*Crochet Today!*

penguin.com